AYAH

AYAH

A Tale of Survival, Love and Revenge

Thushani Weerasekera

Ayah is dedicated to the memory of my father,
who has always been, and will
always continue to be... an inspiration to me.

ABOUT THE AUTHOR

Thushani Weerasekera is a British-Asian actress and writer born in South West London and of Sri Lankan origin. She has acted in several television dramas and has performed at The Royal National Theatre, The Crucible Sheffield, The Birmingham Repertory Theatre, The Soho Theatre London, The Manchester Royal Exchange, The Contact, Manchester and The Dukes, Lancaster. She has participated in productions for BBC Radio as well as taking on the role of '*Storyteller*' for BBC Radio 3 Schools.

Thushani began writing at the Theatre Royal, Stratford East as part of the New Writers' Programme She wrote and performed a short monologue for The Museum of London as part of the gallery actors programme in which she played 'Jemima,' an Indian ayah abandoned in London by her English memsahib. After researching the plight of the ayahs, Thushani's interest in the subject deepened, inspiring her to write her first novel, *Ayah*.

Thushani lives in London.

AYAH

'*Ayah* is a magnificent love story about the forbidden relationship between an English gentleman and his Indian servant. Thushani Weerasekera takes her readers on a gripping journey from imperial India to the slums of Victorian London and opens our eyes to the horrendous treatment of Indian women abandoned in the capital. Ayah is full of memorable characters who could just as easily find a home in Dickens. It is an utterly compelling story, beautifully written. I would recommend this book to any reader of serious fiction.'

Danny Scheinmann, Best-selling author of *Random Acts of Heroic Love*

PART ONE

India 1866

CHAPTER 1
GOODBYE CALCUTTA

Jemima had heard the port of Calcutta hailed as the 'gateway to the East Indies,' but as far as she was concerned it might as well have been the gateway to the entire world. Sightseers, explorers, sailors and seasoned wayfarers mingled with merchants and traders selling their wares in an environment bursting at its seams. Hawkers bellowed into the ears of unsuspecting tourists, their baskets crammed with every edible commodity the city had to offer. Housewives, fishwives and gaudy-face eunuchs puffed on cheroots and gossiped behind veils fashioned from their rainbow-coloured saris. Seated on the fringes and poised like stick insects, bare-chested old fellows with protruding ribs and blood-shot eyes shifted every so often to adjust their *dhotis* or spit out mouthfuls of *paan* that skimmed the air like viscous rubies. The city's beggars pleaded, whilst behind them dusty-faced children hustled to a backdrop of mystical melodies and native beats. How bloated the docks looked to Jemima; its guts seemed to spill out in every direction, spewing a heady concoction of colours, smells, sights and sounds that inspired the locals and besieged the newcomer. Calcutta's paraphernalia cast a giddy spell upon the world within its embrace, but despite this raucous spectacle, the *Bengal Star* – the vessel that would carry Jemima away – sat proudly in the harbour, silently observing the circus around it.

Jemima had never left India before. With the exception of her birthplace – a village in Midnapore – and the district of Krishnagar in which she worked for almost five years, she had never ventured beyond the confines of Calcutta. In her customary environment, life was simple and life was good. Rising every morning at sunrise, she would eat two plantains and some mango for breakfast and then wake the children to prepare them for the day. The mistress would be waiting to be festooned in her fine and fancy dresses and as Jemima coiled the tresses of the lady's soft brown hair, her senses would turn to the world outside the window, where monkeys scampered up tree trunks to steal ripe coconuts and mongooses scuttled across the veranda's wooden slats in search of snakes slithering in the nearby undergrowth. Menacing black crows would gather on the slate rooftops above, whilst beyond them in the distance, the Hooghly River suddenly became the sea that was lit magnificently by the sun's warm and ample rays. The air was alive with damselflies, beetles and locusts, whose call grew more hectic as darkness cloaked the sultry city and then how different the scene would become as Jemima sat in the nursery, singing the children to sleep. Creatures from the river peeked in through the windows, trying to slip in between the wooden slats of the closed shutters. She would chase each mosquito trying to feast on the children's young blood, not resting until she had swatted every last one of them. A few moments would be squandered on the fireflies clustered around the hibiscus bushes; how she loved to see them smoulder in the garden's dusky air. As a child, she had loved the way they illuminated the shadows around her parents' humble home. Yes, of all Calcutta's creatures, fireflies were her favourite; they reminded her of home… of Calcutta and Bengal; *her home.*

And now on the brink of sailing west, the prospect of leaving India's shores terrified and tantalised Jemima in unknown measure. She shivered at the sheer magnitude of the vessels moored in the harbour and the scene made an indelible impression on her unworldly mind. Anxiety rose like a mountain and she almost retched as she recollected the words that prompted the great adventure she was about to undertake. *'The sahib and I are to return home to England.'*

She had not anticipated such a declaration when she was summoned to the memsahib's chamber that day. She had prepared herself for the likes of... *'Jemima, I would like you to wash and dry Sophie's pink dress in time for the picnic on Sunday afternoon.'* Or, *'Jemima, you haven't finished mending Robert's pantaloons.'* Instead she heard, *'We plan to leave in a month's time. The children are of schooling age now and...'* The words floated by in imperceptible murmurs and Jemima could only consider the implications and how it would grieve her to say goodbye. But she was an ayah and being parted from the youngsters she had grown to care for was a disadvantage she had had to get used to. Nevertheless, it took a moment to acknowledge the news and her heart sank with bitter disappointment. She must find another position: an unfamiliar family with unfamiliar children and the bonds of trust and reliance would have to be built again. The curt call of her name harnessed her wandering thoughts and then the memsahib uttered the words that would unbeknownst to Jemima, change her life forever. *'I am in need of a servant to attend to the family during the journey home. The voyage is long and arduous and we could be out at sea for several weeks. Once we have arrived and the children have settled, I shall no longer require your services and you will return to India. We will pay for your journey there and back, and provide for you when necessary. Do you understand?'*

It was hard to think with a head floundering in uncertainty. Jemima needed more time than the measly seconds, during which she was expected to respond. However she soon realised that the memsahib's declaration was not an appeal; it was a command and dutifully, she muttered her reply. *'Yes, Madam, I must come with you.'*

Four weeks later and moments away from departing, Jemima's thoughts were drifting between terror and sadness and she would have remained sinking in this pitiable limbo had Abdul – the sahib's personal servant – not rescued her with a nudge of his elbow. Pulling on the buggy reins, he mumbled a 'whoa' of some sort and ordered Jemima to unload the family possessions in the overweening tone of voice that she had come to detest. But since this would be the last time she would have to take orders from a sluggard like Abdul, Jemima gritted her teeth and hurled the pieces of baggage into his arms.

In the distance, warehouses and factories bustled with seaport activity and coolies of a Chinese as well as native variety heaved an assortment of cargo from the many ships that had sailed far and wide. The drinking holes were chaotic too, selling temptation to sailors seeking solace in shots of hot, unwholesome toddy. Along the coast, British clippers were leaving with consignments of spices, tea and silk. Others dropped anchors with imported freights of textiles and unwrought metals. Indistinct dots on the horizon evolved into schooners and frigates whilst an array of colourful buoys bobbed in between *budgerows* and rowboats brimming with plantains, coconuts and freshly-caught fish. Jemima sensed the exhilaration of children and adults alike: people eager to climb on board their particular class of transport, be it the splendid vessels of the Empire or the more humble palm-shaded *panchway*. But whatever the choice or restriction imposed, the thrill of a sea-based escapade lay heavy in the air and the infectious enthusiasm of others seemed to fortify her nerves. Seconds ago, she was a dithering fool, frightened of the future and the

world beyond Calcutta, but somehow in a moment of contempla-
tion, Jemima's eyes were blazing brightly again. *England.* How
wonderful! What an opportunity! What an honour. In any case,
if she disliked the place, she would eventually be coming home.
The warm brackish air comforted her skin as she climbed down
from the buggy and took her place beside Abdul. Instinctively,
she tugged her muslin shawl further over her brow, for amongst
the clatter of *caranchies,* bullock carts, oxen and buggies, she saw
that the master's carriage had finally cantered up behind them.

William Hayward dismounted the carriage and surveyed the
scene around him. Extending a steadying arm to his wife, he
blinked hard in the intrusive sunlight as the chaos of the port
unfolded about him. He next assisted his children. Crowds were
swelling and a stream of *caranchies* veered towards their shuffling
feet, missing their toes by inches. With a protective hand held
out against the mayhem, William guided his family to the shoreline, accompanied by a chorus of his wife's incessant moans. 'The
stench is unbearable,' Elizabeth Hayward grumbled. Clutching
a rose-scented handkerchief to her nose and mouth, she muttered, 'It's most disagreeable.' In a valedictory serenade to the
ships leaving Calcutta, a row of Indian drummers thumped native rhythms from the brightly hued drums draped about their
necks. Tourists called for an encore but Elizabeth Hayward
cringed and covered her ears. 'Infernal racket!' she huffed. 'I
shall be relieved to get home.'

Native boatmen waved and pointed to a line of tethered
catamarans and William beckoned one from the group and a
skinny, shirtless native man – his lower regions swathed in tatty
cotton – pushed past the others to stake his claim. 'Boat Sahib!
Boat Sahib!' he cried. 'I take you to ship?'

William delved inside his inside coat pocket and withdrew a
leather purse. 'It'll be much easier to reach the ship this way,' he

said, handing it to his wife. 'Looks like there's bedlam ahead of us... by the way, I wouldn't pay the fellow until he's taken you all the way but give him a little extra, Elizabeth... these men barely earn a pittance.'

Elizabeth scoffed as she trailed the boatman down the narrow steps of a *ghat*. There, a rickety boat bounced alongside dozens of others and she squirmed at the thought of having to travel inside one. 'Now there's absolutely nothing for you to worry about,' said William. 'I'll close up the house and send the servants on... and I'll be perfectly fine... Abdul will take good care of me, won't you Abdul?'

William's concern made Elizabeth squirm further. Her gloomy disposition was hardly due to his pending domestic arrangements as he so liked to think. She analysed his face: a façade of good intentions and then focused her gaze on the gormless cow mooching beyond the *ghat* steps. William beckoned his son and daughter. 'Children, I want you to be on your best behaviour. No tears please, Sophie.'

'I don't want to leave, Papa,' the five-year-old whimpered.

'Don't be foolish, child. You're returning home... back to England. Everyone will be delighted to see you. Won't you be delighted to see them?' he replied, crouching on his haunches.

She nodded as a child would do under reluctant circumstances: laboriously with a quivering bottom lip.

'Promise me you'll behave?'

'I promise,' she sighed, fiddling with the silver buttons on her red summer coat.

'Where's Papa's kiss?'

She planted a tear-stained kiss upon his cheek and he showed his affection by way of a tight embrace.

'Robert, you're the fellow in charge,' he said, looking to his son. 'You're seven-years-old now... practically an old man,' he added with a smile. 'Take care of your mother and sister for me. I'm relying on you.'

'Yes sir,' the boy said, trying not to cry.

William gently swept his fingers through his son's golden curls. 'It's all right, my boy... I'll be on the next ship home,' he sighed, squeezing Robert's shoulder. He stood up to face his wife. 'Take good care,' Elizabeth, he said, offering her a kiss. 'Please tell the family I'll see them shortly.'

'Goodbye William.' Her reply sounded bleak. She took hold of his hand but could not bear to touch him further. Her eyes were fixed on the boatman until the sight of his cracked, mis-shapen toenails forced her to search for Ayah. 'Get in the boat, Jemima,' she ordered.

Jemima wondered how foolish her mistress could be. *'Are you made of stone?' she thought. 'If only I were you... how I wish I could be you.'* She pictured herself in a passionate embrace with William Hayward and almost tumbled as she clambered into the catamaran.

'Take very good care of them, Ayah,' he shouted from the steps.

The sound of his voice made her head spin. 'Yes, Sahib,' Jemima replied, adjusting the shawl that had fallen over her head. She was not sure if he heard her response, for he was great-ly preoccupied with his tense wife and sombre children. It was only Abdul who shot a glance in her direction, albeit a noncha-lant one.

The boatman pushed his paddle against the concrete bank and the catamaran floated out amongst the stream of dinghies and barges heading towards the steamer. When the fellow had found his rhythm, he launched into a dexterous pattern of row-ing which propelled the boat speedily towards the ship's gang-way. William pinned his eyes to Sophie's red coat, at least then he thought, he should not lose his family within the herds of vessels congregating around them. His wife's face was taut, possibly pondering the voyage ahead but Elizabeth Hayward was in fact, trying to calm herself, for she could not bury the deep resentment she harboured towards her husband. And as he shrank into nothingness amongst the crowds, the walls of Jemima's heart pulsed and shivered.

The crew of the *Bengal Star* were waiting to assist passengers on board their temporary floating home. Elizabeth and the children seized the first available fingers and clambered onto the gangway, relieved to finally be on board the mighty vessel that would take them part of the way home. Jemima passed some coins into the boatman's bony hand and the fellow jiggled his head and then rowed away as effortlessly as he had rowed his passengers towards the ship. Her eager eyes then scoured every inch of the *ghat* they had left behind but she could no longer see the sahib among the mayhem of people on the banks, though he *was* out there somewhere, whispering wishes into the salty sea air – wishes for the safe passage home of his wife and children.

A bell rang in the distance and the drummers resumed their deafening beats. William Hayward looked back once more at the majestic ship about to carry off his family and wiped a lustrous layer of sweat away from his forehead. 'Do you think they'll be all right, Abdul?' he asked, his tone mixed with guilt and relief.

'You not worry, Sahib,' Abdul chirped. 'Memsahib and children will be fine... they are safely on ship now.'

'I hope so, Abdul,' William said, making his way back to the carriage. 'I really do hope so.'

As the *Bengal Star* set sail, over a dozen ships moored side-by-side drifted by in a line reaching almost two miles down the bank. The ship sailed past Fort William, the impenetrable hexagonal hub of the British Army, separated from the rest of the city by the Esplanade – a former expanse of jungle that now housed the city's white-walled, flat-topped civic and military buildings. The sight of the majestic colonnade of Calcutta's High Court and the Governor's Palace with its Corinthian columns and oriental-style verandas made Jemima marvel and gasp. The Hayward's house in Dhurmotollah Street was situated not far from those very buildings and she had often glimpsed the white masts of the clippers from the nursery's high windows. But the far-away vista of Calcutta's harbour had always appeared to her as an intangible dream or an imaginary world of some sort, in which she would have been a certain intruder. Curling her fingers around the ship's rail, Jemima sighed at the vivid scenes surrounding her. Garden Reach, the chief residential centre for the city's British inhabitants was beautiful and breathtaking. Pretty villas sat alongside elegant houses, their lawns extending like lush green carpets that almost touched the sacred Ganges flowing out before them. Groves of coconut trees tilted in the breeze and distant sprays of tall bamboo swayed to a melancholy rhythm, as if to whisper goodbye.

The ship eventually emerged amid emerald green forests and marshes thick with swamp vegetation and Jemima recalled how a cyclone had hit Calcutta only two years before, luring boats to their destruction and adventurers to a watery grave. But choosing to ignore how perilous the elements could be, she allowed the encompassing splendour to seduce her imagination and watched with eyes agog as plantations of rice, sugar cane and coco-palms swept by in the distance. Thatched, mud-wall cottages rose into view, reminding her of Birshingha – the village in which she was born. Dragonflies danced about the heads of tethered cows and bullocks munched on foliage stretching as far as the eye could see. Half-naked children skipped along the banks, waving their small hands amongst a scattering of banyan trees. The scent of ripe vegetation saturated the air and a chorus of grasshopper chirps built to a crescendo, hailing the jungles of the Sunderbans. Next came the haunting howls of jackals and the threat of prowling tigers, and if her journey had ended there and she was to be dragged off into a shadowy corner of the jungle by one such creature, Jemima would have been content to die having seen the glorious countryside of her native Bengal. Meditating quietly, she concluded that life need not be a struggle when it came to the might of her emotions. She was a servant and her feelings must be controlled... purged even. Well, she had tamed them for over two years now and so, how hard could it be to try and forget? And with the burden of her heartache seemingly lifted, Jemima whispered a prayer into the languid sea air and bade the Motherland a fond farewell. *'Aashi aamar priyo Calcutta, aaber dheka hobe.'* Goodbye Calcutta, I'll see you very soon.

But it was not that easy to banish the sahib's hazy image from her mind and try as she might it was not that easy to forbid those scant reminiscences of his striking face. The faint sound of his voice was forever purring in her ears and how could she forget the first time she ever set eyes on him in the house back in Calcutta.

CHAPTER 2
THE SAHIB

Jemima first ventured to the Hayward house in the early summer of 1864. She was told to look for Tipu Sultan's Mosque: a shrine built by Prince Ghulam Mohammed in memory of his father, Emperor Tipu Sultan, 'The Tiger of Mysore.' She spied the corner minarets from Chowringhee Road. The sacred edifice was situated at the junction of Esplanade East and Dhurmotollah Street and the Hayward abode could be found about a quarter of the way down – a handsome two-storey building with a flat roof and high white walls that boasted the type of architecture favoured by the British. She spotted a turban-clad, bearded fellow crouching on his haunches, eating papaya behind the tall iron gates. Now and again, he would peep towards the house and failed to notice Jemima as she approached from the roadside. He could have been one of her charges, she thought: a child caught in the act of disobedience. She watched him a while longer before making her presence known. 'I am Jemima,' she said.

His shoulders jerked suddenly and he eyed her through the gate railings. Satisfied that she was no one of importance, he dragged his teeth over the remaining papaya pulp before flinging the peel into the surrounding bushes. 'You are the new ayah?' he asked, stretching and yawning like a lazy lion.

'Yes.' She noticed some beads of papaya juice sparkling in his black whiskers.

'Come, come,' he said, unlocking the gates. 'Memsahib is waiting...'

Heedful of his lecherous gaze, she pulled her sari train over her shoulders and mustered the nerve to ask him a question. 'What is your name?'

'Abdul,' he answered, wiping his papaya-stained hands on the back of his white *kameez.*

Abdul led her into a generously proportioned but sparsely decorated hallway with a short corridor running down to the kitchen quarters. The lofty ceilings were supported by thick wooden beams and possessed *punkas* – huge frames of white cotton – that swayed back and forth to create a breeze when the appropriate servant pulled on its cords. Daylight threw its sunbeams through the open shutters, warming the rather understated pieces of wicker furniture scattered about the rooms. The memsahib appeared at the top of the staircase and then floated down the steps in a manner that was both commanding and serene. She ordered Jemima to open her small valise and proceeded to rifle through the unobjectionable contents before turning to inspect her new employee. Investigating and absorbing every aspect of her new servant's figure, Elizabeth Hayward's eyes crawled from the tips of Jemima's sandal-clad toes and along her single plait until – offended by a partially exposed midriff – they came to rest on Jemima's forehead. Her new ayah was petite and slim. The folds of her sari accentuated the contours of her childbearing hips, which had, so far, not borne any offspring. She possessed a heart-shaped face with eyes that brought to Elizabeth's mind the outline of two large almonds. Her pupils constricted in the sunlight but spread into big brown buttons when she sought respite in the shadows. Scraped back and tied into a bun, Jemima's hair glistened magnificently and carried the faint smell of coconut. And secretly, Elizabeth Hayward acknowledged her earthy beauty. 'That garment is not suitable at all,' she remarked, referring to Jemima's sari.

Jemima's spine sagged. The sari was good enough for her previous employer, but it appeared as though this lady was going to be far more of a challenge. She was cut from a superior cloth woven by the lady herself. Still, the green sari *was* a little frayed around the edges but it was Jemima's best one and she only wore it on important occasions.

'You shall borrow a skirt and blouse from Alice,' the memsahib suggested, pacing back and forth rather solemnly. Crossing over to a small bureau in the corner of the room, she opened a drawer and spent a moment sifting through some papers. 'I have received a letter from Reverend Finch and his wife... they also handed me a letter from your first employer...a Dr Mukherjee. Both gentlemen say that you are able to read and write in English. Is this correct?'

'Yes, Memsahib.'

'How extraordinary! I was under the impression that native females... servants especially... were not encouraged to seek an education. Who taught you?'

'Dr Mukerjee's wife, Memsahib.'

'An Indian woman taught you?'

'Yes, Memsahib, she was a teacher.'

Jemima's voice sounded girlish. 'What age are you?' the memsahib asked.

'Twenty-five years, Madam.'

'Good heavens! I wouldn't have imagined you past an age of eighteen! Are you married?'

'I was Memsahib,' Jemima replied.

'Do you have children?'

'No, Memsahib.'

A weighty pause passed.

'What happened to your husband?'

'*Why does she want to know about my personal matters? What right does she have to ask? What does my husband have to do with her?*' A good servant Jemima may be but that hardly stopped her from thinking defiant thoughts. Subservience, however, always won the battle for power and more importantly, she needed the work and so she answered in a manner befitting the servant she was. 'He died, Memsahib.' She had kept that part of her history tucked inside the vaults of her past. To speak of her husband and the way he had passed was to speak of her parents and the manner in which they too had suffered. This was *her* business and no one else's and she was thankful not to be asked to elaborate further.

Meanwhile, Elizabeth Hayward's cheeks had begun to twitch with unruly displeasure. Her knowledge of her servants' personal histories was minimal to say the least. She had never shown any interest in their next of kin nor had she asked any questions pertinent to their backgrounds but now she had discovered more in one morning from Jemima than she had learned from any of the other servants in the six or so months they had been by her side. Beyond an ability to cook, clean and care for her children there was nothing more she needed to know. She did not want a reason to feel sorry for Indians. She did not want to sympathise with their unfortunate circumstances. Her interest lay in their servile capacity and the less she knew about them, the less human they appeared to be. And so, Elizabeth Hayward decided to digress. 'Obedience, honesty, neatness in attire, cleanliness... especially in the company of children... are of supreme importance. I insist on the children being spoken to in English... *always*.' A few exceptions to the rule existed. For example, if an equivalent English word did not exist then the *Hindi* one was permitted.

The odd native song could be sung or a rhyme recited but on no occasion was it ever to be taught. 'I do not wish to hear either of them speaking in a *chi chi* accent.' That rule was non-negotiable.

Mistress and ayah proceeded to the kitchen – a domain chiefly inhabited by the male members of the household staff, who grunted and groaned as the lady talked of 'the terrors of India'. 'The children must be protected from the heat and dust... one can catch so many diseases.' Ignorant of the surreptitious smiles blooming behind her back, she continued. 'Both milk and water must be boiled thoroughly and the children must eat only wholesome English food... nothing spicy *whatsoever* is ever to be given.' At that point, she stared menacingly at one of the servants standing in the corner. 'In the event of a slow bowel movement...a condition to which the children are especially prone... one tablespoon of castor oil should be administered, if need be, while the nose is pinched tight.' And on that direction, she pointed to a large bottle on one of the pantry shelves.

Jemima had heard the speech before; the same scenario in a continuing domestic drama, only now the cast of characters had changed. It ended with the knowledge that she would also have to perform the same menial duties expected of a lady's maid: dusting and cleaning, so on and so forth. Later on, she would learn from the other servants that apart from sunstroke, the odd insect bite and a bout of fever, Robert and Sophie had been uncannily lucky in India and had never suffered as many other youngsters had done. Despite their mother's fears, their days in Calcutta had been, thus far, blithe and disease-free.

She was relieved to leave the male-dominated kitchen, for it was a domain in which she felt uncomfortable. She trailed the memsahib up the stairs, where, at the top, the lady pointed to another set of steps. 'You will retire to the attic,' the memsahib said, moving swiftly onto the first room along a corridor. She then twisted the brass-plated handle, which squeaked as she pushed open the door. Shrill voices rose and fell. 'This is the nursery,' the memsahib said. 'Come and meet the children.' Jemima caught sight of legs randomly kicking the air. They belonged to a small boy lying outstretched on a Persian rug, mercilessly bashing the heads of his two tin soldiers together. 'This is Robert,' the memsahib said. 'Straighten your collar, Robert!' The boy dropped his playthings and immediately set about flattening the wayward lapels on his blue and white sailor suit. 'From now on, Alice will care for Robert... you are already acquainted with Alice, I believe?'

Seated on a chair in the corner of the room was Alice. But it was not Alice that commanded Jemima's attention, for perched within the folds of Alice Ayah's skirts was a doll-like creature adorned in a blaze of white lace and crimson linen. Jemima acknowledged Alice with a nod but her eyes pursued the girl fidgeting on her knees. 'Come here, dear,' said the memsahib, smiling for the first time that day.

Like two gilt curtains, the girl's flaxen ringlets tumbled onto her shoulders as she slipped off Alice's lap and toddled over. 'This is Sophie,' the girl's mother said, pulling the child's crumpled dress into place. 'Sophie, this is Jemima Ayah... she is your new nanny and she will be looking after you.'

Jemima wished she could embrace the child and pinch her apple-like cheeks. However, this was an occasion that called for restraint and the use of her very best English. 'Good morning Sophie,' she chirped. 'I am very pleased to meet you.'

But for the tin bath which took centre stage and the washstand upon which an inverted china jug and basin stood, the children's bathing area was grey and stark with the lingering odour of disinfectant. Besides the aforementioned items, nothing else was permitted: no cupboards, no chairs, no towels or clothing stands. 'That way there are less places for snakes to hide,' explained the memsahib. 'Alice Ayah sweeps and cleans the entire room before each child takes their ablutions. You must do the same.' It was while they were stooped over checking for spiders and such like in the corners and holes that a voice boomed from the corridor outside.

'Elizabeth, where are you?'

The memsahib immediately abandoned her stance of a sour old matron and hurried out of the room, leaving Jemima wondering to whom the virile voice belonged. She dared herself to look beyond the slightly ajar door and could not help but listen to the ensuing conversation.

'I wasn't expecting you home at this hour. How lovely...' the memsahib crooned.

'I've returned for a change of clothes,' the man said. 'Spencer's invited a few of the fellows for drinks at the club. He's been posted in China and leaves within the week. I'm very certain I mentioned it.'

Curious to see what the gentleman looked like, Jemima peeked through the hinged slit of the door and saw a tuft of fair hair flash by. She caught sight of a tall figure; other than that, it was hard to make much else out and the scene was further restricted when the memsahib walked towards the gentleman. 'Must you go, William?'

Jemima felt bold. Reaching out ever so gingerly she edged the door open, praying it would not creak or make the slightest noise. She managed a gap of a few inches before succumbing to nerves but found that if she settled into the alcove nearby, she could see more of the pair as they conversed. His hands lay across his wife's drooping shoulders but she drew away from him, wary of the servant nearby. 'Where are the children?' he asked.

'In the garden... with Alice.'

'I must see Spencer off, Elizabeth. I'll see Robert and Sophie before I depart.'

The atmosphere was tense and Jemima wondered whether the lady would lose her temper. Then, for a while, nothing else was spoken and the pair drifted about in an awkward silence. But Elizabeth Hayward was wondering about her evening ahead. Would she sew before dinner or read after the children had gone to bed? Or would she choose the more likely alternative of resenting the moment she set foot in the godforsaken country that had stolen her husband away? She cleared her throat to eradicate the threads of enthusiasm she had felt on hearing him call out her name. 'The new ayah has arrived,' she said.

'Splendid!' he replied. 'At least Alice Ayah won't shoulder the burden anymore.' And then he crossed to the middle of the room and directly into Jemima's view. 'She was run ragged by the little scoundrels!' he laughed. 'Be sure to tell them not to do the same to... what's the new ayah's name?'

'Jemima,' Elizabeth spat. 'Anyway, she's *their* servant as well as mine, William. She's here to do as they command.'

'That may be so, but I shan't excuse mischief and rudeness to anyone... Jemima and Alice included.'

Jemima peered out beneath the makeshift hood she had fashioned from her sari. Her eyes registered his face but a brief moment later she could offer no explanation for the state of her emotions. Instinctively she looked down but she betrayed her resolve to admire him again. He was rolling one of his son's tin soldiers between his fingers whilst scraping the flaking paint off with the nail of his thumb. Two buttons on his waistcoat were unfastened and his silk cravat remained slack around his neck. His shirt was messy – partly tucked into his waist and partly hanging out – and he brushed aside some locks of blond hair from eyes that were just as blue as his son's and daughter's. '*How kind the sahib is... and what a fine and handsome face he has. What strong shoulders... and a stunning smile,*' she thought. His beauty made her skin sear and he reflected a splendour that explained why the children looked the way they did. He was the most perfect man she had ever seen and a peculiar feeling pulsed in her stomach. It was careless and rash and she felt bewildered and ashamed; bewildered for experiencing such enchantment and ashamed for being attracted to her white superior.

A rush of blood to her head made her retreat inside the alcove again. Neither he nor the memsahib spoke in that passing moment. He glanced down at the toy in his hand and then across to his wife before saying, 'I shall bathe and change... and then I'll see the children.'

Elizabeth shot him with an icy stare. 'Very well,' she said, before turning away.

That one sighting of William Hayward was enough to alter Jemima's state of mind. She rarely crossed paths with the man but she carried his image around as if it were a prized trinket. As an ayah to his children, she could count on her hand the number of times she encountered him: a time when she brought the children in for breakfast; another when she took them to say goodnight. Sometimes his absences stretched to weeks and she ached for an opportunity to see his face. But she and Alice took care of his wife and children and it was Abdul and the other males that tended to his needs. Finally, when he did return, she would often hear his voice from an upstairs chamber or catch his shadow passing in the hallway below. Once, she stole across the hallway to spy on him through a gap in the drawing room door. 'I shall always love England,' she heard him say, 'but India has given me a real purpose... a challenge... even an education! We have as much to learn from its people as they do from us.'

Censure and anger always echoed in the memsahib's voice but a fire of sincerity in his own told Jemima that he loved her homeland as much as she did. But it was the incident with Alice Ayah that confirmed her adulation for him, for when Alice was caught red-handed stealing soap from the storeroom, she was dismissed without being given a second chance. And as Jemima passed the memsahib's bedchamber, she overheard the discussion inside.

'I cannot abide thieves,' the memsahib said, 'and Indian ones are the worst kind.'

'Whatever do you mean by that, Elizabeth?' her husband asked.

'She had already asked if she could take some soap home for her mother and I had already refused her.'

'You mean to say that you refused Alice Ayah when she was honest enough to ask you in the first place?'

'She wasn't best pleased, William. I should have known that she would be up to no good.'

'Good gracious, Elizabeth! Her family is viciously poor and you denied her one or two bars of soap?'

'If I had granted her request, William, who knows what else she'd ask for next. Food? Clothes? This very house?'

It was just before the sahib left for Murshidabad the next day that he entered the nursery and called Jemima aside. She was so taken aback by his presence that she started to tremble a little as she pulled her shawl over her head and bashfully made her way over to him.

'Do you know where Alice lives?' he asked, clasping a box in his hands.

She nodded once and averted her eyes.

'When is your next free day?'

'Tomorrow, Sahib,' she mumbled.

'Good. I must ask a favour of you, Jemima. I'd like you to hide this box in your room for now and when you have the chance, I'd like you to take it to Alice. I shan't go against my wife's wishes and have her back, you understand? But I can do something to help her and her family. Will you do this for me?'

Jemima would jump into a roaring fire for the man. She nodded again.

'Thank you. Oh, and take one for yourself if you need one
too.'

He passed the box into her hands and she admired his long,
lean fingers. He turned and left and she hurried upstairs and
opened the box to find six white bars of soap and an envelope
with 'Alice Ayah' etched on the front. Jemima was certain it contained money and her heart exploded with a heady blend of love
and joy. He was unlike any white man she had ever met – a god
perhaps, in her estimation – at the very least she thought him
worthy of being a king, who ruled his realm with justice and compassion. However, she was under no illusion. On the rare occasion he was ever home, he was pleasant, polite and benevolent
enough, even though in the past, he had sometimes mistaken
her for Alice. But Jemima did not care. Her ardour for him was
her own little secret: a pointless fantasy, a worthless dream, but
hers nonetheless. Yes, she was a native female and her worth was
measured by her capacity to serve; other than that, she was insignificant and invisible. But in the private world of her imagination – where she directed the players on her own stage – she
adored the sahib and the sahib adored her, though, in reality he
had never once given her the slightest second look.

CHAPTER 3
THE SHIP

Known as *The Baltic* when it was first built in 1855, the ship in which Jemima and her memsahib presently sailed was initially chartered by the British Government as a means of army transport used during the Crimean War. The vessel was constructed in the dockyards of Rotherhithe, London and was later refitted, re-decorated and transformed into the handsome looking ship that was now the *Bengal Star*. Currently travelling the route from Calcutta to Suez, the only reminders of the original vessel came in the form of the rather garish figurehead of a lion and the suspension rods of the lower deck's wooden beams, over which, the congested hammocks of British soldiers formerly hung. Now, a motley mix of sailors comprised the crew: Muslim lascars in the engine room, Hindus on deck and Roman Catholic Goans taking the more favourable positions of ship stewards. There was room for up to a five hundred and thirty eight passengers, an assortment of which, strolled along the commodious decks. Diplomats, soldiers and investment bankers brushed shoulders with teachers and civil servants claiming overdue sabbaticals. In the leather sofas of the steamer's elegant smoking rooms, a plethora of lawyers puffed away on a chain of cigars, whilst families heading home for Christmas mingled with clergymen and members of their flock. And waiting amongst this amalgam of masters were the dutiful servants: the maids and the ayahs, the valets and the grooms; the barbers and the baggage handlers – heads lowered, ears cocked – ready to attend to their every whim and fancy.

However, down below in a world disengaged from the grandeur of the upper decks, the engine room lascars were feeling the strain. Nauseous and disorientated, they carried coal on moving decks, stumbling over each other's feet whilst shovelling ash on a ship that plunged and rocked in the rolling waves. Cool draughts of air blown down from the upper deck's ventilation shafts were some temporary respite but the lascars would compete for the relief it brought from the sweltering heat of the ship's demanding boilers. The work was relentless and the conditions appalling; the men in charge were hard-hearted and cruel. No sympathy was given to the fledgling sailors and no clemency shown for their inexperienced hands. No beds or hammocks were provided for their rest and relaxation; only damp, dark spaces with crates piled at one end and animal cages stacked down the other, constituted their meagre quarters. They congregated as far from the beasts as they possibly could, especially the pigs that were considered offensive, but for one lascar in particular, a fellow called Ibrahim, the strain of sailing the ocean waves was about to turn into an unimaginable nightmare.

Three days earlier, in the depths of Calcutta's dockyard, Ibrahim had stood in a scruffy recruiting office in front of a *ghat serang* – a moody man with a cleft lip – who snorted his way through a procession of cheroots. 'Since you have no sufficient experience of the sea, you will earn less than the other seasoned lascars.'

Ibrahim thought the terms reasonable. 'Very well,' he replied.

'A monthly wage of thirty rupees will be paid for the voyage from Calcutta to England and thereafter, a weekly maintenance allowance of ten shillings whilst you await passage home.'

'Excuse me, sir... I only require one-way passage... I am not thinking of lascar work as a career.'

'I will make an exception for you,' the agent sniggered. 'Special treatment! Now sign your name here.'

Ibrahim etched his signature on the flimsy contract without finding the need to read its stipulations.

'You will be sailing on the *Bengal Star* this coming Friday. Come before sunrise and ask for Rajesh Naidu. He is the *serang* in charge... show him the paper.'

'And this is a one-way arrangement?'

'Oh yes. One-way!' the agent chuckled. 'Stupid bloody fool.'

Ibrahim failed to hear the man's insult and left the recruiting office with a spring in his step.

The *Bengal Star* cast a cool but mammoth shadow over the queue of novice lascars waiting to climb onto its decks. Many of them had never seen a vessel of such immense proportions and were greatly intimidated by the prospect of sailing the unpredictable seas. Some distracted themselves by exchanging names and backgrounds whilst several stood in worlds of their own, saddened at the thought of leaving their loved ones behind. Waiting quietly amongst them, Ibrahim traced the ship from stem to stern. He heard a British naval officer bark orders to his second-in-command, who then bellowed his sailor-speak to the experienced Asian lascars waiting on the shore below. Hired navvies lugged crates and winched cages, blaspheming each time the ropes got caught in the pulleys. Cows bayed and pigs grunted, objecting to the pitiless manner in which they were dragged along the gangway. A glut of chickens clucked and flapped, butting their busy heads on the metal bars that stole their freedom. Not knowing if he shook from the coolness of the ship's shadow or the anticipation of travelling into the unknown, Ibrahim felt a wonderment that made his stomach churn. The men ahead of him were having their papers stamped before entering a brand new world. He huffed impatiently when the line ground to a halt, for a new recruit had misplaced his contract and was searching for them in his knapsack. 'Not again!' Ibrahim moaned, dumping his belongings onto the ground. He tapped the shoulder of the man in front and a rather tubby fellow with plump cheeks and a shiny forehead turned around. 'First time?' Ibrahim asked.

The man nodded.

'Mine too. Where are you from?'

'Bengal,' the tubby fellow replied. 'My name is Abu.'

Ibrahim shook his hand. 'I am Ibrahim.'

It felt good to make a friend. Ibrahim was twenty-four years old – a good ten years younger than Abu – but he had worked with men of differing ages and did not feel akin to a particular generation. Abu's kin and roots hailed from a village in Sylhet. 'I was born into a family of fishermen,' he said. 'My father taught me how to handle boats from an early age.' Abu had a tendency to gloat. 'The sea is my home and I am a very skilled sailor. Still... I did not expect to see a ship this big! My wife will not believe me when I tell her.'

'You have left a wife?' queried Ibrahim.

'And three children... I need money and many say lascar work pays well.' The queue moved on a little. 'What about you?' Abu asked. 'What brings you to the sea?'

Ibrahim decided to gloat too. 'Oh... I want to see Europe. I am a skilled chef!'

'A chef!' laughed Abu, his dimpled cheeks inflating with each guffaw. 'Somehow I cannot picture a skinny cook like you trying to command the ocean waves.'

Ibrahim bristled but saw the funny side of Abu's comment. The queue moved on, taking the pair swiftly to the front.

Abu handed over his contract; it was stamped and he was promptly sent up the ramp. Next in line was Ibrahim. 'Rajesh Naidu, sir?' he asked.

The man seated behind the table lifted his head and nodded. Ibrahim smoothed down the creases in his contract and presented it under the boatswain's nose. Greatly amused by his misfit manners, Naidu delicately placed a stamp on the agreement before indicating the way up the ramp, as if his recruit was a fragile English memsahib. 'Excuse me, sir,' Ibrahim asked, straying near the table. 'I am on one-way work passage, yes?'

The *serang* stared back at him. 'What?'

'The *ghat serang* agreed this. He said "one-way passage," sir.'

Naidu placed his hands squarely on the table and called out to a circle of men immersed in a cloud of *bidi* smoke. One fellow sauntered over and Ibrahim recognised him as the *ghat serang* he had seen in the recruiting office three days ago. Naidu stood up and whispered into the man's ear and they sniggered like schoolgirls with their heads curled together. 'One-way work passage. Just for you,' Naidu crooned as he sat back down.

'Thank you, sir! Thank you, sir!' Ibrahim replied, galloping up the ramp.

Slipping in and amongst the new recruits, Ibrahim watched the *serang's* assistant – a man known as a *tindal* – divide the men into groups after determining their religious affiliations. 'Why do they want to know our faith?' he asked.

'Maybe for food,' Abu replied.

Moments later the Hindu lascars were called away to the upper decks, leaving the group of animated Muslims to speculate on the type of work they would be offered. A second *tindal* arrived causing much conjecture when he blew into his tin whistle and ordered everyone to follow his lead. Ibrahim and his band of Muslim brothers scuttled through a dark corridor where the clamour of steel and the growl of boiler fires assaulted their ears and set their sweat glands bubbling with over-activity. Their journey ended in the domain of the engine room, where the sound of coal crashing down metal chutes battered their eardrums. Their induction was swift and incredibly succinct: they must study how the accomplished lascars did their jobs and then get on with it themselves. Simple enough, Ibrahim thought, however this was not the area of work in which his particular talents lay. 'Excuse me, sir,' he said, approaching the *tindal*. 'I am a chef and I am unfamiliar with this kind of work. Is there...' He was cut off mid-sentence when the *tindal* departed, leaving a rather careworn lascar-in-charge to assign the posts. Ibrahim and Abu were chosen as stokers: lascars responsible for keeping the furnaces loaded and grates free from ash.

'Perhaps I should speak to Naidu and tell him I am a cook,' Ibrahim said, contemplating the impropriety of the work.

Abu shrugged and the supervising lascar puckered his brow. The man's face was scarlet and overly shiny and Ibrahim could almost see his own image reflected in his forehead. 'If I were you,' he said, 'I would shut my mouth and get on with the work. And that goes for all of you!' he yelled, pointing a shovel in their faces.

Silenced by caution and hesitant in their feelings, the men considered their future lives in the realm of the engine room. Encased in a giant oven where copper banged against steel and coal collided inside fiery furnaces, their world had transformed into one of torrential sweat and searing heat. And as the temperature rose and the air grew oppressive, so did the doubts in Ibrahim's head.

CHAPTER 4
A HEAVENLY BLUE

William Hayward had reserved two cabins below the poop deck of the *Bengal Star*. They were spacious, tastefully furnished and only available to those first-class passengers who were able to afford them. After taking one herself, Elizabeth claimed the other for Robert and Sophie. A special arrangement had been made for Jemima to remain with the children, but with only two berths available, she would have to make do with a long straw mat extended along the floor, upon which, she hoped to fall asleep. At worst, when the sea was choppy and the cross winds particularly fierce, she would wake to find her skirts soaked by a film of water seeping in under the cabin door, but suffice to say, she preferred the occasional drenching to the discomfort of being housed amid ship with strangers for company.

'*Such long days,*' she often mused, whilst others passed by fleetingly. But Jemima never tired of the sea and its limitless possibilities, for what existed beyond its horizon made her heart burst with excitement. '*Soon I will be in England!*' she told herself.

She imagined England to be clean and civilised – a reflection of its people – well, that is what Memsahib Hayward had always said. It was not too hot, although she expected the sun to shine magnificently and it was not too cold, even though she had heard of snow that lay like white blankets over pretty English towns called Hampshire and Wiltshire and Shropshire – she had read about them in a book called *English Towns and Villages.* There would be picnics, parties and moonlit evenings, glamorous dances and spectacular balls. English ladies would prance about in gargantuan gowns whilst clinging to the arms of men in cravats and smartly pressed suits. The memsahib had asked *her* to travel to England and she felt a sense of pride. Life had presented *her* with a new path and she could barely wait to set foot upon it. She was leaving India for the first time, sailing on a steam ship for the first time and now she would be seeing England for the first time. Yes, England – the beautiful and kind Sahib's home. In the meantime, she would continue to care for the children before the memsahib appeared with her orders for the day. 'Amuse the children, Ayah. Take them for a stroll. Do something with them… only I wish to be left alone.'

Jemima thought it peculiar that the lady chose to spend her days without her son and daughter for company. Sometimes, she would spy her mistress on the upper deck, staring into the ocean for hours on end and there she would remain, a desolate figure peering out to sea until she was forced to strike up conversation with one or two others who had arrived to admire the ocean view. And when the clouds rumbled and the sky turned black, the mistress's disposition would often match the atmosphere. 'Go with Ayah, children!' she would say. 'I do not wish to come for a walk. I've many letters to write and I must finish them before the next mail ship sails past.' But the cabin shutters would remain drawn during the day and the books she had brought on board were still hiding in her case. The writing implements were hardly ever used, leaving Jemima to deal with the children's never-ending questions.

'Ayah, where's Mama?'

'Why is Mama sad, Ayah?'

'Has Mama been crying?'

She guessed the children were feeling responsible for the sombre expression in their mother's eyes, but when it came to the memsahib, the answers often eluded Jemima. In her own humble opinion, there were three basic qualities a servant would do better to possess: an abundant reserve of patience, the energy to accomplish the ceaseless demands and knowing, instinctively, when not to cross the invisible threshold of familiarity. And since the threshold surrounding her present mistress was rock solid and impassable, Jemima found this particular lady rather intriguing. She was pursued by a cloud so icy not even the sizzling Indian sun could do its best to melt its chilly mists and then there was that embittered look: an obscure expression stirring in the eyes and veiling perhaps, a host of secrets. Had trouble started the night Jemima overheard an argument in the house on Dhurmotollah Street? It was a day not unlike many others; the children had taken supper and were ready for bed. Robert had pointed to a picture that had suddenly shuddered against the wall and then the raised tones of a female voice wafted through the floorboards. Jemima contemplated whether it was wise to take the children downstairs to say goodnight. She stole a look through the doorway but the rooms along the corridor were silent and empty. No one appeared to be in her attic room upstairs and so she continued to listen without moving a limb until the thud of footsteps sent her scuttling back to the children.

The altercation sounded serious and would have certainly explained the memsahib's shifting moods during the voyage home. At such times, Jemima was grateful for the games and puppet shows arranged for the ship's younger passengers, for they would occupy the children's attention for a while, though some days they were easily distracted by the show of racing sharks and the sight of porpoises and whales lolling about in the waves. The approach to the Red Sea stimulated the more pious traveller and when the ship passed the age-old mountains described in the Bible, spiritual and contemplative feelings rushed to the fore. Opportunistic missionaries used the epic scenery as an excuse to convert a few more heathens to their faith and Jemima – recognising the signs – swiftly moved away. She much preferred to stare into the crystal clear waters, though she was puzzled as to why something so blue was called the Red Sea. If anything was such a misnomer then it had to be this: the Red Sea – where the desert meets the ocean. It was easy to be held spellbound by the eternal blueness of its waters, for it was such a heavenly blue. Yes, blue was her favourite colour. 'The colour of *his* eyes...'

Jemima gazed into the lapping waves and contemplated how quickly circumstances could change. She had felt such disappointment after discovering the sahib would be delaying his voyage home, for she had so looked forward to seeing his face and she had thought that if he *had* come along, then perhaps she would have been called upon to attend him, for in the absence of Abdul, who would have taken care of the sahib's needs? She would, of course and maybe he would have noticed her face despite it being perpetually plunged behind a scarf or a shawl; such was the custom for native female servants in the presence of their masters. How she wished she could stray beyond the confines of servitude to have him, just once, look at her face.

Exotic fish zigzagged beneath the water's iridescent surface in a balletic display of silver and green. Jemima chased their movements until they vanished beneath the waves and then she scolded herself for allowing her thoughts to dwell on *him*.

CHAPTER 5

ELIZABETH AND
THE CHILDREN

Night fell arm in arm with humidity and passengers threw caution to the wind and invaded the decks with their bedding in tow in a desperate bid to remain cool that evening. The music of a lone violinist strengthened everyone's flagging spirits and soldiers seized their wives and waltzed with only the light of the embryonic moon to illuminate their movements. Singing and merriment floated through portholes, disturbing those who had retired early to bed and after hearing evidence of drunken behaviour arising from the ship's cuddy, Elizabeth Hayward was amongst the first to complain. Taking her evening meal in the privacy of her cabin, she blamed her subsequent lethargy on the muggy air outside. 'I shall have an early night,' she moaned. 'Jemima, attend to the children, please,' she said, disappearing behind her cabin door. But that night, Elizabeth Hayward tossed in her berth, not knowing whether to blame the oppressive heat or the habitual assaults of paranoia for stealing her *joie de vivre.* She longed to annihilate the murk inside her head but the pessimistic persona governing her thoughts was all too commanding and taunted her sanity without respite. Had she made the right decision to leave India? She was certain she had but since William had decided to stay behind for an extra month, should she have remained behind too? He insisted that she and the children leave ahead of him and so could there be another reason why he wanted to stay? Once, excited by the thought of a home in India, Elizabeth pondered how after almost three years it had all turned wretchedly sour.

Elizabeth Beatrice Hayward had it all, or so it seemed. Arriving in India at the age of twenty-four, she embraced her duties as proud mother and loyal wife in support of her industrious husband, William Hayward. The attractive couple with attractive children to match were welcomed into a very British society recreated in a faraway land. Thus, Elizabeth began her new life with gusto and drive. She supported her husband's career as a judiciary official: a position entailing the enforcement of land treaties drawn up between the Crown and the former rulers of India's princely states. However, with no one for company but her children and servants, Elizabeth soon pined for her life back in England. But loneliness and tedium only played minor roles in Elizabeth's motives for leaving. There was another reason – a reason she was disinclined to discuss. When it came to the subject of William, she was convinced her friends had heard the rumours but never broached the subject out of decorum; at least not while she shared their company. Amongst the other ladies, she projected an air of ignorance laced with a measure of her ever-present pride. And though she yearned to talk to someone, *anyone*; Elizabeth knew that the commanding heat of the Indian sun could snare anyone whose fears were apparent. And the nights were just as misleading, for the dark, sticky air could weave a web of illusory comfort around those who lay alone in their beds, reaching out for someone who would listen. But Elizabeth Hayward always resisted.

It had taken six months for Elizabeth to extricate herself from the social scene of Calcutta's elite: a self-imposed decision made after discovering she had become the focus of gossip circulated by the women she had once thought were her friends. The idea of squandering time on the duplicitous wives and jealous tell-tales – who never really liked her in the first place – turned her stomach and made her skin itch, and there appeared to be no one trustworthy with whom she could spend the last of her days. Her husband, of course, was another matter. 'We simply cannot allow you to take William away, Elizabeth,' his friends would say. 'We shall miss his company at the club!' Yes, he was the popular one, the one everyone loved to talk to and the one everyone liked to talk about. She imagined their snarling comments, holding her responsible for his departure, blaming her for forcing him to leave. But she would only have to tolerate their insincerity for a few weeks longer; until then she would continue to smile and nod as she so often did. But Elizabeth's remaining days in India were not as she had planned them, for William's decision to delay his departure made her temperamental and resentful. Consequently, she absconded like a thief, seeing no one, saying nothing but leaving a trail of intrigue blazing behind her.

The blare from the upper decks soon diminished into a mumble of tipsy voices and Elizabeth nestled into a pillow and tried to silence the din inside her head. But in the next minute or so, she would encounter another sound – a woozy sound gliding through the adjoining wall and curving its way towards her body. The lilting melody would soothe her brow and she would recognise the tune, for it was one she had heard many times before. It possessed an uncanny power and curious magic that could send a wilful child to sleep and calm an troubled adult in an instant. Its soporific qualities would appeal to her agitated senses and slowly, she would allow herself to unwind. She had no idea what the words meant, for she had never asked for the meaning of Jemima's nightly serenade but in those forthcoming moments, Elizabeth Hayward cared not for a translation, for Jemima's lullaby was just what she needed.

Soja bacche soja
Saanp khud mein mud gaya aur so gaya
Soja bacche soja
Haathi Leyt gaya aur so gaya
Soja bacche soja
Sher ne dahadana bund kiya aur so gaya
Soja bacche soja
Ab tu bhi aankhein bund karke soja

Sleep baby, sleep
The snake has coiled up and gone to sleep
Sleep baby, sleep
The elephant has lain down and gone to sleep
Sleep baby, sleep
The tiger has stopped roaring and gone to sleep
Sleep baby, sleep
Now close your eyes and go to sleep

It took three renditions of Jemima's lullaby to cast its spell on Robert and Sophie. Soon they were sprawled in their berths, moaning softly as their sleep became more potent. Jemima peered up at Robert: a hazy figure stretched out beneath his netting like a caterpillar within its cocoon. Tiny globules of sweat sparkled on the boy's brow. His hair and nightshirt were soaked too. Jemima peeled off the sheet that clung to his chest and placed another over his slumbering body. In the berth below, Sophie's eyeballs flickered beneath the immature flesh of her eyelids. Locks of damp hair were plastered to her cheeks and brow. Such soft, beautiful hair, Jemima thought; it was like cascading yellow silk. She had been awestruck at the first sight of it, for never before had she seen hair that colour. Only in the tinge of some flower petals or the fleeting wings of a butterfly, or even the beams of the sun itself, had she witnessed a similar golden hue. And then there were the eyes: the vivid blue eyes – intensely striking at times and only vague when camouflaged against the cloudless cerulean sky. '*What kind of children are these blond-haired, blue-eyed creatures? Unearthly beings? Angels perhaps?*' Jemima recalled how drab and insignificant she felt beside them and how compelled she was to stare. She explored every feature and investigated every trait, from the smudges of dark pink that appeared across their cheeks to the scattering of faint freckles emerging on their backs after staying too long in the sun. They looked more like their father than they did their mother, thus she could not help but look upon them as special and extraordinary.

As she plumped Sophie's pillow, something hard brushed against Jemima's fingers. Sliding her hand underneath, she extracted a silk purse, out of which, a *daguerreotype* tumbled forth coming to rest on the child's body. Sophie stirred as it bounced against her stomach but she was too weary to open her eyes and did not wake up. A small portrait lay across her waist, in which she and Robert were pictured, seated on two stools whilst a demure figure knelt at their feet. In fact, it would have been difficult to recognise Jemima had it not been for her big brown eyes staring out from the picture.

Jemima remembered the day the portrait had been taken. It was not long after Alice Ayah had been dismissed for stealing. The memsahib had summoned Jemima into the drawing room and permitted her to take a seat. '*You have proved yourself to be diligent and loyal,*' she said. '*You shall be rewarded by having your image captured with the children.*'

There was a photograph of Abdul standing beside the sahib and his son already on the mantelpiece. Now it was her turn and she felt rather proud. Jemima returned the *daguerreotype* to its hiding place and snuggled down beside Sophie, wondering whether sleep would come to her as swiftly as it did to the children. But soon her eyelids began to flutter at the sound of the girl's soft whimpers, whilst her ear enjoyed a caress from the child's moist, warm breath. Slowly her fingers slid from Sophie's hot, plump cheek and within seconds, she had joined both youngsters in their world of weighty slumber.

CHAPTER 6

LIFE BELOW DECK

The lascars compared the bowels of the *Bengal Star* to Hell; only the idea of Hell's heat seemed marginally more tolerable. By the end of their first day, they were coated from head to toe in gritty coal dust and their bodies resembled a legion of lost souls with only the whites of their eyes to prove they were human. The days at sea disappeared in haste but as the men accustomed themselves to the rigours of the engine room, their muscles grew lean and toned and Ibrahim considered it some consolation for having to work his fingers to the bone. Voices drifting down from the upper decks made him pine to be amongst the privileged passengers in their relative world of splendour. He rarely saw their faces but he sensed their movements and he wondered how different life was for those who existed above his head. Sometimes the scent of frying onions floated down from the galley kitchens; another day, the aroma of roast chicken and braised lamb tantalised his nostrils. How he wished he could taste the lavish fare on offer in the upper decks; dejectedly though, he resigned himself to the bland nourishment provided by lascar food.

Ibrahim's hands trembled as he dragged a wet cloth across his aching legs. Sweat, coal dust, oil and steam were a difficult combination to remove and after a while the water was so black that any further washing seemed a pointless exercise. Abandoning his ablutions, he joined the other men in the supper queue, wishing it had been him who had been chosen to cook their food instead. 'Not rice and dried fish again,' he muttered, receiving his share.

'Maybe we should say something,' said Abu. 'We deserve better than this.' He placed his plate down on the deck floor and headed towards the cook, a chap known as Chami. 'Chami, my friend, we are grateful for the food in our mouths but is there anything else we can have for our supper besides dried fish?'

Chami blinked furiously. 'Are you joking?'

'These men work hard all day and we have been eating dried fish for the past three weeks. Is there anything else?' appealed Abu.

Chami's forthcoming outburst was thwarted by the arrival of Rajesh Naidu, who having overheard Abu's comments, made his way over from the engine room. 'What is it you men would like to eat?' he shouted.

Abu spoke up. 'Perhaps some meat, sir... and vegetables.'

'Meat and vegetables,' repeated Naidu, directing his comment to the cook. 'Make a note, Chami.'

Abu thanked Naidu for granting his request but paused before turning to leave. 'Excuse me, sir,' he mumbled, looking back at the boatswain. 'The meat... it has to be *halal*.'

Naidu's stare bore down on Abu like a fiery beam. 'Did you get that, Chami? The meat has to be *halal*.'

Chami gave a flummoxed nod and watched Naidu stride away.

The following morning, Chami spent hours in the kitchen with the door slammed shut and the mere absence of dried fish in the air caused much supposition. Thus, when the supper bell rang and he emerged clasping two large pots in his hands, every man rushed over, eager to ogle the fruits of his labours. 'Spicy chicken!' he bleated, lifting the lid off one large pot. A euphoric cheer exploded and plates were thrust impatiently under his nose. Chami dumped his concoction onto each and every one of them and encouraged the men to sample his creation.

Faltering on the side lines, looking deeply concerned, Ibrahim pondered that in all his years spent cooking, he had never smelt chicken of the sort that was being served that day. He hesitated before inserting a spoonful into his mouth and scrutinized the morsels lying on his plate.

'What's wrong?' asked Abu, stuffing his face.

'It doesn't smell like chicken.'

'Why are you complaining? It's tasty,' replied another lascar.

Ibrahim glanced over to the area where Chami had prepared the food. A moment later, he abandoned his plate, marched past the cook and forced his way through the kitchen door.

'Hey! Where are you going?' Chami shouted, rising from his place against the kitchen wall.

Ibrahim's eyes urgently searched the room. The cupboard doors were left open and the work surfaces were covered in vegetable peelings and splodges of sauce. Then he saw them sitting in one corner of the dirty floor: four pig's trotters drowning in a pond of blood beside the bloody severed head of a pig. 'Stop! Don't eat! Don't eat! It's pork! It's pork!' he cried, almost knocking Chami over as he sprinted out of the room.

Mouths froze and one fellow spat his food out onto the deck floor. Other lascars followed suit by throwing their plates down in disgust and retching over their feet. Abu flung his plate down and pushed past the doubled-over men in his path. Seizing the cook by the collar, he pinned him against the kitchen wall. 'You bloody devil! Bastard!'

By now, an irate mob of lascars had formed a semi-circle around the pair, egging Abu to punish the wrongdoer and teach him a lesson that he would never forget. But Ibrahim began to panic when he saw Naidu and his men wielding whips and sticks in their hands. One of the *tindals* reached for Abu's shirt sleeve and both men toppled backwards, breaking the line of Muslim rebels who then scattered in all directions. A second *tindal* yanked Abu up and then swung him down at the feet of Naidu, who by now had beckoned the other men forward. The first *tindal* secured his arm around Abu's neck and used his other to force Abu's right hand into the small of his back. Abu lashed out with his free arm until a large wooden truncheon came down hard across it. He shrieked with pain and the men about him cringed and gasped.

'Silence!' yelled Naidu. 'Stand back!' he said, circling the offender. 'I take it you didn't like the food?'

Abu panted like a dog. 'Chami fed us pork... he insulted us.'

'You think you are at home with your wives?' Naidu screamed. 'You think we are here to serve you?' he yelled. 'You bloody fools are here to do what I say. You work when I tell you! You sleep when I tell you! You eat what you are given and if you complain, I will make you eat your own shit! *Halal* meat? *Halal* meat? You Muslim bastards can go to hell... Mr Singh!' he growled. 'Tie him up!'

Mr Singh, the second *tindal* – who had dealt the blow to Abu's arm – made a sweeping gesture with his fingers and Abu was frogmarched over to the wall, where the fumes from the boiler room billowed through a grate. Abu was pushed up against it and tied with length of rope. His hands went numb and his forehead scraped against the wall when his shirt was ferociously ripped from his back. Mr Singh then cleared the path for his superior who brandished the whip that would do the damage.

The fisherman's screams were loud and piercing but towards the end, he stifled his cries and accepted his chastisement without as much as a whimper. Flinching only when the final few lashes tore the skin from his back, he heard how Naidu forbade anyone to cut him down; otherwise, there would be hell to pay. 'Let him be a lesson to the rest of these bastards,' Naidu cursed. 'Now keep your bloody mouths shut and do your work or you will know... *you will know!*' he roared, striding away.

Abu's wounds began to heal but the repercussions of the incident manifested themselves in the little changes made to the lascars' routine. The wake up bell was rung at two-thirty in the morning instead of three and they finished much later in the day with not much time left to eat their meals. Plain rice was the only food on offer. Overcooked and often burnt, it was eaten without airing a single grievance. The cook was replaced but his successor was equally as scornful, though from time to time, Chami was seen sheepishly performing his duties in another section of the hold.

Yearning to leave behind his cruel life at sea, Ibrahim considered escape when the ship docked in the red peninsula of Aden. Almost every lascar available was called to heave coal that day and as they emptied the fuel down the chutes, it occurred to Ibrahim that only two obstacles interfered with his plan to flee. Firstly, the men had not yet been paid and secondly, even if they had been, Aden was nothing but a desert wilderness for miles and if the rumours were true, and the place full of pirates and yellow-haired savages, would he make it out alive?

The crew were permitted to rest after their re-fuelling duties but the heat pierced their skins like a million hot needles and Ibrahim and the other engine room lascars returned below deck to relax within the relative coolness of ship's vast hold. The heavy slam of footsteps heralded the arrival of the *tindals* and Rajesh Naidu followed on from behind, ordering the lascars to stand in a queue whilst he ticked off names and distributed their wages.

The first lascar to be paid walked past looking disappointed and rather confused. Fingering the coins in his packet, he asked, 'How much are we owed?'

'Thirty rupees,' replied Ibrahim.

'There's only twenty in here.'

Ibrahim tore into the man's pouch and counted. *Twenty.* 'How much do *you* have?' he asked, turning to Abu.

Abu poured the coins into his palm and counted. 'Twenty.'

A tangle of discontented whispers soon evolved into a wave of resonant voices, all demanding to know the reason for their lighter purses. Pushing his way to the fore, Ibrahim hovered moodily in front of the boatswain. 'I wish to speak to you.'

'What's the problem?' asked Naidu.

Ibrahim's voice throbbed. 'You promised us thirty.'

Naidu laughed. 'Promised? I never promised you anything.'

'The *ghat serang*... back in Calcutta... he said thirty! We signed a contract. You have to pay!'

The *serang* laughed again and his men moved their hands to their truncheons. 'You signed a contract with *him*... not me... and you should be grateful that you are getting this money with all the trouble you bastards have caused.'

On the advice of the others, Abu had stayed well behind the crowd, but his emotions were about to get the better of him. Elbowing his way forward, he broke through the line of men as his hand formed a fist and the coins in his fingers scattered on the ground. Thrusting his body in Naidu's direction, Abu launched a series of punches into the boatswain's face, causing him to reel backwards and topple into Mr Singh. Before the rest of the henchmen could leap into action, Ibrahim had already propelled his body into the chest of an approaching *tindal* and in a split second, arms and legs were kicking and punching all over the place. The affray came to a head when a cold heavy object slid across Abu's forehead. He released Naidu in an instant when he saw it was a pistol and held his hands aloft in an act of surrender.

Naidu tasted blood on the surface of his lip and prodded the tooth that had come loose from his battered gums. He stretched his jaw several times before spitting blood and the detached incisor onto the deck floor. 'This troublemaker again,' he sneered, his eyes bulging like a demon's. With all his might, he heaved a foot into Abu's stomach, snarling and cursing as the offender clutched his belly and buckled from the pain. 'Tie these mongrels up,' he roared, 'and get the chains.'

Rajesh Naidu needed to inflict a punishment severe enough to make a man think twice about mutiny. But he also had to be sure that the punishment did not render his men incapable of work. In spite of being accountable to the British Chief Officer, Naidu was master of his own little universe and was permitted to exercise his own rules in a separate world existing below deck. The lascars had no choice but to live by his conventions, for his power was resolute and he could discipline lawbreakers in any way he saw fit. However, he did fear the consequences of too many lascar deaths, as this would affect the management of the ship and thus cause his British superiors to doubt his competence. Nevertheless, one or two 'reprobates' were dispensable and in his opinion, Abu and the others were going to pay.

The men who had not participated were made to stay and watch as Abu, Ibrahim and the other culpable lascars were strung up and thrashed pitilessly. Eight men stood side-by-side, bare-chested, with their hands bound to the engine room grate. To smother their screams, the *tindals* crammed shirts into their mouths and then issued thirty blows to their backs: a lash for each rupee the men had demanded. Naidu made sure that there was not too much damage inflicted, for the men were needed to work in the engine room later that day, though he did take it upon himself to execute Abu's beatings personally and it gave him immense pleasure to do so.

Whips whistled as they sliced through the air, stinging the men's torsos as skin split into two. Bodies turned purple and ashen streaks appeared. Blood accumulated under bloated bumps, though some had already erupted and were bleeding profusely. Shoulders throbbed, mouths screamed; eyes bulged with pain. The horrified onlookers averted their eyes and silently prayed for the violence to stop. Abu's previous wounds had already opened but when the thirtieth stroke had made its mark, Naidu could not resist the urge to mete out a few more and by now, Abu's flesh was spraying the air in a grisly shower of ripped skin and blood. As for Ibrahim, he had already lost consciousness and passed out.

He woke up a few hours later surrounded by lascars. They had done their best to wash his wounds and at first, Ibrahim felt nothing, for it seemed that he stirred from a ghastly dream. Then agony took hold of his ribs and he was writhing and shuddering against the deck floor. 'Drink some water,' said a young man called Saheed, who stooped low to speak into his ear. 'You have been tied to the grating for many hours. We were not allowed to cut you down until we finished our work in the engine room.'

The water stung as it spilled over his mouth but it loosened Ibrahim's lips which had been fused together by a crust of dried blood. 'Where is Abu?' he croaked.

'We do not know. When we came to cut you down he was not there.'

Ibrahim heard the boy's words as a faint echo. Again, he lowered his head to the deck floor, closed his eyes and succumbed to sleep.

It was pitch black when he stirred again. Stretching his arms with difficulty, he peered into the night, noticing some silhouettes shifting about in the darkness. With arched backs and raised heads, the men were listening to curious noises in the distance. The beasts were restless too. Disturbed by passing shadows and peculiar sounds, they bayed and bleated endlessly.

'What is it?' whispered Ibrahim.

Saheed struck a match and the meagre light made his ghostly pale face looked like that of a frightened child's. 'You better come... there is something you should see.'

Gulzar, another engine room lascar, had staggered half asleep to the piss bucket at the other end of the hold. The rusty pail provided for that purpose was situated alongside the animal cages and whenever Gulzar heard a porcine grunt or groan, he was driven to utter derogatory comments such as 'filthy swine' or 'dirty hog' and this night proved no different. Turning to insult the beasts as normal, Gulzar noticed something different about them. It was difficult to see in the encircling darkness but two of the creatures were standing on all fours and one appeared slumped in the corner. The upright pigs were grunting around their motionless companion and as Gulzar moved in for a better view, it became apparent that the creature stooped against the bars was not a pig at all. Ibrahim and Saheed found Gulzar distraught and on his knees, trying to shoo the pigs away from the heap in the corner and when Ibrahim realised what it was, the tears rose in his eyes.

Abu sat slouched, bound and zombie-like against the bars. His upper left eyelid was stuck to his lower and his head rolled absurdly from side to side. His face was severely bruised and a length of frayed rope separated his swollen lips. Something was protruding from his mouth and Ibrahim was horrified to see that it was a rotting pig's trotter. Ignoring his own pain, he squeezed an arm between the cage bars and lunged at the air, trying to knock the decaying trotter from Abu's mouth. Powerless to reach it, he frantically searched for something that could release the pig's foot. A collection of crooks stacked in a dark corner drew his eye. The navvies used the crooks to pull the sheep and cattle onto the ship's gangway. 'Bring one quickly!' he yelled to Saheed.

The boy released a crook and immediately handed it to Ibrahim, who fed it through the railings and swiped the pigs away. With some effort, he manipulated the instrument around Abu's gagged mouth and shook the rope until Abu's head bounced forward and the gag fell loose. The unfortunate prisoner remained silent but his unharmed eye flickered to let everyone know that he was still breathing. He was unable to spit the trotter out and it stayed in his mouth a few moments longer but with one last smack, Ibrahim batted it out and it hurtled across the cage floor to baffle the pigs, who quickly assembled around it. Abu's inflamed lips prevented any speech but there was something in his flickering eye that said he had finally given up. With his spirit broken and beyond repair, there was nothing more Naidu and his men could do to humiliate him. And because there was nothing more he could do to help his friend, Ibrahim collapsed to his knees and wept.

Nothing was said and nothing was done in retaliation. With sad faces and wounded hearts, the men laboured as usual when the work bell rang. By the time they were called for supper the next day, someone had noticed that Abu had gone. It was not until late evening that Mr Singh entered the hold, flanked by Naidu's men, and ordered everyone to remain quiet. He said that earlier in the day, Abu had fallen ill and died. They had placed his body into a sack and tossed it overboard. Mr Singh added that this was the custom for those who died at sea.

Thus began Ibrahim's darkest hours. That night, he woke in a sweat after seeing Abu's bruised and bloated face in his dreams.

A few nights later, Abu visited again, but this time the fisherman's face was perfectly unblemished and he smiled and asked after his lascar friends. Then in an instant, his face ballooned to abnormal proportions and rotten blood spilled out from his bulbous eyes. Four putrid pig's trotters sprouted from his limbs and yellow saliva drooled from his mouth. *'Get up, Ibrahim! Get up! They will come for you too. Run! Run! Jump!'* he shrieked.

Ibrahim spent some fearful moments gasping for air before he realised the grisly apparition was a figment of his imagination. Earlier that day, he had received a beating for accidentally spilling clinker ash over Mr Singh's shoes and now his wounds were leaking again. Gone were his hopes of travel and fulfilment; depression and torment had slipped into their place. Obsessed with finding a way out, he wondered whether he should wait until the ship docked in Suez to make his move but doubted if he could he remain on the ship until then. Perhaps the only alternative was death. Should he take his own life? Should he let *Allah* decide his fate? Whatever happened, survival or death, it would be in the hands of his God. *'No. Yes. No. Wait! Wait until Suez!'* And so it went on: fearful scenarios and conflicting thoughts quietly driving him insane.

CHAPTER 7
THE STRANGER

It was the dead of night when Jemima stirred from a deep sleep. She told herself that she must have been dreaming, although she failed to remember the dream. Instinctively, she looked to her charges. Robert's groans were consuming the dainty sighs floating up from Sophie's mouth but nothing seemed to be out of place. The room was hot and stuffy and in need of some air, Jemima stepped out of Sophie's berth and slipped into her sandals before creeping over to the door. She lingered a moment to see if the children would wake, but they remained lifeless and kidnapped by their dreams. She opened the door and tiptoed to the memsahib's cabin. Since no sound or lamplight filtered through the crevices, she returned to the children's cabin, locked the door and then ascended the companionway steps with the key enclosed within a sweaty fist of fingers. The breezy air was a welcome change from the clammy heat of the cabin and if not for the faint hum of music and a few faraway voices, the deck seemed virtually deserted. A myriad of stars were out that night: stars that winked and blinked and shot across the great mass of black. It was the perfect setting in which to ponder the mysteries of the universe and, perhaps, entertain a few furtive fantasies of the sahib. Thus, Jemima did not notice a flicker and a motion of some sort occurring further along the deck.

A noise of a curious nature prised her dreamy eyes open in a flash. She caught sight of a shadow darting about and changing shape. She surprised herself by tiptoeing towards it and moments later, spied the figure of a man peering out to sea. When the wind lifted his long black tresses, he appeared much like Medusa and her serpents preparing for attack. He curled the grubby toes of one foot around the ship's rail and launched his body upwards before slamming his foot down again. Then he dragged his slender fingers through a mane of matted hair and Jemima swore she heard him speak, though his words were garbled and gobbled by the incoming wind. Certain the stranger's muffled speech was not of an English kind, she decided that it would be best if she did not linger to find out what language the queer creature spoke, for it would be sensible to return to the cabin lest he be mad or drunk, or both. But as she stole away, the compulsion to look back once more prevailed and it was then that she saw him mount the rail again. One hand was raised to the sky whilst the other seized the metal bar so manically that she could see his knuckles turn white from where she stood. Teetering precariously, he announced to the world, '*Allahu Akbar!*' *Allah is the greatest!*

'*What was this crazed individual trying to do?*' Jemima thought. As her bewilderment intensified, his purpose became clear but panic was screaming into her ears. '*What if he were dangerous? What if he were a man of questionable character...a man capable of heinous deeds?*' Instinct moved her foot forward and then the other followed. Before she had time to answer her own questions, she was running; and she was running towards him.

'Stop... please!' she cried, grabbing the stranger's tattered shirt.

He stumbled back on one leg but steadied himself by hopping onto his other foot. He turned and stared at Jemima with such feral intensity that she immediately regretted opening her mouth. Lunging suddenly, he pressed a moist salty hand over her mouth and pushed her back into the shadows. *'Chupkar!' Quiet!*

Jemima would have collapsed had he not been gripping her so forcefully. Her legs trembled wildly and her arms wilted like two thirsty flowers. He buried his hand deeper into her mouth and she lurched as his sour body odour overcame her senses. Trying to remain silent was futile; a sob squeezed past her lips and out through his long, sweaty fingers. Again, he said, *'Chupkar!'*

Jemima imagined the repercussions if this man were to do his worst. If the children were to wake and find her gone, Sophie would crumple into one of her fits and Robert would become distressed after attempting to open the locked cabin door. The memsahib would curse her for thinking she had abandoned them all and nobody would know that only the night before she had been murdered by a crazy man and her body thrown overboard. Tears dribbled down the slant of her nose and onto the hand that stood guard over her mouth. She shook in a manner beyond her control but it seemed that her fear made the stranger peel his fingers away from her lips. 'Forgive me...' he whispered, his eyes melting in disgrace. 'I'm sorry... I did not mean to frighten you.' He waved both hands at her. 'Go...go... please! But do not tell them you see me!' he begged. 'They will beat me if you tell.' His stare bore deeper into hers. 'Go... but please, say nothing. I will not hurt you. Please say nothing and I will not hurt you... I'm sorry I frightened you... they will beat me if you tell.'

The glow from the deck lamp threw a soft beam upon the man's body and Jemima registered more of his figure now. He was slim in frame and his face bore jet black eyes that peered out beneath finely arched eyebrows. Tousles of unkempt hair flopped about his jaw, masking cheekbones that rose in the most elegant of arcs. But despite these raw-boned qualities and the capricious demeanour of a madman, Jemima sensed the anguish of a misunderstood and gentle soul. His face collapsed again as the sound of distant voices drifted about in the air. He slumped to his knees and muttered and rocked and pleaded to *Allah*. Something on his shirt invited Jemima's attention; there were blood stains dotted here and there. He was obviously hurt and looked so desperate. Should she do as he asked and leave? Or should she stay and help him? 'Come with me!' she said, walking over to him.

'What are you doing?' he asked, as she seized his arm. 'I beg you not to tell... I will jump if you tell!'

'I'm not going to tell. Let me help you,' she said, pulling him towards the companionway steps.

Cautious of her request, the man allowed her to take the lead. 'They will beat me if they find out I tried to escape,' he kept saying.

'Who will beat you?' she whispered, coaxing him down the steps.

'The *serang*,' he whispered back.

'Who...?'

'The boatswain... I am a lascar.'

'Is that why you want to die?' she asked.

The question baffled him and he glared at her little. 'Die?' he said. 'I not want to die. I want to escape!'

They loitered not far from the children's cabin and Jemima made him crouch in the dim deck light. Suddenly her fingers felt gooey and she saw blood filtering its way through his ripped cotton sleeve. 'What happened to you?' she asked, cringing.

'They flog us,' he said, wincing at the memory. 'When we ask for our money... or more food...they don't like it. When we ask again, they beat us.'

Jemima wiped her fingers on her skirt. 'Wait here,' she said. 'Stay down in the darkness and be *very, very* quiet.'

Only the faint glow of lamplight remained a beacon in an almost black space when Jemima opened the children's cabin door. Robert and Sophie were still snoring away and she did her best not to wake them. The memsahib had packed everything needed in the event of an illness and one of the cases inside contained all manner of medicines. To beckon sleep, the lady was often prone to lacing her glass of milk with a teaspoon of laudanum and Jemima wondered whether the mistress had taken the case for herself that night. Kicking away Robert's discarded sheet held the answer: the medicine bag was concealed underneath. She rifled through the carefully stacked contents, upsetting the stocks of syrups, powders, balms, creams and oils until she found a vial labelled, *'Tincture of Iodine.'* She plucked it out along with two rolls of calico and sneaked over to the buckets at the side of the door. Dipping one piece into the pail of salt solution, she squeezed gently, hoping the squelching sounds would not disturb the slumbering children. And then she found him where she left him, shrivelling in the darkness like an ill-treated animal. The dripping saltwater formed a puddle beside his callused feet. 'Try not to shout,' she whispered, as she gently peeled off his blood-soaked shirt. She winced at the sight of his bruised and battered body and watched as he buried his head into his knees and hissed in pain. She wondered what this man had done to warrant such cruelty but she did not have to wonder for long, for he looked up at her with his terror-filled eyes and explained.

'They treat Muslim lascars very badly here...they lied to us and made us eat pork. It is a sin to eat pork. We might as well be slaves because they take our money and they beat us very badly when we complain. My friend... Abu... they tied him up and they...they...' He stifled his sobs into his arms and then tossed his head from side to side, as if he were releasing the unhappy memory like a wet dog would release water from its fur. 'That is why I want to escape.'

Jemima studied the crusty wounds on his back. 'You will die if you jump into the sea.'

'Drowning is better than slaving on this ship. Animals are treated better.'

'But why did you become a lascar and choose this work?'

'I was easily fooled,' he said, a wry smile appearing on his face. 'I wanted to see places and countries. Before this, I work for a *nawab*... the Prince of Awadh. I cook for him and his family.' He seemed proud of his association with a prince and as he unravelled more of his glorious past, Jemima noticed that the desolate expression haunting his eyes was quickly being replaced with the glow of a fond reminiscence. 'I hear about all the countries the Prince and his guests visit... England, France, Italy. When the British send him to Calcutta, I go with him... but then I decide to leave India and have an adventure.' He winced as she swabbed his scars again. 'I decide to become lascar and sail on ship to pay for my passage. I wanted to make my fortune in a foreign land.' The mellow look in his eyes began to fade. 'They lie to me! They say I can leave this ship when I reach England but now they say I cannot and they will not pay me my money. They lied to us and beat us... I know they killed my friend... Abu... they killed him! So, I must get away... I must get away!'

For a moment, Jemima wondered whether he was telling the truth or whether he was just a sailor driven mad by the turbulence of the seas. 'Perhaps, you could speak to someone... the English Captain? Tell him about this boatswain and the way you have been treated?'

'No!' the man barked. 'Nobody cares for us... you're not going to tell, are you?' he asked. 'Let me go if you are going to tell.'

Something in his voice told Jemima he was telling the truth. The scars at least bore witness to the horrors he had endured. 'I won't tell and I'm sorry about your friend... and the beatings you have suffered, but if you jump into the sea you will drown or you will be eaten by sharks. I have seen them.' He glanced towards the companionway steps and heaved a sad sigh.   'What will you do now? Please... do not try and jump again,' she appealed.

'You not worry,' he said. 'I will not jump. I was stupid... but I escape somehow...as *Allah* is my witness, I *will* get out from here.'

Jemima uncurled the second piece of calico and he twisted his body this way and that, enabling her to wrap him within her makeshift bandage. 'What is your name?' he asked, peeping across at her serious face.

'Jemima.'

'You are with English family?'

'Yes.'

'Going to England?'

'Yes.'

'Ah,' he said, 'ayah?'

Jemima finished tying the two ends of the calico together and nodded.

'I am Ibrahim Omar Akram Kareem.' He declared his name with such pride that Jemima knew that here was a man born to do more than scrubbing measly decks. She hoped one day if their paths were to cross again that she would be able to remember his name with ease, but he assured her that 'Ibrahim' would suffice as that is how he was commonly known.

The calico bandages were rather uncomfortable and Jemima loosened them a little, growing concerned that the inky blue patches would attract unwanted attention. She suggested Ibrahim wear his lascar shirt and slowly guided it over his head, steering his hands into the armholes – a particular activity she was used to doing with the children she had cared for over the years. 'It is quiet,' she said, checking the companionway steps. 'You should go back before they find you. Wait!' she said, running a few paces ahead to see if the deck was clear. 'You can go now.'

'A thousand thank yous, Jemima,' he whispered. 'I will not forget your kindness.' He took a moment to remember her face. '*Inshallah.*' God be with you.

'Goodbye, Ibrahim. Please take care.'

With his arm curled around his waist, Ibrahim prowled calmly in and out of the lamplight, so unlike the frenzied madman Jemima had encountered earlier. As he inched further along the deck, she felt a surge of emotion: the kind a mother would feel worrying after a child. He paused, waiting for an opportune moment to return to his station and then in a blink of an eye, Ibrahim Omar Akram Kareem was gone.

CHAPTER 8
KALI REVISITED

Robert's snores were audible through the ship's walls as Jemima tiptoed back to the cabin and unlocked the door. She peered inside to see Sophie's twisted body almost hanging out of its berth and immediately ventured over to haul the child into a more snug position. The ship pitched and rolled and Jemima tripped over her feet, knocking her old brown valise onto its side. That valise had been everywhere with her and reminded her of the times she had been uprooted. It charted her movements from one family to another; as it opened and closed, so did the various chapters of her life. Two blouses, three sets of saris, two cotton skirts and some self-sewn petticoats lay folded inside. She had also packed a few innocuous items: a comb, a handkerchief and a linen pouch containing some cherished trinkets. But buried beneath them, an object wrapped several times in faded white silk rested in disguise. Jemima released the item from its smooth glossy robe and placed it onto her sleeping mat. The flickering light of the oil lamp shed monstrous shapes on the cabin walls but the belligerent Kali – illuminated in all her glory – sat at Jemima's bended knees, presiding over her audience of one. If the mistress ever discovered the deity in the depths of her suitcase, the consequences would be severe. The lady would scream with horror and dismiss Jemima without a doubt. Indian religions and their native customs were severely frowned upon. No mercy would be shown; she and Kali would be tossed out onto the streets.

It was Alice Ayah who smuggled the four-inch effigy into the Hayward house. Wrapping Kali in a cotton napkin and storing her within a basket of pomegranates, she took great pleasure in recounting the tale of how she had brought the statue into the Hayward abode. 'Here, Madam, some delicious fruit for you and the children,' she said, presenting the pomegranates with all the innocence of a wide-eyed child.

'Oh... thank you, Alice,' the memsahib replied, averse to the idea of strange foreign fruit. 'Take them to the kitchen and give them a thorough scrubbing.'

As she ambled to the kitchen, Alice transferred the religious contraband to her apron pocket and then proceeded to draw some water from the well. She washed each fruit as coolly as her nerve would allow, but when she heard the native gardener call the memsahib into the courtyard, she dropped the pomegranate she had chosen to purge and sprinted up the staircase with the proficiency of a Chinkara gazelle trying to avoid capture from a hungry Bengal tiger. 'Clever, clever Alice,' she laughed, as she thrust Kali onto the highest shelf of the wardrobe in her attic room. And by engaging in secret prayers and midnight offerings, she shared the goddess with Jemima in spite of the risks involved.

But Alice's luck ran its course when she was discovered stealing soap from the kitchen store room. Immediately, she was told to pack her bags and leave, but having fooled the memsahib by honouring Kali, she revelled in that notion and lived up to her furtive disposition by leaving a parting gift for Jemima under her bed. She left Kali reclining in a corner of Jemima's valise and there the goddess remained, shrouded in silk, waiting for an opportunity to emerge once again.

Hunched over to shield the statue from the children – lest they should wake and see the much-misunderstood effigy – Jemima reasoned that this was her only act of defiance and so far she had not been caught. Closing her eyes, she bowed her head and drew her hands together in prayer. With Ibrahim in her thoughts that night, she wondered whether it was recklessness or bravery that drove her to help a manic stranger. Either way, she felt different – more confident – and it thrilled her to feel that way. Whispering her mantra, she remembered the ones she had loved and lost and then covered the goddess back in its pallid mantle before returning it to the seclusion of her travelling case.

The hushed jingle of something precious reminded Jemima of a bygone time. Raising the valise lid again, she spied a linen pouch sitting beside the cloaked Kali and opened it up to be greeted by the red and white sparkle of five gilt bracelets. Squeezing her fingers through the glittering coil, she watched each one line itself beautifully against the other. Taking the wrinkled paper package, she peeled back a layer to reveal the saris that Kali had been sleeping upon. Jemima wondered why she had packed the native garments. They were keepsakes of some sort; symbols evocative of her past. The red one in particular – a silk piece with simple silver embroidery – often made her melancholy. It felt so fragile between her fingers that her mood turned sombre, just as she expected it would. Too feeble to bury her memories, she opened a door and allowed them to enter and then heaved the kind of sigh that told a poignant but guarded tale.

CHAPTER 9
BEFORE JEMIMA

Snatched from an aching womb in a blaze of blood, tears and trauma, the child that would become Jemima was born on the second of October 1840, in Birshingha, a village nestled in the West Bengal district of Midnapore. The local physician, Dr Mukherjee, placed her into the fervent arms of her mother, Madhumita Dev, and crossed the room to her father, who was weeping quietly by the door. 'You have a daughter, Subhas,' he said. 'She's healthy and she'll most certainly live.' Subhas shut his eyes to ward off the disappointment that came with the arrival of a girl and allowed the relief to crash over him like the deluge from a waterfall.

Madhumita Dev – or 'Madhu' as she was generally known – had suffered miscarriages in the past but on this occasion, she had managed to reach full-term with her third child. The subsequent labour lasted two days and was fraught with complications. Poor Madhu was never the same again. Her blood-curdling shrieks not only scattered the birds from the coconut trees but sent the pariah dogs scrambling for cover in the nearby undergrowth. The villagers too were not spared the horror of her pain and flinched from the incessant screeching seeping out of the

Mavadia hut. The sight and stench of the blood-soaked sheets alarmed the sturdiest of men and prompted the Hindu priest at the local temple to lead prayers for the welfare of Madhu and her unborn child. Following speculation on her possible demise, the village community was relieved to hear that Madhu had cheated death and finally produced a child. And though the emergence of a prized baby boy would have been so much preferred, a female child, it would seem, was better than no child and little Anupriya's arrival was notably celebrated.

However, Madhu was told that the implications of the birth were severe. 'You will die if you ever conceive again,' Dr Mukherjee warned. And convinced that she had understood his prognosis, he ended his counsel by congratulating the parents and philosophising on life's unforeseen treasures. 'Do not be sad for what you cannot have. Be thankful for what you have been given... and you have been given a most beloved daughter. Be joyful that she is healthy and finally in your arms.' Uncurling the baby's tiny fist of fingers, the doctor then placed a one-rupee coin in the palm of her hand and cooed, 'for luck!'

That fate had intended to bless Madhu and Subhas with only one child was a certainty the couple were forced to embrace. Two hours passed before they settled on the name; two hours of anxiety, reflection and acceptance. The name bestowed was 'Anupriya,' and it was a name inspired by the doctor's choice words. The meaning, '*beloved daughter*' was never more poignant, for Madhu looked upon her daughter as all her ghostly children rolled into one. The girl was a beautiful amalgam of the offspring that had once sat blossoming in her womb. Hence, she dedicated Anupriya to the memory of their missing spirits and cherished her as no other low-caste girl was cherished before.

Subhas and Madhu's association with the doctor did not end with the birth of their daughter. The couple were already employed in his household – she as a maid and he as a carpenter. The Mukherjee residence was one of a handful of flat-roofed, brick buildings separated from the straw-roofed, mud-huts of the village's low-caste community. But it was under this roof that Anupriya flourished and she grew up in the company of servants, masters and ever-escalating socialism. The doctor and his teacher-wife, Jagattarini, hailed from a breed of Indian philanthropist who fought on behalf of India's subjugated masses. No strangers to controversy, the couple enjoyed challenging the rituals accompanying the traditional caste customs. For example, they would not wait for *kangali-biday* (the distribution of alms during the funeral rites of the Bengali elite) to offer alms to Calcutta's poor; they gave charity simply whenever the fancy took them. They encountered resistance when their attention turned to the campaign for the rights of the Indian woman but that hardly stopped the Mukherjees, who started the crusade from within the walls of their very own home.

Using her powers of persuasion, and a little emotional blackmail thrown in for good measure, Jagattarini coaxed Subhas into considering the possibilities if his ten-year-old daughter were to learn to read and write. 'If Anupriya is educated... just think of what the girl could achieve. Education leads to better employment... better employment leads to better wages... which means a better living. Do you want your daughter to live well? Or do you want her to end up living in poverty like those poor wretches in Black Town?' When she put it like that, how could Subhas refuse? And not wishing to offend the lady – especially since her husband had ensured the safe delivery his child – Subhas succumbed to his mistress's wishes and permitted his daughter to learn to read and write.

Anupriya progressed exceedingly well and looked forward to her lessons. Her enthusiasm prompted Jagatterini into going a step further. 'Why stop at Hindi?' she mused. 'She learns quick-ly... I shall teach her English.'

However, in the village of Birshingha, the precept of caste ruled with a mighty hand and bristling at the thought of his mistress's endeavours, Subhas feared for his child if it became common knowledge that she had been reading books instead of sweeping floors. Thus, in a veiled attempt to allay his fears, Jagatterini encouraged Anupriya to become the servant her parents wished her to be and employed the girl in her household, so that she could be freely seen to embrace a legacy of servitude whilst still receiving her clandestine education. And the birth of Jagatterini's third child did nothing to curtail the lady's passion to teach. Promptly, she handed her newborn over to Anupriya, who washed, fed and cradled the baby whilst she recited the letters of the English alphabet and read from the pages of the epic *Mahabarath*. It was then, some might say, that she – a ten-year-old girl – began her profession as an ayah.

By the age of eleven, Anupriya could read and write Hindustani and Bengali in the most confident of fashions. A year later, she was fully conversant in the basics of the English language and even attempted to read the first chapter of *Gulliver's Travels*. Amazed and impressed, Jagattarini began fostering hopes for the girl that would propel her life beyond that of a humble servant's. 'You are the proof, Anupriya... the living, breathing proof that a low-caste female can learn just as well as anyone else... if not better. You can break the chains of your caste, my girl. You could be an excellent teacher yourself one day. How about that Anupriya? Would you like to be a teacher?' she asked, staring into her student's bashful eyes.

Only a timid smile would flutter on Anupriya's lips, for she loved her life as it was. She loved her parents, she loved Jagatterini, and she loved the other members of the Mukherjee family. The secretive nature of her schooling was exciting in itself. What more could a low-caste girl want? But slowly and surely, Anupriya learned from her formidable mistress that there *was* more a low-caste girl could want – hopes of a better life at least. Yes, Jagatterini had taught her to read books and write in languages such as English and Hindi, but more important than that, her beloved mistress had taught her how to dream.

CHAPTER 10
BECOMING JEMIMA

During the adolescent years of Anupriya's life, the juvenile quality of her facial features lost their plumpness and bloomed into a simple but appealing beauty. She had roused the interest of many a village man who considered her an appropriate match for their bachelor sons and soon a clutch of them would come knocking upon Subhas's door. Accustomed to marrying young – and some as young as six or seven – most of the village women considered an age beyond twelve for taking a husband as rather old. But Subhas and Madhu would not be swayed and kept hold of their daughter for as long as they could. Thus, when Anupriya remained unmarried in her fourteenth year, the rumours spread like dysentery. Duty-bound to prove his daughter's worth, Subhas conceded to a matrimonial match and betrothed Anupriya to the son of a local potter.

For Madhu, however, the years shared with her daughter had soared by in a second. It seemed only yesterday that a child had finally blessed her life. When she learned the news of the betrothal – not from her husband but from the potter's overexcited wife at the local market – she staggered home in a state of disbelief. 'It's too soon... too soon! She is my life! My world! I cannot let her go!'

That night, Subhas lay awake listening to his wife's outpouring of woe and in the days that followed, he watched her cling to their daughter in a fit of depression. 'I will never let you go...' she muttered. 'I will never let you go.' The force of a mother's love would then manifest itself in the marks appearing on Anupriya's shoulders and arms and Subhas could only prise Madhu's fingers away after conceding to her hysterical demands.

As he walked the mile and a half journey to his future son-in-law's home, Subhas searched for a way to solve his predicament. Daylight was fading fast and he turned to the indifferent sunset for answers. Night descended rapidly and, devoid of any stars to wish upon, seemed blacker to him than ever before. But later that evening, seated on the veranda with the boy's father, he explained his quandary and then presented a solution that was surprisingly conjured up by the humid night air. If the potter agreed to postpone the marriage for two years, Subhas would double the amount of his daughter's dowry. A short period of silence passed, during which the potter rubbed his pockmarked chin. Then, after squashing the mosquito drinking from his ankle, he thrust a clay-stained hand into the air and found a carpenter's hand reaching out to take it.

Subhas dreaded the consequences of his spontaneous bargain as he wandered back into the starless night. It had taken an eternity to raise his daughter's dowry and now, thanks to a tenuous solution plucked from the sky, he had recklessly promised to double it. With only two years to achieve what had previously taken a lifetime, he knew it would be more than a struggle to honour his pledge. In the meantime, however, he would remove the millstone from around his neck and return home to tell his wife the good news she had been waiting for.

Two years passed by as swiftly as feathers on a breeze and Subhas worked tirelessly, saving whatever paltry money he could muster from doing whatever miserable work was on offer. In addition to his carpentry jobs, he thatched roofs, carried water, built huts and harvested rice. And though his wages were hastily spent, he stayed true to his word when the time came to honour his pledge.

Jagatterini grieved privately; how could Anupriya become a teacher now? The journey would have been hard enough alone but with a husband and his family to care for what was the point? Anupriya would belong to another man and he would simply not allow it. The time had come for her pupil's thoughts to dwell on other matters and they were matters that begged no interference from Jagatterini or her husband. Even so, the couple insisted on paying for the wedding attire: a gift of a beautiful red silk sari, edged with simple silver embroidery, whilst Madhu parted with the five gold-plated bracelets she had worn on her own wedding day. There was no avoiding the tears; they came in torrents and Subhas hardly uttered a word. Dutifully, he escorted his garlanded and sparsely bejewelled daughter out of his home for the very last time.

The name of her betrothed was Ishwarchandra and she would meet him for the first time on her wedding day. He was waiting by the local shrine, watching the small bridal procession through a curtain of flowers attached to his connubial headdress. Anupriya had been instructed to keep her eyes lowered but she could not resist taking a peek. *'He has a pleasing look,' she thought. 'A little skinny perhaps... I must fatten him up.'* All in all, she was content with her father's choice of husband.

It was a simple wedding with no fuss or celebration: a religious ceremony followed by a journey on horseback to his parent's home. The house was larger than expected and his room more spacious than her own. She sat at the end of his modest bed – eyes dipped, head tilted down – contemplating her forthcoming wifely duties. She tried to remember all the little tips that had made her blush and giggle into her pillow at night and anticipated a touch or a signal that would summon her into his arms. But Ishwarchandra was not ready. He was pouring himself a glass of limejuice from the flask his mother had left on the bedside table. Taking a substantial sip, he drew his tongue along his nascent moustache whilst proceeding to remove the flower garlands from his willowy neck. He wriggled out of his *kameez* like a worm escaping a child's tight clinch, whilst still and beautiful, his young wife waited, not knowing that in only two weeks time, Ishwarchandra – her husband – would be dead and gone.

The day after the wedding, Subhas found the potter standing outside his door, smiling at the thought of reaping the financial reward of the pact they had made two years before. But the potter's smile was soon wiped away as Subhas confessed to his dearth of money and desperate need for more time. The potter was not amused and raised his mottled chin for attack and in his fear and hopelessness, Subhas turned to the doctor for help.

A solution came swiftly to Dr Mukherjee. He and his wife had been invited to speak at a charity event in Krishnagar and could do with a servant to mind the children. If the potter's son agreed to let Anupriya accompany them, the Mukherjees would compensate him well for having to part so swiftly with his bride. Ishwarchandra made no objection. If it meant that she would be paid a good wage, he would willingly part with his wife. And it was not hard for her to leave him. After only two days of being a wife, Anupriya had already begun to feel misplaced and suffocated in the world of her in-laws. She embraced the turn of events with subdued enthusiasm and reassured her parents that she would work hard to earn the money that would restore her father's dignity.

Ten days passed before a letter arrived in Krishnagar, addressed to Dr Mukherjee and his wife. Birshingha's village writer had written the news that Ishwarchandra had collapsed from a sudden illness. His fever was dangerously high and his vomiting was relentless; it was time for his wife to return. The doctor quietly suspected cholera or typhoid and accompanied Anupriya on the journey back to Midnapore, where, upon their arrival, they were told by distraught relatives that Ishwarchandra and his family had not survived the sickness that had so ruthlessly struck them down. Anupriya could tell from the way some villagers avoided her gaze, and from the way others tenderly reached for her hand that her beloved parents had been taken too. The doctor's suspicions were proven correct: cholera had snatched their lives via a deadly trail. Subhas had caught the disease whilst nursing the already frail Madhumita and she had become infected whilst helping to care for the stricken Ishwarchandra. His fate was sealed after playing with his nephew, who had carelessly sipped water from the Hooghly River. A hysterical neighbour summarized the rapidity in which their lives were claimed. 'Here one day... gone the next!' she howled.

The corpses were bound in sacks and Anupriya was benumbed when she saw them. Swollen heads, black and blue, lay slumped upon bodies that were puckered like rotting fruit. She was grateful for their subsequent cremations; she would rather remember them as dust than as the ghoulish figures she had been forced to witness that day. She said a prayer for her fleeting husband, Ishwarchandra, but for Subhas and Madhumita, she wept and wept and wept. She gave alms in their honour and prayed for the safe flight of their souls. She carried her father's smile in her memory and her mother's abundant affection deep in her heart. But when it came to Ishwarchandra, her recollection of him became vague and murky – a fleeting impression of a man who used to be her husband with her wedding sari as the only proof they had ever met. And just like Ishwarchandra's charred remains, her memories of him soon turned to dust.

As her first year as a widow passed, Anupriya bore witness to the astounding events occurring in the Mukherjee household. It all began with the doctor's association with Reverend George Finch – a chaplain for the British Army stationed in Bengal. He had made the Reverend's acquaintance back in Krishnagar, where they had forged a firm friendship after meeting for *tiffin* one day at a mutual friend's house. Reverend Finch revelled in debate that was spirited and intense and the nature of his discourses often centred on India and its diverse religions. 'The immorality of Hinduism' was his favourite topic of discussion. 'The Muslims at least worship one God!' he would often declare.

Anupriya overheard his comments and privately raged. 'How dare he belittle my faith?' Doctor Sahib will put him straight.'

But far from being offended, Dr Mukherjee permitted the clergyman to dismantle the religion he no longer fully practised and listened to his argument for the presence of a single God. Reverend Finch was eloquent, charismatic and committed to dousing India in the born-again sentiment preached by his contemporaries and the doctor found it hard *not* to admire the man's dedication to his faith. Anupriya was puzzled. '*Why does Dr Sahib receive this pompous man? Why is Dr Sahib reading the Bible and listening to Christian sermons in church?*'

She heard the doctor reciting holy passages and singing hymns to an audience that consisted of his bemused wife and children. And when the reports of butchered English women and children in the towns of Meerut and Cawnpore reached his ears, she witnessed the defining moment of Dr Mukherjee's life, for this news incensed him so much that he became further convinced that Christianity was the answer to India's problems.

'Indian brutes! Bloody murdering Indian brutes!' he bellowed through an open window. And yearning to show that not all Indians were murderers and thugs, he made it his mission to urge the British to not judge the Motherland by the actions of a sadistic minority. 'I must speak to the reverend!' he shouted as he packed a bag and left for Krishnagar in a state of panic.

He returned three days later, serene and quiet, and it was under this peaceable aura that he announced his news. 'I am a new man... a man chosen to walk the path of Jesus. I will be baptized in the village church this forthcoming Sunday. Reverend Finch will be conducting the ceremony. He also insists that I volunteer for missionary work in Assam. So I will go wherever the people are in need of salvation.' He hoped that everyone would understand his calling and stunned everyone again with his subsequent words. 'I will no longer be Bidhan Mukherjee... Reverend Finch suggests that I take the name, Joseph Carr.'

Jagatterini needed a seat for fear of fainting. 'Anything else you'd like to tell me?'

'Oh yes...' the doctor began. 'We will all be departing in one month's time.'

Jagatterini suspected that the doctor had taken leave of his senses but dared not disparage his new found beliefs. It took days for her to recover from the shock of his revelations but she adored her husband and out of a deep love and respect for him, she packed her bags in support of his astonishing new vocation. Anupriya was to leave with the Mukherjee family but unbeknownst to Jagatterini, the doctor had made other plans. 'Anupriya is a loyal ayah. She is honest, hardworking and above all, trustworthy. She will restore your faith in Indians,' he said to Reverend Finch.

Anupriya's world collapsed. She had been with the Mukherjees all her life and now she was being offered to this tiresome 'man of the cloth'. It was another bitter blow to Jagatterini but her parting words would re-visit Anupriya in the years to come and make more of an impact than she or her beloved mistress would ever know. 'I begged my husband to take you with us but he has promised you to Reverend Finch. You have sense and intelligence, my girl. Do not be afraid to think for yourself. Challenge those who try to keep you down. Fight against those who mean you harm. There is a world out there, Anupriya... a whole world of choices and possibilities. Who says that it has to belong to the privileged few? The world belongs to everyone... including you. Remember that.'

The doctor and his teacher-wife had seen beyond the submissive servant and wished her to develop beyond the confinements of her caste. And though she was grateful for their support and kindness, Anupriya knew that without Jagatterini by her side, it would be impossible to rise above her station and fulfil some kind of ambition, whatever that might be. Still, it thrilled her to know that the Mukherjees thought more of her than she did herself and she would treasure that reassurance and seek consolation from its sentiment whenever she felt downhearted and alone. She never saw the Mukherjee family again but they mentioned her in letters sent to Reverend Finch and his wife. Assuming her new position under the directive of Mrs Maud Finch, Anupriya was promptly renamed, 'Jemima,' after the beloved pet poodle the new mistress was forced to leave behind in Suffolk – the reason according to Maud, 'They both share the same big brown eyes!'

Lounging across her sleeping mat, Jemima suddenly realised that everything was beginning to make sense. A message was being sent from the depths of her battered travelling case. Kali, goddess of death, destruction, life and creation was speaking to her from its darkness and she finally understood what the deity had been trying to say. Death and destruction had come and gone with the passing of her parents but now she was embarking on an exciting adventure with Kali showing her the way. *'What an adventure I am having!' she thought. 'I have already saved a lascar's life! What would Memsahib Mukherjee think now? Look teacher-memsahib! Look at me! I saved a man's life! His name is Ibrahim. He listened to me and I helped save his life. Yes, teacher-memsahib, I understand now. There is a world out there for me and tonight, the world belongs to me!'*

Ibrahim, meanwhile, had stolen back down the ship's steps as stealthily as a fox. He had passed the engine room with ease and tiptoed past other sleeping lascars, stopping only at the rusty pail that served as a makeshift urinal. There, he untied his *dhoti* and felt overwhelming pain and relief as he squeezed his penis and emptied out his bladder. Looking around, he noticed the appearance of four wooden crates stacked on top of each other and shoved beside the animal cages. The boxes were sitting in a puddle of bilge water and the edges of the bottommost crate were splintered with a layer of mould creeping up its sides. It seemed the ship's rats had dined on its corners and the consequential holes appeared to reveal the presence of something shiny inside. Ibrahim tapped his fingers against a fractured section until a damp corner felt as though it might give way. An area of gnawed wood eventually caved in and something smooth brushed against his fingertips. He plucked at the broken shards until a crevice became large enough to force a hand through and his fingers pulled something out into the lamplight – a tin of *barfi* – Indian sweetmeat.

Ibrahim extracted two more cans before some noises in the distance made him retreat. He pushed the boxes back, making sure the broken sections was turned against the wall, and returned to his resting place, carrying three tins wrapped within his shirt. Turning his back on the other sleeping sailors, he removed the loose deck plank lying underneath his blanket and placed the tins into the murky darkness below. His determination to flee – but by safer and more sensible means – was flourishing by the second. It seemed that unburdening his troubles on Jemima had done him the world of good. She had been gentle with him – his beacon of hope – and the power of human kindness had renewed his faith in the world. His thoughts were quick and lucid as he pondered how many days remained until the ship reached Suez; then he would take the opportunity and flee. He hoped to find Jemima and thank her again for what she did. Above all, he wanted to see her face once more and look deeper into those warm brown eyes. And since fewer days remained than he had originally thought, Ibrahim began to put his plan into action.

CHAPTER 11
THE SERVANT

Elizabeth Hayward lay in her berth the next morning waiting for Jemima's customary knock on the cabin door, but no knock came. She imagined the chiding she would unleash on her servant but immediately regretted entertaining that thought, for had it not been for Jemima, she would have surely had a restless night. Good ayahs were hard to find, especially ones like Jemima. How would she have managed without her? She came on the recommendation of not only a clergyman but by a highly respected doctor too. She was literate in three languages and had coped admirably since Alice's dismissal, never complaining once about having double the workload. Jemima was a godsend; Indian or otherwise, trustworthy nannies were rare to find, though she had to admit that there were times when she felt insanely jealous. Yes, jealous of her servant and the way her children loved that native servant. She would often glimpse them in the sunlight; three ever-increasing silhouettes: a taller one standing amid two smaller ones in a perfect depiction of a mother and her children. Only they were not Jemima's children. These blond-haired, blue-eyed offspring, whose fingers were lovingly entwined within

those of a brown-skinned, low-class woman, were her children...
her children.

It bothered Elizabeth that Sophie would leap into Ayah's
arms like a chimpanzee only comfortable in the arms of its keeper. It bothered Elizabeth that the girl would only reach for Ayah's
earlobe at night to rub the fleshy mound of skin between her
little fingers; a soothing habit that sent her to sleep at bedtimes.
It also bothered Elizabeth that Robert would plead Ayah to tell
him native fables of man-eating snakes and terrifying tigers and
he would sit transfixed as Ayah spiritedly narrated those tales in
a way that only Ayah could. When the children were informed
of their return to England, it bothered Elizabeth that their out-
bursts could only be pacified by Ayah's soothing touches and
only the revelation that Jemima would be by their side would
keep the horrendous tantrums at bay. Indeed, Elizabeth could
have mentioned that detail much sooner, but the idea of a native servant being the sole person capable of allaying the children's fears tossed uncomfortably in her mind. It peeved her to
think that her own flesh and blood preferred the company of an
Indian inferior to that of their own mother; nevertheless, she was
relieved when the children's fury subsided and watched, albeit
begrudgingly, as Jemima reassured their flustered minds. Ayah
would bring the colours of India with her: the calming lullabies,
the thrilling tales of tigers and snakes, and the coconut-scented
embraces; things that the children's mother would not and could
not do. No, Elizabeth Hayward could not cope without Jemima,
however disconcerting her power was.

The children opened their eyes shortly after sunrise. Sophie
was busy tickling her ayah's nose with the seagull feather she
had found on the deck the day before. The previous night's adventure had not left Jemima with much sleep and it was Sophie's
playful actions that woke her from a heavy slumber. She heard
the memsahib's movements from beyond the cabin wall and rose

in a panic, cursing herself quietly for falling asleep in her clothes. There was no time to change and she prayed her dishevelled appearance would go unnoticed. Bracing herself, she rushed next door to her mistress's cabin but hesitated as she spied two drops of blood on the cuff of her sleeve. On further scrutiny, she saw a faint red stain around the hem of her skirt; other than that, her clothes seemed to be free from any additional bloodstained evidence of her meeting with Ibrahim. Tugging at her cuff, she hoped her fingers would mask the dark spots of blood. Breathing deeply, she rapped on the door.

With the exception of their first meeting at the house in Calcutta, Jemima had never given her mistress reason to question her appearance. She was always dressed appropriately in clothes that were clean and neat; surprisingly though, the memsahib appeared to be in high spirits and chose to ignore her tardiness that morning to explain instead that only a few days remained before the ship reached Suez. The lady did make her disapproval known, however, when Jemima opened her mouth and yawned. 'One must cover one's mouth when one does that, Jemima,' she scoffed. 'It's most unsightly'.

Jemima's efforts to disguise her exhaustion failed. She yawned again.

'You seem especially tired today,' the memsahib said, curiously.

'I did not sleep very well, Memsahib.'

'I suppose the sea air can play havoc with one's disposition,' Elizabeth replied, positioning a bonnet around her head. 'All the same, I don't want to find you napping in a corner somewhere. It's going to be an incredibly busy day.'

'Yes Memsahib.'

'And if you must yawn… do it where the other passengers cannot see you. I don't want anyone thinking I have a vulgar maid. Now, I shall take a turn about the deck,' she muttered, passing through the cabin door. 'Have the children dressed and ready for breakfast when I return.'

'Yes Memsahib.'

Jemima watched on as her mistress ascended the companion-way steps. The lady had not noticed the blood stains on her cuffs and hem, and though under normal circumstances, she would never have presented herself in such a state of disarray, she was content on this occasion, to allow the memsahib to believe that her otherwise immaculate standards had fallen.

CHAPTER 12
THE COUNTERFEIT EGYPTIAN

Later that day, thoughts of Ibrahim played on Jemima's mind as she witnessed a trio of lascars hoisting their bodies across the ship's rigging ropes. She could barely look up at one fellow when he shuffled precariously across the yardarms, unfurling the topgallant sails as he went. '*What would happen if the ocean turned rough?' she thought.* She certainly hoped that it was not Ibrahim all the way up there. When several men began making their way down to the lower decks carrying holystones and sand sacks over their backs, Jemima pondered whether Ibrahim was among them and hunted for his face amid the deck hands and stewards. The sea had been calm these past few days; had he changed his mind and jumped? Did he survive and swim to safety? Or was his skinny body dashed about the rocks and devoured by hungry sharks? Then, remembering that he had been a cook, and not just any cook – he had fed the likes of the Prince of Awadh no less – Jemima decided that his talents had been put to better use and he was chopping vegetables and carving meat in the galley kitchens. Yes, she decided, Ibrahim was preparing lunch in the galley kitchens. She would rather picture him there because the alternatives did not bear thinking about.

But Ibrahim was not preparing lunch in the galley kitchens as Jemima had hoped. He was busy shovelling clinker ash away from the ship's furnaces whilst keeping a keen eye on the supervising lascar. When the fellow finally turned his back, Ibrahim took an empty coal sack from the dozens dumped in the corner of the engine room and stuffed it into the open pipe behind the door. After asking for permission to urinate, he snatched the coal sack and headed straight towards to his bed. There, he lifted the loose deck plank and dropped the sack over the tins of *barfi*. That same evening, he sneaked back towards the decaying crates and stole from the ones positioned on the floor. After locating the weak points, he burrowed mercilessly until his cracked fingertips touched the items inside and for the next three consecutive nights, Ibrahim's hands came out clutching tins of *barfi*, boxes of dates, packets of figs and sachets of dried spices. Thus, as the *Bengal Star* drifted into Suez's harbour, Ibrahim prayed to *Allah* and prepared for escape.

When the commotion arising from the upper decks told Ibrahim that the ship was about to drop anchor, he knew the time had come. He dumped his bag of clinker onto the ground, scuttled down the corridor and calmly walked over to his bed. Tugging at the plank below his blanket, he then grabbed his sack of edible treasure and hurled it across his shoulder. As soon as his toes reached the metal steps, he climbed to the top like a man possessed. With hundreds of travellers and hired labourers working on the construction of the nearby canal, all he needed to do was climb overboard and merge into the chaos.

Native boats were already swarming around the vessel and the boatmen were calling for passengers to be taken ashore. Ibrahim spied a boy and his father beckoning him to join them but people were jostling and shoving, keen to observe the sights of the port. He took one last look behind him and was dismayed to see that the boy and his father had gone. He spotted them further along inviting a young couple into their boat, but what did that matter? Suddenly all the boatmen were curling their fingers in an attempt to coax him on board and when one came, they all came and his heart throbbed violently within his skinny chest. He hurled his sack into the nearest dinghy and threw a bony leg in after it. The boatman grabbed his arm and pulled him in. 'Go, go!' Ibrahim cried, pointing manically towards the shore.

The wary boatman negotiated his way through the traffic of vessels and had the advantage of reaching the shoreline before most of the others. 'Money! You pay!' he said, holding out his palm.

'I'm sorry,' Ibrahim said, 'I have no money.'

The man muttered a curse in Arabic and reached for the long wooden stick resting by his foot. Ibrahim raised a hand in defence and used the other to tug at the rope around the neck of his sack. He plunged a hand inside and brought out a tin of *barfi* into the light of day. Next, he reached for a cluster of chillies and a piece of ginger and offered it to the boatman in place of the fee. 'You take this...please...you take.'

The bewildered Egyptian perused the selection of foodstuffs at his feet and peered up to see Ibrahim's torn *kameez* slipping from his shoulder. The previously hidden gashes were now on display and the boatman turned away in horror, reasoning that even within his own struggle for survival, he had never seen any-thing more pitiful than the sight of the beaten fellow sitting in his boat. Returning his stick to its place by his feet, he then pro-ceeded to hand each of the gifts back to Ibrahim. 'Go,' he said, pointing towards the shoreline. He knew Ibrahim was grateful; he could tell from the tears sliding down his cheeks.

'God be with you,' said the Indian, shakily climbing onto the shore.

The man nodded, raised his oars and pushed his boat back out to sea.

It was difficult to find a peaceful spot in which Ibrahim could relax and catch his breath. Traders were pestering him to buy their goods and guides were insisting that he take a ride on their camels. He spied a secluded area beyond several stalls and hid amongst some bushes to pacify his nerves. When anyone passed, he ducked behind some date palms, paranoid that he would be lugged back on board the ship and flogged to within an inch of his life. But nobody stopped to question him and so he wiped away the sweat and lingering tears from his face and rested in the cool shade provided by a canopy of palm trees. Leaning against a tree trunk, Ibrahim soaked in a new world and noticed the local attire of the males: pieces of cloth wrapped around their faces to shelter them safe from the sand and dust. It gave him an idea and his attention turned to the nearby scarf seller. Ahead of him, the stallholders were preparing their merchandise, but fate seemed to be smiling on Ibrahim that morning, for as soon as the passengers alighted in the harbour, the stallholders rushed towards them with their baskets full of goods. Most of the fellows were standing only a short distance away but some had ventured as far as the incoming boats to ply their wares under travellers' noses. The scarf vendor left his stall in the custody of his young son for only a few minutes, but that was all the time Ibrahim needed. Edging closer, he feigned interest in the hectic scene further down the port and as the boy also turned to observe the commotion, Ibrahim snatched a black robe from a hook and pilfered a yellow scarf from the top of a pile. Hurrying back to his place in the shadows, he draped the robe over his shoulders and it fell like a curtain and disturbed the layer of sand on the ground.

By wrapping the yellow scarf around his head, Ibrahim mimicked the turban style of the locals but now that he was ready to disappear amongst the crowds, he faltered beside a line of date palms, contemplating the time he had stolen as a child. He had suffered the consequential beating from his father's stick but now that he could flee incognito, Ibrahim's remorse was hindering his chance to escape. If he had the money, he would have gladly paid for all his clothes, but his precious foodstuffs were all that he possessed. Ibrahim reached for the tin of *barfi* he had proffered the boatman and prowled over to the scarf stall. He deposited the can, along with a few pieces of ginger on top of a pile of neatly folded robes. He mouthed a 'thank you,' to the boy and his father and then made his way through the sandy bazaar.

A broken basket sitting by a palm tree attracted his attention and when he was quite sure it had no owner, he placed his foodstuffs inside and reasoned that he must get away from the *Bengal Star* as swiftly as he could. It would be safer for him in Alexandria but with no money and no means of reaching his destination, he fretted over how he would accomplish this feat. A group of camel owners nearby were offering tourists a more traditional means of transport but Ibrahim thought the donkeys baying in the distance would provide a cheaper alternative. He then promptly abandoned the idea of travelling astride an ass, for he wished to be amongst the westerners in their horse-drawn buggies.

The French were out recruiting healthy Arab men to work on the canal, and Ibrahim thought it an attractive option, for it would certainly help pay the fare to Europe. But how long would the hard labour last before he had saved enough money? And would he be treated fairly? Whilst mulling over his options, he moved out from the path of an old Egyptian woman who, much to his surprise, placed a shrunken hand into his basket of wares and began rooting around inside. She helped herself to a stem of ginger, a bulb of garlic and a handful of chillies and then asked, 'How much?'

Startled by her boldness, Ibrahim placed his basket on the ground and splayed out ten fingers. The woman muttered something in her native tongue and then poked around in her purse. Subsequently, she deposited ten coins into his palm and tucked the purchased items into a cloth bag. Ibrahim quickly peeled down the edges of his sack and brought out six tins of *barfi* and an assortment of dates. He quoted a selection of random prices but she dismissed him and wandered over to a group of ladies standing beside the tobacco stall. After bantering a few moments, she pointed in Ibrahim's direction and the ladies began heading his way. They, too, prodded and nudged the goods in his basket and by the end of several exchanges, he had earned some more money, although of course, he had sold his goods at prices much cheaper than normal. But it mattered not that Ibrahim was ignorant about the Egyptian cost of spices; all he wanted was enough money to get to Cairo and now, he knew what he needed to do.

In Suez, the passengers invaded every nook and cranny of the Egyptian harbour, eager to make their connections and continue on with their journeys. Jemima watched over the Hayward baggage whilst her mistress stood amongst her acquaintances, contemplating the quickest route to Cairo. Nearby, the Hayward children sat cross-legged on a patch of sandy grass, charmed by the entertainment provided by a native man and his acrobatic monkey. Jemima's gaze wandered slightly when a local man, keen to sell his wares, began encircling her. 'Chillies? Turmeric? Garlic? Cloves?' he chanted.

Jemima shook her head and gathered the bags closer.

'Chillies? Turmeric? Ginger? Cloves? I give you very good price, Madam.'

She waved him away but he was persistent.

'Chillies, Turmeric? I have lovely ginger... lovely dates.'

His refusal to move on made her irksome and impatient. He pestered her a while longer, whilst forever pushing back the yellow turban wrapped shoddily about his head. The section masking the lower portion of his face stifled his words when he spoke and suddenly a strange sense of *déjà vu* descended on Jemima. 'Ibrahim?' she gasped.

'Shush,' he whispered, tugging the scarf away from his mouth. 'You not say my name out loud... I have escaped! This is my disguise. I am Egyptian man now. They will not find me like this.' Just then, some lascars ambled up the banks and Ibrahim tossed his scarf around his face and resumed his *souk* persona. 'Chillies, garlic... turmeric!' he cried, keeping a stealthy eye about him. The men moved on and he turned back to Jemima. 'I'm so happy to find you. I want to say a thousand thank yous.'

'But where will you go now?'

'I do not know... England, perhaps.' He delved into his cloth sack and rummaged around for a second. 'I want to give you this... to say thank you for saving this foolish man's life.'

Jemima's eyes brightened. '*Barfi*?'

'I wish I could give you something better, something more...'

'Where did you get this?'

'I took it from the ship with these...' He pointed to the spices in his basket.

'And your clothes?'

'I stole them,' he confessed, looking rather ashamed.

'Thank you, Ibrahim...' Jemima whispered. 'My mistress is coming... you should go now.'

'I am hoping very much that we will meet again soon, Jemima. I cannot forget you. I cannot forget what you did for me...a thousand thank yous,' he smiled. 'Goodbye.'

'Goodbye Ibrahim,' she smiled.

With one last look from his silky black eyes, Ibrahim hurled his robe over his shoulder in the most dramatic of fashions and retreated into the crowd, leaving Jemima to glance down at the *barfi* in her hands. It was a reminder of her homeland and she had just enough time to slip it into her valise before the memsahib arrived with the children. She passed the bags into the possession of a coolie and took her place at her mistress's side as hoards of people waited for a ride to the local station. Merchants were going about their daily business and sweaty men were making a living from the construction of the canal. The monkey screeched as its limbs tumbled through the air and tobacco vendors whistled and cajoled, luring sailors with the promise of mind-altering hookah. And somewhere amongst the sandy chaos, a counterfeit Egyptian with a laughable yellow turban and a broken basket was attempting to sell his stolen wares. And just as he predicted that night on the *Bengal Star*, this counterfeit Egyptian had reclaimed his spirit and had somehow escaped.

CHAPTER 13
WHEN THE WEBSTERS MET THE HAYWARDS

In Alexandria's port, a second ship named the *Viceroy* waited to take Jemima and the Haywards on to their final destination. It was far less impressive than the *Bengal Star* and its accommodation quarters were rather dreary and compact. Many passengers longed to complain but thankful to be safely on board the vessel, merely decided to retire early to bed. The children's cabin was limited to say the least, but Jemima was too exhausted to care and guided Robert and Sophie into their berths without finding the need for the customary lullaby. Their eyelids fluttered until they sealed tight and fluttered no more and Jemima curled up like a baby herself after substituting the shawl around her neck for a makeshift pillow.

The weather was clear and warm across the Mediterranean Sea and the *Viceroy* sped along at a rapid pace. Two days away from the coast of France, the Captain gave permission for dancing and jollity to take place upon the main deck and so the army troops volunteered their best musicians and passengers – rich and poor alike – dressed for an evening beneath the stars. The band struck up the opening verse of *'The Girl I Left Behind Me'* and revellers rushed to partake in the evening's first dance. Elizabeth sipped sherry and strolled to the sound of carefree music. She passed judgement on the cavorting behaviour of several drunken sailors and turned down the offer of a dance with a dashing young soldier. She watched him approach an unattached young lady, who was far too riveted in him to notice anyone else. And suddenly Elizabeth was no longer taking notice of them, for she was staring into the inky black sea, thinking of William and how they had danced together on their wedding day. In fact, Elizabeth Hayward's eyes could not have blazed more brightly than when she first laid eyes on her prospective husband. Not only was he a member of the landed gentry, he was young, handsome and would lead her into London society as a bona fide member of the upper classes.

What else could be said of William Hayward? He was the second of three children born to Lord and Lady Hayward, whose respective bloodlines ensured their position as one of the families sharing the monopoly of land in the county of Surrey. The Hayward fortune was amassed from the family's great oak estate, which supplied timber for the ships of the Royal Navy fleets and like all formidable patriarchs of his class and generation, Lord Victor Hayward entailed his entire estate to his eldest son, Raymond, whose duty was to inherit the title and run the family businesses. And since their youngest child Constance was already betrothed to the son of a property tycoon, all that concerned Lord and Lady Hayward was to arrange an agreeable union for their second son, William.

At first, he felt slighted that he had not been left a share of the family wealth, but after witnessing Raymond's sacrifices, William relished the freedom to follow his own will and necessitated the steps that would initiate his calling as a solicitor in London. Using his own income, he bolstered the small allowance his father had permitted him to receive and lived a life in London that was carefree and enjoyable. He loved visiting the theatre and dining at the supper rooms, but soon formed friendships and acquaintances that were deemed by his social class as 'the wrong sort'. He fraternised with artists, writers and poets, who challenged societal conventions and encouraged free thought. He shared their yearning for a more compassionate world and agreed as they criticised England's reign of oppression in colonies that were collected like valuable trinkets. Back in Surrey, Lady Hayward fretted and fussed over her son's most unsuitable associations. She loved her second born dearly; to her, he should have been the one who inherited it all. Thus, she made it her mission to find William a wife; and one that came with a substantial amount of money.

Further north in the county of Yorkshire, George Webster, a successful middle-class businessman, was prospering exceedingly well from the two wool-manufacturing factories bequeathed to him by his father. As one of the first northern businessmen to introduce factory equipment in place of his plebeian workers, George Webster Senior soon found his investment paying off and slipped away from the world, leaving his booming businesses to his one and only son.

George Webster Junior was welcomed into the higher echelons of society, albeit reluctantly. But like the clichéd moth to the flame, he hobnobbed in places frequented by aristocracy and revelled in a world of upper-class dinners and balls. Coveting the grandeur and power of the noble fellows about him, he yearned to further improve his name and social standing – an aspiration shared with his ambitious wife, Agnes, who was always considered a promising snob. Now officially smug and affluent, Agnes obsessed over securing a marriage for her one and only child in a union that had to achieve two significant goals: social prestige and a better name. The importance of 'marrying up' was thrust into her young daughter's malleable mind and at the tender age of ten, Elizabeth Beatrice Webster mirrored the same ambitions as her indefatigable mother. Finding a suitable match, however, proved more difficult than Agnes had first hoped, but she soon crossed paths with a young man whose Yorkshire-based family fortune was made in coal. She robustly encouraged him to pursue her young daughter until an agreement was settled upon and a marriage date was set. But when the Websters met the Haywards at a dinner in London, henceforth, everything changed.

Lord Victor Hayward struggled to make small talk at a supper held to celebrate the triumphs of the British businessman. His contempt for the *nouveau riche* was especially difficult to suppress that night, for he believed that the bourgeoisie was usurping its way into a historic tradition of legacy and power and the Webster family was a typical example of the ever-increasing *parvenu* who lacked the necessary finesse and, more importantly, old blood, that bequeathed them the right to trespass into his world. As he whispered disapprovingly into his high-born friends' ears, Lord Hayward was promptly silenced by his wife, who, having shared banter with Agnes Webster from across the table, learned that this particular *parvenu* had an eligible daughter who came with an allowance of thirty thousand a year. The transaction was simple: wealth for social power and reputation, which meant that Elizabeth's engagement with the coal merchant's son had to be broken off.

Lady Francis Hayward also schemed and planned. When William next returned home to Surrey, she summoned him to her bedside, feigning sudden illness. 'My darling boy, my nerves are spent... my delicate disposition gets worse by the day. Your father has a troublesome heart and I worry ever so. And then there's my darling boy alone in London... struggling on a paltry wage. The doctor insists I rest... no needless concerns, you understand? Who knows how long I may have left in this life and I long to see you settled and happy.'

'There's no need to worry, Mother... I'm happy enough,' William declared.

'There's a girl, William... a dear, sweet girl. Elizabeth Webster... she'd be perfect for you...'

'But Mother...' William remonstrated.

'Trust me, darling boy! Mother knows what's best. Do you remember when you were a child and you cried when your father took Raymond horse-riding and not you? You'd run into my arms and weep until my embraces made you feel better. Raymond was, and is, your father's favourite... but *you*, William... *you* were *my* favourite and remain so until the day I die. Do you remember how you'd stay wrapped in my arms whilst I rocked and petted you? I always said that you deserved the very best in life.'

'Yes, Mother. I remember... I always felt different from Raymond...even Constance... but you seemed to celebrate that in me instead of pushing me aside... like Father.'

'You were a special little boy... always running and laughing... skipping and jumping... climbing trees, rolling around in the grass...too free for your own good. Nevertheless, you deserved the very best.'

'Father never thought so... I seemed to embarrass him much of the time.'

'Forgive him, William. He's staunch in his ways...but he does love you. He's getting old and tired... we both are... and it would give us both peace of mind if you were to marry and settle down.'

'Marry and settle down with Elizabeth Webster?'

'Yes, William. If not for your father, do it for me.'

It was the accepted thing, William reasoned. Gentlemen married and settled down. They spawned offspring to carry on name and tradition and then they would grow old and eventually die

– like his father would do. But William was not ready and he wished to marry for love. He had enjoyed liaisons with women in the past but they had never quite stirred the passions within him. It was a trying time for William but after constant badgering from the entire Hayward family, he conceded to their wishes in spite of knowing that they went against his very own. He thought he could learn to love Elizabeth Webster, for she was not the kind of woman that usually attracted his eye. She was sensible and safe; winsomely pretty and eager to please. It was not for her money, for he had learned to live without the family wealth and even enjoyed the anonymity his modest lifestyle had brought. Still, he married Elizabeth Webster in the summer of 1858, though their incompatibility surfaced during the honeymoon, when, after exploring Vienna and its surrounding avenues, they encountered an impoverished mother and her three gaunt children begging in the city's streets. William spoke a few words of German and discovered that the woman's husband had recently died from consumption. She was penniless and homeless with three starving children in tow and her desperation to survive almost moved him to tears. Consequently, he handed over almost every last note in his wallet, leaving his new wife suitably enraged.

'That money was intended for our supper at the hotel!'

'They were starving Elizabeth. Besides, we can eat at an inn instead.'

'An inn? Where the commoners go? How can you even propose such a thing? This is our honeymoon!'

'And that's their lives, Elizabeth,' William stressed, pointing to the woman's three skeletal children.

The disagreements continued over the home they would purchase on their return to London. He suggested a modest house in Islington, where the offices of his law practice were within easy reach. She could only scoff at the mere idea. 'Charlotte and her husband, Frederick, inhabit an impressive seven bay, three-storey house on the east side of Grosvenor Square. 'You cannot expect us to entertain them in detestable Islington.'

William succumbed and purchased a home in fashionable Carlton House Terrace. Four months later, his eyes seemed to re-capture their sparkle when Elizabeth told him that she was carry-ing his child. His face glowed like that of the Archangel Gabriel's when she finally delivered a boy into his arms and Sophie's arriv-al seemed to make his happiness complete until the news of a vig-orous recruitment drive in India reminded him that he was tired of whiling away his days dealing with the mundane legalities of various estates, businesses and wills at the offices of Simeon & Howarth. The dismantling of the East India Company was now paving the way for lawyers, solicitors and judges to help establish effective judiciary systems in the major Indian cities. *'I shall be able to make a real difference over there,' he thought.* And so, in need of more meaning and adventure in his life, William accepted the invitation without thinking twice.

CHAPTER 14

THE SILK CITY

William Hayward's final weeks in Calcutta were spent helping his colleague, Mortimer, ease into the position of assistant to the Chief Justice of Bengal. He explained the tedious wording of land treaties and contracts, whilst writing a plethora of formal letters and detailed reports that would introduce Mortimer to the *maharajahs* and *nawabs,* who would, no doubt, be dismayed to hear that they would have to negotiate terms with another new Englishman. But once his successor was firmly entrenched in his former shoes, William Hayward instructed his servants to pack his belongings and close up the house in Dhurmatollah Street. Thus, whilst Abdul filled two large trunks with clothes and possessions, William sat up late into the night, mourning his transitory but exhilarating life in India.

It took William Hayward a while to adapt to his hectic surroundings when he first arrived in India. He could not decide which was more overwhelming: the scorching heat of the Indian sun or the ubiquitous dust of its landscape. The constant high-pitched buzz of the mosquitoes almost drove him to lunacy and he recalled the time he found a foot long centipede curled up in one of his boots. As warned by others, the food and water failed to agree with his delicate European disposition and just as predicted, he fell foul to a mild case of bacillus dysentery. But whilst convalescing, William Hayward began to delight in the ambiguity of India, for as he lay in bed, staring out of the window, the rise and fall of the spectacular sunrises and sunsets simply took his breath away.

On his travels around Bengal, he found the vast lands of the *maharajahs* and *nawabs,* coarse and menacing one moment, and lush and exquisite the next. The history behind each palatial fortress and sacred temple made him feel small and unworthy despite the country and Empire that he himself embodied. Everything captivated him from the toothless beggar crouching on the street to the women washing their clothes at the riverside. Even his servant, Abdul, from whom he had learnt a few words of Hindustani, felt more like an old, reliable friend with whom he could share a laugh and joke; not like the gruff, stuffy servants that had surrounded him in his father's house. He even took to wearing a cotton *kameez*: it was cooling in the evenings and he liked how it felt against his skin. But things suddenly changed when Elizabeth arrived, for her obdurate ways made him realise that India symbolized freedom: a freedom wrapped inside an enthralling madness that only fuelled his love affair with the East.

It had often crossed William's mind that he had made a terrible mistake marrying Elizabeth, for they were as different as two people could be. He had always been a free spirit; a liberalist even – his free-thinking friends had made him realise that, whereas India had only confirmed it. Obsessed with tradition and wealth, his wife was petulant, demanding and unwilling to take a risk. He had tried his best to make their marriage work but he reasoned that he *must* try again, especially since having their almighty argument. In fact, it was an argument that he would never forget. He was seated at the drawing room table, holding his head in one hand, whilst the fingers of the other were drumming the base of the candelabra. 'Forgive me,' he said. 'I've agreed to help Mortimer settle into the post. It'll only take a few weeks and then I'll be on the next ship home.'

'You promised to return with me,' she said, pacing the room.

'I *shall* be returning,' he appealed, 'just a little later than expected... just until Mortimer's settled.'

'Is there not someone else who can assist him?'

'If only it were that simple. He needs to be briefed accordingly and the only fellow who can do that...'

'Is you ...' she interrupted, claiming the seat opposite him. A moment passed and then she said, 'I must ask you, William. Are you having an affair?'

He stood up with such force that the table rocked and the chair came thundering down behind him. 'I can scarcely believe your words,' he retorted, marching a little about the room.

'Please answer the question.'

He shook his head. 'I am not having an affair.'

'You're not telling the truth, William.'

'This is absurd!' he laughed.

'I insist on the truth!'

'Have you gone insane?' he roared, 'I shall tell you, Elizabeth... ever since arriving in India you've whined and complained incessantly. I hardly forced you to come... *you* insisted. You knew what my position entailed and you agreed to come.'

'I am your wife, William,' she hissed. 'Did you expect me to sit at home and wait? I came to support you... '

'Support? Is this your idea of support? I resigned for you... I gave up my career for you. What more do you expect? You abhor everything here... you're never satisfied. You hate the people... you hate the country... "William, it's exceedingly hot. William, there are too many insects. William, I detest the food!" And now... above all, you accuse me of having an affair!'

'It's her isn't it?'

'For goodness sake! Not Ettie again. She's a dear friend.'

'Liar!'

'How dare you accuse me of such nonsense? Ettie and I are friends and frankly, I'm at a loss as to what to do or say anymore.' He stuffed a hand through his jacket armhole and prepared to leave. 'Perhaps it's for the best that you're leaving ahead of me. It would be wise for you to think about how preposterous you've been.' He turned the door handle and glared at her one last time. 'I shall be at the club. Under the circumstances, I think it's best if I stay in their rooms tonight.'

Yes, William Hayward remembered every little detail of the exchange and now as the house in Dhurmatollah Street grew dark, still and increasingly empty, he felt desperate and ashamed. Guilt and sorrow tore his heart into shreds. 'I must make things right again,' he said, 'for the sake of my children at least... I must make things right.'

The very next day, William Hayward embarked on a journey one hundred and thirty-seven miles north to Murshidabad – a district known as the Silk City of the *Nawabs*. His buggy passed the Palace of a Thousand Doors and trotted around the Pearl Lake of Moti Jhil, where it halted further along the banks of the Bhagirathi River. A pale pink house rose up in the distance; it seemed to watch him as he wandered over to its ornamental gates. William peered up at the balcony and thought of the beguiling creature waiting inside before pondering how he would say his final goodbye.

He had first feasted eyes on Sonal at the Ivory Palace: a mansion tucked away in the depths of Murshidabad, where men of wealth and open-mindedness could experience India's heady delights. The hallway was ablaze with fiery light and thick fumes of incense intoxicated the nostrils of the more languorous visitors nearby. A line of richly costumed eunuchs tiptoed barefoot across the soft Persian carpets, illuminating a world of music and poetry with their torches of fire. The host clapped his hands twice and three musicians arrived, signalling her presence with their gentle humming voices. Daintily, she stepped into the room and paid her respects to the space in which she was to perform. She was swathed exquisitely in shimmering gold silk and a myriad of bracelets tinkled and gleamed every time she moved. She assumed a dancer's stance in the middle of the floor and stayed perfectly still until the music swelled into the space. Tonight she would give a rendition of the famous kite dance, and at first, her movements were slow and set to an expressive melody played on the *sitar*. She unfolded her slender arms and curved a knee before rotating a hand with some gesturing fingers. She flicked her eyes upwards and swayed her hips from side to side, holding the audience spellbound as she imitated a lone figure flying a kite in the Indian sky.

William stayed until daybreak, enjoying the sensual pleasures of Indian music, song and dance. He wanted to meet the enchanting dancer who had performed so beautifully before a legion of admirers but she had disappeared into the secret rooms of the Ivory Palace, leaving him giddy with the impression she had made on his heart. When he finally crossed the threshold of her boudoir, he was astonished by her exquisite manners, her knowledge of literature and her experience in the arts. She was conversant in French and adept in Spanish and had even travelled to cities such as Paris and Rome. Her beauty was mysterious... the beguiling eyes, the painted lips... and she danced and sang and made love to him in her private pink house by the river.

Rules and regulations bound him during the day but when evening shed its dusky light, he would cast off his chains to enter her room of incense and flowers. He would loosen his cravat and toss it to the floor; she would unbutton his waistcoat and peel off his shirt, whilst reciting poems in Sanskrit and recounting age-old tales of courtesans who had fallen for handsome British officers. And as William listened to the hypnotic verse, he plunged himself into a trancelike fantasy, believing that Sonal existed only for him. But standing beneath her balcony now, seeing her gorgeous silhouette through a curtain of billowing pink silk, William witnessed another shadow overtake hers: a masculine form that engulfed her sylph-like figure with its greedy arms and probing lips. And in that moment, William did not feel jealousy or anger, for he finally accepted Sonal for what she really was, and he finally accepted himself as the dreamy, tortured fool that he had become. Sonal and India were one and the same: a beautiful drug that had hurtled him through his deep discontentment with such unfathomable intensity that any life hereafter could only be listless and uninspiring. He loathed himself for betraying his wife, but Sonal seemed to make the unbearable existence with Elizabeth more tolerable. 'Goodbye,' he said, walking away, and as a cavern of loneliness appeared in his heart, William felt a part of him made no sense at all. Only emptiness lingered and it was the kind of emptiness not even his children – no matter how much he adored and loved them – could ever fill.

PART TWO

CHAPTER 15

RAIN, RAIN, RAIN

I t was a Saturday – the twenty-ninth of September 1866 to be
exact – when Jemima finally arrived in London. Three days
before her twenty-sixth birthday, she hurtled into Charing Cross
Station on a train that arrived at thirty-seven minutes past nine
in the morning. She had been fortunate enough to secure a seat,
but the carriage had throbbed with the prattle of people excited
to be home and too weary to engage in conversation, Jemima
had elected to snooze against the mucky train window instead.
Outside, a barrage of icy English raindrops pounded the trussed
arch ceiling of the station roof and drizzled down the length
of the train doors, spraying Jemima's fingers and face as she
stepped somewhat groggily onto the wet platform floor. *Rain,
rain, rain; the incessant rain.* It had rained the entire train journey
from Marseille to Boulogne and whilst they had sailed on the
steam packet mail ship to Folkestone. How could she appreciate
the famous English countryside when it was shrouded behind a
watery torrent? *'Is this really England?' she thought. 'It's so cold and
dark.'* The breeze tasted damp and stony, as if she had sipped
water from a glass left idle for days. It did the trick, however,
and lured the lethargy out from her bones as sure as if she had

been slapped across the face with a frosty hand. She hoped the weather would improve; she was already missing the Indian sun.

Sophie was jumping up and down further down the platform. 'We're over here, Ayah! We're over here! This is London, Ayah, we're in London!' she shouted. Jemima raised her skirts to prevent the hems from sucking up the moist filth of the platform floor and made her way over to the girl. Revitalized by the thrill of being in London, the child nuzzled her head into the folds of Jemima's shawl. 'I'm happy that you came with us, Ayah. I want you to stay with us forever,' she said through a soft whisper.

Moved by the child's tender words, Jemima cupped Sophie's cheeks with her hands. 'Ayah is here. Ayah is here, my precious doll... my little, yellow-haired, precious doll!' She had been instructed by the memsahib to keep her pending departure a secret but Jemima made a silent promise that whilst she was by their side, the children's needs would always come first, as they had always done. But even if she had been permitted to enlighten Robert and Sophie, she questioned whether she had enough heart to do so. Looking across at the boy, she noticed that he was in a petulant mood, irritated by his mother's ceaseless banter.

'I thought Grandfather was supposed to be meeting us,' he groaned, as his mother finally tore herself away.

'He ought to be outside, dear,' Elizabeth smiled. 'Now where's that porter?'

There had been a remarkable change in the mistress's demeanour. Gone were the peevish moods and selfish solitary desires; the lady had been high-spirited and almost unflappable these past few days. 'Are you excited to be seeing your Grandfather George?' she asked her children.

'Yes Mama,' they replied together.

'Gracious me! He could be anywhere in this crowd!' she gasped.

Reunion was the theme for some; farewells and tears for others. Husbands, wives, brothers and sisters; friends, lovers, parents and children – all were gathered on the concourse, offering sentiments of every nature. But Jemima preferred to study the woman kneeling beside one of the station pillars. She was cradling a dirty baby in one arm and pleading passers-by for money with the other. Her face was swamped by a mop of matted hair, disguising what were once lustrous blond locks. Her stick-thin body wore torn and faded clothes. Two mismatching shoes dangled upon her emaciated feet – a man's battered brown boot on one foot and a muddy black slipper upon the other, and such was the threadbare nature of the latter that a grimy big toe poked through a tattered hole. Jemima wondered whether the pitifully gaunt woman was in fact, a ghost – a fearsome apparition that had haunted London for a hundred years. Convinced that she was hallucinating due to the lack of sleep, she turned her gaze towards the children and then back to the station pillar but sure enough, the wretch was there, holding the mewling infant inside an old fraying blanket, caked with dried vomit and encrusted excrement. *'What happened to them?' Jemima wondered. 'Why is no one helping them?'*

'Keep up, Jemima!' Elizabeth cried, shattering Jemima's train of thoughts.

The miserable impression of the woman and child lingered with Jemima as she trailed her mistress and they only meandered a short distance before their path was intercepted by a barefoot boy, who yelled, 'Matches, missus! Buy me matches?' His scrawny physique suggested an age of seven or eight but his eyes were somewhat older and reflected horrors that no child should have to witness. He curled down the edges of his little cloth bag and plucked out two boxes of matches with fingers that were thick with grime and gnawed right down to the skin. The boy's face appeared to be injured by a blow to the cheek, and like the woman and her baby, he too was undernourished and shabbily dressed.

'No matches, thank you,' said Elizabeth, shooing him away. He studied the children enviously and they stared back at him with paralleled interest. 'Come away children,' Elizabeth hissed.

The foul stink of urine emanating from the mother and her famished child made Jemima's nostrils retreat and her throat fit to retch. *'Why are these English people suffering like this?' she asked silently.*

The woman presented her snivelling bundle to anyone showing the slightest interest but she soon abandoned her lament to scrutinise the Indian standing close by. 'What you starin' at blackie?' she squawked. 'If you ain't got no money to give us... then bugger off!'

Jemima took heed and hastily joined her mistress.

A well-groomed, bespectacled man was waving in the distance. Jemima guessed correctly that this was the aforementioned grandfather and indeed it was, for George Webster hastened his steps to greet his daughter. 'Elizabeth! My dear, Elizabeth!'

'Father!' she exclaimed, her face plump with delight.

Coy and cautious, the children nestled back into their ayah's skirts as father and daughter engaged themselves in an affectionate embrace. 'Gracious, you're soaked!' Elizabeth declared, brushing the wetness from her father's shoulders.

'Nonsense! It's only a little rain!'

'One can hardly call it *a little rain*, Father. It's been pouring the whole day,' she laughed. 'But I'm happy to be home... even if it is raining.'

Grandfather George then engaged in some levity. 'Where's Robert and Sophie, Elizabeth? Did you leave them behind in Calcutta?'

Robert grimaced and Sophie looked perplexed. 'We're over here,' the boy said, looking serious.

'Well, well!' Grandfather George exclaimed, 'There you are! Goodness, how you've both grown. Come here, children!'

Robert politely extended his arm but found it and the rest of his body yanked into an embrace. Then it was Sophie's turn. The girl was swung playfully into the air before being given a whiskery kiss or two. It was a lively reunion and Jemima recalled how her own father had often greeted her in the same jolly way. It had felt supremely wonderful for one so small to be embraced in the arms of one so big but after hearing Sophie's chuckles spilling into her grandfather's arms, she had to admit, that she was feeling more than out of place.

'This is the children's ayah, Father,' said Elizabeth. 'Her name is Jemima.'

Jemima pulled her shawl further over her brow and waited for him to speak. He managed half a smile but was evidently more preoccupied with his grandchildren. 'Well, come along now, I've a growler waiting. I just hope the rain stops.' With Sophie locked in his arms, Grandfather George charged towards the exit, flanked by his doting daughter and grandson, whilst Ayah trailed dutifully behind.

The rain had begun to recede but Jemima stepped into a puddle and bristled as the icy dampness crept up her legs. Still shivering, she watched the porter as he struggled to load the roof of the growler – a four-wheeled carriage with a compartment for luggage. George Webster urged the cantankerous driver to climb down from his seat and assist the man. Begrudgingly, the man hopped off and tossed the remaining valises into the carriage as Elizabeth and the children climbed inside and Grandfather George claimed the last available space.

Battered suitcase in one hand, shawl tightly gripped in the other, Jemima stood on the pavement, trembling at the thought of being left behind.

'What about Ayah?' Sophie appealed.

'Oh...' George replied. 'I forgot about her ... I suppose she'll have to go up with the driver.'

The driver, a tall man with mutton chop sideburns and a conspicuous Roman style nose was more than ready to guide his horses out into the road.

'I say!' George cried. 'She'll have to sit beside you!' He waved Jemima over. 'Up you go, girl!'

Mounting the carriage required some assistance and Jemima hoped the driver would come to her aid. However, the man was clearly tetchy and turned his head to the other side of the street.

'Well, help her up man!' George roared, wondering why Jemima was still standing on the pavement. 'We haven't got all day!'

The driver extracted some black leather gloves from his pockets, into which, he inserted his hands most furiously. Pointing to Jemima's case, he demanded she pass it up first before seizing it from her fingers and hurling it into the space beside him. His indignation was apparent as he lugged Jemima up onto the seat and wedged her valise firmly between them, in case some part of her body made contact with his. Snarling like a rabid dog, he whacked the reins across the horses' flanks and muttered indiscernible phrases as the growler pulled away.

Jemima wanted to assure the man that she was not happy with the seating arrangement either, for the concoction of sweat and alcohol festering on his clothes was repulsive to say the least. But it was not difficult to avoid any kind of conversation with the surly fellow and paying no heed to him, she took in the sights of the metropolis instead.

Never had she seen so many horses. Carts, drays and a hotch-potch of wagons hauled human and inanimate loads across London's hectic streets. The clamour of iron-shod hooves was thunderous to her ears and whenever a horse-drawn tram or an omnibus piled high with passengers drew up beside the growl-er, Jemima quivered at the thought of being so close to several neighing beasts. The stench from the manure-strewn roads made her head rock and her eyes water; that aside, she was content to watch British people going about their lives. Fashions were dif-ferent: women wore bonnets instead of *topis*, but still magnificent and colossal, their crinoline dresses swished and swayed as their hems dipped into puddles and soaked up the rain. Rich men took cover under tall black hats and workmen laboured in neck-erchiefs and clogs with leather straps strung around their trou-sers to stop the rats from running up their soggy legs. People ducked in and out of public houses, pawnshops and second hand clothing stores to take refuge from the rain under the shops' colourful awnings. Women rattled collection boxes and orphan children scrapped with cheeky go-betweens paid a shilling to carry notes between smart-suited gentlemen. Across the road, the postmaster conversed with a pie man and two homeless mu-sicians braved the misty rain to play a tune on a tin whistle and a decrepit hurdy-gurdy. The growler moved on, passing blocks of well-proportioned houses with soaring white pillars standing back from wide, curving roads. There were plant pots lined up on their wrought iron balconies and Jemima recognised the ar-chitecture as the blueprint for the British houses back home in India. Forgetting the dismal weather and the bad-tempered com-panionship provided by the driver, she quickly became intrigued by the sights of the capital city. But then Jemima was suddenly witnessing something else in London's streets and it made her lurch in disbelief.

She saw *English* people crawling in and out of gutters; she saw *English* people rocking in the sodden roads. They lived in ramshackle hovels right beside the more respectable houses and they were hungry, destitute and begging for money with their scrawny white hands. Time and time again, Jemima had been told that India was inferior and its poverty and inadequacies were rightly called to attention, but the British never mentioned that their streets were full of misery too. Memsahib Hayward had said that England was a shining example to her colonies. It held out a charitable hand to those less fortunate and with the other, paved the way forward for progress and civilization. '*Why are these values not upheld here?*' Jemima thought. '*If England's subjects are equal, why are so many of them living in squalor in the city's streets?*'

She had been told that it would be an honour for her to visit the stronghold of the Empire, but as she absorbed more of the mottled sights, Jemima told herself that this was not the England she had expected to see. In comparison, it seemed Calcutta was not that bad after all.

CHAPTER 16
THE MATRIARCH

By the time evening had fallen on her first day in London, Jemima had met Agnes Webster. The introduction was not a formal one; on account of a prior engagement, Elizabeth's mother had arrived at Carlton House Terrace an hour after her daughter and grandchildren, and Jemima was upstairs at the time, unpacking the children's possessions and had thus gone unnoticed. However, she was unceremoniously stumbled upon, slouched on the nursery floor with the children's possessions spread out before her and the sight had caused Agnes's nostrils to ripple with horror. 'And who might you be?' the lady asked in the most sober of tones.

Jemima was struck by the remarkable likeness shared by mother and daughter. Elizabeth and Agnes possessed the same eye colour, the same bone structure and the same haughtiness. 'I am Jemima Ayah, Memsahib,' she stammered, raising herself from the floor.

Agnes was clearly outraged and left the room to find her daughter. 'Can she speak English? Can she be trusted? She called me something quite odd... something beginning with an *M*.'

'It means 'mistress,' Mother... and yes, she can be trusted, she's been with us for over two years.'

'You could have warned me she was there, dear. I got such a fright when I walked by and saw her black face in and amongst the bags like a little thief.'

'You knew she was accompanying me, Mother. I wrote and told you, remember?'

'Does she have family?'

'No Mother... none whatsoever.'

'Well that's one thing I suppose. What if she runs away?'

'She won't. In any case, where would she go? This is her first time in England. She hardly knows how to get to the end of the pavement let alone the city.'

'Still, I would hold onto her wages if I were you... as an assurance... that way, if she absconds with the family silver, she won't get far.'

'Honestly, Mother!'

'Elizabeth, now that you're home, is there any need for her sort?'

'Mother darling, I'm exceedingly tired and there really is no need to fret about Jemima. And as for her wages... I always intended to keep hold of them until she returns to India.'

Agnes drew a reassuring breath.

They returned to the nursery to find the children's clothes and possessions set in several neat piles. Sophie had since clambered into her ayah's arms and was nuzzling her sleepy head on Jemima's shoulder. Jemima was astutely aware that Agnes Webster was poring over every one of her features. She was wearing her dark brown European skirt, along with a white, high-necked cotton blouse and she held Sophie in a way that was foreign to the other women, for the girl nestled well in her arms and moulded her limbs to fit every curve and bend of her ayah's embrace. Agnes's glare was telling and its menacing power made Jemima painfully aware of her connection with another woman's child. 'Come closer girl,' Agnes commanded.

Jemima brushed Sophie's hand away from her ear and swung the girl down onto the floor. She prepared herself for some kind of tearful backlash but before the child could even think of re-monstrating, she was ushered out of the room by her uptight mother. Jemima walked towards Agnes Webster praying that her previous relaxed behaviour had not caused too much ill will.

'You speak English well,' the lady said.

'Thank you, Memsahib.'

'How do you like England?'

Jemima had not expected such a cordial enquiry from the matriarch of the family in front of whom she hardly made a very good first impression. 'It is very nice, Memsahib...very nice indeed.'

Elizabeth interrupted. 'Jemima, now that you're in England, I'd like you to use 'Madam' when referring to myself and my mother. Do you understand?'

'Yes Mem... Madam,' Jemima replied coyly.

She was dismissed soon after, conscious that Agnes's fear-some gaze was following her out of the room.

'She seems well-mannered enough,' Agnes remarked. 'I sup-pose her lack of family means she'll be less trouble. We can do without the tears and tantrums of a homesick Indian, though... she won't be needed for long. I've taken the liberty of finding an excellent governess for Sophie, not to mention a marvellous butler and the most handsome footman. Just say the word and I'll arrange the interviews.'

Elizabeth's face puckered. 'I do appreciate the help, Mother, but there really is no rush.'

'No rush? Elizabeth, I think it's highly irregular to keep a heathen savage girl in one's home... no matter how house-trained she is.'

'Really, Mother... heathen perhaps, but do you think I'd have a 'savage' looking after my children?'

'There's a place for her kind, dear... people who could take her off our hands.'

'No need, Mother. I will be arranging Jemima's passage home soon after William returns.'

'But I've heard of a place...'

'It really won't be necessary.'

'Very well,' Agnes scoffed.

Jemima heard snatches of conversation from the children's bedroom and it had been a while since she had heard the master's name uttered. He had not been dwelling in her thoughts recently and she thought the fact peculiar and even a little sad. Still, she was rather relieved to think that she might finally be overcoming her absurd infatuation with the man.

She was directed to a little room at the top of the house. It was much smaller than her room in Calcutta and possessed only a bed and a washbowl placed in one corner. Larger rooms existed along one side of the corridor below but they remained locked and reserved for the English servants. Jemima liked the Hayward's London home. It was faintly reminiscent of the house back in Calcutta but definitely built on a much grander scale. Crammed with all manner of polished silverware, the rooms possessed elaborate crystal chandeliers that caught the light magnificently and sparkled like gigantic stars. Gilt-framed photographs rested on mahogany tables and ornate porcelain figurines posed upon chests of walnut wood. Elegant timepieces of varying sizes tinkled on the mantelpieces and chimed along the hallways whilst the floors were shrouded with flamboyantly patterned carpets. The streets were much cleaner in Carlton House Terrace and though England was in the midst of its autumn, Jemima noticed that some gardens were still leafy and green with an array of proper chrysanthemums still blossoming from the window boxes – flowers that had shrivelled swiftly in the inhospitable climate when the memsahib had endeavoured to grow them in India. This was more like the England that she had expected to see. Perhaps the beggars were an illusion after all.

She spent her birthday emptying trunks and boxes. She entered her twenty-sixth year invisible and ghost-like, for nobody knew of it, not even the children. As a child, she had celebrated the day with a visit to the local shrine, where she had prayed with her parents and received blessings from the local Hindu priest. A simple meal of rice and fish would follow and then Dr Mukerjee and Jagatterini would arrive with their annual treat of *bon bons* purchased from the expensive sweetie shop in White Town, Calcutta. Her parent's gift was always given in private. When times were good, it was one they had worked hard for: a small doll or a ribbon for her hair. When times were not so good, it took the form of some sherbet or a spinning top that Subhas had crafted from a piece of wood lying idle in the yard. The day came to an end as she played on her father's lap or listened to Madhu's soothing lullabies in her cot at night. As time went on, the celebrations became more and more modest. Now, orphaned and alone, Jemima preferred her advancing years to wither away without special mention. And they had done so for the past ten years.

CHAPTER 17
THE SHAWL

Two weeks after her return, a letter arrived for Elizabeth, sent by her close friend, Charlotte Godwin. It spoke of a dinner party to which, Elizabeth and her parents were cordially invited. Elizabeth had known Charlotte for over ten years. She had been a bridesmaid at Charlotte's wedding and Charlotte had been present at the births of Robert and Sophie. They had met at their day school in London, where a friendship had bloomed behind the wooden easels of their watercolour painting class. Indeed it was Charlotte's shoulder that Elizabeth cried her middle-class tears upon when the other high-born girls questioned her right to be amongst the elite. But with Charlotte's support, she endured the spiteful storm and vowed to cast off the mantle of inferiority to achieve through marriage what she had been unable to through birth.

Since being away in India, Elizabeth had craved her best friend's company and greeted the invitation with utmost glee. The letter stated that she was to be the guest of honour and the event would herald her recent homecoming. Surprisingly though, Elizabeth thought it best to decline in favour of completing all the endless chores that needed to be accomplished before

William's return. However, Agnes simply would not hear of it. 'You must accustom yourself to society again. Everybody wants to see you. They want to know all about India.'

'I'm trying my best to forget about India,' her daughter remarked.

'That may be so, but I insist you attend. And I recommend a trip to the dressmakers. It would be nothing short of scandalous if you were to be seen in an out of season gown!'

Two days later, they ventured to Oxford Street, enabling Jemima to experience a little more of London whilst her two mistresses perused the stores for fabrics and knick-knacks. She was even permitted to take a seat inside the carriage and already the cold November day seemed considerably brighter. With Sophie chatting merrily on her lap and Robert's concentration ensconced in '*The Little Boy's Handbook*,' Jemima admired the sights of Piccadilly and Regent Street whilst Agnes and Elizabeth discussed the latest couture.

The carriage pulled up outside a dressmaker's shop in Bond Street. The proprietor, Mrs Leeming, an experienced seamstress, had attended to Elizabeth's clothing needs in the past. She exchanged hellos and some pleasant banter before presenting her customers with several rolls of silk, numerous swatches of lace and samples of coloured velvet. Various young women entered with their arms full of dress pattern books and an hour passed before Elizabeth finally settled on a French pattern inspired by the famous *House of Worth*. 'I'd like the dress to be recreated in the sapphire coloured silk... and I prefer the lavender yarn-dyed taffeta.'

'And the petticoats?' asked Mrs Leeming.

'Five please, in turquoise silk.'

'One mustn't forget the *pantalettes*!' bleated Agnes.

'Of course,' replied the dressmaker, 'One pair of *pantelettes* befitting the style of the dress.'

'And hair ornaments!' Agnes bleated again.

Mrs Leeming recommended the *London Emporium* department store for hair ornaments. The place was a veritable treasure trove and stocked everything from Darjeeling Tea to cologne and floor disinfectant. Elizabeth and Agnes frittered the time over the haberdashery counter, captivated by an array of feathers, ribbons, beads and baubles. They took an age before settling a silk flower each – a small lilac orchid with fuchsia pink accents for Elizabeth and a traditional white organza rose for Agnes. Elizabeth then instructed the store assistant to fetch a toy drum from one of the shelves whilst another was asked to measure and cut some pretty yellow ribbon for Sophie's hair. Unexpectedly, she then turned to Jemima. 'Your shawl is quite unbefitting and not to mention, old. Come along, Jemima,' she said, selecting a black woollen wrap which she placed beside the items waiting to be purchased. The counter clerked wrapped everything in brown paper and string before handing the parcels over to Jemima. 'Take exceptional care of the shawl,' Elizabeth said, walking out of the store. 'You must wear it instead of that old green rag of yours.'

The mistress had never given anything old to her Indian servants, let alone anything new that cost money. Now it seemed she cared enough to buy her ayah a shawl. During the carriage ride home, Jemima cradled the brown paper package in her arms and was overcome by a rush of guilt...guilt that saw her falling at her mistress's feet and begging forgiveness... forgiveness, that is, for secretly coveting the lady's husband. The edges of her green stole were certainly old and fraying, and Jemima pondered what she would do with it when she returned to Carlton House Terrace. Maybe she would discard it or maybe she would hide it in her valise as another keepsake. It really did not matter now because her mistress had cared enough to buy her a new one.

Elizabeth woke especially early on the day of Charlotte's soiree, eager for an evening of social gaiety. She wished to make a significant impression on her erstwhile friends and spent most of the time preparing for some appropriate dinner party conversation. She summoned her servant to her chamber at three o'clock and Jemima found her sitting on a stool, puffing up the limp coils of hair that had been flattened during her siesta. Jemima had always admired the memsahib's beauty; everything about the woman seemed so precise. Her hair fell about her face in a rush of soft brown ringlets; her skin twinkled with a delicate layer of perspiration, despite being rubicund from the severe Indian sun. There she was, perched on a stool, refreshing herself with lotions and powders as her petite chest rose and fell within a tightly laced bodice. Jemima often wondered how her heart could pulse freely within such a strange contrivance, but it never seemed to hinder the lady, for Elizabeth Hayward always carried herself with such effortless grace. A mist of lavender cologne perforated the array of stiffened petticoats concealed underneath Elizabeth's day dress. She allowed the aroma to invade her senses and there she remained, meditating in a cloud of perfume – eyes closed; body perfectly still – unaware that she was under her servant's admiring glare.

Jemima had often imagined what it meant to be Elizabeth Hayward. She had even envisaged herself as a sophisticated lady with flowers and ribbons pinned in her hair. She would have to contend with those complicated dresses and equally complicated private affairs, whilst giving the impression that life was a perfect continuum of happiness when everyone else in the world knew it was not. But as alluring as the fantasy was, the reality seemed alien to Jemima and she abandoned her daydreaming to make her presence known.

'You may enter, Jemima,' Elizabeth said, preparing to be undressed.

Jemima was well practised it the art of attending a lady. She had overcome her particular bewilderment of the dress hoop and had skilfully mastered the intricacies of lacing a bodice to twenty inches or less. In the beginning, she had looked away in disgust, for her mistress had often worn such brazen dresses, which pushed her breasts out to the fore. *'These shameless white women might as well walk around naked,' she had thought. 'What must the men be thinking?'* However, she did enjoy the task of arranging her mistress's hair and in turn, the lady found her tender touches relaxing.

That afternoon, Jemima used a pomade of rose musk oil to smooth down Elizabeth's brown tresses before braiding them together two fine plaits. She wound the plaits into a low-placed bun and tucked it inside a velvet brown snood. Finally, she pinned the silk orchid on top. 'This shall do very nicely,' Elizabeth said, admiring Jemima's efforts in her small looking glass. 'I suppose it is time to inform you that the master will be returning soon and we will be choosing a school for Robert and a governess for Sophie... and we will subsequently book your passage back to India. You do understand, Jemima? That was the agreement.'

'I understand, Madam,' Jemima replied, feeling a little dispirited.

'Good, I shall make the appropriate arrangements next month.'

Elizabeth crossed to the centre of the room and stepped into her dress hoop. One corset and four petticoats later, the specially made dress of silk and taffeta was drawn over her shoulders and Jemima set about puffing the bell-shaped sleeves and plumping the copious underskirts. Scurrying over to the bed, she then reached for the large flat box that masked the concluding piece of her mistress's magnificent attire: a midnight-blue velvet cape bordered with a mink fur trim. The sumptuous wrap was placed around Elizabeth's shoulders and Jemima watched as her mistress admired herself in the full-length looking glass. Elizabeth slipped her fingers into her white silk gloves, already knowing she looked exquisite; observing her reflection was a mere formality. 'I shall say goodnight to the children now. Please stay with them until I return,' she said, floating within the doorway that framed her figure so well.

'Madam!' Jemima called out suddenly.

Startled, Elizabeth turned back. 'What is it, Jemima?'

'Tonight ... you look very beautiful.'

Accustomed to condemning improper comments uttered from the mouths of her servants, Elizabeth, on this occasion, found Jemima's transgression strangely empowering. 'Thank you,' she replied, before continuing on to the nursery.

Jemima witnessed the mistress's carriage depart from the children's bedroom window just before seven o'clock. Robert looked pensive as she returned to his bed and settled into a seat. 'Do you miss India, Ayah?' he asked, sliding beneath his bedcovers.

'Yes,' she replied.

'What sorts of things do you miss?'

'The sun... the coconut trees...the fireflies.'

'Perhaps Mother will allow you to return one day... for a vacation. I miss India too. I should like to go back. I don't want to go to school, Ayah.'

Jemima said nothing. She recalled how her former mistress, Jagatterini, yearned to educate every Indian child, regardless of their caste. Mirroring the lady's beliefs, she said, 'Children need to go to school. Education is very important.'

'Mother and Father are going to send me away. I heard them talking in our house in Calcutta.'

The boy was right. His parents *had* made plans but it was not Ayah's place to divulge them. 'You will be happy there,' she said, knowing her words were insufficient consolation.

'I shan't! I'll hate it!' he snapped, diving under his pillow.

Sophie peeped up from behind her blanket. 'Is Robert sad?' she asked.

'A little,' Jemima replied. She reached over and patted Robert on his back. 'Sometimes, something may be bad or horrible at first... but later, it can make you feel good and lead to something better in life.'

Sophie replied in lieu of her brother. 'Do you mean when Mama says that we should be brave soldiers and take our medicine when we are feeling unwell?'

'I suppose so. You see, the medicine tastes bad and you cry... but then it makes you feel better and you smile.'

Robert huffed. 'I do understand what you're trying to say, but... I still don't want to go. Anyway, I'm rather tired now and I want to go to sleep. Goodnight Ayah, goodnight Sophie.'

'Goodnight Robert,' the girl replied.

The boy hid beneath his bedcovers, no doubt contemplating his impending confinement at school. Jemima gently stroked his back and then took her place at Sophie's side.

'Lullaby please, Ayah,' the girl said, reaching for Jemima's earlobe.

Jemima turned the lamplight low and began her usual nightly serenade.

CHAPTER 18
CHARLOTTE'S PIANO

'So you survived the East!' exclaimed Charlotte. 'By the way, you look exquisite... your dress is simply charming! Come Elizabeth, you must meet everybody... they want to know about all your Indian adventures.'

Charlotte Godwin's drawing room was littered with an assortment of guests; some of which Elizabeth knew, some of which she did not. But like a prize-winning pony, she was paraded before each and every one of them to Charlotte's frequent preamble of... 'She's just returned from India!'

'I've heard the weather is horrendously hot,' said one guest.

'How did you find the natives? Were you safe in the house with them?' said another. 'My sister went out to Bombay a year ago. She had quite a time figuring out which servant was supposed to do what.'

'I had the very same problem!' laughed Elizabeth. 'It's such a chore telling them apart!'

There were reunions with old friends and snatches of formal conversation with newly made acquaintances. The dress sparked a whirlwind of fashion banter and, according to Agnes, was a 'roaring success.' Elizabeth took a seat beside her much-pleased mother, satisfied she had achieved what she had set out to do even before having sat down for dinner. And her popularity did not end there, for the ladies flocked to her side, keen to hear about her exploits in the East.

'Charlotte mentioned that you'd brought one back with you,' said a woman with a peacock feather protruding from her hair.

'Yes, I've brought a female with me... she takes care of the children.'

'One cannot be too trusting of these Indian nannies,' Agnes scoffed. 'They have to be watched constantly and they have peculiar ways.'

'Yes!' exclaimed a rather heavy woman called Kitty. 'I heard a rather alarming story of an ayah who gave opium to her charges to calm them at bedtime! Can you imagine that? Feeding opium to a child?'

'I'm quite sure that Jemima is not giving opium to my children,' Elizabeth said.

'Oh... is that her name? Is she... clean?' Kitty asked in a lowered voice. 'The same ayah I just spoke of... well I heard she hardly bathed and her breath smelt horrendous!'

Elizabeth raised an eyebrow. 'Jemima bathes before she takes charge of the children. Her English is very satisfactory and she can read and write too.'

Kitty grimaced in disbelief. 'Really? Can she cook?'

'She cooks, cleans and dresses hair,' replied Elizabeth, distracted by the supple peacock feather in the interlocutor's hair.

'Upon my word! How did you come by her?' Kitty asked.

'She came highly recommended by a doctor and a minister of the church.'

Agnes facial muscles quivered as she spoke. 'I just hope the creature values the opportunity she had been given to see the land of her rulers. How many Indians can say they've been offered such a prospect?'

Having overheard the conversation, Charlotte trotted over to the ladies. 'Will you keep her or send her back?'

'I shall send her back of course… although I shall be very sorry to see her go. Good Indian servants are so hard to find.'

'Not to mention so cheap! One can get eight Indians for the price of an English scullery maid,' Agnes declared.

'Ooh! May we come around and take a peek?' asked the peacock-feather adorned lady.

Elizabeth answered all questions concerning India with eloquence and flair. She threw in the odd anecdote about a gormless Indian servant and described the native female attire as 'a never-ending perplexity.' Her stories provoked raucous laughter from some quarters and profound disgust from others; nevertheless, she slipped back into the elite London scene as if she had never been away. Her ego bruised momentarily when the focus briefly shifted away from her.

'We're just waiting on Violet and Nicholas,' Charlotte said. And she had only just finished speaking when the butler, Willoughby, officially proclaimed the aforementioned pair's arrival.

Just then, a young man marched into the room accompanied by his skinny younger sister. 'We're not late are we, Charlotte?' he boomed.

'Not at all!' she replied sarcastically. 'Elizabeth Hayward, allow me to introduce Nicholas Beaumont and his sister, Violet. Violet has only just returned from India… she was visiting her cousin, so I'm sure you'll both have much in common.'

'I'm pleased to make your acquaintance, Mr Beaumont.'

Nicholas dipped his head. 'As I am yours, Mrs Hayward.'

Facing Violent, Elizabeth said, 'How do you do, Miss Beaumont? How did you find India?'

Violet rolled her eyes to the stucco ceiling and scowled. 'It wasn't entirely to my liking. Certain aspects of the country seemed tolerable but I'm glad to be home now.'

Elizabeth thought Violet Beaumont was rather goose-like and spindly, so unlike her brother, who appeared quite boyishly handsome. An awkward moment passed, during which, Violet's facial expressions danced about bitterly.

'Which part of India did you visit?' Elizabeth asked.

'Madras, Bombay, Allahabad... all over really,' Violet flapped. 'Oh, Calcutta too... I think I've heard your name mentioned once or twice...in fact, I believe my cousin, Eleanor, whom I was visiting, is acquainted with a friend of yours.'

It was not so much what Violet said but more the manner in which she said it that triggered Elizabeth's guard. She was grateful for the appearance of Charlotte, whose intervention, she thought, was more than timely. 'Ladies, I'm afraid the chitchat will have to wait. Willoughby is about to inform us that dinner is ready to be served.'

A gloved finger lazily brushed against Elizabeth's elbow. 'We shall have to continue our little conversation after dinner,' Violet teased. Winding an arm around Nicholas's bicep, she sauntered off and disappeared in and amongst the hierarchy of couples heading towards the dining room.

Twelve sat for dinner that night, not including the host and hostess. The crystal tinkled and the silverware sparkled as the guests bantered around the magnificent rosewood table. A centrepiece of pink roses and orchids commanded the eye and sixteen white tapering candles illuminated the adornments most beautifully. Dinner arrived in courses of soup, platters of lobster and salvers of braised beef. A dessert of fresh fruit and Neapolitan cakes followed, all washed down with three decanters of Madeira wine. The topics of conversation ranged from Empire politics, which the men mainly discussed, to the difficulty in finding good British servants, which the women mainly discussed. By the time they had reached a matter in which both sexes could freely participate – Charlotte's new *Bosendorfer* piano – Elizabeth had already reached the zenith of her agitation. Having spent the entire dinner trying to fathom out Violet Beaumont – with whom she exchanged unnatural smiles and fake courteous glances – she knew she had to speak with her again, if only to discover the identity of their 'mutual friend.' Thus, when the sumptuous banquet eventually came to an end and the ladies abandoned the men to their port and cigars, Elizabeth followed Charlotte into the drawing room, where both women claimed seats on the mahogany sofa and seized the opportunity to catch up with each other. 'Tell me more about this magnificent piano, Charlotte.'

'It was such a delightful surprise but heaven knows where I'll place it...it's sitting in the back parlour for the time being. You simply must see it, Elizabeth. Frederick was a dear to buy it for me. I'm attempting a lovely little piece by that German fellow, Brahms... his *Waltz in A flat Major*... I'm not very good though!'

With one ear straining to hear Charlotte's conversation and one eye fixed on the drifting figure of Violet, Elizabeth feigned interest in her best friend's banter. Violet took a turn about the room but soon sidled up beside them. 'Charlotte, forgive me for interrupting but I was just telling Elizabeth...before dinner...that we have a mutual acquaintance. I stumbled upon her whilst in Calcutta.'

'Really? How interesting,' grinned Charlotte,

'I was acquainted with so many people in Calcutta. I can't quite think who it could be,' Elizabeth scoffed.

'Henrietta.'

'Henrietta?' said Elizabeth, genuinely baffled. 'I'm afraid I'm not familiar with a Henrietta. You must be mistaken, Violet.'

Violet placed her glass down on the rosewood table and feigned carelessness. 'How silly of me... she's better known as Ettie. Ettie Henderson.' Elizabeth abandoned her teacup and saucer to the table for fear that they would slip from her grasp.

'Yes, she often mentioned your name,' Violet continued, 'and now I return to London and here you are! I wasn't aware that you and Charlotte were old friends. How small the world seems to be,' she said, punctuating her sentence with a little menacing laugh.

Elizabeth winced. 'I've encountered Ettie once or twice but I don't really know her that well.'

'That's strange... she seems to know your husband exceedingly well. Actually, I hear they're very great friends.'

And there it was... Violet's *coup de grace*.

'Do you think William will miss the tiger hunting when he comes home?' Violet asked. And rambling further, she concluded that William *would* miss the tiger hunting since all men were mad for the sport and it beat the thrill of the English foxhunt hands down. 'Ettie says, "Give a man the choice between a tiger and his wife and the tiger would win every time!" She says the most amusing things. Don't you think she says the most amusing things, Elizabeth?'

Elizabeth found the air hard to breathe.

'Here come the men!' Charlotte boomed, sensing the prickly atmosphere. 'Frederick had a bottle of that brandy Nicholas likes sent over from France, Violet. Why don't you ask Willoughby to pour a glass for him?'

'Very well.' Violet rose from the sofa and sauntered off.

'Are you all right, Elizabeth, dear?' Charlotte whispered. 'You seem...upset. Is it Violet? Nicholas insists that she can be rather wearisome at times.'

'I'm perfectly fine,' Elizabeth said coldly. 'Really I am.'

The evening trudged on.

In order to catch a moment alone, Elizabeth excused herself to admire Charlotte's praiseworthy piano and advanced along the hallway, hoping her decision would not encourage her parents to follow her lead. As she approached the back parlour door, a trickle of voices alerted her ears and peeping inside, she saw Nicholas seated on the piano stool, playing discordant melodies and inharmonious chords. A crescendo of tinkling piano keys drowned out the sound of his voice, whilst ahead of him, Violet mouthed some words, which for Nicholas's harsh playing, Elizabeth could not hear. She turned away from the door but the cacophonous music ceased and it was only then that she heard the venomous tone in Violet Beaumont's voice. 'I tell you, Nicholas, for someone so middle-class she has the airs and graces of Queen Victoria. Ettie is absolutely right about that woman.'

Elizabeth tiptoed back to the door and prayed that Nicholas would not resume his miserable attempt at producing music.

'Such a lofty manner!' Violet spat.

'Really Vi, she seems perfectly decent to me.'

'She's so intensely vain! And the way she condescends is most disagreeable.'

'You're hardly one to talk about that, Vi,' mocked Nicholas.

Violet flounced over to her brother and edged her way onto the piano stool. 'She thinks she's better than all of us,' she squawked, hitting the middle C note quite viciously. 'I shouldn't blame her husband for keeping a mistress.'

Elizabeth wanted to run down the hall, open the front door and disappear into the night. But all the strength she could muster was invested in keeping herself from tumbling to the floor. She witnessed Nicholas closing the piano lid and gulp down his leftover whisky. 'Honestly Vi,' he said, smacking his lips together. 'That's quite enough. I detest gossip. Now come along, let's go back and tell Charlotte how stupendous her piano is.'

Elizabeth's body shook violently. Hurrying back to the drawing room, she found her parents enjoying a game of whist but quietly demanded they all leave immediately. From the corner of her eye, she spied Nicholas and Violet entering the room and proceeded to say her adieus succinctly as she could.

'Whatever is the matter?' Charlotte asked, noticing distress in her friend's eyes.

Elizabeth wanted to confide in Charlotte but with her perplexed parents standing beside her, she held her tongue.

'Shall I call on you tomorrow... eleven, perhaps? We can have some time to ourselves... talk privately?' Charlotte added.

Elizabeth nodded. In agony, she whispered her goodbye.

During the journey home, the image of the two adulterers was imprinted in Elizabeth's mind with intense colours and uncouth shapes. Could Ettie be the real reason William had delayed his return? She had first encountered Ettie whilst holidaying at a hill-station in Kashmir. The woman had flirted with William the entire time and it was a biting comment uttered from her lips that set the cat amongst the pigeons. 'If he wasn't hers, he'd be mine,' Ettie was overheard to say.

That night, Elizabeth's interminable tears soaked her bedcovers. In the morning, she remained beneath them, numb and perfectly still. The dress that had fitted so beautifully around her figure lay in a crumpled heap on the floor and Jemima's heart sank when she saw it discarded like a piece of litter. She thought it best to shed some light into the room before she endeavoured to rescue it, but as her fingertips moved towards the curtains, the austere tone of the mistress's voice shattered the silence in which she moved. 'Leave them closed. And go away. I don't wish to be disturbed.'

The dark cloud had returned.

Elizabeth eventually emerged with evidence of an emotionally turbulent night carved in the contours of her face. She had tried her best to dab down her swollen eyelids and pinch her pale cheeks back to life, but the strain of concealing her misery had only made her appearance worse. At breakfast, she absently picked at her food and her frustration revealed itself through a variety of behaviours: profound sighs of irritation, restless pacing across the living room floor; raising her voice at the servants and children. She was unable to concentrate on any of the domestic tasks that were usually handled with the exactitude of a sergeant major and expended an hour staring out of the living room window, willing Charlotte's carriage to appear.

Charlotte arrived a little after eleven and was speedily shepherded into the living room. It was there that Elizabeth chose to divulge the events of the previous evening, confessing that rumours of her husband's illicit behaviour had stretched as far back as two years. She exposed her own humiliation at the hands of Violet Beaumont and recounted the details as calmly as she could. But her spirit quickly buckled and before long, she was sobbing freely on her friend's shoulder.

'Forgive me, Elizabeth,' Charlotte gasped. 'I had absolutely no idea that Violet was such a troublemaker. I would never have invited her if I'd known.' She used her handkerchief to catch Elizabeth's plentiful tears. 'I met her briefly before she went out to India. Frederick and I are more acquainted with Nicholas and he's always been perfectly decent.' Coiling her arm around Elizabeth's shoulder, she asked, 'What does William say to all of this?'

'He denies it of course... says it's idle gossip.'

'Well then, that should put an end to it. It's just as William says... idle gossip! There's no proof that he has been unfaithful and some scandalous remarks from a few busybodies can hardly qualify as reliable testimony. You've been the victim of malicious tittle-tattle, my dear. There's nothing more to it. As for Violet, well, I'll deal with her personally.'

And with that, Charlotte Godwin went on her way.

Elizabeth felt better after Charlotte's visit and considered how paranoia had taken the place of rationale. It was easy to be misguided when one was always left alone and she felt wretched for calling her husband a liar and desperately wanted to make amends. She wanted to make everything better, for she was missing William terribly and wished they had parted on friendlier terms. She consoled herself with the idea that India had been responsible for all their problems and swore things would be different when he finally returned. She would make a concerted effort to banish their troubles and live the seemingly happy life that they had once shared. However, the remaining weeks were slow to pass and sure enough, Elizabeth's resolve began to crumble. *'Was Violet telling the truth? If William was innocent, why had the rumours followed her back to England? Was William going to confess and leave her for Ettie?'*

He would be home in two days and she would make sure that his reception was executed with open arms and hearty embraces. However, sooner or later, she would have to confront him again but this time, she would be armed with Violet Beaumont's testimony.

CHAPTER 19
THE HOMECOMING

The clatter of horses' hooves against the concrete road was clamorous enough to be heard from the furthest corner of the Hayward house. Then the doorbell rung in such an infuriating manner meant that it could have only resulted from the actions of a child. Indeed, Sophie was the culprit. She loved to hold the bell pull for such a ridiculously long time, knowing it would annoy everyone within the house's four walls. Nonetheless, it was these sounds that signalled her father's return. A smart fellow of forty-five years with a fine-featured face and soft gossamer-like hair solemnly opened the door. He was eager to make a good impression on his new mistress and now his new master, but shuddered as the children bounded into the hallway. 'Father's here, Cole!' Robert bellowed, bumping into the new butler.

Elizabeth allowed the others to approach William first and observed the scene from behind the living room door. She watched as he greeted his mother and sister with an affectionate embrace and then engaged in an enthusiastic handshake with his father, Victor. He had lost a little weight, she thought, and his eyes looked small and sallow. But his charming looks – the handsome jaw line, the intense blue eyes; the captivating smile – surpassed his fatigue and Elizabeth accepted that most women would, at some point or another, want to be the object of William's affections. Sober ladies often metamorphosed into the most horrendous flirts in the vain hope that he might notice them. She thought such behaviour was brazen, inappropriate and executed without a thought for her feelings, but could she accept that William might have returned more than just a gesture? She tested his every move, his every word and his every smile.

'Where's my wife?' he asked, looking beyond the bodies congregated in the hallway.

Emerging regally, she said, 'I'm here.'

'Hello, Elizabeth.'

'Welcome home, William.'

'It's good to be back.' He kissed her gently on the cheek.

So far, she thought, he was passing the test.

Jemima had been given the afternoon off. It was a pointless gesture, since she had nowhere to go and no idea how to get about London. Even if she had some knowledge of the city, there was hardly enough time to engage in anything worthwhile and so she had no choice but to hide in her room until she was called to serve her purpose. She opted to mend the loose hems of her skirts and expended many an hour stitching, mending and guessing whether the master had finally come home. It was the jarring chimes of the doorbell that made her venture onto the first floor landing. There, she hoped to spy on the happenings below. An echo of sonorous male voices made her earlobes twitch but she could not tell which one belonged to the sahib, for he and his father sounded so alike. The conversation was lively. Even the new servants wandered to and fro, passing judgement on the master.

'He's so handsome!'

'Ain't he just...'

It was difficult to see much from where Jemima was hidden. Nevertheless, she persevered, spying and eavesdropping like a mischievous child. She beckoned him out through her silent wishes and when he did emerge, he collided with the parlour maid and apologized profusely for his clumsy conduct. Kneeling down outside the living room door, he scoured the contents of a large carpet bag. 'It's here, somewhere, Father,' he said, extracting an item from its depths.

Jemima glimpsed the back of his shoulders and some locks of blond hair but she missed his face, for it flashed before her without a chance to be admired. She had fooled herself, she thought. The feelings she had tried to cast out like demons were still very much alive... desire, adoration; dare she say it, 'love'... nothing had changed and she shuddered from knowing he was just beyond the bottom of the staircase. It was just as well that she was leaving soon, for her passion had grown and was no longer bearable. Any further attempts to capture his visage were abandoned. She returned to her room and resumed her needlework, hoping that she would see his face when she was summoned to take the children away.

Meanwhile, Elizabeth was watching Robert and Sophie bask in the glory of their father's return. Sophie was eagerly tearing the wrapping away from the gift her father had brought and a set of brightly painted sandalwood elephants tumbled into her lap. She yelped with delight as she lined them up in order of size upon the small side table and then became distracted as Robert attempted to play the bamboo flute his father had purchased from the bazaar in Chowringhee Road. William held the instrument to his lips and puffed gently across the mouthpiece as the boy looked on lovingly. It was a precious moment and it aggrieved Elizabeth to think that by her own hand, she would soon wreak havoc on the heart-warming picture. She had managed to restrain herself throughout the reunion but now the other members of the family had taken their leave, she wanted to send the children away in order to confront her husband. However, the joy in the youngsters' faces was pure and momentous; to finally be in the company of their father was a pleasure they had so often been denied and so, Elizabeth did not have the heart to spoil the touching display of intimacy and she decided to delay her plan of action. Familiar with the exhaustion brought on by the passage home, she suggested William take a nap. Thus, with a kiss and an embrace, he left his family and ascended the stairs to his room to relax. Subsequently, Elizabeth issued Cole with a set of instructions: supper was to be prepared punctually for seven, but before that he was to wake the master and inform him that she would be waiting in the dining room. They were not to be disturbed. In truth, Cole and the other servants were to be discharged earlier than usual but she would expect them early the next day. Then she would wait... wait until she and William were finally alone.

CHAPTER 20

THE EMERALD NECKLACE

Bleary from sleep, William descended the staircase with only the ominous glow from a lamp to light his journey. His wife was already seated at the dining table and he took the chair opposite as the fire crackled and the light from the sconces hurled long shadows across the burgundy walls. Tonight, he would enjoy a large bowl of leek soup, a cold supper of beef slices and creamed potatoes. 'I shall be serving you this evening, William. I've dismissed the servants. I hope you don't mind,' Elizabeth said, her stare unnerving him.

'Not at all.'

'I requested that cook prepare something light on account of this afternoon.'

'Good idea, I'm still full from the sandwiches and cakes.'

She raised herself out of her chair and ladled some soup into his bowl.

'I have a gift for you,' he smiled, burrowing into his jacket pocket. 'You didn't think I'd bring everyone a gift, except you?' he said, walking toward her as she reclaimed her seat.

'What is it?' she said, filling her bowl.

'Open it up and see.'

Elizabeth lifted the gilded catch of a red velvet box and her eyes feasted on an emerald surrounded by a circular border of tiny diamonds.

'I had it made especially,' he said.

'It's beautiful,' she whispered. She was telling the truth. The jewel was superb.

'I'm home now, Elizabeth, and everything is going to be as it should.' He kissed her in a manner that some might have interpreted as strained, as if he had been told what to do and when to do it. But it produced the desired effect, for Elizabeth was now considering her recent behaviour as silly, selfish and paranoid. She stroked a finger across the stone's smooth surface but cringed as several winking diamonds dragged sharply against her skin. And in that bitter moment, she remembered Violet Beaumont's stinging words and considered how easy it was for a man to seduce a woman with the help of an alluring trinket. Women often accepted expensive jewels in lieu of their husbands' fidelity. For such pretty gems, they remained silent and compliant and so, was the emerald necklace given for the purpose of sealing her lips? And yet, an eternity had passed since she had shared a romantic interlude with William and tonight, it would seem that he had made a tremendous effort.

'I'd like to forget our unhappy times in India and start afresh,' he continued. 'Father's written to Simeon and Howarth and it appears I'll have my old position back at the firm. Then there's Robert's school... your father prefers Rugby and mine, Charterhouse.'

Elizabeth pushed the lid down on the box and it snapped shut like the jaws of an angry reptile. 'I must ask you something, William,' she said.

'Of course.'

Briefly she saw Robert's face flickering in his, eager for a sympathetic touch or a tender embrace; at times, father and son looked so alike. And since it was a trap into which she so often fell, she looked away to ask the one question that had for so long plagued her mind. 'Are you acquainted with a lady called Violet Beaumont? She's recently returned from India.'

He flicked his eyes from side to side. 'I can't say I am.'

'Well she knows of you... in fact, she knows a great deal about you.'

'Really? Like what?'

The tranquil manner in which she recounted the incidents surrounding Charlotte's dinner party surprised William. But the mulish way she sliced through his smokescreen filled him with utter dread. She demanded an explanation, and when he was finally given the chance to speak, he narrowed his eyes and muttered through gritted teeth, 'I am not having an affair with Ettie Henderson.'

Elizabeth vented her fury on the bowl of soup that sat before her getting cold. The bowl splintered into a million pieces and the contents sprayed the table and floor. 'Tell the truth, William!'

'I am not having an affair with Ettie...'

Elizabeth slammed her hands down against the table. 'Why is it that I cannot believe a word you say, William? Tell me the truth! I demand to know the truth!'

William dropped his head into his hands. 'I think you should sit down, Elizabeth.'

'I do not wish to sit down,' she sneered.

'Very well then...I was seeing someone...but not Ettie. It was a brief affair... long finished now.'

Elizabeth's initial feeling of vindication was swiftly replaced with an overriding sense of bewilderment. 'Who?'

'What does that matter? You don't know of her... nobody does. It was just... madness.'

'What's her name?'

He slid deeper into his chair as her hands slammed the table again. *'What is her name?* I must know!'

'Sonal,' he whispered.

'What?' She asked him to repeat the name and then shrank at his answer. 'An Indian…a native?' she gasped, for that particular visualisation was a hundred times worse than the idea of him and Ettie together. 'A native?' she snarled.

He nodded.

'A filthy native?!'

She snatched the necklace up in her fingers and hurled it across the room. 'How could you?' she shrieked, rocking back on her heels. 'With a dirty… dirty coolie? You repulse me!'

Elizabeth would be damned if she let him see her cry. She rushed out of the room, only to collapse halfway up the stairs, shedding a river of tears. A gentle hand on her shoulder gave her cause to look up. 'Madam? What is wrong?' Jemima asked, trying to help her mistress to her feet. But Elizabeth Hayward's wrath suddenly became fierce and instead of seeing a hardworking servant extending a comforting hand; instead of seeing her children's devoted ayah standing on the step above, she saw Sonal – the disgusting native who had bewitched her husband and enticed him into her bed.

'Away from me, you savage!' she roared, slapping Jemima's hand. 'Never touch me again!' she hissed as she pictured William writhing around naked with a 'brownie.' 'Dirty savage!' she cursed, hesitating only when she caught sight of Robert cowering by the bedroom door. The boy's face was frozen in horror but his demeanour did nothing to calm his mother's rage. 'Stay away from my children!' she screeched, waving him back into his room.

Too stunned to question or cry, Jemima fled up the attic stairs, not stopping to rescue the candle that had slipped from her quaking fingers. She cowered on her bed, knees drawn to her chest, wondering why the mistress was so outraged. Her prayers to Kali were fraught that night. There was a plea for protection, a request for understanding and a desire for forgiveness, for whatever it was she had supposedly done. The seemingly infinite night forewarned misfortune and doom. She fell asleep but woke shortly after and must have done so a dozen times. Soon, not a sound was heard from the house below; only the sound of her heaving heart.

Noisy footsteps woke her from her sleep. Peeping up from her blanket, Jemima wondered why nobody had come to wake her, for it was almost midday and never before had she slept in so late. Whoever it was hesitated before banging on the door and too frightened to face them, Jemima closed her eyes as the door handle squeaked and turned. A young woman – fourteen or fifteen years old perhaps – plunged her face into the room. It was a small and pretty face but it eyed Jemima as if she were a caged animal in a zoo. 'Get up, girl!' she shrieked. 'The mistress wants you downstairs right now. You understand, girl?'

Jemima understood the words but not the reasons why and after delivering her message, the cocky girl invited herself into the room, curious to see how an Indian lived. Realising that there was nothing much to see, she dragged her feet over to the bed and frightened Jemima further when she snatched the bedcovers out from her fingers. 'Pack – yer – bag! An' get your brown arse downstairs now! Chop, chop!' she said, finishing with a little clap. She left the door swinging on its hinges and galloped down the staircase, whistling a merry tune.

Jemima found the mistress waiting in the vestibule. The lady was staring into the large gilt-edged looking glass that hung on the central wall. The house was deathly quiet and lacked the warmth it had known the morning before. 'Do you have all your possessions?' she asked.

'Yes Madam.'

'Good... because you are no longer are in my employ.' She leaned towards the kitchen. 'Cole!' she cried.

Cole advanced in his usual grave manner. 'Yes Madam.'

'I shall be gone until early evening but I shall return for supper.'

'Yes Madam, the carriage is waiting outside.'

'Am I going home, Madam?' Jemima asked, hoping the children would come bounding down the staircase to say their farewells. But there was no activity. No sign of them at all. 'May I say goodbye to the children, Madam?'

'No.'

Jemima started to tremble. She followed her mistress up the pathway to the awaiting carriage and raised a hand to the driver, but it was then that Elizabeth Hayward said, 'Come inside the carriage, they won't take you if catch a chill and fall ill.'

How strange, Jemima thought; one moment aloof, another worried about her ayah's welfare. Surely an Indian doctor could tend to her needs if she became ill on the ship? She quickly climbed into the compartment before the lady changed her mind but the gloomy silence inside was agonising and remained that way as the carriage pulled out of Carlton House Terrace. 'Madam, have I done something wrong?' Jemima asked.

'Your services are no longer needed,' Elizabeth said, focusing on a passing streetlamp, a child playing hopscotch and the street's many horses; anything but Jemima. And though she considered her forthcoming actions as rather cruel, Elizabeth prickled at the notion of having a young, Indian woman – and an attractive one at that – living under the same roof as her cheating husband. The children's ayah was a constant reminder of the filthy coolie woman who had seduced William; therefore, she must get the Indian as far away from him as possible and her mind was too busy racing with her husband's revelations to set about arranging a sea passage to India. Indeed, Elizabeth could think of nothing else but the impending scandal.

'Am I going home?' Jemima wondered. Her excitement was growing by the second. London was not for her, she decided. 'Madam, am I going home? Please...where am I going, Madam?'

'Stop asking questions!' Elizabeth hissed. 'You'll know soon enough, Jemima. You'll know soon enough.'

CHAPTER 21

THE BROKEN PROMISE

The sky was charcoal grey and its clouds were ready to spill out at any given moment, but the winter sun was out there somewhere, trying its best to show its face. St Paul's Cathedral loomed ever closer reminding Jemima of the Empire governing her homeland. She loved its regal features and elegant architecture, and thought its surroundings were rather splendid, but after witnessing the magnificence of Monument and Tower, she spied a number of miserable souls wandering the streets in poverty and destitution. There were men urinating in alleyways and women, asleep or dead – she could not tell – lying prostrate in the filthy gutters. Soot-faced children chased soot-faced rats and stacks of discarded rubbish lay strewn across the dirty drains. London's poor huddled in doorways or sought refuge under railway arches and everyone breathed in squalid air that made the rows of clean washing dirty again. Numerous lines of petticoats, pantaloons and stockings provided coarse adornments to the filthy windows. Some had come loose in the breeze and drifted into the mucky, wet puddles lying on the pavements below. 'Hackney Wick Metals' and 'The Hackney Tavern' were two among many establishments that drifted past the carriage window. The driver then made a turn into the wide thoroughfare known as Mare Street and drew the carriage to a halt outside a row of terraced houses. He jumped down and knocked on the door of a large, shabby house and two women wandered out on to the pathway. One was plump and stern looking, whilst the other appeared small and mousey in frame. The latter clutched a grey handkerchief into which she habitually plunged a very red nose.

'Mrs Shade?' said Elizabeth, as she approached the house.

'That'll be me, Ma'am,' replied the plump woman.

'I am Mrs Hayward and this is Jemima.'

'Righty ho, Ma'am.'

'Shall we take our business inside?'

The woman called Mrs Shade allowed Elizabeth to pass first whilst the mousey girl beckoned Jemima along a splintered stone path bursting with weeds.

'We can do our business in 'ere,' said Mrs Shade, ushering Elizabeth into a small room.

In a dismal hallway with only the mousey girl called Ruby for company, Jemima looked up to a cracked ceiling with walls that were soft to the touch. The carpet beneath her feet bore a floral pattern that had faded well beyond recognition, whilst above her head, clusters of cobwebs packed with dead bugs and flies wilted from the filthy lamp fittings. Ruby blended in perfectly with the dreary surroundings and seemed not in the least bit curious or surprised at the foreigner standing beside her. 'You from the East?' she asked, pulling her loose apron strings into a firm knot.

Ruby and Mrs Shade's particular way of speaking puzzled Jemima. She nodded once, not knowing how else to respond. Ruby sneezed twice and then the office door swung open. 'As you can see, Jemima is of a healthy disposition and I'm certain that she'll be no trouble at all,' said Elizabeth emerging from the room.

'Good Ma'am...'cause we don't take ones that are pale and sickly. Too much trouble Ma'am... too much mischief,' replied Mrs Shade, following on from behind.

'Goodbye, Mrs Shade. Please thank Mr Pendlebury for finding a place so swiftly and please pass on my mother's good wishes to him.'

Elizabeth hastened her steps as Ruby released the bolt on the door. Jemima quickly trailed her mistress only to be stopped in her tracks by Mrs Shade, who proceeded to yank her arm quite loutishly. For the first time that day, Elizabeth looked her ayah in the eye. 'You will not be returning with me, Jemima. From now on, you will be staying here.'

'Am I not going home, Madam?'

'You'll have to make your own arrangement to return home.'

Jemima's wet and worried eyes glimmered in confusion. 'But our agreement...'

'There is no longer an agreement. The sahib and I have decided that you are no longer our responsibility. In fact... this was *his* wish.'

On that declaration, Elizabeth Hayward walked away, flinching only when a thick droplet of rainwater splashed across her face. And as Ruby leaned in to close the door, Mare Street lodging house closed in on Jemima and like the rain outside, her tears came tumbling forth.

CHAPTER 22

THE HOUSE OF FORSAKEN WOMEN

'Stop your caterwauling and follow me. And look lively! I ain't got all day.'

Mrs Shade was not the sympathetic kind. Standing in the hallway, crabby and impatient, she guessed that Jemima's first instinct might be to unbolt the door and run away. But no attempt was made to restrain the new arrival, for Mrs Shade knew that Jemima would be back within minutes of discovering that she was in a strange part of the city without a hint of where to go. 'Where's this one goin'?' she yelled.

'I think there's room in number three,' Ruby snorted, plodding up the stairs.

'We might as well start up there,' Mrs Shade replied, beckoning Jemima with a podgy finger.

Jemima passed the room where the 'business' had been conducted and hesitated as a swell of contained voices snatched her attention. 'Come on!' crowed Mrs Shade. 'These stairs will be the death of me,' she grunted. 'Up an' down all bleedin' day!' she said, peering towards the summit as if she were about to tackle the mountainous heights of Kilimanjaro. She wobbled like a blancmange as her enormity filled the width of the staircase and Jemima wondered how quickly she would have reached the top if she had been fortunate enough to be in front, for Mrs Shade stopped frequently to mop her brow. Finally when the housekeeper reached the topmost step, she ambled along the landing and entered the room that Ruby referred to as 'number three'.

'There's space for her in the corner,' Ruby coughed, pointing to the area by a window.

The room was pitiful. Several boxes and crates were pushed up against the walls and on closer inspection, what Jemima thought were pillows were in fact carpetbags and travelling valises covered with shawls and various items of clothing. Three of these crude resting places occupied one half of the room, whilst the other held host to two: one either side of a fireplace whose embers struggled to glow behind a busted iron grate. The space by the window – made vacant by those reluctant to be near the draught – was a haven of spider-infested nooks and crannies. Jemima dropped her case onto the chipped wooden floorboards and silently asked herself how she came to be in such a woebegone place.

'We haven't got enough beds...' Mrs Shade barked. 'First come first served, you see. You'll 'ave to wait until we get some more boxes, so for now... you're on the floor.' Rubbing her hands together, she geared herself up for the descent of the staircase. 'Right then, now everything's sorted, you can come downstairs... you too Ruby.'

The miserable twosome trudged on down and turned into a narrow hallway veering off to the right. There were two rooms on the left hand side of the carpeted corridor and Mrs Shade immediately opened the door to the first. 'This is where you'll eat and be grateful for what you're given.'

Were it not for three pictures of Jesus Christ and one large portrait of Queen Victoria, the walls would have been bare and mottled with patches of grime. A hefty table claimed the centre of the room with a dozen or so chairs pushed underneath; it carried a stack of off-white plates, mismatched teacups and a mound of rusty cutlery. Since there was not much else to see, all three women walked the short distance to the adjacent room with Ruby continuing onto the kitchen at the end of the corridor. Mrs Shade hesitated somewhat before opening the second door. 'This here's the Visitors' Room, where you take your Bible class and receive them that wants to give you charity.'

The sound of laughter rose and fell, prompting Mrs Shade to slap an ear against the door and then hurl it open, as if she was expecting to catch the perpetrator of an unsolved crime. Several pairs of eyes looked up. The eyes belonged to faces: black faces, brown faces, yellow faces and red. The faces belonged to women seated behind several little desks, their heads bobbing and dipping, as they tried to catch a glimpse of the stranger in the doorway.

'Right you lot!' squawked Mrs Shade. 'We got another one here and she's from...' She turned to Jemima. 'Where are you from? India ain't it?' Jemima nodded. 'She's from India... like you ladies...' Mrs Shade pointed out three women huddled together in the middle of the room. 'Her name's...' Turning to Jemima again, she asked, 'what's yer name?'

'Jemima.'

'Jemima,' repeated Mrs Shade.

There was a short silence and then...'Good morning, Je-mii-maa!' It was said in unison like schoolchildren greeting their teacher in class.

Jemima was not entirely sure what she had expected to find at the dismal lodging house but she had certainly not expected to see the remarkable collection of women sitting before her.

Fifteen female faces of differing ages and nationalities – Chinese, Indian, African and Burmese – stared back with kind eyes and sympathetic smiles. Bibles lay on some laps but many were passing needles in and out of large squares of cotton. A few were dressed as she was, that is, in blouses and skirts, but many wore their own particular native attire. The sound of the front door slamming shut unnerved Mrs Shade and she jostled Jemima out of the room, denying her the chance to get acquainted with its occupants. Ruby was dawdling in the hallway outside. 'Pendlebury's here,' she sniffed, stuffing an over-used nose rag into her apron pocket. 'He's gone inside.'

Mrs Shade pounded the office door and seconds later, a rather distinguished-looking gentleman poked his head out of the room. 'Good day, Mrs Shade,' he said, peering over his spectacles.

'Good day, Mr Pendlebury. The new one's here, sir. She was dropped off just this afternoon and the lady what brought her says to thank you for finding a place so quickly.' Mrs Shade glared at Jemima. 'This is Mr Pendlebury from the London City Mission. He's here to help you.'

'Come in, girl,' Mr Pendlebury said.

Jemima dithered under the scrutiny of three strange faces. *'Who is this Mr Pendlebury? In fact, who is this woman called Mrs Shade and who is this sickly girl called Ruby? Why have they suddenly entered my life? I should be on a ship sailing home to Calcutta but why am I standing in a dirty hallway surrounded by three strange faces?'*

Mrs Shade looked fit to explode. 'Well go on girl!' she huffed, shoving Jemima through the doorway. 'Honestly, I don't know how you have the patience, Mr Pendlebury. You try and help their sort and do they appreciate it?'

Having heard the familiar rant before, Mr Pendlebury closed the door on Mrs Shade's face.

'Take a seat,' he said, pointing to a chair opposite the fireplace.

Jemima thought Mr Pendlebury had the benign look of a wise old owl, though whenever he peered over his glasses, he tended to examine her like a microscopic specimen mounted on a small glass plate. 'Your former mistress, Mrs Elizabeth Hayward, has passed all wages to date on to Mare Street lodging house. Every week, a shilling will be deducted to pay for your food and board. Do you understand?'

Jemima nodded. 'Sir... how long will I have to stay?'

'That depends on how long your funds last and also on your circumstances. You may advertise your services in the local newspaper at your own expense of course, but unless you have other means by which you can travel back home, then announcing yourself as a lady's maid, waiting to accompany a new mistress back to India is the only way you could possibly return.'

No effort was involved in convincing Jemima otherwise; she promptly agreed and asked if she could write the advertisement there and then. Mr Pendlebury invited her to sit at the bureau and like a professor tutoring his student, he watched over her as she penned the details of her notice. She paused frequently to take his advice but he was impressed with her high standard of written English and offered to place the notice in the paper himself. It read as follows: *'Any lady requiring a maid for passage to the East Indies may be advantageously supplied with a female servant native to that region. Jemima is her name and it no longer suits her former mistress to keep her. She is available forthwith to attend a lady on her journey to India and to also serve, if the lady so wishes, a period after arrival. She is a good servant who speaks and writes English well. She is particularly skilled in caring for children; she cooks, cleans and dresses hair to a high standard. She may be reached by sending correspondence to Mr Rudolf Pendlebury of 'The London City Mission,' 36 Cambridge Heath Road, Bethnal Green, E.2.'*

Jemima closed her eyes and made a wish for such a lady to whisk her away back home. She would make certain of it by praying to Kali that night. She thanked Mr Pendlebury for his kind assistance and patiently waited for permission to leave the room. He fiddled with his spectacles for a time before walking over to the tallboy in the corner and rummaging around in the topmost drawer. He was holding a book when he turned around. Its outer sleeve was inscribed with two familiar words: The Bible.

'Now Jemima,' he began. 'Do you believe in God?'

Thus, a sermon on the importance of Christianity in the life of the heathen spilled out from Mr Pendlebury's pious lips. Jemima listened dutifully and after falsely promising to embrace the son of God, she was allowed to leave the office, but not without a copy of the Good Book thrust firmly into her hands.

The ubiquitous chatter inside the Visitors' Room dwindled into a prying hush as Jemima turned the door handle and stepped inside. Her eyes searched for an empty chair and though there were a few dotted here and there, she felt too bashful to claim one and wished she could be left alone to make sense of the day. A young woman sitting between the upright piano and a dusty bookcase pointed to the empty seat beside her. Jemima timidly made her way over and sat down. Suddenly grateful for the book in her hands, she pinned her eyes to the first page, hoping it would draw her attention away from the curious faces around her. She ran a finger down the book's spine but could not resist peeking across at her neighbour.

'I saved this seat for you,' the young woman said, lowering her voice into a whisper. 'It is so nice to have someone here my own age for a change. Most of the women here are old enough to be our great grandmothers.' The young woman was right; the other women seemed a great deal older and if they were not, they certainly looked it. 'All they ever talk about is illness.'

The young woman then mimicked their voices. *'Oh my eyesight is getting worse! Oh I have a terrible pain in my back. Oh my feet ache so much!'*

A smile pushed against Jemima's lips.

'My name is Nuwani.'

'I am Jemima. Are you from India?'

'Close by... Ceylon.'

Talk of 'the new girl' whirled about the room. One of the three older Indian women responsible for the gossip pushed forward a vacant stool and Nuwani chuckled. 'You should introduce yourself. They are really very nice... a little nosy... but very nice.'

On Nuwani's advice, Jemima crossed the room and settled on the stool. *'Namaste,'* she said.

'Namaste.'

'My name is Rani,' said one woman.

'I am Indira,' said the second.

'Sita,' said the third.

Jemima sensed poignancy in the women's eyes, as if she reminded them of a daughter or sister they had not seen for a while. All three were amiable as Nuwani suggested and possessed the kind of maternal influence missing from Jemima's life. She divulged some details of her background but the information sparked a plethora of questions.

'How old are you?'

'Are you married?'

'Do you have children?'

'Which village are you from?'

Once again, Nuwani was right. The women *were* rather nosy. But Jemima was content to be amongst her compatriots and answered each query as politely as she could.

'That makes four of you Indians now,' Nuwani boomed. 'You are almost catching up with the Chinese.'

'Welcome, Jemima!' smiled Rani.

'Yes, welcome,' snorted a disembodied voice from across the room. 'Welcome to the house of forsaken women!'

Jemima turned to see the person responsible for uttering such a phrase but she was hidden behind a trio of Chinese women hunched over their squares of embroidery.

'Ignore her,' Nuwani said, folding her fingers over her knees. 'She's a miserable old goat.'

Sita shook her head. 'Always in a bad mood, that one.'

Jemima gave up trying to identify the culprit. 'How long have you been here?' she asked Sita.

'Almost two months.'

Jemima thought she misheard. 'Two months?'

'And I have been here for three!' Indira exclaimed.

Others moved in to partake in the conversation and Jemima quickly realised that she was not the only one waiting to go back home. Amahs, ayahs, servants and maids from China, Africa and Ceylon told similar tales of neglect and abandonment. One amah had been deserted at a train station; another had been mistreated and ran away. Some knew their contracts were coming to an end but had no idea that they would be condemned to a rundown lodging house in an impoverished part of London. How it saddened Jemima to hear such tales but she took comfort in the knowledge that she was amongst those who understood her plight.

She spoke of the notice she had placed in the newspaper but had hardly finished speaking when a stream of witchy cackles rose up into the air. Looking beyond the gathered bodies, she noticed the brittle shoulders of a diminutive Chinese woman bobbing up and down. Her face was gnarled like an elderly oak tree, giving the impression that she had lived for an eternity. Two gold loops swung from her shrivelled earlobes, whilst the skin from her jaw hung like the jowls of an old bloodhound. 'We have all placed advertisements in the newspaper,' she laughed. 'And six months later, I am still here.'

'Six months! *Six months?*' Jemima thought.

'You must not lose hope, Jemima,' Nuwani said. 'It depends on many things... whether there is a ship sailing to your country... whether an English lady is travelling there... whether she will choose you for her maid. It depends on luck and fate. It could be different for you.'

'That's true. Remember the English lady who came to take Yen-Yen?' Rani said.

'She was from China... she was very, very lucky,' Indira smiled.

Jemima's eyes glimmered as the women spoke of the girl who had been fortunate enough to go home. But Yen-Yen's fellow citizen – simply known as 'the China woman' – tittered on as the others hypothesized on the advantages of placing a notice in the newspaper. 'It also depends on how much money you have left before they throw you out!' she cried, slinging another cynical bone into the pot. 'I was considered rich before I came here... in fact, I could have gone back to China on my own... but they tricked me and the only things they haven't taken are the clothes off my back. No doubt, they'll soon be after those too!'

'Don't listen to her!' Rani said, 'she's never happy about anything!'

'Yes, don't listen to me... listen to those fools!' the China woman hissed, pointing to the Indians. 'They will still be here in fifty years time waiting for an English woman to come.'

'I hate to agree,' Indira frowned. 'These people don't care about us... they just take our money.'

Somebody muttered in agreement and someone else urged everyone to remember the girl called Yen-Yen. Discussion descended into argument and the China woman's lips curled into a snigger. Jemima's faith swiftly dissolved into the painful reality that like her fellow lodgers, she too, could be stranded at Mare Street for much longer than she hoped. But someone would answer her advertisement; she was certain of it. Like Nuwani said, things could be different for her. She was young and eloquent in more than one language unlike the others who were older and rather limited in their capabilities. And so, she would not allow herself to descend to the sceptical depths already reached by the China woman. She would hold onto hope with every last fibre of her being; for without it, she had nothing.

CHAPTER 23

THE CUPBOARD FOR FALSE IDOLS

Jemima did not relish sleeping on the cold, dirty floor of a draughty room shared with five others. Rummaging around in her valise, she searched for something that she could use as substitute pillow and found the black shawl recently bought by Elizabeth Hayward scrunched up beside Ibrahim's tin of *barfi*. A gift from a once-trusted mistress was now a reminder of her bitter abandonment. 'Damn that woman!' she cursed under her breath. 'Damn the sahib, too!' How could she adore a man who had conspired to send her away to this hell-hole? 'How could you do this? I thought you were kind. I hate you!' she quietly snarled. 'I will never think of you again. You promised to send me home and you and the memsahib broke your promise. So damn you both! Damn you all!' But that would mean damning the children too and try as she might, Jemima could never damn *them*. Robert and Sophie were innocents who had done no wrong. Fighting the urge to hurl the shawl across the room, Jemima exiled it to the eternal confinement of her valise and in need of all the heat she could muster, she tugged her

nightgown over her clothes and fed her shivering arms through
its sleeves. The sudden appearance of Mrs Shade, however, almost made her leap out of her skin.

'What the bleedin' hell is that?' yelled the housekeeper, pointing a forefinger towards Kali, who was sitting on top of Jemima's
travelling valise.

'It is my goddess... she is for worship only.'

'Well, it looks like the bleedin' devil himself!' A second later,
Mrs Shade was screaming for Ruby and everyone's ears wept at
the force of her magnificent lungs.

Ruby traipsed up the stairs and pushed her way through the
crowd that had now gathered in room number three. 'What is
it?' she snorted through a blocked nose.

'The new girl's got one of those heathen statue things,' she
said, shoving Ruby in front of the offending article. 'Stick it in
the cupboard with the others.'

Ruby clamped her hands over her mouth and let out a terrified squeak. 'Blimey Mrs Shade, it's horrible. I don't want to
touch it! Please don't make me,' she cried, wiping the flowing
snot away from her nose. 'It's even worse than that ugly elephant
thing of Sita's.'

Sita glared at Ruby.

'All right, all right,' said Mrs Shade, deciding to do the deed
herself. 'Give me yer duster.'

Ruby lifted an old rag out from her apron pocket and tossed
it over to the housekeeper.

'No, please do not take her,' Jemima wailed, raising her hands
in supplication. 'She is not bad, she is sacred... a goddess. I am a
Hindu, she is for worship only.'

Mrs Shade flung the duster over Kali. 'It's disgusting. I won't
have that abomination under this roof.' And grimacing at the
idea of having to touch it, she grasped the covered idol and held
it out from her body as far as her chubby arm could stretch. 'I've

got my eye on you, girl,' she said through contorted lips before exiting the room with Ruby cringing at her side.

The cupboard for false idols was positioned under an alcove in the cellar under the stairs. Ruby unlocked one of its doors and the sudden light streaming in from her lamp illuminated several mysterious deities sitting silently on one of the shelves. There was one Buddha, three Shivas, two Krishnas and Ganesh. Mrs Shade thrust her hand onto the uppermost ledge and forced Kali to take her place amongst them.

Jemima curled across the floor, imagining the moment she would strike Mrs Shade if she ever tried to confront her again. Of course she would never really do such as thing, especially to a white woman, but with Kali gone from her side, her mood had turned into a belligerent one. Life had suddenly become unbearable and she wanted to lash out, and if not for a gentle hand stroking her back, she would have gone stiff with fury. 'We have some boxes for you,' Nuwani said, pointing beyond Indira, Sita and Rani's legs.

Four freely donated crates waited to be fashioned into a bed. Nuwani manoeuvred them into the space beside her own resting place whilst the others helped arrange Jemima's shawls into ample covers for the night. They encouraged her to lie down, but alas, the crates were more uncomfortable than the floor and there seemed to be no snug position into which Jemima could settle her weary bones. But despite her show of indifference to their help and advice, they wished Jemima a peaceful night's sleep and left her to her own devices.

Jemima glimpsed Nuwani's face, moonlit and pretty, staring back at her in the darkness. Her feet dangled into the space where a crate used to be but it seemed not to bother her in the slightest. 'The first day I came here, Mr Pendlebury took away my statue of the Lord Buddha,' she whispered. 'My father gave it to me when I was a child. It was very precious to me.' She leaned her head against her hand and sighed. 'Try to be strong, Jemima... if you have faith in your heart, you will never be alone.'

Flinging her dark locks of hair across her back, Nuwani smiled. 'Goodnight Jemima, I *really* do hope you sleep well tonight.'

PART THREE

CHAPTER 24

LITTLE MAN AND
THE CAPTAIN

Ibrahim had bonded with one of the caravan leaders, a small man called Sebak, who had been guiding a caravan route from Suez to Alexandria for almost ten years. They had become friends after Sebak loaned Ibrahim a small hammer and chisel, with which Ibrahim managed to open a tin of *barfi*. When the caravan stopped for its periodic rest, the two men swapped stories of themselves, whilst tucking into pieces of the Indian sweetmeat and Sebak learned of Ibrahim's desire to sail to Europe. The Egyptian was certain that work could be found in Alexandria's port, for the ships' boatswains were always looking for men to join their crew; particularly the ships sailing to Europe.

Ibrahim spent his first night of freedom in the humble company of Sebak and his wife, Mosi, who inhabited a small mud-walled hut on the outskirts of Cairo. Though they could only offer him a simple meal of rice and beans, and a straw mat laid across the stone floor for a bed, Ibrahim did not complain. To him, the food was all the more delicious and his mat felt like it was made of feathers. That night, he stared into the darkness and wept for many reasons. He shed tears of gratitude for those who had treated him with respect and concern, but his tears were mainly ones of relief, for he had survived on sheer wit and a few tins of *barfi* and now he would sleep very soundly, for he must rise early to join another caravan route to another city, where there would be another port, in which he would have to find work. But this time, he would be alert and canny, and this time there would be no reason for him to hide.

The journey to Alexandria took its toll on Ibrahim. Tiredness weighed him down like a heavy mantle, pushing to the fore the aches and pains that were hidden within the strain of the past few weeks. Bruises reared their ugly heads and those that had been there a good while longer exhibited colours not dissimilar to the rich Egyptian sunset. Bravely, Ibrahim soldiered on, enduring severe discomfort and pain, but the soft trudge of the camel's feet was strangely soothing, though the noises of the desert were unmistakably distinct. Conversations ebbed and flowed under the thunderous rattle of the passing trains and the sound battered Ibrahim's ears until he heard nothing at all. Bolt upright on a camel and blind to his surroundings, Ibrahim appeared to be in the midst of an epiphany. His eyes had closed but his mind had opened and he would have remained that way had the sharp poke of Sebak's stick not summoned him back to the universe. 'You were asleep... you almost fell. Be careful!' Sebak shouted. 'It is not long before we reach Alexandria. We will stop and have refreshment in Mansheya before I take you to the port.'

Ibrahim had not fallen asleep. In a transient blaze of enlightenment, his jaded view of the world had transformed into one of incredible contentment. '*Inshallah*,' he whispered. 'Ibrahim Omar Ahmed Kareem is ready now.'

A brand new Ibrahim had entered the world; a defiant one, an ambitious one: one who vowed to relish every experience from that moment forth. His stomach roared for food in a way it had never done before and he thought of the meal he would prepare when the first opportunity arose. He pictured a banquet of *fish shorba* and *shammi kebabs* followed by a dish of *Chicken Noorjehan* and spicy mutton stew. Both concoctions would swim in a thick sea of meaty gravy, into which he would dip a golden strip of *shirmaal roti*. To accompany the dishes, he would make a bowl of fragrant *biriyani* tossed with shredded coriander and the plumpest of raisins. Yes, Ibrahim decided that these culinary creations would definitely suffice, and as he visualized his feast for one, a trickle of saliva meandered its way from the corner of his mouth to drench the hairs of his bearded chin. It seemed his senses had returned with a vengeance.

Mansheya was a small city stamped with the history of Alexandria's military skirmishes and its centre was alive with all manner of activity. The ever-present French were recruiting labourers, whilst a plethora of tourists and swaggering sailors wandered about, keen to experience the exotic atmosphere of the port. Sebak tied his beasts to the trunks of some palm trees and sent Ibrahim to the bench nearby before a drunken tramp claimed it for his bed. After handing a fig to the vagrant and shooing him away, Sebak sank into a seat beside his friend and washed down some chunks of Mosi's home-made bread with several gulps of water. 'There will be English ships sailing from here. You can get work as a sailor. After we eat, I take you to Mubarak's place.'

'Mubarak's place?' questioned Ibrahim, his teeth jammed with bread.

'Everyone knows Mubarak's place. We will find men there who will give you ship work.'

Mubarak's place was an infamous gin hole renowned for its intoxicated foreign clientele. Situated in Abou-Qir, it nestled between a tobacco shop and an unruly boarding house for sailors, and supplied all manner of alcohol to the travellers passing through the port. The place was a favourite haunt amongst sailors and wayfarers, partly due to its convenient location and partly due to the fact that the owner, Mubarak, supplied the town's whores as well as the booze.

Ibrahim and Sebak walked into an environment of hookah pipes and sea talk, where glasses clinked and men guffawed beneath clouds of potent substances. Ibrahim retreated into a dark corner whilst Sebak bantered with a group of lascars lounging by the veiled window. It was difficult for him to see anyone's faces, for the atmosphere was dense and hazy. Heads swayed beneath a blanket of hookah smoke and the air tasted spicy. Ibrahim was just about able to recognise the pocket-sized figure of Sebak wandering ghost-like towards him. 'Come, come, Ibrahim,' he called, hauling him towards four Indian sailors staggered across a table.

'You want work?' said one man, puffing on a fat cigar.

Ibrahim's eyes roamed to the unusually long nail that was fashioned into a sharp talon on the man's third finger. It made a scratching sound whenever he scraped the areas around his hairy nostrils. 'I have work for lascars on my ship sailing to England,' the man boasted. 'You know lascar work?'

'No,' Ibrahim lied. 'But I can learn. I am a hard worker.'

'Good!' the man smiled, 'because there is plenty of hard work on my ship.'

'What is the name of *your* ship?'

A gust of cigar smoke raged through the man's nostrils. '*Victoria*. We sail in two days time.'

Ibrahim suppressed a laugh. '*His ship!*' The vessel belonged to the British and already he sensed delusions of grandeur.

'Are you a Muslim?' another sailor asked. Ibrahim nodded and the fellow rapped his fingers against the table. 'Don't worry... we cater very well for you Muslims!' He exploded with laughter and his ridicule was more than offensive. Ibrahim only stayed a moment longer out of a duty to Sebak who, in all good nature, had tried to help him secure some work.

'How much do you pay your lascars?' he asked through gritted teeth.

The long-nailed man dragged a hirsute finger across his thick lips and grunted heavily. 'Twenty rupees per month, but we pay you the bulk at the end of the journey... when we reach England.'

Here was another lying boatswain, Ibrahim thought. The scoundrel had a different face but he spoke the same fraudulent language. A similar character back in Calcutta had spun him same line and as a result, he had been hoodwinked into a voyage of torment and violence with no wage to show for his pains. 'I think about it and let you know,' he replied nonchalantly.

'Don't think about it too long,' the boatswain groaned, flaring his bushy nostrils again.

Sebak was loafing on a grassy bank outside the gin-hole when he spied Ibrahim striding towards him. 'Did he give you work?' he asked, making room for his friend to sit down. The chef's expression spoke a thousand disappointed words. 'What happened, Ibrahim? He told me he has work on his ship.'

'He does have work, Sebak, but he is not a good man.'

'But... '

'You are a good friend, Sebak, and I am a thousand times grateful for your help, but believe me when I say that he is not a good man.'

The Egyptian took his word on the matter and spoke of other boatswains who could offer work on their ships, but Ibrahim explained that it would be a futile exercise, for there would always be a *serang* in charge of the native sailors and for that reason alone, he would not risk suffering the same degradation as he had suffered on the *Bengal Star*.

'What will you do?' the camel guide sighed.

'I know not, my friend. I know not... but I will think of something.'

Relaxing side-by-side, the two men then explored the possibilities of supper and a bed for the night and since the weather was exceptionally warm, they settled for sleeping in the open air. As the sun gradually dipped, Ibrahim fell asleep and Sebak dozed off shortly after until a prodding sensation in his buttocks soon woke him from his catnap.

'Wake up little man!'

Two men stood over Sebak: a stocky, bearded Italian fellow wearing a seafarer's hat and a slimmer, younger chap, who looked overly serious. 'Captain Gasparro!' Sebak cried, clambering up on all fours.

'Little man!' the bearded fellow roared, embracing the Egyptian robustly. 'I have not seen you for some time. Have you been hiding from me, eh?' he asked, cocking a suspicious eyebrow. 'Now tell me, has your wife finally thrown you out? Is that why you're sleeping in a dirty ditch?'

Sebak laughed. 'Oh...it is a long story!'

'I like long stories!' the Captain roared. 'Come inside with your friend... have a drink with me or... mango juice is what you like, eh?' Turning to his companion, he cried, 'Stefano! Two beers and whatever these two gentlemen are having!'

Stefano claimed a free table and summoned an attendant, who subsequently arrived with a tray of hookah pipes and an assortment of dates. The Captain and his mate each took a drag and reeled from the soporific effects. Sebak recounted how he had acted as a tour guide for Gasparro and his crew on the first day they docked in Alexandria. 'They raced my camels on the dusty desert tracks!'

'We were idiotically drunk!' the Captain chuckled.

Sebak creased over with laughter. 'He toppled from his beast three times!'

Ibrahim enjoyed listening to their joyful memories and then it dawned on him that the solution to his problem might be seated across from him. Gasparro was in charge of his own vessel and if Ibrahim could sail to Italy, perhaps he could make his way to England from an Italian port instead? Politely, he interrupted the banter to ask whether there was work on the Captain's ship.

Sebak frowned. 'But I thought you wanted to go to England.'

'I do, Sebak... but perhaps I can travel there from Italy instead.'

'We have enough men!' Stefano snorted on his captain's behalf. 'Remember, Guiseppe, you are on probation.'

'He is right, my friend. I have been brought before the powers that be for giving too many positions to too many men. They don't like it!' Gasparro declared, rubbing a thumb across his fingers. 'Forgive me, Ibrahim. I like you... I like you very much and wish you could join my crew, but you heard Stefano... I have enough sailors.'

'I do not want sailor work!' Ibrahim exclaimed, almost out of his chair. 'I am a chef... a cook of fine cuisine and I have worked for the Prince of Awadh!'

The Captain was astounded. 'Stefano!' he boomed. 'Do we have work for the Prince of Awadh's cook?'

'No, Captain!' Stefano cried, almost choking on a date. 'We *cannot* pay any more men!'

'Then I will work for no money! I will earn my passage by cooking for your passengers. Please Captain, I beg you!'

Captain Gasparro threw his hands up in the air, stood up and spanked Ibrahim vigorously on the back. 'Welcome to my crew! We set sail tomorrow!' he bellowed, hauling Ibrahim into a manly clinch. And such was Ibrahim's happiness that he thanked the Captain a thousand and one times and even spent some moments hugging sour old Stefano until a long-nailed finger tapping his shoulder caught him by surprise.

'You thought about it, yet?' asked the Indian boatswain he had spoken with earlier.

'Yes,' Ibrahim scoffed. 'I do not need to work on *your* ship. I am sailing to Italy instead!'

Sebak punched the air and the Captain yelled for more drinks. Stefano heaved a sigh that was long and exasperated but tempered by the hookah swirling in his veins, he toasted the new recruit with a third tankard of beer and was merely content to joke with his companions until the sun slid against the dusky sky and faded beyond the purple horizon.

CHAPTER 25
WILLIAM AND ELIZABETH

Elizabeth Hayward had often considered how it was commonplace for a man to indulge in the odd affair. She had also considered how it was even acceptable for some to keep a mistress. But no matter how hard she tried, Elizabeth Hayward could not come to terms with the fact that her husband had shared his bed with an Indian, for he had plummeted so far in her estimation that it sickened her to look at his cheating face. Moreover, there was nothing to be done about their sorry state of affairs; unless William admitted to subjecting his wife to mental cruelty – or something more sinister – the law forbade their marriage to come to an end. Yet, he could not divorce her unless she was the perpetrator of the crime and he, the innocent party, and if news of his affair reached her family and friends, it would prove too much for her to bear: the scandal, the mortification, the effect on her children. No, Elizabeth Hayward could not risk that kind of humiliation; not after she had worked hard to achieve a position in society and had been nothing short of an exemplary wife. She had left England's shores to be with her husband and had suffered the deplorable conditions in India to make a comfortable home... when all the while he was... she could not even bring herself to say it. William had made a fool of her, but they must stay together in spite of the acrimony and so she would quietly make him suffer. By God, she would make his life unbearable.

Though the servants speculated on why their master's clothes and personal effects were being transferred to another chamber, not even Cole dared question the mistress on the reasons why. She kept her husband's dalliance a secret, for Elizabeth could not bear the thought of *anyone* knowing. Her moods were tolerable at the best of times but the workforce bore the brunt of her anger whenever they failed to measure up to her lofty standards. She refused to share her meals with her husband unless the children were present and only then would she engage in some semblance of normality. Just as expected, news of Ayah's departure had not gone down well with the children. Heartbroken and bewildered, they struggled to make sense of Jemima's startling exit. In a fit of fury, Sophie had hurled her toys against the nursery walls and lashed out at the new maid, Molly, who had to call upon her master to carry the child weeping and wailing to bed. It wounded William deeply to see his children hurt and bereft. Sophie, at least, could vent her disappointment through her paroxysms but Robert, without Ayah by his side, bottled his feelings tightly.

'I want Ayah!' Sophie wept, writhing eel-like beneath her sheets. 'Please bring her back, Papa!'

'I would if I could, my angel,' he whispered. 'But Ayah had to go home to Calcutta.'

'Why didn't she say goodbye?' asked Robert.

A voice from the doorway overtook William's, saving him from having to concoct a lie. 'Ayah *wanted* to go back to India,' Elizabeth calmly replied. 'Would you like a story?' she asked over her daughter's whimpering. 'Where's your handbook, Robert? Shall I ask Molly to read you a story from that?'

'But it's for boys!' Sophie retorted.

'I've already read it anyway,' moaned Robert.

Sophie began to sob again. 'I want my lullaby!'

Elizabeth's face turned red. 'I shall call for Molly.'

'I want Ayah's lullaby!'

'Nonsense, Sophie!' Elizabeth hissed. Your new nanny will be arriving soon... a proper English governess... and there'll be no time for ridiculous *Indian* lullabies! You'll learn *English* songs and listen to *English* stories, you understand?'

William stepped forward. 'You're hardly helping matters, Elizabeth.'

'Allow me to deal with the children, William,' she snapped, glaring back at him.

'But Mama, I want Ayah!' wailed Sophie, sitting up. 'I want Ayah!'

Elizabeth breathed deeply. 'Very well, I shall leave now but Ayah has gone forever and may that be an end to it!'

That night, Sophie cried herself to sleep and for the very first time, Robert looked forward to leaving home and attending school. He remembered how Ayah had said that every child needed to go to school and his recollections forced William's guilt to grow that much stronger. It should have been *him* who uttered those words to his son; not a simple Indian servant, whose face he could not pick out in a crowd. She had loved and cared for his children in a way that he and his wife would never understand and he wished he could conjure her right there and then; not only for his children but also for himself. He wanted to say thank you to Jemima for cherishing them through his many selfish absences. Crossing paths in the corridor outside, William lingered to ask his wife a question. 'You're quite sure Jemima went back to India?'

'Of course,' she lied, her voice hardly faltering. 'I waved her off myself.'

'Even so, you really ought to have let the children say goodbye.'

He failed to see her scathing expression as she disappeared behind her bedroom door, but later on, having reflected on all the recent events, William astounded himself with the decision he had made to confess all to his wife. It would have been far easier to lie about his Indian lover, for he could have made Elizabeth believe that he had strayed with a woman as white as the snow on the pavements outside. She would have ranted and raved but she would have forgiven him, but then it occurred to him that deep down, perhaps, he wanted her to know.

CHAPTER 26

THE BEST FRIEND, THE DO-GOODERS AND THE PAINTER

The passing of two weeks signified a bitter benchmark for Jemima. If the Haywards had kept their word, she would have been bidding goodbye to Europe on the first of two voyages that would have taken her back to India. The never-explained reasons that had brought her to Mare Street were distressing enough and this, in turn, was confounded by the monotonous routine of the lodging house: a repetitive schedule of breakfast, Bible reading, needlepoint and lunch, with not much recreation time left before dinner. An intermittent sprinkling of pious visitors was welcome relief to the day's predictable agenda. Consequently, a degree of excitement lay in guessing which charitable organisation would be calling on them next.

Jemima spent most of her days analysing Mrs Shade's puffy hands for signs of a letter from a prospective employer. But more often than not, Mrs Shade came and went offering only commands and criticism. The lodgers were affable on the whole but Jemima kept her distance from the old Chinese woman whose gloomy opinions always dampened everyone's spirits. Languages and customs provided barriers with some, whilst unsolicited motherly attention separated her from others. However, she had grown closer to Nuwani, and came to look upon her as the sister she never had. Nuwani was twenty-five years old and had left behind a husband and two children. On arrival in London she was told by her English memsahib that her services were no longer needed and instructed to seek out the offices of the London City Mission. Jemima admired her sanguine spirit. In spite of everything, Nuwani always spoke heartening words. She laughed, joked and only had to poke fun at Mrs Shade's portly frame by stuffing a shawl under her blouse and waddling like a duck. Sometimes she would feign a thunderous sneeze and shuffle her feet in testament to the ailing Ruby. At other times, she would wrap a scarf around her head, double-over and pull a face as sour as a lemon to imitate the China woman at her worst. It was these hilarious impressions that forced Jemima to forget her woes, for she would be too busy howling with laughter to remember them. One day however, Jemima noticed a change in Nuwani's demeanour. She seemed unusually quiet as she stared out of the dining room window.

'What is it, Nuwani?' Jemima asked.

'Nothing.'

'Nothing? I don't believe you. There is something wrong... I can tell.'

Nuwani succumbed. 'Just before you came here, Jemima, Mr Pendlebury told me that I have very little money left and that I may have to leave. I begged him to let me stay until the end of the month... to see if a lady will come for me. He agreed, but the days are passing quickly and no lady has come.'

'Where will you go if you have to leave?'

'I will have to go to the workhouse,' Nuwani frowned, 'and then I will never get home. Ruby says they do terrible things to darkies in there. They hardly ever come out alive. I must get home, Jemima. My husband and children are waiting for me.' Her voice cracked. 'It is my daughter's birthday next week. She will be four years old.' Tears slipped out of Nuwani's eyes. 'I cannot go to the workhouse. If I go to the workhouse, I will never see my family again.'

'That won't happen, Nuwani.'

'How do you know that?'

'I will find out how much money I have left and if there is enough I will pay for your board myself.'

Nuwani squeezed Jemima's fingers. 'I cannot let you do that and I know you will not have enough to keep us both here. You will need every penny yourself. This place may be dull but at least we are safe here. I wouldn't want to spoil your chances of going home too.'

Jemima curled an arm around her friend's shoulder and stared out of the window at the rain-sodden streets. 'We still have time left before the end of the month. A lady may come for you, Nuwani. You must not lose hope.'

Nuwani looked across at Jemima and smiled. 'You sound just like me.'

'Yes, Nuwani...' she said, smiling back. 'I sound just like you.'

It seemed that Nuwani's plight had forced Jemima to confront her own regrets, for that night she lay awake wondering how Robert and Sophie had taken the news of her departure. She pictured the mistress's new maid brushing Sophie's golden hair and invented images of Robert listening to another servant's stories. When she thought of Nuwani's children, oceans away, not knowing if they would ever see their mother again, Jemima considered how she was glad to be childless, for under the present circumstances, it would be too painful to be a mother.

As a fourth Saturday dawned at Mare Street, Jemima stared into the habitual bowl of porridge and contemplated missing breakfast. She realised of course, that it would be sensible to remain healthy and strong in the event of being chosen by a potential employer and so, she dipped her spoon into the watery mixture and urged herself to swallow a mouthful. The slop slipped down without leaving a trace of flavour and she wondered if it were made from a concoction of rainwater and flour, for it certainly tasted that way.

'What I'd give for some *kiri buth* and *seeni sambal*,' Nuwani spluttered, forcing the bland fusion down her throat.

'What is that?' asked Sita.

'Milk rice and onion chutney.'

Rani's shoulders bobbed. 'Mmm... delicious.'

An array of culinary musings rose from the lodgers' heads. 'I dream of eating fish and rice,' said Indira. 'You know... my husband is a fisherman. Every day he would bring home fresh mackerel and I would say, "Oh no! Not mackerel again! How about catching some swordfish for a change?" But now I could eat mackerel all day.'

Sita lifted her spoon of porridge into the air. 'I don't know how the English eat this. Look at it... wobbling like a jellyfish. It has no taste. It is pale and colourless... it needs some flavour... some spice.'

The China woman waded into the debate. 'You think the English eat this?' she sneered. They don't eat what they feed us.'

'All the same,' Sita snapped, 'it needs some sugar, some spices; cinnamon and nutmeg perhaps... to make it more exciting.'

'You could say the same thing for the English,' replied Nuwani.

Rani's giggles infected the row of women seated at the table. Even Jemima could not refrain from chuckling and for her it was a much-needed release. Apart from her friendship with Nuwani, there had been so little to smile about lately, but now her laughter was unstoppable and only subsided when Mrs Shade peered into the room. 'What are you lot cacklin' about? You got visitors today from the Strangers' Fund, so sup up! They'll be here soon,' she said, departing.

Nuwani pointed her empty spoon towards the doorway. 'If anyone needs some spice... that fat one surely does.' Laughter erupted again.

At three minutes to ten, Ruby opened the front door to three breathless, wind-swept females laden with an assortment of boxes. A slim, rosy-cheeked woman, bearing a crate full of old shoes, volunteered to speak first. 'Is Mr Pendlebury there, girl? Tell him, it's Miss Bellamy from the Strangers' Fund.'

Just then, Mr Pendlebury tore out of the office room. 'Welcome Miss Bellamy,' he fussed, brushing Ruby aside to relieve the young women of their loads.

Miss Bellamy looked exhausted. 'May I introduce Mrs Charles,' she said, pointing to a rather strict-looking woman. 'And this is her niece, Miss Caroline Lacey.'

'Welcome ladies,' he said. 'The women are in the Visitors' Room. Please follow me.'

Mrs Shade was about to organise refreshments when the sound of the doorbell ringing again sent her careering back up the hallway. She opened the door to a rather peculiar gentleman perched on the doorstep. He was wearing a tall blue hat, matching blue gloves and his hands were resting upon the amber globe of a black lacquered walking stick. He appeared to be an age of around thirty but Mrs Shade noticed that some strands of his brown hair were exceptionally white in places and that his face exhibited a rather pasty hue. But whatever colour the man lacked in his skin was certainly compensated for in the flamboyance of his clothes, for he was dressed in a light blue day suit and sported a red velvet cravat drawn all the way up to his neck. It gave Mrs Shade the impression that he had something to hide. 'Good day,' he said, placing a shiny boot on the doorstep. 'May I speak with the good proprietor of your lodging house?'

'The what?'

'Mr Pendlebury.'

'Oh... yes. Wait here, please.'

She left him standing in the hallway without asking for his name. He spotted the plentiful cobwebs and decided not to lean against the wall for fear that his Savile Row suit would snag against the grime. He absorbed the crude surroundings and sneered at the lack of decoration. Then, conscious of his appearance, he pulled his cravat further up to his chin.

Mr Pendlebury was emptying the contents of a wooden box when Mrs Shade burst into the room, wide-eyed and breathless. 'I do declare, Mr Pendlebury! There's a peculiar gentleman waiting to see you.'

'Who is it, Mrs Shade? Can you not see that I am rather busy?' he huffed, catching a shoe before it fell to the floor.

'Dunno sir,' she shrugged. 'But he looks like the spectre of me Great Uncle Horace.'

Mr Pendlebury cast a flummoxed look in the housekeeper's direction and left his guests in the company of his tenants.

Outside in the hallway, Pendlebury eyed the pallid stranger with quiet caution. 'You wish to see me, sir?'

'Mr Pendlebury,' the gentleman began, throwing out an arm in friendship. 'Please accept my humblest apology for the unexpected intrusion. My name is Sylvester Lawrence and I am painter and patron of the arts. I happened to encounter three ladies who recently entered your establishment... a Miss Bellamy, I believe. I foolishly forget the names of the others.'

'Mrs Charles and Miss Lacey,' interjected Pendlebury.

'Yes, I remember now. Well, the good ladies informed me that there are natives from the colonies seeking shelter here.'

'That is correct, sir... and what of it?'

'Well, sir, being an artist in constant pursuit of inspiration, I wondered whether you would be so kind to permit me to meet your tenants? I have been asked to paint a scene indicative of our great Empire... for an exhibition in fact... and in order to do so, it is necessary for me to see its subjects... for purposes of research, of course. One soon tires of painting the humdrum bowl of fruit or the grave Lady of the Manor with her spaniels panting at her feet.'

'There are only women residing here, Mr Lawrence,' Pendlebury frowned. 'And most are of a timid disposition. Under the circumstances, I'm afraid I must decline your request. I do hope you understand.'

'That's a very great shame, Mr Pendlebury,' the artist said, dragging the tip of his boot along the well-worn carpet. 'Miss Bellamy also informs me of the admirable work being carried out by the London City Mission under the selfless instruction of persons such as yourself... and there was I... hoping to make a sizeable donation of five or even ten pounds to your wonderful charity. What a shame, sir. What a very great shame. Never mind, I shall bid you good day.'

Mr Pendlebury dithered and then hastened his steps before the front door closed before him. He hoped the painter had not gone too far out of sight, but there Lawrence was lurking along the pathway, pretending to fiddle with the buttons on his peacock blue overcoat. 'Sir, forgive my brash manner!' Pendlebury pleaded. 'I'm certain we can come to an arrangement.'

Sylvester Lawrence threw his cane a little into the air and naturally, he caught it before it hit the ground.

Pandemonium had erupted in the Visitors' Room. Old clothes and second-hand boots spilled over chairs and toppled off tables. Donated gloves and knitted scarves lay scattered across the piano and strewn upon the bookcase. The benefactresses of 'The East London Strangers' Fund' had quite a time keeping up with the lodgers as they rifled through the charity boxes in search of items suitable for their size and build. The vigour displayed was not dissimilar to that of a pack of scavenging hyenas and the visitors watched on in alarm as the lodgers scoured the crates for some appropriate attire. No one noticed Mr Pendlebury when he entered the room. No one heard his voice as he called for attention. Order was eventually restored after he began issuing a series of slow, loud claps. 'Ladies we have another guest. May I introduce Mr Lawrence? He's an artist.'

Nobody listened because nobody cared. Apart from the visitors who had recognised the man they had met in the street, none of the others took the slightest interest in the brazen individual standing in the doorway. But he was taking a great deal of interest in them. In actual fact, the scene in the Visitors' Room amused Lawrence greatly. Women were wearing clothes several sizes too big. Petticoats and pantaloons were being tossed into the air. Two tenants were arguing over a pretty silk corset and pulling it between them in a thrilling tug of war.

'You say that the women are of a timid disposition, Mr Pendlebury?' Lawrence smirked.

Mr Pendlebury turned beetroot red and recruited Ruby to settle the dispute between the warring women.

Lawrence prowled about, observing each female in his path with utter delight. He spotted the China woman engaged in the scrutiny of an old shawl and tapped her on the shoulder. 'My, my...' he grinned. You look like a wise old bird.'

She frowned and blinked. He smiled and continued on.

Having found a pair of leather gloves to suit her small hands, Jemima was now struggling to lace a pair of old boots that were, frankly, too big for her anyway. She kicked them loose and handed them to Nuwani, who was just as determined to find a pair of slippers that fit. Jemima then noticed her face reflected in a pair of men's shoes. She liked the way they were polished to perfection. But the shoes possessed legs and trailing them upwards, she saw the colourful figure of Sylvester Lawrence staring down at her most curiously. 'My, my...' he declared. 'What a charming face you have.' Lawrence moved his trespassing eyes to her lips and then, with the luck of a man who had suddenly struck gold, he squatted on his haunches and politely asked for her name.

Jemima almost forgot to reply, for she was preoccupied with his red cravat. It was such a striking colour against his funny pale skin that it clashed somewhat with the dappled white ends of his wavy brown hair. He asked her to stand and as she rose to her feet, the scent of his fancy cologne tickled her nostrils. 'Enchanted to meet you, Jemima,' he said. 'And where does a heavenly little creature like you come from?'

Jemima looked for a shawl to cover her head. 'India, sir.'

'My name is Sylvester Lawrence,' the artist replied, taking the boots from her hand. 'Well, these are far too drab for an exotic being like you,' he teased, releasing the boots from his grasp. They bounced against the box and hit the floor. 'Look up, my dear... that's it... no need to hide those big brown eyes from me. Tell me, do you own a garment called a sari?'

Jemima hesitated before nodding and his eyes shone with glee. 'Perfect,' he beamed, 'just perfect.'

Lawrence examined the length and breadth of the room until he spied Mr Pendlebury in the corner. Turning back to Jemima, he whispered, 'I bet it's just beastly living here... imprisoned within these four drab walls each and every day... nothing to do... nowhere to go.'

Jemima silently agreed, *'How did the man know?'*

'Would you like a little adventure?'

Jemima's eyes creased in suspicion.

'What I mean is... how would you like to earn some money?'

Her eyes brightened. 'Money, sir?'

'Yes... money for doing a little work?' The man was odd to say the least, but perhaps he had a wife and children that needed an ayah, Jemima thought. This work he spoke of could help pay for her voyage home. 'I shall have a word with Pendlebury,' he continued, stepping away. 'It's been an utter pleasure making your acquaintance, Jemima. I do believe we shall meet again.'

Lawrence weaved his way in between the room's occupants, dodging the strewn clothing and dishevelled boxes in his path. After whispering into Mr Pendlebury's ear, both men exited the room.

Nuwani nudged Jemima's shoulder. 'What did he want?'

Jemima shrugged. 'I'm not sure.'

'Who is he?'

'I think Mr Pendlebury said he was an artist.'

'Looks strange... did you see his skin?'

Jemima nodded, but it was not his ailment that bothered her.

Meanwhile, in the hallway, Sylvester Lawrence shared his thoughts with Mr Pendlebury. 'I have another favour, sir, and I do hope that you will indulge me. The Indian girl... Jemima... I would very much like to paint her... such a becoming face.'

Pendlebury's cheeks sagged. 'Oh... I'd rather imagined that you would paint all the women with their tutors by their side.'

'No sir. Only the girl... I would, of course, expect to paint her in my own studio.'

'That would be highly inappropriate,' Pendlebury huffed. 'This establishment thrives on charitable donations and does not have the means to pay for carriages to take these women to and fro.'

'I will pay for her transport,' Lawrence insisted. 'It would only be for a few hours a week.'

'Even so, we provide Christian teaching here and it would be most detrimental to Jemima's moral development if she were to miss her religious instruction.' On that note, Pendlebury edged back towards the Visitors' Room as a sign that he was ready to end the conversation. 'Now, I'm afraid that you will have to excuse me, sir.' He called out for Mrs Shade, who emerged somewhat sheepishly from the confines of the office room. 'Mrs Shade, please show Mr Lawrence out. Good day, sir.'

'Good day,' Sylvester Lawrence sighed, walking up the hallway.

'Excuse me, sir! I couldn't help but overhear your conversation,' said Mrs Shade with her back facing the door. Much to Lawrence's befuddlement, they continued walking in a strange sort of unison, as if they were performing a waltz at the local Hackney dancehall. She opened the door and then pulled it until it was masking both their bodies. Then, stretching her neck several times, she lowered her voice and said. 'Mr Pendlebury ain't here all the time, you know.'

'I beg your pardon?' said Lawrence, baffled.

'I'm the one who's really in charge, 'cause I'm the one who works her fingers to the bone for them darkies in there... and I get paid a pittance for it,' she squawked, extending a sausage-like finger towards the inside of the house. Lawrence was content to while away a few minutes listening to Mrs Shade's nonsensical mutterings. 'What I'm saying is that Mr Pendlebury only comes here once or twice a week at the most and come Sunday, he's off to Scotland or Ireland or some godforsaken place to save some more darkies and he'll be gone for weeks, or so he says.'

'And?'

Mrs Shade rolled her eyes. 'I'm saying that if you want to paint the darkie, I can send her to you and Pendlebury need never know. It'll be just between you and me... our little secret.'

Suddenly, Sylvester Lawrence understood.

'Like I said,' continued Mrs Shade, 'I get paid a pittance for all the work I do for them lot and they get treated better than I do. They're like a bleeding bunch o' Queen o' Shebas and there's me with me bad back an' all.'

Lawrence was already searching for his pocket book. 'Don't worry Mrs...'

'Shade.'

'Mrs Shade... I understand entirely. I shall send my carriage next Friday at nine. She'll be back by two and I shall pay you handsomely for your trouble... starting from now of course.'

Three shillings slipped into Mrs Shade's hand and her eyes protruded at the mere sight of them. 'Oh, thank you, sir.'

'*Thank you* Mrs Shade... it's been utterly enlightening. Oh... and please inform Jemima that I will pay her after the session.'

Mrs Shade's mouth fell open. 'Pay her?'

'Yes,' Lawrence stated, 'I intend to recompense Jemima for her time.'

Mrs Shade's blood began to boil. 'No, no, no!' she began, before attempting to calm herself down. 'I mean... sir... I shouldn't think it would be wise to give the money to her directly... she'd only spend it on ... well, I haven't a clue what her kind spend their money on... but I'd imagine it'd be something good Christian people wouldn't approve of.' Lawrence raised an eyebrow. 'Best give it to me, sir... I'll look after it for her.'

'Very well,' smiled Lawrence, passing an extra shilling into Mrs Shade's hand. He pointed to the housekeeper's vast waist with his walking stick and with a short, sharp poke, displaced the woman into the weed-infested flowerbed. On reaching the end of the pathway, he quickly spun on his heels. 'Please tell Jemima that she must bring her sari with her.' Mrs Shade nodded and again, he pointed his stick in her direction. 'Our little secret,' he smiled, bringing the top of the cane to his lips.

'Our little secret,' Mrs Shade nodded.

CHAPTER 27

THE COLONEL AND MRS MALVERY

Time did nothing to douse the flames of hostility flickering between William and Elizabeth, but as far as the children were concerned, their father had come on leaps and bounds. Guilt and regret had handed him over to them like a sacrificial offering and he spent every free hour of his time racing around the nursery with Sophie straddled over his back, whinnying and trotting like a pet pony. Whenever Robert was home from school, he accompanied the boy to his archery lessons and made a concerted effort to quell his fears of school by reminiscing about his own didactic experiences. On one of their 'father and son' walks, he remarked that school often involved a mountain of hard work but he would forever remember his time there as a string of halcyon days during which, he learnt to swim, fish and make a cluster of friends. More importantly, he emerged from university knowledgeable, confident and ready to take on the world. Comforted by his father's words, Robert packed his trunks and left for Rugby, relieved that he would no longer be privy to his parents' battles.

Elizabeth watched on, smarting at the unruliness of Sophie, who only seemed obedient and calm in her father's presence. Having made arrangements to pass the winter months in Adel, she insisted the girl accompany her for no other reason but to undermine the father and daughter bond. William gave his permission and reluctantly waved Sophie off. He took his breakfasts alone in a dining room once animated with the children's vigour but opted to spend his evenings at the premises of Simeon & Howarth, where he would take a seat in his dimly lit office and allow his thoughts to dwell on India. This particular evening, however, he decided to visit *Whites* of London – the Gentlemen's Club he so often frequented before he left for the East. He had taken supper there and was now relaxing in a leather chair, away from the pockets of dark-suited men conversing on the periphery. With a tumbler of whisky set at his side, he perused the pages of the *Times*, feigning interest in a report of the ongoing French-Mexican War. Club members wandered through, nodding their greetings but William much rather preferred it if nobody came to join him and sinking deeper into his chair, he recollected his joyful days at the Bengal Club in Calcutta and considered how in many respects, the two establishments shared many similarities. Perhaps, the only difference lay in the attendants, for back in India they wore turbans and smart native suits.

His colleagues had toasted his arrival in Calcutta by cementing his membership at the renowned Bengal Club, where gentlemen could partake in traditional British pastimes such as drinking, smoking, billiards and cards, as well as the favoured cultural pursuits of tiger hunting and polo. It was there that William received two kinds of welcome: sedate from some quarters and rambunctious from others. From the latter, he heard stories of the maharajahs and princes, whose generous hospitality was gamely bestowed upon well-to-do Englishmen. To see the real India, these royal gentlemen insisted that one could only experience the country's magnificence after the daylight hours had well and truly passed. According to them, India only came alive when the British were climbing into their beds at night and so, to witness the fruits of this provocative chatter, British men risked venturing beyond the perimeter of sobriety to indulge in the spirit of the *bidi* house and *nautch* party.

William's eyes drifted whimsically across the darkened club rooms until they settled on the figure of a rather jovial gentleman crossing the floor to shake hands with two other fellows. The man then reached for a cigar from a box proffered by an attendant and leaned in for a light, puffing several times until the cigar was glowing nicely at the tip. He exhibited a convivial manner that made William want to watch him a while longer and soon their gazes met, prompting both men to nod courteously. William ended the greeting by plunging his face behind his broadsheet but a second later, he was peering beyond its pages in response to a polite-sounding voice. 'Excuse me, dear fellow.'

William came face to face with the gentleman he had noticed earlier – a fellow of about fifty, whose dark brown hair, streaked with delicate lines of silver, bestowed a distinguished charm to a face that William already considered classically handsome. His clothes were stitched to perfection and indubitably made by the finest tailors in Europe, whilst his shiny shoes reflected the flickering flames from the club's elaborate sconces. 'Forgive me for intruding, sir, but... have we had the pleasure of meeting before?' the gentleman asked.

William looked for a clue in the man's face. 'Sir, I regret not.'

'My abundant apologies, I must have mistaken you for somebody else. I may as well introduce myself while I'm here. My name is Colonel James Malvery.'

William stood up and shook the man's hand. 'I am William Hayward.'

'Honoured to meet you, Mr Hayward but... were you ever in India?'

William was taken aback. 'Yes, I was, sir, I am little over a month returned.'

'Perhaps that is why you seem familiar,' said the Colonel.

'I was based in Calcutta. Does that shed any light on the situation?'

The Colonel pursed his lips. 'I have visited Calcutta many times. It's your face... it seems... I suppose our paths may have crossed at some time or another... I don't suppose you'd care to join us in our little corner, Mr Hayward?'

William agreed.

A solicitor and an accountant were seated at Colonel Malvery's table: Mr John Campbell and Mr Cecil Richards respectively. Both men were in the Colonel's employ and had been discussing the possibility of him purchasing a property in Sussex. 'The Colonel already possesses two mansions, Mr Hayward... one in London and one in Hertfordshire, both bequeathed to him by his father. What on earth he needs a third one for is beyond my comprehension,' laughed Mr Richards.

The Colonel sucked on his cigar. 'It's my wife, Mr Hayward, she adores the south coast... says it reminds her of back home. I understand that breathing in the sea air is extremely good for one's health. I've already toured two properties... one in Brighton and the other in Hove and I'm quite undecided. Which do you prefer?'

William offered his opinion. 'They say Brighton is more fashionable...'

'With his wealth he could buy both,' interjected the solicitor.

'Or better still... build a new one!' added the accountant.

At this point, all three gentlemen chortled into their drinks.

'That might be an idea,' the Colonel sniggered. 'Grandfather would have been most impressed.'

William laughed out of politeness, though he had no clue of the intended joke.

'Yes, they could be called 'Malvery Manor Two' and 'Malvery Manor Three,' quipped Mr Campbell.

All three men chuckled again, attracting attention from the more mature members of the club who scoffed disapprovingly. The Colonel registered William's bemused expression and settled himself. 'Forgive me for leaving you out in the cold, Mr Hayward. My grandfather worked for the East India Company. He served under Robert Clive's administration shortly after Bengal became a company province. As one of Clive's senior advisors, he made his fortune from property acquired from the defeated ruler, *Siraj-ud-Duala*. India made my father an extremely rich man... a *nabob* is what they called his kind.'

'Yes, I'm familiar with the *nabobs*,' William replied.

'My grandfather bought a mansion in Berkeley Square and then had a second one built in Hertfordshire. The first he called, 'Malvery House,' the second, he referred to as 'Malvery Mansion.' The grounds I now own in Hertfordshire are known as 'Malvery Park,' and my carriages and traps bear the name, 'Malvery Coaches.' And so... one can see why many thought my grandfather, a narcissistic and self-indulgent fellow... hence, our little joke.'

'However, one shouldn't be too facetious about the Colonel's grandfather, Mr Hayward,' crowed Mr Richards. 'He left the Colonel and his father, two very wealthy men.'

'Very wealthy indeed,' interjected Mr Campbell.

William tapped the ash off the end of his cigar and eased himself into the jaunty company of the Colonel and his friends. 'I heard a great number of stories about the *nabobs* and their wealth before I went to India. I trained as a solicitor myself, Mr Campbell. I went out three years ago to help set up the judiciary system in Calcutta… help the Indians … make sure the princes adhere to the land treaties… that sort of thing. I just wish I could have stayed out there longer and learned more from the people… the country is quite remarkable.'

'Learned more from the people?' asked Mr Richards, looking puzzled.

'Yes… there's a tremendous amount we can learn from the Indians.'

'Do you not think that there's a tremendous amount they've learned from us?' Mr Campbell scoffed.

'Like how to build decent roads and railways… and an efficient telegraph service,' added Mr Richards.

'You misunderstand, gentlemen. I do not refer to those sorts of feats… I refer to the condition of the human spirit…the meaning of what it really means to live.'

Looks of horror passed over the solicitor's and accountant's faces, which made the Colonel smile.

'What the devil are you on about, Mr Hayward?' snapped Mr Richards, rising from his seat. 'I'm a proud God-fearing Christian gentleman and my human spirit is all the better for it. Now I must take my leave of you Colonel.'

Mr Richards hastily instructed an attendant to fetch his coat.

'Can I not interest you in a nightcap back at Malvery House?' asked the Colonel, smirking.

'I'm afraid not, sir. Mrs Richards will be wondering as to my whereabouts.'

Mr Campbell, the solicitor, finished his drink and set the empty glass down on the table. 'I shall join you, Richards. Perhaps we can share a hansom.'

Richards agreed and instructed the waiter to bring Campbell's coat.

'You too, Campbell?' the Colonel falsely remonstrated.

'Sir, the hour is late and I have an early start on the papers *you* have asked me to prepare.'

The solicitor and accountant bade their farewells and disappeared hastily into an awaiting cab.

'Oh dear,' William said, turning to the Colonel. 'It seems I have upset your companions.'

'Nonsense!' the Colonel grinned, 'and if you did, I'm all the more glad for it! Now, do *you* care to join me for a drink at Malvery House?' he said. 'Put those two ignoramus lightweights to shame?'

'Yes, Colonel,' William smiled. 'I think I will.'

Colonel Malvery's carriage turned from Piccadilly into Berkeley Street and cantered up a pathway to the magnificent abode known as 'Malvery House.' William peered out of the window and spotted a rather regal looking Asian fellow standing before the gigantic front door, wearing a white turban that was kept under the most pristine conditions.

'This is Mr Hayward, Kalsi,' the Colonel said, climbing out.

'Good evening, Mr Hayward,' Kalsi replied.

'Good evening... Kalsi is it?' asked William, impressed by the butler's efficient manner.

Kalsi took William's things. 'It is, sir.'

'I have the feeling that Mr Hayward and I are going to be very good friends, Kalsi,' the Colonel grinned. 'What do you think to that?'

'If sir thinks it, then sir must be right.'

'How about a cognac, Mr Hayward?' the Colonel asked.

'Yes, thank you,' replied William.

'Fetch us the Hennessy please, Kalsi, and bring it to the front drawing room.'

With the men's coats hanging elegantly over his arms, Kalsi floated across the hallway and disappeared behind the arc of a sweeping marble staircase, whilst the Colonel led William into an impressive lounge, where an imposing portrait of his grandfather hung above the fireplace. Beneath it, a log fire popped and hissed, bestowing much warmth to the ornate room. Indian tastes were everywhere: a silk tapestry of decorated elephants adorned the wall to the left whilst an elegant porcelain vase carried a clutch of blue-green peacock feathers in the furthest corner of the room. William perused the selection of Mughal cameos lined along mantelpiece and was careful not to tread on the majestic silk rug that boasted a myriad of colours. He studied the two Georgian cabinets carrying a cornucopia of ivory and sandalwood Indian figurines and leaned in to admire the tapestry. 'Your home is incredible, Colonel,' he said, allowing the musky aroma of the East to invade his senses. Moving to the painting of the *nautch* girl, he added, 'Your collection of Indian art is astonishing.'

Malvery clipped the end of a cigar and reached for a matchbox. 'Yes it is. Much of it came from my grandfather but the tapestry and the portrait of the *nautch* girl belong to my wife. Like me, she's a keen lover of art, in fact... I think you should meet her.' He crossed the room and tugged on a cord by the fireplace. Seconds later, Kalsi appeared, carrying a tray of drinks in his hands.

'Is Madam still awake, Kalsi?'

'I believe so, sir,' he said, setting the tray of drinks on a small walnut wood table.

'Ask Champa to call her please... and tell *her* to tell Madam that I have a guest for her to meet.'

'Very good, sir.' Kalsi poured the drinks and exited the room.

Colonel Malvery handed William a glass of cognac and proceeded to enlighten his new friend on the history of his Indian figurines: where they came from, how old they were and how much they were worth. He stopped only in response to the sound of tinkling jewellery echoing from the corridor. 'Ah, my dear, I was hoping you would be awake,' he said to a figure entering the room. 'Come and meet a friend of mine. I met him at the club earlier this evening.'

William set his brandy aside and rose to greet the Colonel's wife. He was quietly amazed at the creature standing before him, for she was adorned in the palest peach silk sari that drifted about like the lightest of mists. A dozen or so golden bracelets glittered on her wrists and her rich dark brown hair enhanced the sparkle of the diamond necklace sitting around her neck. But it was not just the jewels that shimmered in the lamplight, for her fine features bloomed most radiantly as she smiled in anticipation of meeting her husband's new friend.

'My dear, allow me to introduce William Hayward. William, this is my wife, Tara.'

Tara glided over like a stunning peach spectre and held out a dainty hand. 'I am very honoured to make your acquaintance, Mr Hayward.'

William needed a second to recover. 'The honour is mine, Mrs Malvery.'

Her bracelets tickled his wrist as they shook hands and the scent of honeysuckle sailed past his nose as she pulled her sari train against her shoulder. 'Is my husband taking care of you properly? Has he offered you dinner?'

'I dined earlier at the club, Madam, and yes, the Colonel has made me feel very welcome.'

'Good,' she smiled.

'You have a splendid home, Madam, and a very fine collection of art.'

'Are you an admirer of Indian art, Mr Hayward?' she asked, looking beyond him to the painting on the wall.

'Yes. I have only recently returned from there.'

'Really?' she said, reacting with surprise. 'Then you must join us for dinner one evening and tell us about all your exploits. My husband and I can show you the rest of our collection.' She remained in the centre of the room, lost in a moment of reflection. 'May I ask if there is a Mrs Hayward?'

It almost pained him to answer. 'Yes, there is.'

'Then you must bring her also.'

Thoughts of Elizabeth stabbed William's conscience. 'I'm afraid she's presently visiting her parents in Leeds.'

'Oh. Then you must bring her back, Mr Hayward,' smiled Tara. 'Now, if you will excuse me, gentlemen... the hour is much too late and I really should retire. It was a pleasure to meet you, Mr Hayward. Shall we say... a week this Friday for dinner?'

'Very well, Madam, and thank you.'

'Good night, Mr Hayward.'

Tara touched her husband affectionately on the arm and slipped out of the room in a haze of peach silk and honeysuckle perfume.

'Remarkable isn't she?' said the Colonel. 'We've been married for twenty years and she still looks as young as the day I met her. I still catch men ten years her junior staring at her open-mouthed.'

Suddenly, as he stood gaping towards the door, William became agonizingly aware that the Colonel's comment had been directed towards him. Blushing deeply, he turned his gaze to the fire.

'It's perfectly fine, Mr Hayward, I'm used to it. She's a very fine looking woman.'

'Forgive me, sir... yes, she is,' he said, downing his cognac in one.

'Don't concern yourself, dear boy. I'd rather you marvel at her beauty than cower from her colour...which is the reaction she's more familiar with.' He puffed his cigar and poured another drink. 'So! Friday week it is then! I can send a carriage to fetch the pair of you, if you like.'

'Pair?' questioned William.

'Well, you heard my wife... she insists on meeting your better half.'

William fell silent.

'Is there anything wrong?' the Colonel asked.

'No sir...not at all... I was just thinking... that there really is no need to send a carriage. We have our own.'

'Excellent!' boomed the host. 'Then I'll look forward to meeting *your* wife.'

'Yes...' replied William, beaming a smile that quickly tumbled off his lips.

William returned to Carlton House Terrace, giddy with the experience of having met Colonel James Malvery. Here was a man who delighted in India as much as he did, so much so that he even had an Indian wife. Invigorated by their hospitality, William ascended the stairs to his bedchamber to unlock the one trunk he had never begun to unpack. He pulled out his cream coloured *topi* and silk *kameez* – the latter being a comfortable garment he only wore in the company of men who shared his passion for India. But soon William's sentimental longing was displaced by the image of Elizabeth, from whom there had been no news since she had left for Leeds. He considered sending her word, but expecting his wife to visit the home of an Englishman married to an Indian – after what had transpired between them – was simply out of the question. As a matter of fact, anything to do with India was now out of bounds, for the country made Elizabeth squirm with horror.

William buried his *kameez* in the depths of his trunk and grimaced as the edges of some *daguerreotypes* scraped against his knuckles. He had stumbled across them whilst boarding up the house in Calcutta and had wanted the portraits to take pride of place in his London home. He studied the image of himself, his son and Abdul – back straight, arms lowered – standing obediently at his side. Next was the portrait of the entire Hayward family and then sitting beneath that, Robert and Sophie with Jemima Ayah at their feet. William wondered what had become of Ayah. His confession of adultery had not only affected his wife and children, but it had far-reaching repercussions on Jemima too. He felt wretched as he studied her vague impression in the portrait and hoped – at the very least – that she had found her way home. On that thought, he returned the *daguerreotypes* to his trunk and lowered the lid on his former life in the East.

CHAPTER 28

THE DIM-WITTED SUBORDINATE

The sound of raised voices and weeping in the hallway disturbed the morning Bible class at Mare Street. Miss Hornsey – a tutor and volunteer from the East London Mission tried her best to disregard the commotion occurring outside the door. In the absence of Mr Pendlebury, Mrs Shade was the appointed person in charge and she had summoned Nuwani out of Miss Hornsey's class before it had started. Nuwani had remained in Mrs Shade's company for the best part of the morning and the lodgers assumed the ruckus in the hallway was somehow connected to the Ceylonese girl. Their heads whirled at the sudden thud of footsteps rushing up the staircase and shortly after that, Mrs Shade entered the room, asking if she could share a word with the tutor. 'The girl from Ceylon, she won't be returning to class,' she said. 'She's leaving.'

The rest of the lodgers gasped and queried. Had a lady answered Nuwani's advertisement? Jemima guessed that this was not the case and her heart began to ache. When Ruby rung the recreation bell, she rushed up the staircase to bedroom number three and found Nuwani, distraught and tearful, packing her belongings. 'She will not let me stay,' she whimpered, 'and I have no more money.'

Jemima rushed to embrace her friend. 'Ask her again! I'll ask her!'

'It's no use, Jemima. She won't listen.'

Just then, the sound of shuffling footsteps broke them apart. 'Pst! Oi!' came some sounds. It was Ruby. 'Mrs Shade tells me you're being kicked out. You goin' to the workhouse?' she asked, twisting the corner of her crusty handkerchief.

Nuwani burst into tears again.

'You don't wanna go there,' snorted Ruby, 'It's shockin' what goes on ... go in alive, come out dead, I say.'

Ruby returned to the door and slapped an ear against it. When she was quite certain that nobody was listening on the other side, she ambled back across the room. 'Where are you going then?'

Nuwani's tossed a puzzled look to Jemima and Jemima tossed one back. 'I don't know,' she sniffed. 'Somewhere I can get work. Why?'

Ruby buried her front teeth into her bottom lip and shot a quick sideways glance. 'I can help you if you like. See, I know this lady, Ivy's her name and she's looking for girls like you for work. Interested?'

'What kind of work?' asked Nuwani.

Ruby nestled the tip of her dilapidated boot into the ridge of a crate and nudged it slightly. 'Oh... this an' that, this an' that. It's much better than the workhouse though! Interested?'

'Yes... I'll do anything... anything but go to the workhouse.'

Ruby poked her hand inside her apron pocket. 'Take this,' she said, waving a scrap of paper in the air. 'Tell her it was Ruby that sent you but for god's sake, don't tell Mrs Shade or Pendlebury what I've just told you. You an' all!' she snapped, pointing a chewed finger at Jemima.

Nuwani glanced down at the chaotic scrawl that passed as Ruby's handwriting. 'I cannot read!' she gasped, discarding the paper in frustration.

'Keep the noise down!' Ruby hissed as she retrieved the note from the floor. *Ivy Wilson, 59 Princess St, London E.1.* Got that?' She repeated the address several times until Nuwani could remember it with ease and was already out the door before Nuwani had the chance to thank her. Only then did it occur to both Nuwani and Jemima that Mrs Shade's subordinate was not as dim-witted as she appeared to be.

'What do you think, Jemima? Do you think Ruby is telling the truth?' said Nuwani, perking up.

'I hope so...'

Nuwani began tucking her clothes into her valise with a little more vigour now and it was Jemima who appeared overly distraught. 'I want to come with you.'

'Really?' said Nuwani, snapping the valise catches shut.

'Yes I'll come with you. I don't want to stay in this place.'

Nuwani heaved a sigh. 'But you have already paid for your board and what if a nice English lady comes for you? You will miss the chance to go home.'

'And if no one comes?'

'I believe a lady will come for you, Jemima. You are very skilled and you can read and write... but if there is trouble for you... if your money runs out... maybe this lady will give you work too.' She showed Ruby's piece of paper to Jemima. 'Can you remember the words?'

Mrs Shade's bellowing voice shattered their concentration. 'Hurry up and get down 'ere! It's time for you to leave!'

Nuwani adjusted her shawl and picked up her valise. 'Be patient. A lady will come.' Taking Jemima's hand, she descended the staircase to find Mrs Shade, hands planted on hips, and Ruby shifting indifferently against the wall. The women too had congregated in the hallway.

'Let her stay please!' Jemima begged, 'just until Mr Pendlebury returns!'

'What do you think this is... a free doss house for darkies?' Mrs Shade yelled.' She's got no more money. She's out!'

Nuwani tugged Jemima to one side. 'Don't worry. I'll be all right.'

'I'll come with you!' Jemima wailed. 'Wait! Let me get my things...'

'You ain't going nowhere!' said Mrs Shade, digging her nails into Jemima's arm. 'Grab her Ruby!'

The women threw their hands up in alarm as Jemima tried to wrestle free from Mrs Shade's iron grip. The tussle came to an end when Nuwani stamped her feet loudly. 'She is staying! Let her go!' Mrs Shade slowly eased her grip and Ruby stepped to one side as the two friends reached for each other's hands. Jemima immediately withered into tears.

'A nice lady will come for you, Jemima. I know it. Stay until the nice lady comes.' Looking beyond Jemima's drooping shoulders, Nuwani shouted, 'Goodbye sisters! Never give up hope!' and holding her head high, she crept along the icy pathway and onto the snowy street beyond before finally disappearing around the corner.

Evening fell and Jemima stared vacantly out of the window as one of the lodgers ladled some broth into her bowl. And it was not just her mood that had darkened, for Rani, Sita and Indira had spent much of the day worrying about Nuwani's safety.

'How will she survive?' Rani asked.

Indira rocked back and forth in her chair. 'If it happens to me, I don't know how I will cope.'

'Whatever your language, whatever your faith and country... pray for Nuwani. I believe God will look over her and keep her safe,' said Sita.

Everyone nodded but it was the China woman who retaliated first. 'You all better pray hard and long,' she hissed. 'If she doesn't die from hunger, she will die from the cold.'

Sighs of horror filled the room. Spoons froze between fingers and soup spilled into laps. Sita was a woman seldom riled but even she found the comments bristling enough to thump her fist down onto the table. 'What is wrong with you, woman? Why are you so cruel?' she boomed, glowering at the China woman from across her bowl.

'I am not cruel!' the China woman cried, banging her chest as she spoke. 'My eyes are open! If she survives in this city it will be a miracle!'

Indira protested. 'Someone will help her... someone will give her some food and a place to stay.'

Then Rani joined in. 'Nuwani is a good girl. She will find some work and someone will look after her.'

But the China woman was not convinced. 'Open your eyes, fools! All of you! You think these English will help us? They hate us. We are the lowest of the low. They take our money and look how they treat us. Look how they speak to us! We are all doomed. We will never go home. Sometimes I think it is better to die.'

The soup rippled in her spoon as she brought it to the edges of her wrinkled mouth. Some dripped onto her clothes and stained her blouse. The China woman had sent the room's occupants whirling into depression and it was only Sita's voice of reason that dispersed the potent murk. Placing her hands on the shoulders of the women beside her, she gave them each a reassuring squeeze. 'Where there is God, there is hope. He *will* look after Nuwani.'

It occurred to Jemima that perhaps the China woman was right and they were all doomed after all. Remaining hopeful under such dismal conditions was not an easy task. But remaining hopeful was the one thing Nuwani urged her to be and so in honour of their friendship, she would try her best to believe that fate would have something else in mind for her. Yes, perhaps fate would engineer a happy ending for her after all.

CHAPTER 29
PAINTINGS AND MUFFINS

It was a Thursday afternoon when Mrs Shade ushered Jemima to one side of the hallway and informed her of Sylvester Lawrence's plans. 'Why that toff wants to paint you, I'll never know.'

Jemima had forgotten about the artist. *'So that is what he wanted,' she pondered. 'He wanted to paint me.'* She began to fret. Why did he want to paint her? She remembered him saying that she had a charming face; still, his flattery was not adequate incentive to make her want to model for him. She then remembered him saying something about paying her; yes, *paying* her. And such an adventure would at the very least, help pass the tedious days whilst she waited for a lady to respond to her advertisement.

'He wants you to take one of them sari things with you... what like Sita wears. You have got one?' Mr Shade bleated. Jemima nodded. 'And another thing, I don't want you saying nothing to Pendlebury or the other darkies. Understand?' Jemima was not sure if she did understand but when it came to Mrs Shade, her approach was to just nod at much of what she said. 'If anyone asks... you're out cleaning for a lady in Stepney. You got that?'

Jemima wondered why her visit to the painter had to be such a secret. She did not welcome the deceitful nature of the operation and it must have shown on her face because Mrs Shade's tone suddenly changed. 'You better do as I say, girl, 'cause if you don't, I can make your life very difficult, especially if a lady wants to take you with her. I can tell her that you've already gone or that you fell ill and dropped dead. Understand?'

That much Jemima did understand and any attempt to question Mrs Shade's motives was hastily abandoned.

As dusk fell, Jemima opened her valise and brought out the crumpled tissue-lined package lying inside. She untied the string that just about held it together and peeled back the covers to find three folded saris and three matching blouses set in a pile. She had only packed them out of a sense of nostalgia; to know they were there was strangely reassuring. But it was not a garment that was well suited to a cold climate and she never dreamed she would be wearing one in England. 'Which one do you like?' she asked Rani.

Rani's eyes roamed to the green sari. 'This is very pretty.'

'It is a little faded and frayed along the hem.'

'This one is very soft,' said Indira, reaching for the blue.

'But don't you think it is plain?'

'No. Why do you ask?'

'No reason.'

Sita admired the third and last sari lying at the very bottom of the package. 'This one is beautiful. Is it silk?' she asked, plunging her fingertips between the folds of Jemima's wedding sari.

'Yes...' Jemima whispered, her eyes glistening. But her melancholy was misinterpreted by the others as sadness for a dead husband, when she was, in fact, remembering Subhas and Madhu as they escorted her out of the house on her wedding day. 'Do you prefer the green or the blue?' she asked, composing herself again.

'Why are you looking at them?' Rani asked.

Jemima desperately wanted to share her secret with the others, but the thought of Mrs Shade ruining her chances to go home was enough to exclude them from the cloak-and-dagger operation. 'Sometimes when I am homesick, I like to look at them.' It was not really a lie. Oftentimes, she clung to her saris to invoke a sense of the familiar. They reminded her of home and so much more.

'I like the green one,' Indira said. 'And don't worry, Jemima... you will go home, I feel it. I just feel it.'

Jemima forced a smile and placed her saris back into her valise.

On Friday morning, a man arrived at the lodging house, asking to speak with Mrs Shade. When Mr Pendlebury was away on business, the housekeeper took up residence in his office and she emerged from that very room to shoo Ruby away from the door. The man introduced himself as Sylvester Lawrence's driver and made it known that he had come to collect the Indian.

'It's not nine o'clock yet,' grumbled Mrs Shade.

The man explained that Lawrence's schedule had changed at short notice and Jemima was needed earlier than planned. And were it not for a pouch of shillings appearing punctually in her hand, Mrs Shade would have chosen to rant and moan a good deal longer.

Jemima was playing with the watered-down slop in her bowl when Ruby poked her head into the room and hollered, 'Mrs Shade wants you!'

It was barely gone half past eight and Jemima wondered what the housekeeper would want with her now. Following Ruby into the corridor, she found Mrs Shade pacing, just as she did when she was anxious of a matter. After banishing poor Ruby to the kitchen again, the woman pinched Jemima's elbow and hushed her voice. 'Go get your stuff... his carriage is waiting outside.'

'Now?'

'Yes! Now! Blimey girl, can't you darkies hear properly? Go and get your things quickly.'

Jemima scurried up the staircase and grabbed her shawl and gloves. There was no time to choose a sari and she came away with the entire package in her arms.

'Hurry up!' Mrs Shade crowed. 'The man's waiting!'

'She'll be back early afternoon,' he shouted.

The carriage jerked forward as Jemima hastily climbed inside. Glancing back, she caught sight of Mrs Shade ogling the shillings in her pouch. *'Horrible woman!' Jemima thought to herself. 'The artist's money will help me go home. The artist's money will help me get out of this country...away from her!'* She settled back and absorbed the world passing outside the window.

The carriage journeyed through the dismal streets of East London, crossing Whitechapel and Aldgate before passing through the City and arriving at its destination. 'Wait here,' the driver shouted, jumping down. He quickly disappeared down a set of concrete steps.

The surrounding streets boasted an array of inns and taverns bursting with the hustle and bustle of London life. Jemima noticed a brass plaque hanging on the iron gates; it read: *Sylvester Lawrence, 21 Theobald's Road.* She then heard the echo of the driver's tip-tapping shoes mixed with the sound of another's and saw the man re-emerge from behind the wall, trailed by another fellow, who handed him a pouch of coins. 'Follow me, girl!' the second man yelled, galloping back down the steps two at a time.

Jemima climbed out of the carriage and followed suit. The second man was hurrying along the passageway below, whilst the window ahead of him was plastered with a layer of inquisitive faces. He flicked his finger towards them and yelled, 'Get back to work!'

The bodies retreated, leaving hot breath and fingerprints smudged all over the glass. 'Sorry, Mr Stubbs…we just wanted to see the brownie,' said one young man, resuming his task of sharpening some knives.

'Well you've seen her now, so get back to work,' said Stubbs, who was gone again in a second.

Left alone with an audience of gaping servants, Jemima jolted with fright when Mr Stubbs popped his head back through the doorway and bellowed, 'This way, girl!'

More steps led into a large hallway and Mr Stubbs told her to wait without touching a thing. The walls were adorned with several works of art, the likes of which, Jemima had never seen. A vast portrait on the wall ahead bore an image of a frowning old man seated in a chair with the snout of a huge black Labrador resting on his knee. On the wall behind, a beautiful stream trickled past a grassy bank with poppies flowering on hills in the distance. Watercolours and pencil sketches of foxes, badgers and birds graced the alcoves and shelves. Moving in further, Jemima noticed some of the charcoals depicted women's body parts: a bare arm perched over the back of a chair, an exposed leg positioned languorously across a bed. Mr Stubbs disturbed her thoughts. 'Come here!' he commanded, pointing through the doorway. 'Mr Lawrence is waiting for you.'

Numerous finished and unfinished paintings rested against the bare white walls of Sylvester Lawrence's studio. Some larger portraits lay flat upon the floor; some leaned against tables or remained propped against chairs. A red, velvet couch took centre stage with a large easel positioned before it and there were paintbrushes of varying sizes laid out like a fan, resting beside a naked palette. A blend of paint, tobacco and linseed fumes hung in the air. The odour seemed to emanate from a trace of smoke twisting up in the corner of the room. Sylvester Lawrence was seated at a small table by the window, holding a cup of tea in one hand whilst balancing a cigarette between the fingers of the other. One leg was crossed over his knee and his tunic was smeared with paint and charcoal. 'Good day, Jemima,' he smiled, 'Did I not say that we would meet again?'

'Will that be all, sir?' said Stubbs, lingering by the door.

Lawrence finished the last of his tea and set his cup down on the table. 'Yes, Stubbs, you may go and I do not wish to be disturbed for the rest of the afternoon.'

'Right you are, sir.'

Stubbs made his exit.

A tray of toasted muffins, a platter of fruit and a pot of hot tea tantalised Jemima's taste buds. Lawrence blew a stream of smoke into the air and patted the chair opposite. 'Take a seat, Jemima,' he coaxed. 'No need to worry, my dear... I'm not going to bite.' Using a paint-splattered boot, he pushed out a chair and Jemima tentatively moved across, trying her best to avoid eye contact with the little banquet goading her stomach. 'What have you got there?' he asked.

'Saris, sir,' she said, registering the milky blotches on his hands. Her hunger made its presence known and she pressed the tissue package into her stomach, hoping it would suppress the sounds of her roaring tummy.

'No prizes for guessing that you're hungry,' laughed Lawrence. 'Now hand me your saris and help yourself to some tea and muffins.'

She was startled by Lawrence's suggestion. As a child, she had eaten with Dr Mukherjee's family but here was a well-to-do white man offering her food from his table and to some it would have been an outrage. Too hungry to care about the implications, Jemima remembered how Lawrence's driver had come for her earlier than planned, which meant she had missed her breakfast

– as horrible as it was – and so, the least the artist could do was to offer her some sustenance. Thus, as he reached over and took the package from her arms, she reached over and took a muffin, which she crammed into her mouth as soon as his back was turned. 'This one is perfect… the colour is heavenly. It will compliment your skin magnificently,' he muttered.

The last morsel of muffin was gliding down her throat when she noticed that Lawrence was referring to her wedding sari. She had never meant to bring it with her and she searched for some courage to explain her reasons not to wear it. *'This man has treated me well… he has even allowed me to take a seat at his table and eat his food. Perhaps there are some nice people in England after all.'*

Lawrence compared his selection of paint colours to the shades in the garment. 'I should be able to match the shade without any problems. Yes, this is definitely the one.'

Jemima helped herself to another cup of tea and smuggled a handful of grapes into her mouth. She felt a little queasy after having eaten everything so quickly but the presence of good food in her stomach restored some much-needed vitality. She contemplated taking more food as Lawrence played with several of his brushes.

'Have you had enough to eat?'

'Yes, sir, thank you, sir,' she replied, gulping down her tea.

'Good. Now come along.'

She flicked some muffin crumbs from her lap and stepped over various paintings in her pathway. 'I'd like you to put this on please,' he stated, handing her the sari and its matching blouse. She half-heartedly took the wedding sari from his hands and waited for him to take his leave, but Lawrence proceeded to squeeze some red paint onto his palette before pointing to a screen in the corner. 'You can use that.'

The space behind the divide was hardly adequate for the purpose of dressing in a garment as long as a sari. The best solution was for Lawrence to leave the room. She spoke up. 'The sari is long and difficult to arrange, sir. I need more space.'

'Very well,' agreed Lawrence, 'you may use the room. I shall leave you for now. Don't take an age now.'

She went behind the screen anyway, unbuttoning her blouse and skirt as she went. She fed an arm through the sleeve of the sari blouse and was staggered to find that it fitted perfectly after more than ten years. She tucked a corner of the garment into her underskirt and with some effort, achieved some semblance of an outfit. The last segment was placed over her shoulder and she wondered how dreadful she must have looked without a look-ing glass for guidance. She picked up her shawl and arranged it about her head before a knock at the door sent her dashing for cover behind the screen again. Without a moment's hesitation, Lawrence walked in. 'Are you ready?' he asked.

She peeped from behind the screen and nodded.

'Well, step out then.'

She stepped out and reluctantly showed him her creation.

'I should like to be able to paint your face, Jemima, so remove that ghastly scarf... or shawl or whatever it is... from your head.'

Jemima reluctantly flung her shawl on top of her folded blouse. As she saw it, she looked a disaster, but to his untrained eye, she was a vision. 'My, my...' he sighed. 'That colour really does flatter your skin tone. Now be seated on the couch.'

Lawrence then decided that the seated position was highly unsuitable and suggested that she recline against the cushions. Such behaviour, she thought, was highly inappropriate but she extended her legs and rested one arm across the back of the couch whilst her other arm rested listlessly in her lap. Snuggling back further, she felt somewhat self-conscious as she pulled her sari further over her ankles and smoothed out the creases in the folds. She looked around the studio and noticed that there were no photographs or prints of Lawrence's family or friends.

Perhaps his wife – if indeed he was married – and his children, if he had any, were in another part of the house. But then again, Jemima pondered, it would take an extraordinarily loving woman to be the wife of such a queer-looking individual. From the corner of her eye, she was aware he was preparing his canvas and paints, but too immersed in her own thoughts of the man, Jemima failed to notice that he was locking the door.

CHAPTER 30

THE COLOURLESS MAN

Lawrence sketched with passion and every now and then, Jemima caught him staring at her, as if he was lost in some secret world, playing out a private fantasy. He paused only to sip his whisky but an hour later, he broke the heavy silence. 'Which part of India do you hail from?'

She was glad he had spoken; her muscles were aching and she needed the opportunity to shuffle into a less disagreeable position. 'Bengal, sir,' she replied, wiggling her toes.

'It has always been a desire of mine to visit the East. I expect there must be some truly remarkable scenes to paint. However...' he glanced down at his speckled hands, 'my skin condition forbids me from venturing anywhere rather hot and mysterious.'

Jemima felt a pang of sympathy for him.

'People assume I was born this way...well, I wasn't. The physicians thought it was leprosy at first and then diagnosed a rather puzzling malformation of the skin. I expect someone like *you* has never seen someone like *me* before.'

Jemima floundered. '*Shall I answer him?*' She answered him. 'Yes, sir, I have.'

Lawrence was astonished. 'Really? Well, don't keep me in suspense!'

'Back home in India, sir...'

'Oh?'

Should she say it? She said it. 'The beggars, sir.'

Lawrence looked wounded. 'Well, isn't that marvellous?' he sneered. 'The people with whom I have the most in common are some filthy, disgusting Indian beggars! Yes, I join the ranks of the vermin and rats whose leopard-like bodies are ridiculed wherever they go... whose amorous advances are jeered at and spurned by every woman with whom they have the misfortune of falling in love.'

Lawrence's tone was simmering into something more dark and edgy and he seemed to turn more scornful through each guzzle of alcohol. 'Fortunately, my talent as an artist proved to be my saving grace, Jemima,' he boasted, pouring himself another whiskey. 'Yes, in spite of it all, I tempt the rich, the conceited and the intensely vain... men and women who are willing to disregard my appearance to be eternally preserved in charcoal and paint. Women, who wouldn't dare look at me twice, come to me because I wield the power to make them look attractive on the canvas. Oh! The irony of it all!' he declared, slurring his words. 'Here I am... a colourless man filling my life with the colours of others!'

Jemima was growing more anxious by the second. She wanted Lawrence to stop talking and paint, but he rambled on bitterly, pausing only to drink from his everlasting glass of whisky. 'Something is not quite right,' he said, almost tripping out from behind his easel. 'The hair, that's it... the hair... unpin your hair.'

Jemima was not accustomed to having her hair loose during the day. It tumbled into her eyes and snagged against her clothes. It interfered with her chores and looked untidy when it was left undone. Though it was as much a part of her as her arms and legs, she regarded it as part of her uniform and only felt complete when it was twisted into a bun. She plucked out a hairpin and a loosely braided plait tumbled into her lap. She unravelled it slowly and ran her fingers through the twisted strands; a wealth of beautiful curls hung about her waist. Gone was the demure servant; a goddess had taken her place. Sylvester Lawrence leaned forward and planted two paint-stained hands upon his knees. 'Drape your hair over the other shoulder.' Jemima placed her hair on the other shoulder. 'No, no, both shoulders.' She dithered, not understanding what he meant. 'Allow me,' he said, slithering over to her.

Lawrence balanced a knee on the edge of the couch and clumsily arranged her curls here and there. He changed his mind several times in the process but his sluggish eyes soon grew intrusive as they soaked up the colours of black and brown against the most crimson of silks. He wrapped some locks of hair around his sallow fingers and felt its silky softness against his dry flaking skin. Envy lurked in his eyes as he plunged himself into a moment of deep reflection. He brought some strands of her hair to his nose and inhaled its musky scent. Then, quite viciously, Sylvester Lawrence yanked Jemima's hair with such brutal force that her head lurched forwards and slammed into his chin.

Cold wood suddenly smashed against her neck. Reeling, she felt a dull pain throb inside her head. Dazed and feeble, she lay there whilst Lawrence's rough hands slid through reams of red sari silk. She heard the sound of ripping and realised that her undergarments were no longer secure. Her hips and thighs were fully exposed and Lawrence's hands were crawling up them. His fingers were now probing inside the mass of thick black hair between her legs and as he licked his fingers, she gasped as he thrust them deep inside her. The pain made her rear up but

Lawrence withdrew his hand and slapped her hard across the face. Jemima fell back again and hit her head.

Stillness and darkness passed, interspersed with patches of dappled light. A strange sort of motion – a lumbering rocking back and forth – forced Jemima's eyes to open. She felt cold and intensely vulnerable and then noticed her sari blouse had been pulled off her shoulders and her breasts were uncovered. Trembling, she drew her hands over them but Lawrence smacked them away before proceeding to knead her bosoms in a drooling frenzy. He positioned his body on top of hers and rutted like some angry beast. His tunic buttons scraped her nipples and she tried pushing and shoving until he eyed her with the look of a wolf about to tear the flesh from her neck. 'I can tell you're enjoying it...even black bitches enjoy it,' he hissed. 'You should be grateful that a white man is giving it to you... even one that looks like me.'

Jemima went numb. A small, submissive voice told her *'You're a worthless servant. What can you do against him...a white man? You're far from home with no one to help you. Let him have his way with you. Be quiet and do as you're told. It will be over soon and he will let you go.'* She felt a strange pulsing sensation inside her stomach as Lawrence fingered her breasts and moaned. A cold stickiness seeped in between her thighs and she cringed as he slipped his hands under her buttocks and pinched them hard. Panting absurdly, he collapsed into a heap and nuzzled his alcohol and cigarette-scented head into her collarbone.

There was no sudden urge to push him off. Imprisoned by the laws of servitude and insignificance, Jemima remained still, feeling nothing but disgust and shame. They lay there for a few minutes, though to her, it felt like a malevolent eternity. His physical misfortune was more visible to her now. The hair on the crown of his head was pale and thinning; the skin under which it lay was pink, flaky and terribly sore. The paisley scarf around his neck had come undone to reveal the abnormal stains upon his neck: huge crusty blemishes interspersed with spots of normal white skin. Eventually, he climbed off and fumbled with his trousers and she saw the red sores on his limp white penis and ashen behind. He smoothed down his out of place mishmash hair and mentioned that he was incredibly thirsty. Reaching for the decanter of whisky on the table, he proposed that Jemima drink a glass too.

Her hands were shaking as she drew her dishevelled underskirt over her knees and the tears welled uncontrollably. She squeezed her eyes shut but one tear escaped; a single, solitary one, which rolled down her cheek and made its mark by way of a small dark spot on her red silk blouse. Reaching up, she touched the large bump at the base of her head and it pounded in agony. She hid her face behind a curtain of ravaged hair and attempted to straighten the sari that had been viciously wrenched apart. She pulled a section over her private parts and felt her buttocks and legs ache with self-loathing and unfathomable humiliation.

Lawrence watched from behind his easel, showing no sympathy or one trace of remorse. 'I shouldn't tell anyone about what just happened, Jemima. Besides, who on earth would believe you? You will be taken to prison, where they will inflict far worse on you for even suggesting a white man would dare look at you,' he smirked, picturing the numerous women who had ridiculed him in the past. Saying that, Sylvester Lawrence picked up his brush and it was only then that he really began to paint.

Jemima wanted to die in bed that night as she recalled the smell of tobacco and the taste of tea and whisky on the artist's breath. His stubble had made her skin pucker and she felt its bitter sting as her cheek swept against her makeshift pillow. He had been bullish and violent, and she had found blood between her legs. It was as if he had wanted to go further and further inside her, not satisfied until he had burst right through her skin, tearing her body apart. He had politely told her to tidy herself up and leave before calling for Mr Stubbs to take her to his driver. Then he mentioned that he had passed one shilling for her time into Mrs Shade's custody and seemed to revert back to the gentleman she had imagined him to be. Now she could only despise herself for thinking he could be 'nice'.

Jemima twisted into a ball as the image of Lawrence violating her body repeatedly invaded her head. She longed to sleep but sleep eluded her, and thoughts of anything else... the lodgers, Nuwani, even thoughts of home... would dissipate as soon as she had conjured them. Ishwachandra was the only other man with whom she had been intimate and his face flickered in her brittle mind. He had possessed an inexperienced touch that was gentle in its manner but she had never loved him because she never had the time. Now, as she reclined across her bed of crates, she longed for Ishwarchandra's protective embrace and tried not to wake the others as she sobbed into her hands. But every so often, she let out a whimper, which floated into the air and dissolved into the sleepy darkness above the other women's heads.

She became more and more reclusive in the days to come. The other women put her depressed moods down to losing Nuwani. She told no one about her ordeal; not even Rani, Sita or Indira. And so, when the footfall of horses was heard on the street outside, Jemima looked through the window, hoping to see Mr Pendlebury's carriage coming up the pathway. Instead, utter horror crept over her face when she saw that Sylvester Lawrence's driver had come for her again. Jemima knelt down and silently screamed.

CHAPTER 31
MAHARANI

A chilly wind whistled down the chimneystacks of Mare Street the day that Lawrence's driver came for Jemima. She noticed the frosty puffs of air appearing whenever he or Mrs Shade spoke. As always, the housekeeper was more interested in the pouch of shillings that warmed her hands than the welfare of one of her lodgers and Jemima wondered whether the woman would be bothered about the ordeal to which she had recently been subjected. Would the woman even care if the driver dragged her into a dark alley to be strangled? No, Mrs Shade would only be concerned with the money that served as her recompense. The icy pavements looked as if they were strewn with layers of pretty white lace and Jemima thought she might take a tumble as she stepped precariously along the pathway. Perhaps she should slip and fall? Perhaps she should feign sickness? What could she do to escape the artist's studio? Too late, she was already seated in the carriage.

Christmas was making its presence known and the streets were full of people caught up in the festive season. Memsahib Hayward once said that the celebrations in India could never replace the ones back home and to witness the best Christmases of all, one had to be in England with all the beautifully lit candles, the roaring log fires and a sprinkling of snow on the streets outside. Jemima agreed; in London, the atmosphere was special. Coloured streamers hung across shops and men leaned upon ladders, trying to attach celebratory lanterns along the windowpanes. Strangers made an effort to exchange conversation and the shop windows were stocked high with pretty gifts and knick-knacks. The city itself was one huge present tied within a bright, colourful bow, but whenever Jemima thought of Sylvester Lawrence, she knew that beneath the wrapping lurked something very ugly indeed. She longed to open the carriage door and flee but where would she go in a city that had become as black as the devil himself? She remembered Jagatterini's parting words, '*Challenge those who mean you harm and try to keep you down,*' and then pictured herself, brave and forthright, sinking her nails into Lawrence's face and gouging his eyeballs out. Could she be capable of that? Perhaps she would take the knife with which he sliced his fruit and twist it deep into that decrepit body of his until his eyes bulged and he breathed no more. Was she capable of killing the man? England was making her think so.

Again she was taken past the gawping servants and asked to wait in the portrait-adorned hallway and as expected, Lawrence was waiting inside his studio. Jemima walked past the beginnings of her portrait not in the least bit curious of the image hiding beneath the white cloth. She plucked the crumpled red sari from her package, not bothered that the edges were sweeping against the dirty, paint-covered floor.

'You shan't be wearing that today,' he said.

Despairing at what the painter might do or say next, Jemima watched him flip open a flat, silver case and lift out a cigarette. 'The most fortunate incident occurred the other afternoon, Jemima. Well, whilst I was strolling along Portman Square, I encountered a rather peculiar establishment called the Hindoostani

Tobacco House. I took the liberty of dropping by and discovered the proprietor to be of Anglo-Indian descent... a fellow called Mr Jhosh.'

The story sounded vague and uninteresting and Jemima imagined what she might do to this man if he ever touched her again. He continued on. 'Just as I was sampling the man's coffee and excellent snuff, it came to my attention that he had other wares... not just tobacco, you know... the fellow mentioned that he could get his hands on practically anything and that's how I procured this.' He crossed over to the table where he took his tea and opened a large box, from which, he extracted a sari of the most exquisite nature. The cerise-coloured garment carried hundreds of gold filigree flowers and there were lines of golden teardrops meandering their way up and down the entire purple border. Jemima could not help but marvel at the rich colours and fine craftsmanship as Lawrence mentioned that it once belonged to the Indian wife of an English *nabob*. 'I'd like you to wear this for the portrait instead of the other one,' he instructed. 'Off you go!'

The sari was so beautiful that Jemima deemed herself unworthy to wear it and under normal circumstances, she would never have been able to afford such a sumptuous article. But she had to keep telling herself that these were hardly normal circumstances and she wondered if she was suspended in a surreal dream. She often experienced peculiar imaginings whenever she napped during the day – afternoon mares, she called them – and they were much stranger than night dreams. They were nonsensical and more alarming, and what was happening now made no sense at all.

The sari blouse was far too big and needed to be taken in an inch or so. She wrapped the expanse of silk around her waist and ventured out from behind the divide. Lawrence had already unveiled the painting and was busy assessing his previous efforts. 'The blouse does not fit,' she said, interrupting his train of thoughts.

'Don't fret, Jemima, it will fit you in the painting,' he replied. 'Now, if you would take up the same position as before and un-pin your hair please!'

Jemima looked over to the door but Lawrence was sure to have bolted it. Shakily, she unravelled the bun she had fixed that morning and settled on the red velvet couch. Lawrence grimaced at the sight of his subject, whose face was plunged behind a shroud of hair. 'Peer up, Jemima,' he said, wading about in the image before him. 'That's better. My...one can easily forget you're just a humble servant,' he smiled, making his way over to the canvas. He dipped his brush into a red-coloured splodge and painted with quick and light brush strokes. He continued on for an hour or so, skilfully blending his colours and building each layer with intense determination. Tired and hungry, Jemima smothered a yawn that pushed stubbornly against her lips.

'How about some lunch?' he suggested.

She devoured four cheese sandwiches, two cups of lemon tea and three *millefeuille*. Once or twice she met his gaze and caught his wry smile scoring the air most impudently. The bastard certainly enjoyed smoking his tobacco, she thought. She could tell by the way he sighed contentedly whenever the smoke careered out from his pasty nostrils.

'Tell me about your parents,' he said, stubbing out the end of his cigarette on a dish.

Why would a rich, white, gentleman-rapist want to know anything about her low-caste parents? Jemima thought the notion quite mystifying. 'They are dead, sir.'

Lawrence twirled a spoon of sugar into a second cup of tea and blew the steam away from its surface. 'How did they make a living?'

Jemima did not want to talk to this man. She hated him. Still, she had to answer him. 'They were servants too.'

'I find that highly difficult to believe,' he said mischievously. 'I'm willing to wager that you're the daughter of an Indian King and Queen. That's it! The daughter of one of those maharajahs I've heard so much about. Here I am looking at you swathed top to toe in exquisite silk and I'm willing to wager that you are a princess... an Indian princess.' A shifting cloud of smoke drifted dreamily from his mouth. 'How do you say princess in your language?'

'*Maharani.*'

'*Maharani*...yes, you're a *maharani.*'

'My father was a carpenter and my mother... a house maid,' she said defensively.

'You're much too beautiful to be the child of servants. Isn't it more thrilling to be a mysterious princess?' he asked, puffing on his cigarette.

Her blood ran cold and she wanted to strike him. 'Servants can have beautiful children too.'

'Evidently so, Jemima...evidently so!' he quipped, impressed by her clever retort.

He painted for a further hour and she was relieved that he had so far not touched as much as a hair on her head. But whenever he moved in closer for the purpose of adjusting her hair or moving an arm, her body recoiled with a justified fear. The old grandfather clock made two thunderous chimes and Jemima's heart leapt when he announced that the session had come to an end. She would quickly change back into her clothes and Lawrence's driver would take her back to Mare Street. Oh, if life were only that uncomplicated, for Sylvester Lawrence was ambling towards Jemima again and unbuttoning his trousers as he did so.

CHAPTER 32
THE WORTHLESS KNIFE

The first snows of December fluttered down like white confetti and instantly dissolved upon the rooftops and pavements of Mare Street. Children ran along the road with their tongues protruding from their mouths, trying to gulp the frosty air and savour the taste of a hundred chilly snowflakes. In alleyways and under railways arches, the poor and the homeless flocked together in a miserable throng, wondering how they were going to remain warm on the streets that night and every other winter night to come. Those inhabitants of Mare Street lucky enough to have a roof over their heads waited for the coalmen to deliver the fuel and complained to their neighbours about the rising cost of heating their homes.

The lodging house windows were dotted with a layer of female faces mesmerised by their first sight of small icy deposits tumbling from the sky; except for the China woman of course, who frankly did not understand what all the fuss was about as it always snowed during the winters in Peking and this particular event was nothing special. It was Jemima's first experience of the British winter too and now the snow was falling thick and fast, she liked the way it disguised the world outside. The roads, pavements, roofs and chimney pots – even the dreary dustbins and drains – all looked pretty under a crisp white blanket. It seemed the snow could transform the darkest alley into something pure and magical and she wished that she could feel clean and pure too. But no amount of snow could make her feel unsullied, not after being tainted by Sylvester Lawrence.

She had not struggled this time. In spite of her imaginings, in which she would torture the artist and then hack him to death, she lay back, closed her eyes and let him do his business. He had called her a 'good, obedient, girl' and then sent her on her way. In time, his driver would come again and she lived each day in fear of his arrival. The thought made her sick to the stomach and she retched whenever she envisaged his face. Never had she felt so helpless and alone.

At supper time, she peered at the stale loaf of bread sitting on a board in the centre of the table. Sliced unevenly, some pieces were as thick as doormats whilst others looked as thin as paper. The knife responsible for the carnage was loose in its holder and blunt as a stone. No one talked much. The women helped stack the dirty china and cutlery into an empty basin and Ruby dumped the bread platter lazily on top. She gathered all the crockery and serving utensils but failed to notice that the bread knife had gone.

Some of the women had already claimed Nuwani's bed of crates and the gaping hole left behind only reinforced the fact that she was no longer there. Jemima fondly recalled how Nuwani had comforted her on her first night at Mare Street and ever since, they had both whispered across the chilly darkness to each other until they had fallen asleep. Reaching into the void that used to carry her friend, Jemima tried to picture Nuwani's radiant smile, but the China woman's sour expression seemed to hover in its place instead. *'We are all doomed. We will never go home. It is better to die!'*

A collage of disagreeable images suffocated Jemima's mind. She recalled the moment Elizabeth Hayward condemned her on the doorstep of the lodging house and then felt the immense sorrow of being separated from Nuwani. Lawrence's thighs were now sliding against her own and all the while, she heard the China woman's words. *'It is better to die! It is better to die!'*

The moon was full and fat that night and a beam of its pearly light shone softly across the room. Jemima slipped her hand underneath her old green shawl and fumbled around until she felt the rusty steel of the old bread knife scrape against her fingers. Clenching the holder, she shivered as she tried to think of something good before drifting into the afterlife. Annoyingly though, her head was as empty as the space that once held Nuwani. She prayed the gods would not punish her too harshly for her subsequent actions and then, in a moment of desperate madness, she turned the knife towards her chest.

Jemima heard the sound of metal hitting the floor. The knife handle was still in her hand but the blade was missing. Being so blunt and old, it had come loose from its handle and had slipped out when she had aimed it towards her heart. Reaching beneath her nightdress, she felt a coarse graze that stung in the space between her breasts and frustrated with the miserable attempt to end her life, she flung the holder across the room. Rani drowsily raised her head but within seconds, she was slumbering again and delivering a crescendo of roaring snores. Jemima tip-toed across the floor and hunted for the handle; she found it lying by the door. She slotted the blade back into its holder and plunged the worthless knife back under her shawl.

The coalman was in the midst of delivering fuel when the women descended for breakfast the next morning. He had left the front door wide open and heard them moan as they scurried into the relative warmth of the dining room. There was no sign of Ruby or even Mrs Shade but Jemima could hear the coalman panting and puffing as he struggled to offload the bulging sack perched on his shoulder. If she were to leave at that precise moment, Jemima reckoned that it would have to be without her belongings, for she had no time to run upstairs and procure them. But she would be wandering the streets of an unfriendly city in search of Nuwani whose whereabouts were unknown. She tried picturing the address on Ruby's piece of paper but had no luck remembering the details. Thus, she would have to corner the maid in private, away from Mrs Shade's prying nose.

The coalman wiped his boots and heaved the second sack of coal onto the floor. As he bent over to settle its contents, he revealed – in the space behind him – the bookish presence of Mr Pendlebury. 'Good day, Jemima,' he said, studying his timepiece. 'You appear to be late for breakfast.'

Relief spread through Jemima's veins like the flames of a magnificent fire. Staring straight ahead at the man – who she now deemed her saviour – she smiled for the first time in weeks. Mr Pendlebury sent the coalman to the kitchen for a warming cup of tea and then turned back to Jemima. 'I would like you to come to the office after breakfast. I have news for you,' he said.

Jemima nodded and joined the other women for breakfast. The bread knife was hidden within the folds of her shawl and surreptitiously, she placed it amongst the scattered pieces of cutlery. She served herself a bowl of porridge and sat down at the table, secretly wondering whether Pendlebury would be the bearer of the news she was desperate to hear.

Mr Pendlebury was leafing through a stack of official looking papers when Jemima took the customary seat opposite the mantelpiece. He was in the midst of signing some official looking documents but after a moment, he cleared his throat, removed his spectacles and proceeded to massage his eyes with two red, knotty knuckles. Jemima noticed the groove on the bridge of his nose – the point where his spectacles balanced – and resisted the urge to rub the notch into oblivion. She was relieved when he restored the glasses to his face, for without them, he looked frail and she much preferred him with his reassuring sense of authority; that is, with his glasses on. Before he was able to say a word, Mrs Shade flew into the room. 'You're back, Mr Pendlebury! I wasn't expecting you so soon! How lovely! How was your trip?'

'Mrs Shade, is it not evident that I am dealing with a matter concerning Jemima?' he snapped.

'Just thought you could do with a nice cuppa tea...'

'No thank you, Mrs Shade.'

'Need me to help you in 'ere, sir?' she asked, dragging a finger across the dust-laden fireplace.

Mr Pendlebury gripped his forehead. 'That will be all, thank you, Mrs Shade!'

She finally departed, scowling as she went.

Mr Pendlebury rummaged around in his briefcase for a time. 'As I mentioned before, I have news for you, Jemima. Just last week, our offices in Bethnal Green received a letter from a lady called...' He pulled out a letter and read... 'Mrs Lavinia Rice-Thomas. Having seen your advertisement in the paper, she has expressed a wish to interview you. She will be travelling to India and is in urgent need of a maid. There is even the possibility of further employment once she has settled in Madras... but I'm certain she'll discuss the particulars with you should she wish to secure your services. My assistant at the office took the liberty of replying on your behalf and the lady in question has since requested a meeting.'

No words could describe Jemima's feeling of ecstasy. She could have fallen at Pendlebury's feet and thanked him as much as her jubilant heart would allow. She wanted to thank Pendlebury's assistant too. She wanted to seek that person out, fling her arms around them and show her gratitude for responding on her behalf. A sudden impulse to shriek with delight was swiftly suppressed as she compared her present feelings to the ones she had experienced the night before. How foolish she felt for trying to take her own life, for salvation had intervened in the guise of a blunt, faulty knife and the impromptu appearance of the wonderful Mr Pendlebury. *'Thank heavens for Mr Pendlebury!' Jemima silently cheered, 'and his magnificent assistant... whoever he or she might be.'* A lady who went by the name of Mrs Lavinia Rice-Thomas had answered her notice and now Jemima would do everything in her power to make sure that Mrs Lavinia Rice-Thomas took her home.

'However, it's best not to raise one's hopes,' advised Pendlebury. 'She may decide that you're highly unsuitable... as has been the case before when many such ladies have been disappointed with the unhealthy dispositions or unsuitable characters of some foreign maids. She may even ask to meet one or two other women but if she does choose you, Jemima... you must remember that she is going to Madras and not Calcutta.'

Jemima cared not for Pendlebury's pessimistic comments. She would make certain Mrs Rice-Thomas chose her and no one else. As for going to Madras and not Calcutta, she would accompany the lady to the moon if it meant she would be leaving England.

'She has requested an appointment to see you the day after tomorrow at eleven o'clock. Thus, it is in your best interests to be clean and presentable. Is that understood?'

The day after tomorrow: Wednesday. It was music to Jemima's ears. Pendlebury asked if she had any questions and since she did not, she left the room walking on air.

Outside, she pondered how she would break the news to the others but decided that until she had met the lady in question and more importantly, the agreement was written in stone, she would not utter a word. Inevitably, her companions would ask a million questions and so, for now, she would tell them that Mr Pendlebury had asked whether she wished to place another notice in another paper. It was plausible enough and the plan worked. Her explanation was accepted without further query and from that moment, she ate each insipid meal with great gusto and even consumed the dregs of food left over on the other lodgers' plates. The women noticed the change in her behaviour and were happy to find her appetite returned. She was determined to bring a glow to her cheeks and so she would eat up everything on offer, even if it meant gobbling up the plate itself.

Wednesday was anticipated with much trepidation and the night before, Jemima found it hard to sleep. Recently, she had been too depressed to make an effort with her appearance but that morning she washed and dressed whilst the others slept. Often, she had seen Memsahib Hayward pinch her cheeks to bring some colour to her face and Jemima did the same herself before arranging her hair into the neat bun she was accustomed to wearing as an ayah.

Miss Hornsey returned with her arms full of hymnbooks, hoping to exercise her musical talents by teaching the women some traditional Christmas carols. After wheeling out the old piano, she played some seasonal tunes but it was a transitory distraction for Jemima, who tried singing each song as enthusiastically as she could. She failed to hear the doorbell under a cacophonous verse of '*Hark The Herald Angels Sing*' and Mrs Rice-Thomas's arrival went undetected beneath Miss Hornsey's crooning voice. Everyone was ordered to turn to page sixty-three in their hymnbooks and '*Oh Come All Ye Faithful*' was selected as the next carol to be sung. But before the women had the chance to wreak havoc on the first verse, Mr Pendlebury entered the room and apologised for his intrusion. He spoke to Miss Hornsey with a hushed voice and minutes later, beckoned Jemima out into the corridor.

Mrs Rice-Thomas was sipping tea from a china cup reserved for a better breed of visitor when Jemima entered the office. 'Come closer girl... let me take a look at you,' she said.

With a hot forehead and two clammy hands, Jemima approached her *hopefully* soon-to-be employer, thinking that if anyone needed assistance during the strenuous voyage to India, then it was certainly the woman seated in the room, for Mrs Rice-Thomas was rather pale and brittle-looking. 'Mr Pendlebury mentioned that you were an ayah.'

'Yes, Madam, I have been an ayah and maid for ten years now.'

'Mr Pendlebury also mentioned that you worked for a former assistant to the Chief Justice of Bengal?'

'That is correct, Madam. Before that, I worked for an English reverend and his wife.'

'You have an excellent grasp of the English language.'

'Thank you, Madam.'

Mr Pendlebury intervened. 'Jemima has fully embraced the teachings of the Christian faith and I'm sure it won't be long before she can be baptized.'

'So heartening to hear, Mr Pendlebury.'

Jemima bit her lip. As for being baptized, she would deal with that particular quandary later on.

'Your notice said that you can cook. Is this so?' asked Mrs Rice-Thomas.

'Yes, Madam.'

'I understand that you have a talent for dressing hair?'

'That is so, Madam.'

'Very practical…very practical indeed… please show me your hands.'

Jemima splayed her fingers and presented her palms. Satisfied they were good and clean, the lady inspected her nails. 'Thank you, Jemima… I am sailing to India to join my husband. He is a general in the British Army stationed in Madras. If you prove yourself worthy, I will consider the possibility of a permanent position for you in the Rice-Thomas household.'

With the sweetest of smiles and the correct posture, Jemima agreed to everything the lady said.

'She's highly suitable, Mr Pendlebury and skilled in many areas… unlike most maids. I'm so very relieved. I thought I'd never find a young, healthy Indian maid… they're so difficult to come by… especially one who knows her place and displays such impeccable manners. My husband will be thrilled. I can finally book my sea passage to the East… he's been waiting a while now. I'm already packed and ready to go! My goodness, is that the time?' she said, peering at the clock on the mantelpiece. 'I must arrange passage… next week in fact. I'll send word regarding Jemima's travel arrangements. Thank you so much, Mr Pendlebury. I'm ever so pleased!'

Nothing and no one could have prevented Jemima from gliding across the hallway that day. She even giggled at the inharmonious chanting of Christmas carols coming through the Visitors' Room door. Now she was really in the mood for singing and the time seemed right to share her news. She told everyone during lunch and, on the whole, the reaction was a cheerful one. But Jemima could sense envy and sorrow as the women pondered the idea of being left behind. 'Ask the lady if she will take us too!' Rani said, intending the question as a joke but Jemima heard her voice crack as she said it.

As wonderful as the news was to Jemima's ears, it broke the hearts of others, who had been lodging at Mare Street for far longer than she. Guilt diluted her joy and, like Nuwani, she could only say, 'Never give up hope.'

News came on the following Monday that Jemima's sea passage had been arranged for the approaching Friday. She counted down the remaining days and made an effort to obstruct the sombre feelings emanating from those she was leaving behind. Her last breakfast at Mare Street was a glum affair and she pondered that if God had asked her to swap places with any of the others, would she be selfless enough to do so? She came to the conclusion that she was not and willed the clock hands to move to twelve, for that was when Mrs Rice-Thomas's carriage would take her away from Mare Street.

At eleven-thirty, a flustered young man arrived bearing the news that due to unforeseen circumstances, Mrs Rice-Thomas had been unable to send her carriage and consequently, Jemima must make her own way to Charing Cross Station in a hired hansom – Mrs Rice-Thomas had sent the fare. She had also sent Jemima her train ticket with the instruction to meet on platform number nine.

Mr Pendlebury sent Ruby to hail a cab from the regular pool that congregated two streets down and advised Jemima to say her goodbyes. Some cowardly moments passed before she was able to open the door to the Visitors' Room but once she did, the women gathered around her eagerly. 'We shall miss you, Jemima,' Rani whispered.

Sita clasped her hands and tried not to cry. 'Take care, Jemima.'

'Don't forget us...' Indira cried.

The kind farewells only made Jemima feel worse. She was undeserving of their consolation, for it was *they* who were being left behind, *not her.* Surely she must be strong for them? Someone tucked something soft and silky into her hand.

Looking up, she saw the hunched body of the China woman. 'Dry your eyes,' she said.

The tears almost jumped back into Jemima's eyes at the shock of seeing the China woman in any mood other than quarrelsome. Jemima did as she was told and used the handkerchief to wipe away the tears. 'Thank you,' she whimpered, endeavouring to hand it back.

'Take it with you,' the China woman said, re-claiming her space in the corner of the room.

Ruby yelled through the door and Jemima knew the time had come. Taking a deep breath, she closed the door of the Visitors' Room and then heard the sound of muffled weeping trickling through the keyhole. It was difficult to tell to whom the tears belonged; frankly, she thought it better if she did not know.

Mrs Shade was determined to mar her good fortune. 'Oi,' she whispered. 'You better not have mentioned nothin' to Mr Pendlebury about Lawrence...'cause I'll break your bleedin' neck if you have.' Keeping a tight hold of Jemima's arm, she sneered, 'Of all the sorry lot of you...you were the only one that was any use to me. Suppose I'll have to send word to Lawrence and tell him you won't be coming anymore.'

The mere mention of the painter's name was enough to send a brutal shudder down Jemima's spine but it was then that she remembered something that had been playing on her mind. 'Where is my money?' she asked, fixing the housekeeper with a stern stare.

Mrs Shade released her arm. 'What money?'

'My money from the painter.'

'I don't know what the bleedin' hell you're talking about!'

'You wouldn't, would you?' Jemima smirked. 'Keep it! I'd rather die than take anything from him.'

Mrs Shade's cheeks turned purple. 'How dare you speak to me – ' she began, stopping when Mr Pendlebury strolled into hallway.

'The cab outside will take you to the station. Goodbye Jemima and good luck. Remember to walk in the path of Jesus...only then will your sins be washed away.'

'Goodbye sir,' she said.

A scruffy hansom cab had already parked up on the roadside. The carriage door was swinging open, inviting Jemima to climb inside. Pendlebury returned to the sanctuary that was his office room and Ruby opened her mouth to say goodbye, but the girl was never given the chance to communicate her farewell, for Mrs Shade had rudely intervened by slamming the door clean on Jemima's face.

PART FOUR

CHAPTER 33

HAPPY HANNUKAH!

A rancid melange of tobacco, alcohol and vomit fumes fes-tered within the hansom carriage walls but the icy wind blowing through the compartment masked the stink that seemed to emanate from every crevice. Elizabeth Hayward's trusty rose-scented handkerchief sprung into Jemima's mind; it was the la-dy's rescue from all smells unpleasant. Jemima held the China woman's silk square over her nostrils and was grateful to find the lingering scent of sandalwood.

What was Elizabeth Hayward doing at this precise mo-ment in time, Jemima wondered? Had she packed Robert off to school? Was she scolding Sophie for sucking her thumb? She had not even seen the sahib before she was cruelly ousted from his house. *'Forget about those people,'* Jemima told herself. *'They sent you to Mare Street and to that disgusting man... that monster, Lawrence. Forget about them. You have a new mistress to care for now. Why do you waste your time dwelling on those who have caused you so much pain?'* Jemima's eyes were weary. She had not slept well for days. Her mind constantly raced with thoughts of Nuwani and she had been unable to repress the nightmare of events that had unfurled at Lawrence's studio. But now she drifted easily in and out of a slumber, opening her eyes once in a while to check the items she had been given were still in her pocket. Satisfied that they were safely contained, she leaned back and dozed off again.

It was not the clamour of the streets or the potholes in the road that subsequently jolted Jemima from a shallow sleep. This time, the abrupt jerking motion of the carriage suddenly forced her eyelids to open. The cab driver had parked on one side of the road and she heard him climb down from his seat and light a cigarette. She had not seen his face upon entering the carriage but it was certain that he had seen hers. She wondered whether or not she should question the man. Burly, unshaven and most probably unwashed, he sported a puffy left eye that was purple from a punch in a street brawl. He loitered on the street corner, taking deep drags and then swaggered over to the carriage window, across which, he folded his arms. Suddenly, he cleared his throat most vehemently and emitted the slimy contents of his mouth out onto the roadside, leaving a trail of spittle dangling from his lips. 'Well… here we are… Charing Cross Station,' he growled, wiping away the lingering drool with the sleeve of his coat.

'Where, sir?' Jemima asked.

A clumsy hand came through the window and pointed to two buildings on the other side of the pavement.

'I do not see it,' she said, asserting herself.

The man's bushy eyebrows – thick like two fat maggots – crawled into an arched position. Rolling his tongue against the insides of his dirty cheeks, he said, 'That's 'cause it's through there!' He pointed towards the alleyway again. 'Can't get me horse through you see.' His breath reeked as he spoke and his teeth were yellow and skew-whiff. 'Now pay me what you owe me and get out me carriage. Or, I can drag you out if you like.'

Jemima could hardly remember how she managed to extract Mrs Rice-Thomas's pouch of money from her pocket, for it had vanished in a second and somehow ended up in the driver's stocky hands. He stuck his fat fingers into the purse and peered inside before stuffing it into his pocket. 'This'll do,' he grinned. 'Now get out me carriage, you black whore.'

She clambered out as quickly as her petrified legs could carry her and could do nothing more but watch him climb back up to his seat and ride away with Mrs Rice-Thomas's money jangling in his trouser pocket. Jemima buried her head in her hands and smothered a scream. Clenching her fists fiercely, she turned and made her approach towards the alleyway.

A rat scampered off at the sound of her footsteps and a wave of displeasing odours greeted her nose. Tentatively she headed inside, expecting to hear the commotion of a busy train station but the alley opened out into a street that gave rise to another, and another after that, and the surrounding buildings looked as if they were sandwiched together in a space that appeared to be much too small. Jemima looked either side of her; to her left, she spotted a male figure seated in the doorway of the adjacent edifice. 'Excuse me, sir,' she said, approaching the man. 'Please can you tell me the way to Charing Cross Station?'

He burped and mumbled incoherently before reaching for the gin bottle standing by his feet and Jemima left without waiting for his answer. She then spied three men shovelling dead leaves and ice further down the street and across to her right, she spotted two women locked in conversation outside a public house. *'Perhaps the ladies will help?' she thought.* One of them, a fair-haired woman, was laughing and joking with her brown-haired companion. Jemima addressed the blond first. 'Excuse me, Madam...' she began.

The blond threw her head back and hooted loudly. 'Get a load o' this Ida... she's calling me, Madam!'

Ida grabbed the ends of her skirts and performed a mock-curtsey. 'Well heavens above if it ain't Lady Nancy Longbottom!'

Jemima would not be put off. 'I am looking for the train station.'

'What station's that then?' asked Ida.

'Charing Cross Station... a man told me it is very close by.'

'Close by? Charing Cross Station? Listen darlin,' there ain't no – '

At that moment, Nancy, the blonde-haired cohort, swung her crony out of Jemima's path. 'Yeah I know where it is,' she said, taking the place of the brunette. 'You go down there,' she said, pointing to the opposite street, 'then take the left... then right, and right again. And then, you just keep going till you see it. Got it?'

Jemima failed to notice Ida's look of disbelief. 'Thank you,' she said, crossing the street.

Ida turned to her friend and laughed. 'Ooh you are terrible, Nancy!'

'I wonder where she'll end up,' Nancy mused.

'From the sound of where you sent her... probably with the Jews.'

'She'll feel right at home then.'

'Left, right and right again,' Jemima said, repeating Nancy's directions. And though she had no sense of time or direction, her resolve to reach the station was fierce and inexorable. Marching on with her train ticket tucked inside her fist, she made the turn to her left and then walked the short distance to a road on her right. Crossing over again, she took another right and realised that the surroundings had become rather claustrophobic. With a dearth of signs to help her on her way, she searched for the final turning which, according to Nancy, would lead to her Charing

Cross Station, but following the path ahead, she ended up in a dead end street with nothing in view but a dog so mangy that it could hardly cross from one spot to the other without stopping to gnaw at its saggy hindquarters.

Jemima decided that she could either collapse into tears or remain resolute and carry on. She carried on. People skulked about on street corners and a group of grubby-faced children played hopscotch in the street ahead. Three gentlemen dressed in similar dark attire commanded her attention. They were engrossed in conversation outside a little shop. All three possessed beards and wore black coats with matching black hats. Two solitary curls dangled each side of their faces and Jemima watched them shake hands and heard them chat amiably to one another. Two of the men departed and the other went inside the shop. A grimy sign above the door said, *'Pawnbroker.'*

Jemima had only just begun to cross the road when she felt a presence at her side. Looking down, she saw the face of a shabbily dressed girl peering back at her in a most enquiring fashion. She had broken away from the other children playing in the street and was of an age of seven or eight. 'Got any money to spare?' the child asked.

Jemima shook her head.

'What you got in your hand?'

'Nothing,' Jemima said, attempting to cross the street.

The girl intercepted her path. 'Go on!' she exclaimed. 'Give us some money!'

Jemima walked around the child and continued on.

The shop had a mysterious nature about it. The sign in the window said, *'Shalom'* and there were various items placed here and there: old boots, clocks, teacups; old violins. Another notice placed halfway down the sooty glass pane bore even more unfamiliar words.

Happy Hanukkah to all our Jewish Brothers and Sisters.
Celebrate with us at Spitalfields Synagogue.

Through the window, Jemima could see the man who had entered earlier. He was laughing with the gentleman behind the counter and all manner of items lay on the shelves behind: eyeglasses, dusty telescopes, battered shoes and Sunday Best Suits; none of which looked new. Jemima opened the door and a little bell rung, making the two men turn around and stare.

'Can I help you, Miss?' said the gentleman behind the counter.

His accent sounded foreign. Jemima had never heard anything like it before. 'Please, sir. Could you tell me the way to the train station?'

'Which station, Miss?'

'Charing Cross Station... I think it is very near here.'

The shopkeeper pulled a face. 'This is the East End, my dear. Charing Cross Station is in the centre of London. You will have to take a hansom.'

Her heart sank so low that she was sure it had plummeted to the floor. Averse to the idea of another cab, for the previous driver had taken all her money, she said, 'If you show me the way, sir, I will walk.'

The man looked confused and looked over to his equally-confused friend. 'He's right Miss,' the friend said. 'It is a very long way. You'd best take a hansom from Whitechapel.'

Jemima was too embarrassed to admit that she was penniless, but she would have traded a sari in return for her fare if she had known the purpose of a pawnbroker's shop. On the other hand, even if she had the money, she would never trust a hansom cab driver again. 'Please show me the way and I will walk.'

The pawnbroker shrugged and entreated his friend. 'Isaiah, please show this lady the way to Whitechapel.'

Isaiah obliged and opened the door. 'Thank you, sir.' she said, looking over to the pawnbroker.

'My pleasure, good luck, Miss,' he said, scratching his head.

Isaiah pointed to a street sign outside. 'This is Brick Lane... see...' He had the same foreign accent as the pawnbroker. 'Walk all the way up until you come to the main thoroughfare of Whitechapel.' He repeated the name until it sunk into Jemima's head. 'Then, turn right and keep going until you see a sign for the City. I'm afraid that you will have to ask someone else from there.'

'Thank you,' she replied.

'Look for the signs to the City. Don't forget.'

'Please, what is the time, sir?'

Isaiah fetched a small timepiece from the inside of his coat pocket and scrutinized its face. 'It is almost quarter past one, Miss.'

She thanked him again and set out on the road ahead with the train ticket safe within her fingers. Adamant that she would make it to the station on time – even if it meant running all the way – Jemima headed along Brick Lane with hearty strides, though she failed to hear the pitter-patter of little footsteps following on from behind.

CHAPTER 34

THE BOY CALLED CHARLIE

Only random sightings of males dressed similarly to the gentlemen outside the pawnbroker's shop distracted Jemima from her purpose as she marched along Brick Lane. When one such individual passed her in the street, she speculated on his origins and customs and it was then that she noticed the same troop of children that had lingered in the alleyways behind. The clatter of their worn down shoes grew louder by the second and she sensed one of them was gaining on her. She quickened her pace, but suddenly a young boy of no more than thirteen years was cockily striding behind her. 'Got any money?' he asked, matching her speed and eyeing her fist for the presence of something tucked inside. By now, the four other scamps had also caught up.

'She's got something in 'er hand, Charlie. I saw it before,' one of them said and Jemima recognised the girl who had asked her for money.

'My sister says you got something in your hand,' the boy said.

'No. I have nothing,' she replied, attempting to pass him.

'Show us! Go on soot bag, show us!' cried a younger boy.

Suddenly Jemima was surrounded and the ensuing moments were something of a blur. She was hauled into an alleyway and struggling to wrestle free from the grip of the older boy, who had now seized her wrist. He shouted instructions to the younger boys whilst the two girls clapped and cheered them on. 'Go on Charlie! Get the soot bag's money!'

'Get 'er case! Get 'er case!'

The older boy tried uncurling her fingers but Jemima stubbornly kept them coiled. But when the younger boys pulled with all their might, the valise handle slipped out of her hand and in the mayhem of the screams and the chaos of the tussle, she let go of the ticket and it fluttered to the ground. The older boy immediately snatched the ticket up and waved it in front of the children's faces. He attempted to read the words on the front but the victorious expression in his sharp green eyes soon shrivelled into a look of severe discontentment. 'It ain't money... it's only a soddin' piece o' paper!' he shouted, subjecting his mistaken younger sister to a disapproving stare. And then to Jemima's horror, the boy called Charlie ripped up her train ticket and tossed its numerous pieces into the cold, sooty air. There was no time to salvage the fragments. Charlie screamed, 'Throw us 'er bag!' and the battle for the travelling case began.

Jemima channelled her fury into the contest over her belongings. She intercepted the case as it was thrown into the air but the girls kicked her ankles and the boys punched her arms and since she could take no more of the onslaught, she let it fall to the ground. Her clothes and possessions spilled onto the mucky, wet cobbles and the young vultures circled, eager to see what was hiding inside. But just as the boy called Charlie bent down to stake his claim, a hand dived across the scruff of his neck and yanked him into the air.

'What do you think you're doing?' someone yelled. 'Leave her alone!'

'I'll beat the whole lot of you!' said someone else.

The other youngsters fled instantly when one of the unknown individuals began giving them chase. Left at the mercy of the other mysterious fellow, Charlie wriggled like a worm caught in the grip of a man who was brown-skinned like Jemima. Then the other man returned; a man of African appearance, who eyed Charlie with steely black eyes. 'Did he take anything?' he asked.

Jemima wailed as the ticket pieces fluttered across the cobbles. Some fragments had blown into the street beyond; others lay perishing in the puddles nearby. Her dilapidated case lay open for all to see, and her property – soggy with alley water – was strewn across the valise lid. Ibrahim's tin of *barfi* had since rolled into a ditch, but nothing had been taken and miserably, she shook her head.

'Get out of here!' the brown man shouted, dragging Charlie out into the lane.

'Or we will boil you up and eat your head!' laughed the African.

Charlie ran like the wind, tearing across the road, hurling insults over his shoulder. The two men glared after him and chuckled as he tripped over his feet in his haste. Then the brown-skinned man peered at Jemima and since she would not move or speak, he leaned forward to gather some of her fallen possessions. He was clean-shaven and his clothes were neat and smart. He sported a waistcoat on top of a *kameez* and both were sheltered by a black overcoat. Bespectacled and well spoken, he looked an age of around twenty years. 'Are you hurt?' he asked, absorbing every aspect of Jemima from the belongings that were flung across the cobbles to the dark locks of hair flopping about her face. 'Are you Indian?'

After a moment, she nodded.

'My name is Navin. Navin Mehta.'

If she had been in a less traumatic state, Jemima would have already deduced that here was a fellow Indian. Incapable of doing anything, she stared straight past him.

'This is Jacob,' he said, pointing to his companion.

Jacob tipped his cap and picked up the can of *barfi* lying in the ditch. He peered at the label and then slipped the tin inside Jemima's case.

Navin Mehta asked for her name and wished to know how she ended up in her particular predicament but Jemima's thoughts had wandered elsewhere. 'What is the time?'

'Almost two o'clock,' replied Jacob, folding her brown shawl.

Seated in an alleyway with two strangers by her side, Jemima watched a serrated piece of train ticket dissolve in a grotty black puddle and allowed her spirit to dissolve along with it. She pictured Mrs Rice-Thomas searching for her along platform number nine and saw the train chugging out from the station without her sitting inside one of its carriages. The ship sailed away without her standing on its deck and lowering her eyes to the mucky wet cobbles, she wept like a sorrowful child and did not care who or what witnessed her tears.

Mehta rescued two bracelets twinkling in the darkness and dried them on his trousers. 'Jacob, go on to the inn. I will meet you there.'

The African closed the valise and placed it in an upright position beside Jemima's feet. He tipped his cap again and departed. Mehta pulled out a cotton handkerchief and held it under Jemima's low-slung head. She remained still and impassive and so he pushed it into her lap. It was the second handkerchief she had been given that day and she thought the fact mildly amusing. Folding the hanky between her fingers, she buried her eyes into its threads and allowed her tears to spill across its fibres.

'You look like you need some food,' Mehta said after a moment. 'Come with me.'

A sudden movement of his hand made her cower like a mistreated cat. Trust was a quality that she had lost along the way and Mehta accurately sensed her caution. 'I am not going to hurt you. I will buy you something to eat and you can leave if you wish. It is your decision.' He paused for a while, waiting for a response but she continued to mope in silence. 'Do you have money?' She shook her head sullenly. 'Do you have somewhere to go?'Again, she shook her head. 'If you stay here, what will become of you? You have no money and what if those children return?'

It seemed she had sunk so low that she cared not whether she lived or died. Staggering to her feet, she brushed the filth away from her skirt.

'Will you come?' he asked.

She nodded but declined his offer to carry her case.

'You speak English?' he asked, taking a left into the street.

She nodded again but never said a word.

They advanced along Brick Lane towards Whitechapel and Mehta held onto Jemima's elbow, making sure she avoided the onslaught of horses hurtling across the thoroughfare. They reached the safety of the pavement on the other side and Mehta stopped and stared at her intently. 'What is your name?'

'Jemima,' she whispered.

He repeated it out loud and seemed most irritated as he said it. 'How did you come to be in such a great country, *Jemima?*'

She sensed sarcasm. 'I came with my mistress.'

'An English mistress?' Mehta asked, making a noise halfway between a huff and a laugh. 'You are a maid?'

'Ayah.'

'Where is your mistress now?' The look on her face said it all. 'She has abandoned you...' he said. Then, after realising Jemima was no longer beside him, he peered over his shoulder and saw her standing perfectly still. 'Am I right?' he asked, walking some paces back.

'How do you know?'

'Do you think you are the only foreigner to be abandoned in London?' he said, nudging her forward. 'Come with me.'

She had to run to keep up with his athletic strides. He turned into a road full of market stalls, where people were selling anything from flowers, fruit, shoes and gloves to freshly baked pies and scrumptious warm bread. Stallholders yelled 'apples for a penny' and 'five pies for a shilling' and their raucous voices harassed Jemima's ears.

'Look around you,' Mehta said, pointing to the glut of people.

She passed her gaze from stall to stall until some rolls of coloured cloth drew her eyes to the haberdashery stand. Reams of coloured ribbon made her think of Sophie and remembering Mehta's words, she looked beyond the stallholder cutting out his fabric to find a figure leafing through a stack of papers. He was Asian in origin and he waved at them when he spotted their faces.

'You see him?' Mehta asked, waving at back the fellow.

'Yes,'

'That is Anil.'

Anil made his way over in shoes that were falling apart.

'*Namaste*, Anil,' said Mehta, extending a hand.

'*Namaste*, Navin,' replied Anil cheerily. 'Who is your friend?'

'This is Jemima,' he said, piercing her with a lofty stare. 'She has been abandoned by her memsahib.'

Anil's face fell. 'I'm sorry to hear that, Jemima.'

'Tell her...' began Mehta. 'Tell her what happened to you.'

Anil tossed his head from side to side and shrugged. 'I came two years ago with my English sahib but he fell ill from consumption and died. The memsahib did not like me... or trust me... she threw me out onto the streets.'

'Tell her what it is that you do to survive, Anil,' Mehta insisted, curious to see Jemima's reaction.

'Well...' Anil laughed, 'Now I pretend to be Christian because that way I can sell tracts from the Bible to earn some money. On a good day, I often sell many. The old English ladies feel sorry for me and give me money! I am waiting for some of them now... they come by here often.'

'I hope you sell many today, Anil,' said Mehta, delving into his pocket. 'Here, my friend, buy your wife and children some food.' He dropped a shilling into Anil's palm and shook his hand.

'Thank you... thank you! Goodbye, friend... goodbye Jemima.'

Anil hid the coin inside his trouser pockets and scuttled back to his place near the haberdashery stall.

'He has a wife and children too?' Jemima asked, following Mehta on.

'He married an English servant girl and they have a son and daughter now. They live in a room with five other families and barely have enough money to buy food.'

Mehta's words were soon drowned out by the sound of beating drums. The noise lured him and Jemima towards a street corner, where three men dressed in native Indian costumes were playing the tom-toms hanging around their necks. They sang to a group of assembled spectators and Mehta urged Jemima to climb on a discarded fruit crate in order to see more of the fellows with ease. 'Those men are the Swamee brothers. They are very well known in London... an English businessman brought them over from India and they gave concerts all over the country. The Englishman turned out to be a crook and fled with their money... there was an article written about it in the *Times* newspaper. Now a lawyer has taken on their case and the authorities insist that they are looking for the man responsible for the theft of their wages. But the brothers have lost faith in British law and are trying to raise some money themselves.'

Mehta showed her a woman from Singapore hawking incense and a man from Malaysia sweeping the streets. He pointed to a Guyanese fellow hustling for money on a street corner and then to some Africans chatting in a darkened doorway. And not only were there Indians, but there were Chinese and Burmese, who had come to see the country that governed their homelands. Others had come with dreams of a better life, but many had come with a master or a mistress on a promise that they would be sent back home, but, as Mehta was quick to point out they had been deserted for whatever reason, just as Jemima had been by her own English mistress. Misery was dwelling in the East End streets and the further Mehta walked, the more Jemima witnessed. East London's deprived neighbourhoods were overflowing with starving English families, struggling Irish workers, frightened Jewish immigrants and destitute Europeans and right beside them lived London's Black poor with abject poverty uniting them all. And though Jemima was relieved to know that she was not alone in her plight, she could not help but feel overwhelming sorrow for those, white and black alike, having to live their lives so dismally.

'Most of these people want to go home but they cannot afford to pay for their passage,' Mehta said, pointing to the assortment of coloured individuals lurking in the streets. 'They must survive the best way they can and that is what *you* must learn to do too.'

Jemima agreed. Until she could earn enough money to return to India, she would have to learn to stay alive on the streets. She promised herself that she would not be reduced to the likes of the fellow, Anil, pushing Bible tracts on kind-hearted English ladies and she would try to avoid the path of the woman from Singapore selling sticks of incense to passers-by. She was a skilled servant and so, she would find some other means of raising the money and then she would leave. Yes, *somehow*, she would leave.

The chaos of the marketplace dwindled as they ventured through the squalid tenements of Wapping and Shadwell. The maze of cobbled streets echoed with their footsteps and Jemima, following Mehta on obediently, found her head raging with questions. '*Where do the Swamee Brothers live? How can the Singaporean woman afford to eat on the paltry money she earns for her incense? Does Anil ever have to steal in order to survive? And what of Mehta himself?*'

Yes, Mehta seemed to be the most intriguing of them all. Articulate and most definitely higher caste, he wore smart clothes and certainly looked out of place amongst the foreign vagabonds roaming London's streets. Jemima dared to ask him about his background but he walked on, sporting an exceedingly serious expression. 'I was a student. I came here over a year ago to study Law. Now I have opened my eyes.' He used the same phrase as the China woman but Jemima was too tired to question him further and decided to save the interrogation for later.

A group of Chinese men with long pigtails and cheeky grins raised their glasses of ale when they spied Mehta and his female companion approaching. They were chatting outside a tavern on the corner and Mehta stopped and conversed with them for a few minutes whilst Jemima – distracted by music and gaiety trickling through the inn walls – studied the curious-looking building. She heard laughter sneak out through the cracks in the windows and smelt beer and food waft out through the gaps in the door. A large wrought iron placard creaked noisily in the wind and looking up, she could just make out the faded letters that spelt out: '*The Shadwell Inn.*'

CHAPTER 35
THE SHADWELL INN

Mehta opened the doors to the Shadwell Inn and what a sight greeted Jemima's eyes. Men and women of every colour, shape and faith were chatting and making merry with each other. African servants, Asian lascars, Irish coal heavers and English dustmen were seated haphazardly across tables, exchanging conversation, and in some cases insults, with Chinese roadsweepers, Turkish moneylenders, visiting Spaniards and passing Greeks. Customers tottered across the floor, spilling drinks and shouting out curses, whilst a thick fog of tobacco smoke levitated over everyone's heads. Men yelled for more beer and spirited women – perched in their laps – swayed to the music played by a drunken violinist. A stout gentleman sporting a handlebar moustache stood at the bar, presiding over his boozy kingdom. He ensured the alcohol was in constant supply, whilst two harassed wenches served it out front. The startled expression on Jemima's face amused Mehta greatly. 'Welcome to the Shadwell Inn!' he shouted above the racket.

Jacob waved from a table nearby. Mehta made his way over and Jemima followed suit. Several other Indian fellows were already seated. Most of them seemed well bred like Mehta, though a few looked rather dishevelled in appearance. Mehta shook their hands and smiled impishly. 'We have a new friend, gentlemen. Please welcome *Jemima...* another Indian thrown to the lions.'

United in their growls, the men expressed their disapproval on Britain and its Empire. One young man stood up and offered Jemima his chair. Nervous at the prospect of being surrounded by so many males, she settled in it tentatively and remained silent as Mehta unbuttoned his coat and greeted his cronies, two of whom, were keen to secure his attention.   Though familiar with the company of men, Jacob seemed disconnected from the group and seemed content to sit on the sidelines whilst they discussed their business. 'Are you feeling better?' he asked, dragging his chair closer to Jemima's.

Jemima had never encountered a black man before. She had seen exaggerated drawings of Africans in books and journals, where they were always portrayed with ebony black skin, bulging eyes and thick red lips, but Jacob looked like nothing of the sort. Still, she was rather uncertain of him. 'A little...'

'You were lucky we were passing otherwise who knows what may have happened to you.'

She had not dwelt on the incident in the alley since she had entered the Shadwell Inn. The collection of foreigners stranded in the East End streets and the miscellaneous occupants of the tavern had driven the ordeal from her mind. 'I am very grateful to you both,' she said, with a frail smile.

'I am glad that we could help...'

His words were interrupted by the arrival of a rather worn-out serving wench, who emerged from the counter carrying a large tray of beers. She thumped the jugs down on the table and licked the alcohol that spilled over her knuckles. 'Anything else?'

'What have you got today, Sarah?' Mehta asked, breaking off from his discussion.

'He's made chicken with vegetables.'

'Bring us two plates.'

Sarah wiped her perspiring brow with the back of her hand. 'You'll have to wait, cos there's others who've been waiting longer. Otherwise you can have pie and mash... me sister's just made a batch.'

'Then we'll *definitely* wait.'

'Two plates of chicken and veg is it then,' she said, marching off.

Mehta resumed his tête-à-tête with the sombre men either side of him and Jemima watched his face grow grim with each sentence spoken. Several times, he pounded his fist on the table, disillusioned with the news coming from their lips.

'Mehta is a good man,' Jacob whispered. 'He is a little reckless at times but he's clever and passionate about what he believes.'

Jacob seemed nice and suddenly, Jemima felt comfortable in his presence. 'He tells me he is a student,' she said.

He supped his ale and nodded. 'Yes... he was.'

'*Was?*'

'His parents struggled to raise money for his education. They sent him here to study Law but he was treated very badly because of the colour of his skin and the rich white men told him to leave. They did not want darkies at their university and Mehta faced their hatred wherever he turned. Now he fights on behalf of the oppressed and wants the British to leave India, though... there are some that think his methods of protest are too extreme.'

'Why?'

'Well... he has broken away from the moderate groups and now he leads a band of his own. They believe that the Raj can only be dismantled by...' Jacob hushed his voice, 'other means.'

'Other means?'

'Yes... force.'

Jemima became mesmerized as she listened to Jacob recount how Mehta and his men had been driven underground for advocating their anti-co-operation propaganda to disillusioned immigrants and angry students. 'London is changing and its share of Black poor is rising by the day. They dwell in the dark parts of the city and Mehta searches for them here... in London's East End.'

'How did *you* meet him?'

'Much like you... only it is *I* who saved *him*.'

Jacob's eyes brightened as he prepared to tell the tale. 'I work as an unskilled labourer in the West India docks and one night I stumbled across him on the waterfront, handing leaflets out to lascars near the gin holes. It was dark and foggy that night and he offered a leaflet to a man he thought to be of Eastern origin. Well, the man was not Eastern at all... he was an English sailor... and he thumped Mehta in the stomach and almost beat him to a pulp.'

Jemima looked horrified. 'What happened next?'

'I remembered seeing lots of papers fluttering in the air and Mehta writhing on the wet concrete below them. I chased the man away and helped Mehta to his feet. We shared a meal and a beer, and have remained friends ever since.'

Jacob's story was fascinating and Jemima was astonished by the volatile life Mehta had chosen to lead. Ravenous at the thought of the meal the student had promised her, she waited patiently as Mehta rose from the table and greeted some more men. 'How are you, my friend?' he said to the Irishman who had come to shake his hand.

'He's a popular fellow,' Jemima thought. But Mehta's jolly expression clouded over when he returned and resumed his rebellious talk. Once or twice, he glanced in her direction and she immediately looked away. Eavesdropping, she cocked her ear to hear what he and his band of men had to say.

'It is too risky to print them at the college,' said one fellow. 'We are already banned.'

'Then we will write them by hand!' boomed Mehta, smacking the table defiantly. Turning to face Jemima, he said, 'You speak English well. Can you also read and write?' .

'Yes,' she said after a while.

Mehta nodded and one man placed a leather briefcase into his lap. After fumbling inside for a few seconds, he plucked out a piece of paper, which he kept hidden under the table. When he had drunk sufficiently from his jug of ale, he snatched the paper from his knees and flicked it under Jemima's nose.

India for Indians!
Home Rule for India
Expel the British!
Support the Free India Movement

'You can help us write our leaflets?' It sounded more like a command than a question. 'Will you help your Indian comrades?' he asked again.

All Jemima craved was a hot meal, a bed for the night and a means of finding her way back home. She tried finding an appropriate response: one that brought no offence and sounded polite; one that sounded intelligent perhaps, for she felt so wholly inadequate in his presence. 'I do not wish to offend but... it is not my business,' she said quite innocently.

A sliver of silence drifted within the ubiquitous noise of the inn and Mehta did not speak for a while but glanced at several of his chums. 'It is not her business, gentlemen,' he said, before chortling into his knuckles. Then, after a moment, he asked, 'What is your name?'

Jemima was baffled. He already knew her name. Why was he asking again?

'What is your name?'

His manner was abrupt and she felt that she must answer him. 'Jemima...'

'That is not your name!' he yelled. 'What is your *real* name? The name you were born with? Your *Indian* name?' His affronted eyes rolled in shame and it was only Jacob who attempted to keep the peace by tossing a disapproving glance in his friend's direction.

'Anupriya!' My name is Anupriya!' Jemima cried above the drunken clamour.

'You see!' Mehta roared, jabbing the air with an aggressive finger. 'This is what the Empire has done to you. 'Jemima' is the name with which the British have branded you. They have put their mark on you like cattle! Before they came to our country, you were an Indian woman with an Indian name. Now you have no identity. No soul! Have you ever stopped to think about how the Motherland has been raped and plundered?' He was out of his seat, towering above her, his immense frustration spurring him on. 'Look at yourself! Look at what they have done to you!'

'I just want to go home,' she whimpered, but her reply seemed to agitate him all the more.

'Enough, Navin,' Jacob said, urging the fellow to calm down.

Mehta heeded Jacob's advice and lowered his voice. 'All right! All right!' he said, reclaiming his seat. 'What if I *pay* you to write the leaflets... then you can earn some money to go *home*. But remember one thing,' he said, eyeing her with contempt, 'if India is not *your business*, then it is not *your home*.'

Jemima felt as small as an ant.

Sarah returned carrying two plates of steaming rice and curried chicken with a portion of vegetables spooned to the side. The aroma was glorious to Jemima's nose and it displaced the acerbic air that had since settled above the table. Sarah passed one plate to Mehta and was directed to deliver the other to Jemima, who, after having antagonised the student, hesitated in accepting his hospitality.

'Eat,' he said, shovelling the food into his mouth.

With Mehta's permission, Jemima finally raised a spoonful of eastern flavoured food to her lips; a pleasure denied her for more than three months. And it mattered not that it was some white man's poor endeavour to recreate some spicy cuisine for his regular foreign clientele. But surprisingly enough, the food was delicious and she gobbled it down with voracious pleasure. Mehta devoured a mouthful too and called Sarah back.

'What now?' she asked anticipating impertinence

'Tell him he needs to make it hotter!'

Everyone fell about the table, guffawing into their drinks. Even Jacob's shoulders bobbed up and down in sheer delight.

'Tell him yourself,' Sarah hissed, turning her back on him disdainfully.

Jemima was ploughing through a mound of rice when she felt a presence behind her chair, but she was too busy wolfing down her food to care for the person who had come to challenge Mehta. The men at the table were howling hysterically and she heard a voice fighting to be heard over the sniggers. 'Mehta... always you complaining!'

'Why can't you put some extra chilli in?' the student joked.

'No one else complains.'

Mehta tilted his spoon in Jemima's direction. 'What do you think?' he asked, interested in her opinion.

Resentful at having been drawn into the debate, Jemima tucked a mouthful of food into her mouth and chewed slowly.

'Tell him,' Mehta said, referring to the person standing behind her chair.

Jemima balanced her spoon against the rim of her plate and peeped over her shoulder. But she almost choked on the rice gliding down her throat when she turned and saw Ibrahim standing there.

CHAPTER 36

GOOD DESTINY/BAD DESTINY

With his hands perched on his slender hips and the colours of his gastronomic endeavours splashed across his long white apron, Ibrahim stood his ground and prepared for attack. He had changed so much, Jemima thought. His jet black hair was combed neatly and tied with a white bandanna to prevent his locks from tumbling into his black-as-night eyes. His face was fuller and softer now and it stared down from a body that loomed over Jemima like a willowy palm tree. And though he was more than ready to deflect all the teasing remarks, Ibrahim's frown was never given the chance to reach the peak of its displeasure, for it had already twisted into a look of utter incredulity. Like a snake stretching in the undergrowth, a huge smile blossomed amongst the whiskers of his black beard. 'Jemima!' he cried in utmost delight.

Mehta gasped, 'You know each other?'

'Yes,' replied Ibrahim, taking Jemima's hands into his. 'She saved my life once.'

The former law student pointed a finger at Jemima. 'So it is *you* who is responsible for his tasteless food!'

The almighty bellow of laughter that followed attracted the attention of the stout man with the handlebar moustache. 'Oi Ibrahim!' he yelled, looking over from the bar.

Mr Meade, the landlord of the Shadwell Inn, and father of Sarah and Jenny, the serving wenches, was well accustomed to the rowdy nature of his East London pub. But he knew it was time to lay down the law when his chef had strayed from the confines of the kitchen to make idle chit chat with the punters. 'Get back in that kitchen! The food ain't gonna cook itself.'

Ibrahim made a placatory gesture with his hands and then turned back to Jemima. 'I finish soon. Wait here.'

Jemima reached out and tugged on his apron strings. 'Ibrahim, the food is really very, very good!'

Ibrahim shot a smug look at Mehta and hurried back to the kitchen under Meade's beady eye. He stopped at the doorway and tossed a look over at Jemima again, just to make sure he had not imagined the encounter and smiled warmly before disappearing behind the kitchen doors.

Jemima anticipated a barrage of questions from Mehta but he chatted on, indifferent to the details of her friendship with the cook. Jacob, however, was intrigued. 'How do know Ibrahim?'

She cast her mind back to that hot and humid night on board the *Bengal Star*. 'We met on the ship leaving India. He was working as a lascar... they treated him very badly and I stopped him from jumping into the sea.'

'Well, well...' Jacob smiled, 'it seems we are all saving lives.'

Jemima agreed. Perhaps all their destinies were intertwined.

'You know, Mehta likes to tease Ibrahim about his cooking,' Jacob said. 'He knows his food is excellent.'

Mehta overheard the comment and leaned across the table. 'Of course his food is excellent! Before he came, the food was not fit to serve to dogs.'

The young man who had given his seat up for Jemima – a fellow called Vikram – hurled his arms up into the air. 'You remember when Meade and his daughter tried to make Indian food for the first time?' he chuckled. 'A blind donkey could have done better!'

The resulting laughter sent the Irish wolfhound sleeping at his owner's feet dashing for cover under the nearby table. 'It was so bad…we had runny shit for days!' cackled Mehta.

Meade's suspicious eyes bobbed in their sockets as the Indians pointed and howled at his nonplussed face. Jemima welcomed the ensuing jollity. It masked the dark thoughts she had carried from the day's earlier events and now that she had been reunited with Ibrahim, she wondered what other surprises were waiting to be unearthed. But the merriment soon dwindled when the talk took on a more subversive tone. She heard seditious words spoken; words like 'demonstration,' 'mob,' 'police' and 'freedom,' and she grew weary of all the provocative chatter. She watched the Irish wolfhound chase a rat into a pile of straw and finally, when she spotted Ibrahim hovering near the kitchen door, she promptly excused herself and hurried over to him. He untied his apron and escorted her to a table in the corner.

'I am so happy to be meeting you again, Jemima. What good luck we both have? I told you I would come to England.'

The subject of luck was debatable, at least for her. 'You look so well Ibrahim… so happy!' she said.

Just then, Sarah stomped over to them and was barely able to look at Jemima. 'Pa says you need to be back in the kitchen in an hour!'

'Yes, yes…' Ibrahim replied. 'I will be back on time… no need to worry.'

'Make sure you are!' she snapped, turning petulantly and sticking her nose in the air.

'Now what was I saying?' he continued, wondering whether he should take Jemima's hands again. He paused as he digested more of her appearance. 'Please forgive me for saying this... but you look a little thin and shabby.'

Jemima was not offended, for Ibrahim spoke the truth. There was mud and dirty rainwater splattered on her clothes. Her hair was creeping out of what was now a forlorn bun. Ibrahim's fare was the first decent meal she had consumed in an age and her complexion had suffered from eating the watered-down porridge of Mare Street. She panicked when he asked his next question. 'How did you come to be here?'

Jemima dreaded having to recall her misfortunes. 'Tell me your story first,' she said. 'How did *you* come to be here?' And no sooner had she asked, Ibrahim stretched out his sinewy legs and launched into his account with loquacious gusto.

'I sailed to Italy on the *Conte Russo*... an Italian ship with an Italian crew. The Captain was good to me, Jemima... he treated me well. We sailed to Venice and he took me to his magnificent home. My goodness, you should see Venice, Jemima... the city floats on water! Such a wondrous place! One day... I will take you there. The Captain wanted me to stay and work for him and his wife, *Signora* Filomena Gasparro. I stayed for three weeks until I earned enough money. You see, the Captain paid me very well. He and his wife, they like my food and I was tempted to stay but... the Italian language is so difficult for me to understand. So I decide... it is better for me to come to England.'

'You came as a lascar?'

'Not this time, Jemima. I travelled as a passenger. When I arrived in Southampton, some lascars told me everyone was going to the capital to find lodgings... in a place called Dock Street... so I came to London. The railway porter was a kind fellow. He told me to take the next omnibus travelling east... have you seen such a thing, Jemima?'

'You mean the carriage with two floors?'

'Yes... a very strange contraption... but the ticket master was a very pleasant fellow too. He told me about an inn, where the landlord cooked eastern food... only...' Ibrahim lowered his voice at this point, 'it was his daughter who cooked it and you could hardly have called it *eastern*... and you could hardly have called it *food*... but it was this place, Jemima... the Shadwell Inn... and I couldn't believe my eyes when I saw all the Indian faces sitting inside!

I asked for a plate of curried vegetables and rice... well... all I can say is that the lascar food I ate on the ship tasted much better...in fact, the ship's rats would have tasted much better... oh the chillies were so withered and the rice stuck together. Jemima, the potatoes were awful... half-cooked... unseasoned... I had to swallow them down with some tea... that was awful too. Even the lascar sitting across from me said his meat tasted like an old shoe. Still, we finished the food and paid the bill because we were so hungry.'

Ibrahim's storytelling was highly animated and Jemima giggled whenever he gesticulated and pulled a face. 'Did you find a place to stay?' she asked.

'I went to this Dock Street, Jemima. Some sailors were smoking on the pavement outside and they told me to see a man called Mr Wimpole... the only fellow who had any rooms left. The house was disgraceful, Jemima... five to six lascars to a room... dirty, smelly mattresses for beds. One fellow called Loopy...don't ask me why he was called that, I cannot tell you... but this Loopy fellow looked half dead. He was coughing and wheezing so much that his chest rattled whenever he spoke! I tell you no lie, Jemima, the fellow was so ill he could barely lift his face...and the story becomes worse... it becomes so bad!'

Jemima laughed. 'How?'

'The washroom! Oh Jemima!' Ibrahim cried, pinching his nostrils. 'It was the filthiest room I've ever seen... patches of urine on the floor... stink coming from the shii...' Ibrahim paused, 'forgive me for using such foul words in your presence, Jemima, but there are no nicer ones I can find.'

'I forgive you, Ibrahim! Please... continue.'

'It was worse than being back at sea... even sleeping in the gutters seemed better because they looked cleaner, believe me, much cleaner.'

Jemima's concentration shifted. 'Ibrahim... why is that girl looking at us?'

'What girl?

'The girl who served the food earlier.'

Sarah was eyeing them again from the kitchen doors. She passed by with a determined sway and stopped to flirt with some customers standing at the bar.

'That's Sarah,' Ibrahim smiled.

Sarah perched her elbows upon the pub counter and glanced over from time to time.

'I don't think she likes me,' concluded Jemima.

'Nonsense!' Ibrahim scoffed. 'Sarah is a little... headstrong. But she is really very nice.'

'Why is she scowling at us both?'

'Please... you do not worry about Sarah... let me finish my story.'

'Yes of course. What happened next?'

'I left Dock Street, but I had nowhere to go. So I came back to this place.'

'And Mr Meade kindly gave you a job?'

'I wouldn't say 'kindly,' Jemima. You see, I was drinking another cup of their miserable tea...brought to me by Sarah, in fact... wondering where I was going to sleep that night, when the fellow seated beside me suddenly stood up and asked for his money back.'

'Why?'

'He said the food was 'stinking awful.'

Jemima giggled again.

'Well, Mr Meade's face looked like thunder had struck it. He called two big fellows over from the bar and they picked up the man and threw him out.'

'Really?'

'Yes but then another fellow sitting next to me said that the man was right... the food was 'stinking awful' and that's when I asked Mr Meade for a job as a cook.'

'And he said yes?'

'Not straight away, Jemima. The fellow had to be persuaded... and believe me, he is very difficult man to persuade!'

'How did you do it?'

'Well, he said he did not have any jobs to give... especially to foreigners... and being a chef for a *nawab* did not impress him either. He said that he did not care if I had cooked for Ghenghis Khan himself... he still had no jobs to give. But I was so desperate Jemima that I asked to cook for him and his daughters and if they liked my food, then I would work for nothing... well... almost nothing. I would offer my services in return for lodgings.'

'What did he say?'

'When I told him that his daughter, Jenny... the one who cooked the food... was driving his customers away, I thought he would get those two big fellows to come over and throw me out too, but Mr Meade agreed that Jenny was more than terrible and allowed me to cook for him that very night! But it was a difficult, Jemima... the kitchen cupboards had nothing but fatty beef and old potatoes and so Mr Meade directed me to the local East End market and I spent the last of my wages buying all the ingredients.'

'What did you make?'

Ibrahim's face bloomed with pride. 'I began with my version of *seekh kebabs* in a bed of green lettuce and a dressing of garlic and lime juice, followed by a main dish of mild mutton *kurma* served with a carrot and capsicum *raita* and a pot of freshly chopped tomatoes blended into chutney. I served it with my father's dish of mashed lentils with coriander, and for dessert... I whipped up a soft vanilla sauce flavoured with slices of sweet peaches.'

'Did they like it?'

'Like it? Goodness! There was nothing left, Jemima! Plates were licked clean... bones were sucked dry... my dessert vanished in seconds. Mr Meade even brought out a box of his cigars and offered one to me.'

'And after that, he offered you work?'

'Yes!'

'How wonderful, Ibrahim!'

'I told him I could produce an excellent eastern menu, Jemima... mild for the western palette... spicy for the eastern... and I was right. Now my food is attracting all kinds of people and Mr Meade is very pleased. He has even bought me a new bed and I have a room of my own... the cellar.'

'Ibrahim, I am so happy for you. You have done so well.'

'*Well?*' smiled Ibrahim. I plan to do better than *well*. I am going to make this place the best eating tavern in town!'

Jemima leaned back in her chair and absorbed Ibrahim's joy. They had both suffered greatly and his journey had been equally as fraught as hers. But Ibrahim assured her that he wanted to forget his past and leave his adversities firmly behind. Life was a good deal brighter now; his English had improved and he intended to make something of himself. Slapping his hands against his thighs, he said, 'Tell me about your adventure now.'

Jemima reluctantly recounted the trouble-free journey from Alexandria to London but her manner turned grave after recalling the perplexing circumstances that led her to Mare Street. There was some respite as she described the inhabitants of the lodging house; yet fond memories of the women she had left behind made her somewhat melancholy. The tale of Mrs Rice-Thomas almost reduced her to tears and she watched Ibrahim grow angry after hearing about the thieving hansom cab driver. He expressed his relief to hear that the Jewish gentlemen had earnestly tried to help her and applauded Mehta and Jacob for their timely intervention in the alleys of Brick Lane. But Ibrahim did not learn everything of Jemima's experiences, for she did not mention Sylvester Lawrence and he missed a streak of agony in her eyes as she attempted to bury her horror again.

'What are your plans now? Where will you go?' he asked.

'Perhaps Mehta will help me.'

'Mehta?' Ibrahim scoffed. 'Trouble follows that fellow wherever he goes.'

The former law student was looking over at them. A second later, he began heading in their direction. Ibrahim urgently leaned forward on his elbows and hushed his voice. 'You can stay here. Meade is a good man. He will give you work... if he doesn't... I shall leave!'

Mehta reached their table and smiled in the same peculiar way he had done during their reunion. 'We are leaving now,' he said, looking at Jemima. 'Vikram says there is room for you at his lodgings in Wapping. The landlord is an Indian brother, he will not mind if you stay.'

'That is not necessary,' Ibrahim said, taking charge. 'She is staying here.'

'Is that so?' Mehta replied.

Jemima nodded in agreement and sensed the student's displeasure as he turned to depart. Inadvertently, she called out to him. 'The work you mentioned... I will do it for you.' She regretted the words as soon as she said them.

Mehta's irritated facial expression flowered into a look of self-satisfied triumph. 'Good. I'll come by soon.' And then with his cronies in tow, he left the inn and Jemima waved goodbye to Jacob, who followed on shortly after.

'What work is this?' Ibrahim said, tapping the table with his finger.

'He has asked me to write some papers for him.'

Ibrahim stared at her. 'You can write? When did you learn to write?'

'As a child... my mistress taught me. She said I could become a teacher if I wanted.'

Ibrahim hid his disapproval. In his opinion, Indian women like Jemima should not pay heed to such things. It could only give them ideas above their station and lead to endless trouble. They should only be concerned with their husbands and children. They should only be concerned with making a home. Ambition was men's business. 'Hmm,' he muttered warily, 'be careful Jemima. Be *very* careful.'

She assured him that she would.

CHAPTER 37

THE PRINCE'S COOK

After being introduced as one of Ibrahim's many cousins, Jemima was permitted to sleep in the cellar in return for some mangling and cleaning chores. Ibrahim insisted that she take his bed, whilst he made himself comfortable on his old lumpy mattress. Seated alone in the cellar, cleaning the scars she had garnered from her encounter in the alleyway, Jemima considered how the morning had started so positively and ended so... words failed her. But at least she had met a familiar face, although she had to admit that she was feeling rather concerned at the prospect of sharing a room with another man who was not her husband. From the dark recesses of her mind – where the figure of Sylvester Lawrence often lurked – she imagined Ibrahim slinking over in the middle of the night and mounting her body against her will. She scolded herself for thinking such awful thoughts. He was a friend she could trust. There was no doubt about that...was there? She tossed and turned in bed that night after drawing the blankets all the way up to her chin. She wanted to make sure every inch of her body was hidden from sight. Was there something hard close by with which she could strike Ibrahim... the candlestick perhaps? She remembered that night on the ship when she first encountered him... the fellow who pressed his hand across her mouth and pushed her hard against the ship wall. He could have assaulted then and there, but he did not. No; Ibrahim did not.

They both lay there in the darkness; she on the bed and he further across the floor, divided by a length of old cloth that bestowed some privacy on their separate parts of the room. 'Are you still awake?' he asked, listening to her restless movements.

'Yes.'

'What is the matter, Jemima? Can't you sleep?'

'I was thinking... thinking of my parents,' she lied.

'I often think of mine too.'

'What were they like?'

'My mother died when I was five years old.'

'I'm sorry...' she said, propping her face on her elbows. 'Do you remember her?'

Certain memories lingered: his mother's hearty laugh, her generous embraces, but it was hard to remember much else. 'My father married again... a woman called Alia. She gave him two daughters but... I was never close to them.'

'Were you close to your father?'

'Yes. He was a chef too.'

'Do you have fond memories of him?'

'Yes, said Ibrahim, chuckling. 'My fondest memory is my earliest memory. I was seven years old and my father scooped me up in his arms to show me the chillies and spices sizzling in his pot. I was mesmerized by the ingredients dancing about in the hot oil, but I inhaled the spicy aroma too deeply and the scent of frying chillies grated my throat like broken glass and my young nostrils jiggled so much that I sneezed some snot into my father's pot! Everyone laughed, except my father... he had to begin cooking all over again in a snot-free pot!'

Jemima instantly felt at ease. 'Tell me about your life in Awadh. What was it like to be a prince's cook?'

'Oh,' Ibrahim smiled. 'Most of the time, it was wonderful. You see... my father, Rafik, and his father before him... had served as chefs in the palace kitchens of Awadh's royal family and I learned the art of royal cuisine when I was only eight years old. My father had to promise on my behalf that I would never speak about the royal recipes to any outsiders. This was an oath many seeking work in the kitchens had to take and offenders were punished by means of a thrashing followed by a shameful dismissal! There were three kitchens in the *Nawab's* palace... the Mughlai, the Hindu and the European... and each was forever trying to outdo the other in order to win the *Nawab's* praise. But it was our kitchen... the Mughlai kitchen... that cooked the Prince's meals.'

'Why three kitchens when the Prince only ate from one?'

'The other two were for his Hindu and European guests... the Prince and the Royal Family were devout Muslims...their *halal* food had to be prepared in a separate kitchen and the other cooks were very jealous.'

Jemima was gripped. 'Jealous?'

'Of course!' bleated Ibrahim. 'There were rivalries everywhere...between princedoms, between kitchens and especially between cooks!'

Ibrahim explained that each of the *Nawab's* kitchens had experts specialising in their own signature dishes and Rafik's area of expertise involved the humble lentil. 'Of course, there were many other excellent dishes that my father could cook but day after day, he made his lentil creations and passed the recipes down to me. I soon became an accomplished chef myself but I was not happy there, Jemima. My father was forever warning me against making friends with the other cooks, who, I was often told, would sell their grandmothers to know the Mughlai trade secrets. But I longed to enter the forbidden kitchens to see how the Hindus and Europeans worked their magic. I grew bored of cooking lentils every day.

When the Prince was entertaining his European guests, I would hear stories of the world beyond India and Jemima, I heard such stories! In cities such as Paris, Milan and Cadiz, chefs were cooking exciting new combinations of food and serving it in fancy establishments called 'restaurants.' I wanted to leave India, Jemima, but I could not speak to my father about my dreams. He would not have understood.'

'Why not?'

'He needed me. He relied on me... and I could not disappoint him. You see, ever since he was young, my father had problems with his eyes and eventually he lost his sight completely. It happened after the British had commandeered the Prince's lands... they were ready to declare Awadh as an annexed state and the Prince was forced to take a smaller residence on the banks of Calcutta. More than half of his servants were released and the weakest and the oldest were the first to go... including my father. I was offered a position in the new Calcutta mansion on the banks of the Hooghly River. In my free time, I would go down to the port and dream of the day I would sail to faraway lands. It was there I heard about my father's death... they say it was his heart, Jemima.'

'I'm sorry to hear that, Ibrahim.'

'I returned to see my stepmother and stepsisters but they did not care for me. My father had left my stepmother his house and money, but still she wanted more. So I opened my wallet and gave her everything. "Take it," I said to her. "I have no more to give. I have no job and no home but it is yours." My stepmother said I was a fool to give up my position in Calcutta. Still, she took my money, Jemima. That woman took all my money!'

I decided that I would never see her or the family again and so the beginning of my new life was bittersweet, for I could follow my dreams but aside from my train fare to Calcutta, I had no more money to my name. I saw the boats anchored in the harbour and the *ghat serangs* looking for men to work as sailors on the ships sailing to Europe. And so I signed up as a lascar and you know what happened next, Jemima... you saved my life.'

Jemima sensed sleep beckoning and closed her eyes. She *could* trust Ibrahim; he *was* her friend and from that moment on, she would sleep soundly knowing that he was in the room. He, on the other hand, was admiring her shifting shadow through the cloth partition. If he could make her forget her foolish notions about becoming a teacher, she would make a most suitable wife. He nestled his head into his pillow and sighed contentedly, whilst his heart fluttered happily inside his chest.

CHAPTER 38

THE IVORY PALACE

After informing the host and hostess that his wife was indefinitely detained in Leeds, William Hayward attended the Malverys' dinner alone. He mentioned that Elizabeth was tending to a mother who was ill with influenza; it was a lie of course but the only excuse he could think to offer. His deceit was further bolstered when he suggested the couple lunch at Carlton House Terrace when his wife returned, knowing full well that Elizabeth would rather die a horrible death than have to make small talk with them. Thus, with his uncomfortable charade put to one side, William took immense pleasure in the time spent with the Colonel and his wife and was thrilled to have finally found a place in which he could belong.

Despite their immense wealth, William thought the Malverys were humble in nature and admired how their love spoke of something special; something more substantial than the tenuous marital unions he had come to know. They possessed a bond built on trust and devotion and it inspired him to yearn for a sense of peace in the relationship he shared with his own wife. And so, when Tara retired, and he and the Colonel retreated into the drawing room, he took the opportunity to find out more. 'What enticed you to India, Colonel?'

'I am a very lucky man, William... a very lucky man. When the old fellow passed on, I inherited it all and my first inclination was to visit the country that had made my family's fortune. Please don't misunderstand me, William, I loved my father and my grandfather very much and I am most grateful for the luxury they have left me to enjoy. My grandfather's wealth enabled me to have the best education and a redundant need to work for a living. I chose to study art and literature. Well... it seemed the natural thing to do having grown up surrounded by such beautiful things. My mother was also an art lover and she taught me a great deal on the subject. She died from fever not long after returning from India and I came back from Oxford to help my father manage the estate like any dutiful son would, I suppose. But I am fully aware that the pleasures in which I bask result from the plunder of riches from my wife's homeland and nothing made me more aware than when I visited India for the very first time.

It was over twenty years ago now. I signed up with the army... I really have no idea why... boredom I think... but I quickly rose through the ranks to command my own regiment. While I was stationed out there, I developed an interest in the people and culture, the customs, the religion and the inherent air of spirituality. I was enthralled by Indian history and heritage and I realised that my grandfather... and many men like him... seized much of that legacy and used stolen Indian treasures to furnish their homes. I donated a share of my fortune to several charities and helped the poor as much and as often as I could. I had schools and orphanages built to clear some part of my conscience... you see, William, I enjoy my lifestyle... my riches... and giving some of it back to India and its people makes me feel better about myself and better about my grandfather.'

'Pardon me for asking, Colonol, but how did you meet Mrs Malvery?'

The Colonel's eyes twinkled. 'I was in Bengal on military business when I was invited to the home of an Indian merchant. This fellow's grandfather had made his fortune by helping the East India Company trade in the Ganga Valley. The family had literally made their fortune overnight from the sale of land in Calcutta... a member of the *bhadralok* classes, I believe. I informed him of my penchant for Indian culture and he held a *nautch* party in my honour. There were dancing girls and poetry recitals and it was there that I met his daughter, who is now, my wife. She was not one of the dancing girls, you understand? But I was instantly taken with her beauty and wit... her calm manner and gentle ways. She put me at ease in a way I have never found with other women. I suppose you find that difficult to understand, Hayward?'

William cast his eyes to the floor trying to conceal the fact that he *did* understand.

'Fortunately, her father was an anglophile and agreed to our courtship, but I knew... I knew she was the one for me the moment she graced the room. Now we have two splendid sons to show for our union. They are both away at college and I can safely say that we are happy... very happy indeed. She accepts me for who I am and the way I am... and I hold her in the highest regard. And what of your own wife, William? How did she enjoy India? Did it agree with her?'

William fidgeted in his seat. 'Mostly... I'm afraid she became rather homesick.'

'Mrs Malvery is *so* looking forward to meeting her. When do you think she'll return?'

'Soon, I imagine.'

'I expect Mrs Hayward will be interested in seeing my wife's jewellery collection...it's quite a spectacle,' the Colonel remarked. 'What do you say?'

William wondered how long he must keep up his foolish pretence. He thought of the lies he had told the couple and felt wretched and unworthy of their friendship.

'My dear fellow, are you all right?' the Colonel asked, noticing the sweat on William's brow. 'Are you sitting rather too close to the fire?'

'I'm sorry Colonel, but my wife will not be coming to your home. She will not be interested in seeing your jewellery collection and she certainly won't be interested in meeting you or your wife. She abhors India and everything to do with it.'

Colonel Malvery blinked repeatedly as William continued on. 'Elizabeth and I are living separate lives. She is staying with her family in Leeds in order to be as far away from me as possible.'

'May I ask why?'

'Because... I had an affair back in India.'

The Colonel swirled the liquid in his glass and scoffed. 'My dear fellow, name me a man in India, indeed the world, who hasn't engaged in an affair of some sort. Give her time... let her have her rant. She'll soon calm down and forget about it.'

'It was with a native woman in Murshidhabad. She was from one of the *bidi* houses.'

The taut lines around Colonel Malvery's eyes relaxed into a realisation of some sort. 'The Ivory Palace...' he muttered. 'I knew I'd seen you before...'

It was easy to confess to the Colonel. He listened patiently as William told him the tale of Sonal. Colonel Malvery knew who she was. He had heard tales of her seductive beauty and talent and had even seen her perform at the Palace, where he had also noticed William Hayward watching her every move. Rolling the stem of his brandy glass between his thumb and forefinger, he said, 'Were you content with your wife before you left for India?'

'Content enough.'

'Content enough? Content enough?' the host jeered. 'Do you love your wife, William?'

'Well...yes...'

Malvery clenched his fists to make his next point. 'I mean love in the sense of... you cannot bear to be parted from her... your heart thumps at the thought of her... and your passion for her, and *her* alone, pulses through you like a raging river. Or do you feel indifference? I wouldn't blame you if you did. Marriages are often based on matters other than love and affection.'

William stared into the fire.

'I am not here to judge you... especially on your choice of mistress. Indeed your affair is of no concern of mine. But I will say this... I am sorry to see a young fellow so bereft of spirit. You see... the one belief I possess is that life is so precious, so fleeting and real love between people so rare to find that I would rather be alone than live a life with someone devoid of love and passion. Now there are those who would strongly disagree with me for saying so and they are perfectly entitled to their opinions, but I am an honest man and I speak my mind and I do as I see fit to make myself happy. And that is all I can say to you.'

The Colonel's words made William's brain spin. 'Elizabeth will not forgive me.'

'Perhaps she never will. But in my humble opinion, it is better to be alone than suffer a dead relationship. Both parties become ever so embittered.'

'Are you saying I divorce her? I have no grounds for divorce and she cannot prove my affair. I cannot stop thinking about my life in India. I was happy there... somehow I felt I belonged. Now I feel trapped and hopeless... as if I'm going mad.'

There was a soft knock at the door and Kalsi entered, asking to be of service. The Colonel sent him away with an order for hot tea and then hushed his voice to a whisper. 'Dear fellow, I cannot tell you what to do... and the stigma from a scandal can be the cause of one's downfall. But you are a young man and you should be savouring life. It seems to me that you and your wife are two very different people. I may be wrong, of course, but I'm willing to guess that you married without getting to know each other's ways. Am I right?'

William nodded. 'But I want everything to be all right, Colonel.'

'Hmm,' the Colonel said. 'Are you sure about that?'

'Yes, I must try to make things right for the sake of my children.'

The Colonel nodded and sighed. 'Well as you say, William. One can only try, dear fellow. One can only try.'

CHAPTER 39
POLITICS AND FEATHERS

Jemima earned her keep at the Shadwell Inn by mangling clothes, scrubbing work surfaces and sweeping floors. She helped Ibrahim round up the chickens and took heed as he placed half in one pen and the remaining half in another. 'Those are for Muslim customers... *halal*,' he said, pointing to the right pen. Pointing to the left, he said, 'Those are for the rest of the customers... *haram*.' He then opened one of the coop doors, grabbed the nearest chicken by its neck and did not warn Jemima of the subsequent beheading that followed. She had witnessed her father sever the heads of chickens on many occasions but this time, the spurting blood made her run away and vomit in the yard. Later that morning, seated alone with blood and feathers stuck to her fingers and the limp, headless bodies of poultry strewn about her feet, Jemima lurched sideways, wondering if she would faint. Her head was hot and her armpits soggy and since the work was not particularly taxing, she questioned what might be causing her feverish condition. The sight and stench of the slaughtered chickens could not have helped and she concluded that the tussle with the children must have affected her more than she had first thought. Her back ached badly and she longed to sleep but there were chickens to pluck and floors to be swept and later on she would have to lend a hand when the inn opened its doors. Now her life revolved around the tavern and its thirsty minions and soon the place would be heaving with festive revellers, clamouring for alcohol and food.

Christmas passed and Sarah sauntered into the kitchen, announcing that Mehta was asking for Jemima. 'I think she's got an admirer!' she teased.

'*If only he were that,' Jemima thought.* Having an admirer was easier to deal with than being associated with a political activist.

'I'll tell him to leave,' Ibrahim said, peering through a haze of steam and spitting broth.

Jemima dried her hands on her apron. 'No Ibrahim, I promised to work for him.'

'That fellow is nothing but trouble. It is better you do not go,' he said, venturing out from behind the stove.

'He helped me, Ibrahim. Now I must help him.'

Ibrahim bristled at her defiance. 'Don't allow him to bully you.'

'I won't,' she said, walking rebelliously through the kitchen doors.

Mehta was seated beside three fellows in the corner furthest away from the pub counter and Jemima recognised the other faces from the first day she came to the inn. The young Indian, Vikram, was sitting amongst them. He pulled out a chair as she approached. 'Sit...sit,' he said, overjoyed at seeing her again.

'I have to get back to work soon,' she said.

'This won't take long,' Mehta insisted. His head turned when the inn doors flew open and in walked Mr Meade singing *Sweet Molly Malone.*

'Alive, alive, oh! Alive, Alive, oh!
Crying cockles and muscles,
Alive, alive oh!'

Tipping his hat, Meade greeted his clientele with vigorous hand-shakes and jubilant hellos, but his geniality diminished when he spied Mehta and his band of followers lounging in the corner. 'Oi!' he cried, pointing a finger at the Indian.

'Good day, Mr Meade!' bellowed Mehta. 'Fine day, today!'

'I've been hearing stories about you,' the publican shouted.

Mehta folded his arms and grinned. 'I'm a popular fellow, Mr Meade.'

'It looks like you're popular with the peelers 'n' all,' hissed Meade. 'Now listen 'ere,' he warned, his tummy quivering as he said it. 'I know you're a troublemaker and I don't want you or your lackeys spouting your rubbish in my inn. The last thing I need is the old bill giving me what for 'cause I let the likes of you sup in my establishment.'

Mehta's insolence sizzled. 'I wouldn't *dream* of it, Mr Meade.'

'Now don't act cocky with me! If I so much as see you do anything short of downing my ale and eatin' my pies, you're out. Understand? Out!' His eyes throbbed at the sight of Jemima. ''ere! Why aren't you working back there?' he cried, pointing to the kitchen.

'She's resting,' Vikram replied.

Meade twiddled his moustache furiously. 'Well, don't take too long... and it would do you good to think about the company you keep!' He threw a last harsh look in their direction and headed off to the bar and Mehta waited until he was well out of earshot before attempting to speak to Jemima again.

'The bag I am going to pass you contains a pen, a bottle of ink and some writing paper. There is also a leaflet... like the one I showed you that day, remember?'

Of course, Jemima remembered. How could she forget? He launched an almighty attack on her shortly afterwards.

'Copy the writing onto the papers,' he ordered. 'It is most important that you do not show anyone, not even your friend, the cook, you understand? Hide it well and I will return in two days' time. Bring me the finished papers and I will bring you some money.'

He placed the bag onto Jemima's thighs and she grabbed it whilst Mr Meade's attention was turned to some men at the counter. Holding it to one side of her skirt, she walked over to the cellar and scurried down the steps, where, at the bottom, she opened up her travelling valise and plunged the bag of seditious items in and amongst her worldly goods.

Thankfully, Ibrahim fell asleep fairly swiftly that night, enabling Jemima to make a start on her clandestine task. Peering inside the bag, she saw two thick rolls of paper fastened with string, one bottle of ink and a pen, just as Mehta had mentioned. There was writing on the inside of one roll and smoothing down the curled edges, she read the following message:

Home Rule for India
Free India! Expel the British!
The Free India Movement accuse the British of stealing our jobs, our land, our wealth, our voice and our dignity. For over two hundred years, the British have plundered the Motherland.
Brothers and Sisters, it is time to rise up against the Empire.
Meeting 1ˢᵗ January 1867, 7pm.
Wells Warehouse, Wells Street E.1.

The meeting was to be held on the forthcoming Tuesday – New Year's Day – and by the time she had written the twentieth copy, her eyes stung from squinting too much in the candlelight. Ibrahim mumbled nonsensically in his sleep; aside from that, all was quiet. Fifty blank pages needed to be filled and she decided to write half then and half the following evening. Only five were left before she could settle down to sleep that night and she battled fatigue to finish the last one. When at last the deed was done, she secured the stopper on the inkbottle and gathered up the newly written leaflets that had been placed in a row to dry. After tying them securely and confining them to the darkness of Mehta's bag, she rolled the pen and inkbottle within the handkerchief provided and stowed all the items in the small sack entrusted into her possession. Worn out but satisfied in her achievement, Jemima blew out the candle and rested.

She finished the task the following Friday and the resulting relief was overwhelmingly immense. Her association with the belligerent student was at long last coming to an end and when he came by the next day, just as he said he would, she passed the concealed items into his hands and watched as he handed the bag to the man on his left. But then the man on his right handed him another, which was promptly delivered into Jemima's lap.

'Here are fifty more,' Mehta whispered. 'I will return on Sunday.'

Displeasure poured out from Jemima's veins as she seized the bag and wrapped it within her shawl. She stormed off towards the cellar, wondering how long she would have to keep on paying her debt.

It took forever for Ibrahim to fall asleep that night. He had been expanding his knowledge of English cuisine by studying the recipes in *Mrs Beeton's Book of Household Management*. The book had belonged to Jenny but she had been ordered to part with it soon after being stripped of her title as Shadwell Inn's resident cook. Ibrahim had already mastered a few English recipes: bread and butter pudding, fish and chips and oxtail soup, and that night, he had been chatting incessantly about the favourable comments his steak and kidney pies had received. He had added his own special touch by experimenting with different herbs and spices, and now that Mr Meade was beginning to make money, he had permitted his new chef to do almost whatever he wanted.

Jemima was especially fond of their nightly chats but secretly, she was willing Ibrahim to fall asleep in order to get on with the task at hand. Sure enough, he dozed off and this time she noticed that there was an extra item residing inside Mehta's bag: a folded piece of parchment with something hiding inside. When she opened it, one shilling toppled onto her pillow. She read: *'One shilling for fifty copies.'*

Mehta had been true to his word and with her efforts now rewarded, Jemima executed her errand with pleasure. But there was a different message on the paper this time.

Indian citizens of every caste and creed,
Rise up and fight the British!
Claim liberation for the Motherland!
The Free India Movement will march from Victoria Park to Parliament.
March with us at 1pm on 5ᵗʰ January 1867

She completed the leaflets over the nights that remained and Mehta came to collect them on New Year's Eve. The place was packed with carousers gathered to welcome in the brand new year and concealed among them, Mehta completed his transaction, undetected by Meade. Jemima was half-expecting another bag to drop into her lap but was pleasantly surprised when a pouch of money appeared instead. 'You did well,' Mehta said. 'But there is something else I need you to do.'

Jemima clenched her teeth, bit into her lip and listened to what he had to say.

'I need you to hand some leaflets out at the meeting tomorrow. I will pay you after.'

The idea of handing out leaflets seemed easy enough. She agreed.

'I will come for you tomorrow. Make an excuse to Meade,' he said, vanishing within the mob of merrymakers.

It was not easy to get the evening off. New Year's Day was one of the inn's busiest nights and Jemima was needed to work in the kitchens. Ibrahim argued in her defence, saying that ever since she had arrived, she had worked like a dog and was due some time off. Meade reluctantly agreed but insisted she make up the hours on another occasion. When asked of her plans that night, Jemima informed Ibrahim that she needed to complete her work for Mehta.

'Where are you going to complete this *work*?' he asked suspiciously.

She reasoned that she had to be going to Wells Warehouse, just like Mehta's leaflet had said, yet, she replied, 'I don't know... I didn't ask, but I'm sure it is close by. Don't worry Ibrahim, Mehta is meeting me outside and he will bring me back.'

'You don't know where he is taking you? Jemima... this is very foolish. I forbid you to go.'

'I must go. He helped me in the alley. He bought me a meal. Now he is paying me to do some work and I need money to get out of this country, Ibrahim. I want to go home.'

Ibrahim's heart sagged each time Jemima voiced her intent to return to India, but he dared not argue, for he noticed something different about her. She had been subdued and frightened when she first arrived at the Shadwell Inn, but within the past few weeks, she had grown resolute and knew her own mind. He could not be entirely sure if this was a good thing for an Indian female and he worried about the company she kept. And though he had no claim over her whatsoever, he resolved to remain in the background and keep a protective eye on her, and perhaps in time, he would persuade her to stay.

As far as Jemima was concerned, the less Ibrahim knew the better. She agreed that any association with Mehta could only spell trouble, but she had to admit that she was grateful for his money, though she was more than wary of the man's irascible nature. Nevertheless, she would do as he asked and hand out the leaflets, then she would collect her dues and leave. After tonight, she would heed Ibrahim's counsel and keep her distance from the quick-tempered Indian and his hot-blooded politics. After tonight, she and Mehta were even.

CHAPTER 40

WELLS WAREHOUSE

The world beyond the Shadwell Inn was a daunting prospect for Jemima, but when she saw the snow on the pavement outside, illuminated by the yellow flare of the street lamps, the scene appeared almost bewitching. It was just like the pictures she had seen in Sophie's books, for the white surroundings and crisp evening air evoked a dream-like quality to her vision of London in winter. A man leaning against a lamppost nearby turned out to be Vikram, devoted follower of Mehta and unbeknown to Jemima, her admirer. Their eyes had met on a few occasions but they had never exchanged any proper conversation. He beckoned her over and asked her questions. He wanted to know about her family, her origins and then asked about Ibrahim and Mr Meade. He seemed good-humoured enough but she thought him far too inquisitive for her liking. 'There is a coffee house in Holborn where coloureds are welcome,' he said, crossing the street. 'I would be most happy to take you there.'

Jemima did not want to go to a coffee house where coloureds were welcome; she wanted to go home, to India. Yet, she told him that she would think about his proposal and hoped his endless chatter would soon cease. He stopped at a street corner and began conversing with a group of students shivering outside a shabby old building. Jemima left them to their talk and watched the snow turn to sleet as it hit the cobbled pavements. The windows of the edifice were smashed and masked in a splattering of yellowy-white bird droppings and though there was no visible indication to the establishment's name, Jemima knew she was standing outside Wells Warehouse.

The foyer inside was dirty and draughty and a dilapidated staircase wound its way into the creepy darkness above. Mouldy crates gathered dust below the high flaking ceilings and two large bricks held open the main set of doors. At the other end of the chilly hall, Mehta and his collaborators were busy meting out stacks of papers. He caught sight of Jemima and barked his orders without even saying hello. 'Take these and hand them out to everyone,' he said, shoving a wad of leaflets into her hand.

Mounds of pamphlets – all written by hand – sat in rows upon a long wooden bench. Foolishly, Jemima had imagined that the leaflets *she* had inscribed would somehow be the only ones on offer, but she saw hundreds more written by different hands but all bearing the same rebellious message. A varied crowd graced the warehouse that evening: Irish activists seeing close parallels between their own fight and the Indian cause had come with ideas of forming an alliance. Members of a nationalist movement from the Ottoman Empire took their seats beside the Egyptian separatists, who sympathised with India's call for independence. Lascars, Indian soldiers, beggars and tramps had also arrived, but the latter two had followed the crowd in search of some shelter from the freezing weather outside. It seemed that Mehta had chosen a good day – New Year's Day – when the English masses were recovering from their merrymaking, leaving the poor, the starving and the disillusioned to search for justice in his arms. Jemima distributed the leaflets to anyone who walked through the doors and smiled when she encountered a few she had written herself. When the students were quite sure there were no more people to come, the doors were bolted and everyone took their positions around the hall.

It was cold and dark but several lighted candles and one or two lamps turned up full flare provided some meagre warmth. Jemima removed her gloves and lingered beside a lamp, grateful for the little heat it bestowed upon her fingers. Some individuals were lucky enough to have obtained a chair but most sat on the boxes heaved in from the grimy foyer. Vikram entered, pushing a crate through a side door. He invited Jemima to sit down and wiped the dust from its surface as she perched herself on the edge.

Mehta welcomed the crowd but that was the extent of the niceties. Eloquent and masterful, he possessed all the right gesticulations to match his stirring words as he instantly launched into a rant on the evils of the British Empire. '*They say that we are heathens because we worship many gods... that we run around bare-chested in the jungle eating one another! How arrogant is the Englishman! How ignorant is the Englishman! They say we are incapable of running our own affairs, that we know nothing of government and law. But we are lawyers and doctors, and businessmen! And we are scientists and teachers and poets! India is a nation of great authors and writers. We have learnt the language of the Englishman and speak it better than their people. Wherever we turn, they try to stop us! They stop us from learning and furthering ourselves. But we have learnt! And we have overcome the obstacles they have thrown in our path and now we are ready to fight!*'

Apart from the education she had received at the hands of Dr Mukherjee's wife, Jemima had never possessed a reason to dwell on matters beyond her role as an ayah. But seated in the draughty hallway of a ramshackle warehouse in East London, she found Navin Mehta's words robustly empowering and for the first time in her life, she was really made to think.

'They say India is not civilized... that we are savages and barbarians. But it is the British who have raped our country and plundered its riches. It is they who are the savages! It is they who are the barbarians! And now it is time to take back what is ours!'

Bursts of applause echoed between the warehouse walls as Mehta's gamut of articulate expressions whipped the onlookers into a frenzy of rebellion. Jemima realised that she was applauding too. She was not sure whether she liked Mehta, but she now agreed that the British were savages, especially Sylvester Lawrence. He was a savage and a barbarian.

Mehta suddenly raised a hand into the air and clenched his fist tightly. *'India for Indians!'* Everyone leapt to their feet and repeated his words. The mantra swept through the hallway, inciting stragglers, strays and drunks, who had accidentally wandered inside, to whistle and chant along with the sympathisers. Vikram stamped and shrieked the motto of the movement; others whistled, cheered and clapped along. But amongst the riotous cheers and mutinous rapture, nobody noticed that the main doors had swung upon and whistles of another kind were being blown.

Within seconds, the Metropolitan Police had rammed their way into the warehouse and were heading straight for Mehta's group of men. Bedlam exploded and everyone dispersed. Some escaped by toppling boxes in the path of policemen, whilst others removed their shoes and lobbed them against the windowpanes, risking certain injury as they squeezed their bodies through shards of broken glass. Too slow to run and hide, the vagrants were rounded up and threatened into submission, whilst beyond them, Mehta and his men retreated into the darkness like cornered animals. With no means of escape, Mehta ran headlong into the arms of the law but was beaten into surrender and warned not to flee.

Frozen with fear against a wall, Jemima felt someone's cold fingers coil around her wrist and saw that they belonged to Vikram. He whisked her through the side door and down a corridor and led her towards an old kitchen, where he managed to unbolt a door and heave it open with all his might. After jumping over a low wall, he turned back to help Jemima do the same and together, they fled across icy grass and slippery cobblestones, stopping briefly in darkly lit corners to clutch their stomachs and pant clouds of cold air back into the night. 'It will be safer in the alleyways,' Vikram insisted, continuing on until the privacy of a narrow passageway drew him within its shady walls. 'That was close,' he said, checking to see if they had been followed.

Jemima panted wildly. 'What will happen to Mehta and the others?'

'He will be arrested and charged. Someone must have found out about the meeting and told the police, or... someone betrayed us. We have to fight to make sure that he and the others are freed.'

As inspirational as Mehta had been, it occurred to Jemima that she had done quite enough fighting for him and his cause. Now, all she pined for was one of Ibrahim's meals and the comfort of her cellar bed. 'Is it safe to go back now?'

Vikram shivered. 'Not yet, the police will still be around in the streets. It is better to wait.'

Jemima remembered that she had left her gloves back in the warehouse and paced the cobbles, scowling at the thought of having to obtain another pair. It dawned on her too that she would probably never receive payment for the work she had done that night.

'Stop worrying,' Vikram said, sweeping his fingers along the edge of her skirt. 'I will look after you.'

She carried on brooding as he rose to his feet. His face was bathed in darkness; hers was bathed in his drifting shadow. He studied her facial features in the dim alley light – the curve of her cheek, the slant of her nose, the far-reaching eyelashes on her large doe-like eyes. 'You are pretty,' he whispered and a ghostly wisp of air slipped out of his mouth. She felt his arm creep around her waist as she moved back against the wet alley wall.

'No,' she said, but his icy finger slid down her cheek.

Vikram pressed his mouth upon her lips and she was surprised by its warmth. Quickly, she pulled away but he locked his leg between her thighs and nudged her back against the wall. The face of Sylvester Lawrence loomed again and she closed her eyes to stave off the memory. When she opened them again, Vikram had taken his place.

Jemima reasoned that if she could not trust a fellow Indian, then who could she trust? It seemed that bad men came in all colours, shapes and forms. 'No,' she silently said to herself. 'Never again,' and as part of her spirit irrevocably hardened, she raised her imprisoned leg and aimed it speedily into Vikram's crotch. He screamed in pain before throwing his hands around his injured groin and stared at her fiercely.

'Coolie bitch!' he yelled.

She could have turned and ran there and then, but Jemima chose to remain for a moment in order to slap Vikram hard on the face. Not only that, she pushed him against the alley wall and watched as he smacked his head and tripped over his feet before landing with a thud on the icy cobblestones.

She was running again. Furthermore, she was running in the opposite direction to the Shadwell Inn. Undesirables were skulking on every corner: drunkards, tramps, swindlers and thieves. Someone shrieked and a cat prowling in an alley fled across her feet. She was beside herself with fear but she would take on any man or beast who tried to block her way. The hollering stranger was a joker, a prankster; a festive reveller and with his drunken breath, he wished her a 'Happy New Year.' He had meant no harm yet she continued to run on, darting in and out of slushy puddles, bumping into people in the dark, dreary roads. She took a chance down a street a sight more respectable than the dingy passageways that had gone before and turned a corner, thinking she would wither away and die. She collapsed to her knees with her head in her hands and did not notice a young woman peering at her from the other side of the street. But for two rouged cheeks, the girl's face was coated in a thick layer of white talcum powder. 'You all right, ducky?' she asked.

'Leave me alone!' Jemima screamed.

The girl jumped back with a start. 'I was only asking... ungrateful cow!' She grimaced and left Jemima descending into abject desperation.

Jemima raised her head and looked about. She registered the street sign and glanced back down in a heavy sulk. Seconds later, she clambered to her feet. Princess St E.1... *Princess St. E1...* the same street written on Ruby's piece of paper. She ran past a row of dismal buildings, forgetting decorum to call out Nuwani's name. She knocked on doors and pulled on bell chains, and then scrambled across the road to do the same. There were hardly any houses in the area; only bleak-looking establishments shut up for the night. She desperately tried remembering the number Ruby had written down for Nuwani, but the road grew darker and the buildings more drab and in a moment of madness, she screamed out Nuwani's name as loud as her lungs would allow.

The property situated further up on the corner appeared just as gloomy and insipid as the rest that went before it, but if Jemima had taken a closer look, she would have noticed an edifice much smarter in form with a light glowing at one of the windows above. Pressed against the pane, several faces tried glimpsing the hopeless creature shrieking in the road, whilst beneath them, a shiny black door opened and a trio of female figures stepped out onto a path.

Spasms shot through Jemima's stomach. Clutching her belly, she fell to her knees and did not hear one of the women whisper something to the second. The third hurried back into the house and Jemima witnessed her as only a vague and murky shadow. A sea of lumpy fluid suddenly burst through her lips and then someone else stooped low and held onto her arm. A mane of auburn curls tumbled into view and a woman touched her lightly on the shoulder. 'There, there, dear.'

Jemima was overcome by a stream of surging cramps. She tried to speak but her frail voice was overwhelmed by the soft, mellow sound of another's. 'Jemima?'

'Nuwani?'

Nuwani looked different; very different.

'So, you do know her?' the redhead said.

'Yes. I wasn't sure before but I am now,' Nuwani replied.

The third female came shuffling along the pavement, holding a blanket in her arms. She hurled it around Jemima's shoulders and helped raise her from the ground. Jemima's sore eyes searched for Nuwani but everything began spinning into a blur and Nuwani's face seemed to melt into a mist. The scene grew dim and the lamplight burned out and before she knew it, she had fainted in her old friend's arms.

CHAPTER 41

MRS WILSON

Jemima had grown accustomed to the noises Ibrahim made when he rose to leave for the markets in the morning. He would try his best to be as quiet as a mouse but she would wake up and see his meandering shadow through the cloth partition, pulling on an overcoat or shuffling the numerous pieces of papers, upon which, his recipes were haphazardly written. The cellar was a dark and dismal place, but he would always light a lamp and warm the room by burning some wood in the old stove that Mr Meade had brought down from the kitchen. However, Jemima's sleep seemed deathly that morning and she stirred on a bed that was unusually soft. When she opened her eyes, the cellar's wooden stair frame had vanished and her eyes looked up to a white stucco ceiling instead. Fortunately, the musty odour of mildew was no longer displeasing to her nose, but much to her dismay, Ibrahim's mattress was no longer there.

A ray of light streaming in from a large bow window illuminated an empty glass coated with a faint residue of white powder. Jemima wondered where it had come from and then noticed that her fingers were clutching a pink-coloured bedspread. Noises rose from one side of the room and peering over her bedspread, she saw the petite figure of a girl crouching down by the mantel-piece. She was stoking coals on the fire and appeared unsteady on her feet, but she managed to straighten herself to show Jemima that she was not so much a girl but a dark-skinned woman of Caribbean descent with a yard or so of orange coloured cotton sheathed tightly around her head. Jemima had a faint recollection of already having seen the woman but before she could ask any questions, she tottered out of the room, banging the coal bucket as she went. 'She's awake... she's awake!' she cried.

Jemima dropped her head back onto her pillow and sighed. Her parched and tender throat longed for some water, for her breath smelt vile and she could hardly find her voice. A damp towel would have come in handy to wipe away the debris of sleep from her eyes and she yearned for someone to soothe her rough and tired skin. Somebody had dressed her in a clean cotton nightdress and she noticed its lace-trimmed sleeves when she attempted to climb out of bed. *'What has happened to my clothes?' she thought.* A moment later, she saw them draped over a chair and whoever had clothed her had been kind enough to fold her blouse and petticoat too. Her underskirt was placed on the seat and her outer skirt was hanging neatly across it, but halfway down the hem, Jemima spied some patches of blood.

She recalled the doomed meeting at the warehouse and remembered running away from Vikram – the blood must have resulted from her falling in the street. A woman with red hair arrived and then Nuwani. Was it really Nuwani she saw last night? Finally, a third woman appeared with a blanket... that is why the woman stoking coals seemed familiar, for it was the same woman who had helped her to her feet last night. Jemima heard soft footsteps along the corridor outside. The door opened and there she was standing in the doorway: Nuwani. She ran towards the bed and hurled her arms around Jemima. The tearful embrace was witnessed by an audience of females, eager to catch a glimpse of the convalescing stranger. Shortly after, the redhead arrived to observe the touching spectacle. 'Off you go girls!' she cried, dispersing the others. 'How are you feeling, my dear?' she asked, planting her behind on the bed.

Jemima attempted to rise. 'I am feeling much better, Madam. Thank you,' she croaked.

'You mustn't get up, dear. By the state of you last night, you've had quite a time of it,' the redhead said. 'The doctor says you'll be as right as rain after you've had a good rest. Anyway, I'll get Butterfly to bring you something to eat and I'll leave you and Nuwi to get re-acquainted.'

Before leaving, she admired her reflection in the small looking glass on the wall and walked off with the skirts of her magnificent green dress undulating behind her.

'Nuwi?' asked Jemima.

'Yes, that is what they call me here.'

'The lady is very kind. Who is she?'

'That's Mrs Wilson. She is... very kind.'

Jemima noticed that Nuwani's hair was especially glossy and there was kohl etched along her eyelids, bestowing a seductive charm to her face. 'You look well, Nuwani... so pretty.'

Nuwani lowered her decorated eyes to the floor and reached for Jemima's hand. 'I'm sorry, Jemima. I'm not sure how to tell you this.'

'Tell me what?'

'You lost your baby.'

Jemima's heartbeat began to stammer.

'Yesterday evening... when we found you in the street... you were weak and you fainted. We found blood on your skirt and Mrs Wilson called Dr Rose. He said that you had been eight weeks with child but yesterday... in the street... you miscarried.'

Jemima's head throbbed with the absurdity of Nuwani's declaration. 'No, no, no. The doctor is wrong. I am... I was not pregnant. I have bruises and scars from the children... that day in the alley. They tried to steal my ticket and they kicked me! That is why there was blood... the children!'

She was out of bed and delirious with denial but Nuwani caught her by the shoulders and guided her back under the bedcovers. 'You did not know?'

Jemima felt as though she would suffocate. Forced to remember Sylvester Lawrence again, she gripped the bedcovers tightly and finally divulged her horrific ordeal through an avalanche of tears.

'Jemima, you are not to blame.'

'Help me Nuwani...' Jemima appealed. 'You said to come and find you if I needed help. You do work here, don't you? Is this where you stay? There must be work here. Your clothes are new and you look so well. Is there work for me too? I will do anything... cook, clean. *Anything!* Then we can save our money and go home.'

How it pained Nuwani to think of home. Her family must think her dead by now.

'Ask the lady, please,' Jemima pleaded, tugging on Nuwani's arm 'Your friend...Mrs Wilson. Ask her if there is any work for me.'

Nuwani's once spirited eyes seemed jaded of late and there was a strange tone in her voice whenever she spoke. 'All right, Jemima.'

Butterfly staggered inside the room carrying a tray of toast and tea. She spilled a little as she crossed the floor. 'Food for the Miss...' she said, in a thick, lilting accent.

'Eat Jemima and rest,' insisted Nuwani. 'I will go and speak to Mrs Wilson.' She kissed Jemima on the forehead and quickly left the room.

'Yes, eat Miss,' Butterfly said. 'You need anything else... just call for Butterfly.'

Jemima's eyes strayed along the length of the maid's skirts.

'You wondering 'bout this ol' thing?' Butterfly bellowed, smacking her right thigh. '*Everyone* wonders 'bout this! Well I'll tell you, Miss...'cause I's not ashamed of it. My old master beat me so hard one day, he broke my leg and it ain't never been right since. So there you are, Miss. You don't have to wonder no more.'

'I'm sorry,' Jemima muttered.

'Is no problem, Miss. No problem at all. I's come back and fetch the tray later.'

Butterfly smiled and limped out of the room.

Mrs Wilson was munching on her favourite sesame crackers when she heard a light rapping on her partially open office door. When she saw it was Nuwani, she abandoned the perusal of her accounts and ledger books and immediately invited her in.

'Close the door behind you,' she said, brushing some cracker crumbs from her skirts. 'How did she take the news about her baby?'

'She did not know about the baby.'

'Didn't know about her own baby? What do you mean didn't know?'

'She did not know that she was with child.'

'What happened to the father? Did he abandon her? Did she love him?'

'No. She did not love him,' Nuwani said. 'He forced himself on her.'

Mrs Wilson patted her lips with a napkin. 'Poor girl! I hope the scoundrel gets what he deserves.'

Nuwani's eyes drifted over the mound of papers and books on Mrs Wilson's desk until they settled on the handsome figure of the woman herself. 'She needs work, Mrs Wilson.'

'I thought she might,' the lady smiled. 'Well, even in the state she's in, I can see that she's a pretty little thing... much like your lovely self, Nuwi. A few weeks of rest and relaxation and a good meal or two will bring the colour back into her cheeks. Come to think of it… I can see her being quite popular.'

'She says she will do anything to repay your kindness. She can cook, clean, mend and sew… she can help Butterfly with the chores.'

'Cook? Clean? What are you talking about, Nuwi?'

Mrs Wilson paused and then her face grew fat with glee.

'Wait a minute! You haven't told her have you?' she cried, hurling her hands into the air. 'Hah!' she squawked, clapping her hands over and over again. 'You haven't told her, Nuwi! You haven't told her!'

PART FIVE

CHAPTER 42
MEHTA REVISITED

For the time being, Nuwani and Ivy Wilson thought it best not to tell Jemima that she was convalescing in a house of ill repute, and though Nuwani was grateful for the reprieve, she spent hours agonising over how to tell her friend that she had since become a prostitute. Of course, Ivy Wilson withheld the nature of her business with an ulterior motive in hand. With only two women originating from the East Indies in her collection of high-class whores, she needed to recruit more; such was the demand. And to avoid the possibility of the potential newcomer fleeing in disgust – if she were to find out too soon – Ivy took exceptional care of Jemima by showering her with kindness and abundant understanding. Jemima's honourable nature told Ivy that it would be exceptionally difficult for her to leave knowing she owed a debt of gratitude to those who had gone out of their way to help her. And to lure Jemima further into the trap, Ivy instructed all her girls to tender the explanation that was given to the authorities, that is, the establishment was a 'work agency' and 'lodging house' for women of the colonies. Hence Jemima was transferred to a room on the third floor and instructed to rest until her health had improved. Whenever she needed assistance, she had to ring a bell for Butterfly, whose mismatched footsteps were often heard echoing along the corridor.

Two weeks passed before Dr Rose was finally able to declare Jemima fit and well, but with endless hours to ponder the vicissitudes of life, the loss of her child pestered Jemima's conscience more than she cared to admit. She grieved in private but her stifled weeping could be heard late at night by anyone who crept past her door. She never could quite explain why she cried for the creature, for it had resulted from an act of violence perpetrated by an odious man. Still, the loss wounded her deeply and she tormented herself with the consequential actions she may or may not have taken had she known that she was with child. Eventually, she tucked away the dark episode, pledging that its shadowy memory would not blight her spirit ever again.

Butterfly's tender touches made her yearn for Madhu. The maid bathed, dressed and tended to her in an almost obsessive way. What a curious creature she was, Jemima thought. Aside from her one damaged leg, the rest of Butterfly's body was as perfectly formed as a body could be. Her eyes were sleek and there were equine qualities to her face that at certain angles made her look impossibly beautiful. She did exactly as she was told and was fiercely loyal to Mrs Wilson, and after a few moments of questioning from Jemima, it became apparent why.

'If not for Missus Wilson, I's probably be dead now. She brung me over from Louisiana... won me in a game of poker the night my master almos' beat me to death. He was one of her ...' At that point, Butterfly's eyes grew large and she buried her top teeth into her bottom lip as she hastily returned to the point. 'I's so grateful to Missus Wilson that I begged to be her maid, even though my leg never healed right. But I'd do anything for Missus Wilson 'cause she freed me from the devil himself.'

Butterfly's anecdotes of a life spent in Louisiana were fascinating enough, but with nothing to do all day, Jemima soon grew restless having been weaned on commands and hard work. She asked Mrs Wilson if she could improve her English by perusing a newspaper or two, and so the next time Butterfly appeared with the usual breakfast of toast and tea, a copy of *The East London Chronicle* lay folded on the tray.

Jemima perused all articles concerning India, but it was while she was circumventing the latest reports on science and literature that she stumbled upon the following headline:

'TRIAL DATE ASSIGNED FOR LEADER
OF THE FREE INDIA MOVEMENT'

With the page almost touching her nose, she scrutinized the report on her former knight in shining armour.

The trial of Navin Mehta, notorious leader of The Free India Movement, continues to engage the anxious solicitude and grave interest of both Her Majesty's government and the great general public. Mehta, a former student of law, arrested at Wells Warehouse, Wells Street, E.1, New Year's Day 1867, for preaching hatred against Queen, Country and Empire will be charged alongside his co-conspirators, Amithav Seth, Raju Viswanath, (son of C.P.Viswanath, proprietor of Wells Warehouse), and Vikram Bonnerjee (caught by The Metropolitan Police soon after fleeing) at Bow Street Magistrate Court, Bow, East London on Tuesday 23rd April 1867.

So the police had caught up with Vikram too. Fearing what would happen to them all, Jemima decided that they would be found guilty of course, and then what? She would have been languishing in prison herself had she not fled from Vikram when she did.

And how fortunate she was to have run in the opposite direction, for if she had returned to the inn, there was a distinct possibility that she would have been arrested too. Her mind then wandered to Ibrahim – poor Ibrahim – he must be out of his mind with worry. When the opportunity arose, she would try to send word letting him know that she was alive and well. But for now, she would have to lie low, at least until this business with Mehta had well and truly blown over.

Ibrahim had indeed been out of his mind with worry and had been ever since Jemima failed to return on New Year's Day. Everyone at the inn was talking about the storming of a political meeting in a warehouse nearby and Mr Meade suspected that Mehta and his cronies had to be involved. That fateful night, Ibrahim had sat up into the early hours, waiting for Jemima to knock upon the door. The next morning, he had stared at her empty bed and then left the premises to ask the locals if she had been seen in the vicinity. As news of Mehta's arrest reached everyone, he rushed to the local police station to see if Jemima had been detained. Returning none the wiser, he blamed himself for not stopping her when he had had the chance.

Meade's comments added insult to injury. 'If something's happened to her... it's her own fault! Foolish girl! I warned her, didn't I? I warned her not to keep company with that vermin!'

And some might say that Sarah should have been glad that Jemima was out of the way, but wilting at the sight of Ibrahim's sorrowful eyes, she declared, 'She'll be all right, you know.'

'Do you really think so, Sarah?'

''course she will. If something's happened to her we'd have heard by now.'

'But she does not know her way around this city and she will be most frightened.'

'Don't mind what Pa says. Jemima's not stupid. She'll be all right.'

Smiling sweetly, she turned to leave but found her fingers grasped within his. 'Thank you, Sarah,' he said. 'You've made me feel better.'

'I'm glad,' she replied, ascending the cellar stairs.

CHAPTER 43

PRIYA

It was mostly at night that Jemima heard strange sounds emanating from the floors below her room. Sometimes she heard scurrying footsteps and hushed voices, followed by a swell of raucous laughter, piercing the panels of her bedroom door. The most intriguing sounds of all included the faint thud of drumbeats and then, in the dead of night, moans of pleasure – male and female. What kind of peculiar world was turning outside her door, she wondered? She had promised not to stray from her room at night and no matter what, she dared not break her word. But one time, she did flout the rule, only to discover that after dark, her door was always locked from the outside.

The last day of January arrived and the sun's rays pierced the clouds to melt the thin layer of snow that had fallen in the early hours of the morning. Both Nuwani and Jemima were in good spirits and they laughed and reminisced about their time at Mare Street lodging house. Nuwani grimaced at the memory of the awful Mrs Shade and chuckled out loud remembering the sickly Ruby forever attached to her snot-sodden handkerchief. This was more like the Nuwani Jemima remembered, but the jollity dwindled somewhat when they recalled the faces of the women they left behind. All in all, they were thrilled that fate had reunited them both and decided to be thankful for such small mercies. As Nuwani proceeded to plait the wavy strands of Jemima's dark hair, she suddenly asked, 'Why didn't you tell anyone about that man?'

'What man?'

'Lawrence.'

Jemima's body stiffened. 'Nobody would have cared.'

'You could have told Mr Pendlebury.'

Jemima glared at her friend. 'Do you think anyone would have believed me against a rich, white man? In our own country we have no rights... what makes you think we have any here?' Jemima noticed the steel in her own voice. She sounded like Mehta. 'The China woman was right,' she declared. 'We are the lowest of the low.'

'I did not mean to upset you.'

'I'm not upset,' Jemima spat. 'Like the China woman said... I have opened my eyes.'

It occurred to Jemima that Mehta and Jagatterini would have been more than proud to know that she was reacting at last. Turning to Nuwani, she then said, 'I've been meaning to ask you... what it is that you actually do in this place?'

The light went out in Nuwani's eyes.

'What is it, Nuwani? Tell me... you can tell me,' Jemima said, softening.

'I came here looking for honest work, Jemima... I did not know what the women did here to earn money.'

Jemima seized her friend's arm. 'What do they do, Nuwani? *What do they do?*'

Nuwani did not answer immediately. Little ridges of skin appeared on her forehead and she frowned. 'Do you really not know, Jemima?'

Jemima said nothing.

'Ruby is one of Mrs Wilson's spies and Mrs Wilson pays her to search for women like us... anywhere Asians, Blacks and Orientals can be found... in lodging houses and workhouses. They must be healthy... speak English well... look nice and pretty. In return, she gives clothes, decent lodgings and another way to make a living. Most of the girls here are from other countries... like us. There are girls from China, Japan, Africa, Italy and Austria. Mrs Wilson pays us and looks after us well. She told me that one girl even earned enough to go home to Africa and that one day, I could do the same.'

'What about your husband and children?'

'You think I have not already thought about them?'

'What if they found out?'

Nuwani frowned. 'How would they know? How could they? They will never find out. I had no choice, Jemima, and I want to go home. Mrs Wilson pays us well. Every month, she takes money for board, food and clothing and there is some left over for us to save. There are rules... strict rules... we are not allowed to leave this place on our own...only the European girls are allowed to leave. But she cares for us Jemima... and if the men are bad to us, she deals with them.' Nuwani rose from Jemima's side and peered through the window. 'She calls this place, 'the Atrium,' and we are her 'birds of paradise'. The gentlemen come willingly and pay willingly.'

'And what are these gentlemen like?'

'Very nice...mostly. Sometimes they give gifts, even money... money Mrs Wilson does not know about.' An odd silence lingered and Nuwani seemed a million miles away. 'Yes, *money*... they give us money... and soon, I will be able to go home to my husband and children.' Moving closer to the bed, she continued. 'It won't be long before I see them again.' Her eyes shone and her manner became almost delirious. 'We are not common streetwalkers like the women who stand on the dirty corners... we are high-class here,' she proclaimed, laughing out loud. 'Back home, we are low class servants, and here... we are high-class prostitutes!' She staggered across the room and laughed, but soon the laughter dissolved into tears.

Jemima snatched the China woman's handkerchief from the bedside table and pushed it into Nuwani's fingers. 'Don't cry.'

'Understand that I had no choice... I had no choice, Jemima... forgive me.'

Jemima remembered how Nuwani had not passed judgement on the scandalous nature of her own predicament. Nuwani had helped her in her time of need. She had asked Ivy to take her in and together, with Butterfly, they had tenderly nursed her back to health. So it was not a question of forgiveness; it was a question of their friendship, and Jemima knew that that was rock solid.

Now everything was out in the open, Mrs Wilson made it clear to Jemima that her earning capacity at the Atrium was far greater than doing menial work in a factory. But if she preferred the life of a drudge, Mrs Wilson was swift to point out that it would take Jemima years to save enough money to go home. She could honour her debt by doing a few menial chores under Butterfly's guidance but after that, Mrs Wilson would have no choice but to turn her out. Perhaps, she would end up in the poorhouse or work for a pittance in a factory or laundry; whatever she ended up doing, Jemima was happy to fetch and carry whilst pondering her fate. Returning to Ibrahim was a possible option, but the police were sure to be looking for her after being seen at the meeting on New Year's Day. Could she even entertain the possibility of returning to Mare Street? 'Never! Never!' she said to herself. Hell would freeze over first before she returned to that miserable place.

The crossroads did arrive, however, when she beheld Nuwani for the very first time, dressed head to toe in her glittering attire. Nuwani's eyes were outlined in kohl. Her hair fell loosely about her shoulders and her lips were rouged in a deep tint of burgundy. Sparkling trinkets adorned her ears and neck and she wore a sapphire-coloured sari that evening. Whenever she made the slightest movement, tiny bells tinkled about her feet. Nuwani looked beautiful. Nuwani looked magnificent. Nuwani looked like a princess and Jemima wanted to look the same.

Soon after, Ivy Wilson welcomed Jemima into her private office. 'I understand that you've made a decision,' she said, leaning against her desk.

'Yes.' There was a moment of silence.

'Well I haven't got all day, dear.'

'I will work for you, Mrs Wilson. I will be one of your 'birds of paradise'.

A sumptuous smile slid across Ivy's lips. 'I am very content to hear that, dear... most content indeed. We will begin your lessons immediately and in the meantime, if there's anything you want or need... just come to me.'

It would be easier for Jemima; she had no husband, no children and no parents to bring shame upon. Already defiled at the hands of Sylvester Lawrence, she would justify her actions by giving her permission and receiving money in return. But she could no longer function as Jemima – the once innocent and dutiful servant – and an age had passed since she had been known as Anupriya, the treasured daughter of parents committed to dust. She must take another name – a transitory name that would sever her ties to the past and disentangle her from her life as a servant. Then she would do as Nuwani did: sell her body for money that would take her home.

'Mrs Wilson, there is one thing I ask.'

'What is it, dear?'

'From now on, I would like to be called Priya.'

'Of course, my dear...you can be called anything you want!'

That evening, the bawd gathered her girls together in the drawing room and offered each of them a glass of wine. 'Ladies, raise your glasses to my newest bird. Her name is Priya!'

Feverish whispers filled the room.

'I expect all of you to help guide her in the ways of the Atrium.'

The girls gathered around 'Priya.' Some greeted her warmly; others judged from a distance.

'So you are one of us now,' Nuwani whispered into Jemima's ear.

'I want to go home just as much as you do,' Jemima whispered back.

'Nobody else back home can ever know.'

Jemima squeezed Nuwani's hand. 'No one back home will *ever* know.'

CHAPTER 44
THE DEBUT

'I never proffer my girls without subjecting them to a thorough medical examination first,' lectured Ivy Wilson as she took a turn about Jemima's bedroom. 'My favoured physician is Doctor Amos Rose… a man I pay handsomely for his diagnoses, prescriptions and more importantly, discretion. Every month he checks the girls for disease and I'm afraid you'll not forego your own share of scrutiny too. There's much to learn about this business, Priya. It's not just a matter of letting a man stick it in and pull it out, you know. The Atrium is high class and caters for gentlemen with individual needs… not like those knocking shops on Ratcliffe Highway that allow any old riff-raff to molest their girls.'

Ivy then made sure that Jemima was well versed in the benefits of a man engaging in *coitus interruptus*. 'There are some who are unwilling to show restraint… especially the elderly ones who are… shall we say… unable to perform the same sense of self-control they possessed in their younger days!' She then filled her new courtesan's hands with condoms of vulcanized rubber and pessaries of a solid and liquid nature, but if those options failed, Ivy ensured that Dr Rose was highly accomplished in the practise of abortion. Once the unpleasant side of the business was dealt with, Ivy sent for Mr Sandhu.

Mr Sandhu was a Parsee Indian merchant who made his living by importing goods from the far-flung corners of the globe. Mrs Wilson had met him when she herself was a high-class prostitute and valued his trade in imported saris, jewellery and cosmetics. As one of the many open-minded merchants who visited the brothel regularly, Mr Sandhu was famed for his ability to procure almost anything and he advised Jemima to sprinkle his scented *attars* into her bathwater and use his perfumes to soften her skin. After permitting her to choose some items from his array of treasures, Jemima opted for a carpet, an Indian painting and some silk cushions. Shyly, she also asked if he might bring her a statue of Kali to replace the one Mrs Shade had heartlessly snatched away.

'Hmm...' Sandhu mused. 'She's considered quite hideous by the English and truth be told, I must agree. It is within my means, however, to acquire a small statue of Ganesh instead, although, in my opinion, he's only a smidgen less ugly than Kali!'

She settled for the elephant god, Ganesh.

Consequently, Jemima furnished her surroundings with paraphernalia conducive to her homeland and conjured a little Indian haven in room number seven on the brothel's first floor. For the finishing touches, she lit some sticks of incense and arranged a clutch of flowers in a pretty porcelain vase. Proud of the intoxicating atmosphere she had created in her bed chamber, she ate well, slept like a cat and began to enjoy the company of the women whose lives were governed by the Atrium.

Ivy was eager to teach her novice the art of seduction and recruited the voluptuous Malaysian girl, Ezrine, to coach Jemima in the basics of Indian dance. 'These movements and poses are drawn from the disciplines of *Kathak* and *Bharatnatyam*,' Ezrine explained. She then tilted her bejewelled toes upwards and executed the perfect pirouette five times in a row.

Jemima achieved three consecutive rotations before feeling dizzy and toppling onto her bed. She accomplished the less intricate footwork with relative ease but excelled at the seductive sidelong glance, which, according to Ezrine, sent the men insane with desire. 'Now,' Ezrine continued, 'Move your neck to the right and then to the left... and lick your lips when you do it.' Ezrine slid her tongue across her upper lip and completed several lateral glides of the neck. Jemima giggled and followed suit. 'Not bad!' Ezrine declared. 'I will tell Mrs Wilson that you are nearly ready.'

As Jemima became equipped with the abilities necessary to seduce her future clients, the reality of a night with a stranger loomed ever closer. With the gaiety of the training well and truly over, Mrs Wilson set about arranging a debut for her ingénue and Jemima could only reluctantly wait for the bawd to name the day. However, Ivy did succumb to the more considerate side of her nature when she suggested that 'Priya' be initiated under more gentle circumstances. 'A new client has requested a private session in three days' time, but don't worry, he may not even choose you. Still, it's the perfect opportunity for you to begin.'

Three days later, the central doors of the Atrium opened and Ivy entered, ringing a bell. The blare silenced the musicians in the midst of their recital and made everyone's heads spin. Ivy marched over to the women seated on the sedan chairs and pointed to the female in the centre. 'Congratulations Priya. The new client is rather smitten with you!'

Everyone showered Priya with applause and innuendo but nobody, except Nuwani, noticed that her hands were shaking. 'Remember why you are doing this,' she whispered, gently squeezing Priya's shoulder.

Ivy led her protégé into the lounge. 'No need to be frightened, dear. He's very respectable... very respectable indeed. Now remember everything the girls and I taught you and go upstairs and please him.' She gave Priya a sprightly shove onto the first step of the staircase. 'Don't disappoint me.'

Priya climbed to the top of stairs with two heavy feet. She continued on, stopping mid-way to wipe her moist, hot brow. She swooned against the wall in search of her mettle and tugged her sari train over her head in an attempt to create a sense of the demure maiden she had been instructed to portray. She mustered the nerve to knock on the door and dipped her eyes as she turned the door handle. First, she spotted two rain-splattered shoes and following the legs upwards, her eyes then settled on a masquerading face.

'Good evening,' the man said.

'Good evening,' she replied, toying with the bracelets on her wrist.

Peeping up, she saw he was wearing one of Mrs Wilson's theatrical masks. An awkward hiatus passed and then the gentleman rose from the bed. 'You look like a frightened rabbit. Come closer, I'm not going to hurt you.'

She tried to remember the sentences she had been taught to say and began with, 'Shall I undress for you, sir?'

'No, no... I just...' His sighs were deep and full of concern. 'It occurred to me downstairs that we both have something in common. It's my first time here too... just as it is yours... Mrs Wilson mentioned it to me... and so... I'm just as anxious as you are.' He patted the bed and she moved towards him. 'Would you like a little wine? Priya isn't it?'

She nodded. Dutch courage would help her through the night. He poured out two measures from the bottle Butterfly had delivered earlier and resumed his position on the bed. She took a self-conscious sip and abandoned her glass on the bedside table. 'Would you like me to undress you, sir?'

He drank some of his wine. 'I really am at a loss to know why I'm here. I just wanted to... talk really. Does that seem acceptable to you?'

Relieved, she nodded.

'It's rather dark and gloomy in here,' he said, bringing the table lamp over to the chest of drawers nearby. 'Priya is a lovely name...as lovely as you are. Do you mind me saying that you are *very* beautiful?'

Blushing at his compliment, she sat by him, making small talk and sharing little silences. He took another great gulp of wine and fiddled with the mask on his face. 'I feel quite foolish with this on. Will you help me untie it?' He turned his back to her whilst she unfastened the knot and lifted the disguise over his head. Rising from her place beside him, she left the mask on the chest of drawers. 'That's much better,' he said, rubbing his eyes.

She caught sight of her reflection in the looking glass. The kohl remained neatly drawn on her eyelids but her mouth looked as dry as a bone. She swept her tongue across her lips and wound a curl behind her ear, but then a glimpse of *his* naked face staring back from the mirror made the vanilla-scented air begin to suffocate her lungs. The ground beneath her feet began to rumble and blinking hard and slow, she reached for the bedpost only to miss the target and stumble into the stranger's arms... the stranger who happened to be her former sahib, William Hayward.

CHAPTER 45

AYAH OR COURTESAN?

'Steady there!' he exclaimed, catching her by the arm. 'It seems the wine's gone straight to your head. It's best to sip it slowly if you're not accustomed to it. Perhaps I should get Mrs Wilson to bring you something to eat? It might calm you.'

Under the circumstances, it would have been impossible for her to keep anything down. She declined the offer and allowed him to steer her onto the bed.

'Please don't fret,' he said. 'I can sense you're a little uncertain of me but I should like to get to know you, that's all... you needn't get undressed.' She dreaded what might happen if they locked eyes but she remained perfectly quiet, unable to articulate an expression in any of the three languages in which she was well versed.

'Mrs Wilson tells me you're from India. Is that correct?'

Drawing her sari train over her head, she nodded.

'I went out to India for a while. I only returned this November gone. I lived and worked in Calcutta. Which part are you from?'

'Bombay,' she lied.

'I have never had the pleasure of visiting Bombay,' he said. 'Calcutta is a fine city... have you been to Calcutta?' From instinct, she nodded and then wondered if she should have lied. 'I lived on Dhurmotollah Street... are you familiar with it?' She shook her head. 'Tell me about yourself. What did you do in Bombay? And how did you come to be in England?'

His last question angered her. *'How did I come to be in England?'* *she thought. 'You and your callous wife brought me and left me here.* *You lied to me. I could expect that of her...but you? I thought you were a* *kind, decent man. I adored you... I loved you.'* How she wanted to say all those things in her head out loud. Instead she said, 'I was a teacher... I came to England for work. I fell on hard times... and now... I do not have enough money to return. But when I have enough... I will go home.'

His forehead wrinkled. 'How unfortunate it is that you've fallen on hard times... I cannot imagine what it must be like for you... though... forgive me for saying this but part of me is glad that you came here, otherwise I wouldn't have had the pleasure of meeting you.'

Jemima's fury was building. *'How unfortunate? How unfortu-* *nate!'* she silently shrieked. But it seemed that William Hayward had not the faintest suspicion that seated beside him was his children's former ayah. Yes, she had only served his wife and their children and yes, they had barely crossed paths, but was she really that worthless for him to have no idea who she was? Did she really look that different through her face paint and fancy sari? He had never concerned himself with the Indian women who watched over his children; they were minor domestic details who answered to his wife. But his ignorance, no matter how much it piqued her, made it so much easier for her to lie.

William Hayward spoke of India and the happy times he had spent in Bengal. He loved most things about the province and expressed disappointment at having to leave. Much braver now, she looked him in the eye, but all through his recollections of the life he had lived in Calcutta, he never once mentioned his wife or his children. 'I expect that you miss India terribly... I know I do,' he said.

She glanced at him contemptuously and was surprised to see him looking immensely sad. 'I feel utterly dreadful on your be-half...what I mean is... having to resort to doing this.'

Again, she saw genuine compassion and signs of humanity – characteristics of the sahib she once treasured and adored.

Time passed in a heartbeat and a knock at the door herald-ed the end of their tryst. Butterfly shouted, 'Time up, sir!' and William Hayward's melancholic expression slipped into a frown.

'That hour went rather quickly,' he said, beginning to pace the room. 'May I come back and visit again? How about the day after tomorrow? Yes, Wednesday. I would very much like to visit on Wednesday.' His fingertips touched her elbow and she resent-ed how it made her shiver for reasons other than being recog-nised. 'I shall return on Wednesday.'

Butterfly knocked again. 'Sir...time up! Time up!'

He snatched his mask from the dressing table and kissed her on the cheek. He asked her to fasten the ties of his disguise and she obliged, using ten trembling fingers. 'Until Wednesday,' he said, staring back at her one last time.

Ivy Wilson's eyelids flickered under the influence of her third glass of brandy. Lounging slothfully on an ottoman, she allowed her body to sag and her satin slippers to dangle freely from her toes until the thud of William Hayward's footsteps made her sit up to attention. She stuffed her feet into her shoes and straightened her dress before rushing to his side. 'How was it, Mr Hayward? Was the experience satisfactory?'

William looked deep in thought.

'Is everything all right, Mr Hayward?'

'May I have one of those?' he asked, pointing to her glass.

'Certainly,' she said, crossing the room to the drinks cabinet.

'I wish to make an arrangement with you, Mrs Wilson. Is that possible?' he asked.

'Well, that depends what the arrangement is,' she replied, handing him his drink.

William emptied the entire contents down his throat and felt the alcoholic heat spread through his veins. 'I would like Priya to be kept exclusively for myself.'

'I beg your pardon,' Ivy reeled.

'What I mean is... I don't want her to be exposed to your other clients. I'll compensate you handsomely but no one is to touch her, do you understand?' he said, extracting his wallet.

Ivy pulled a face. 'Well, I'm not sure. I've never ... '

'How much?'

Ivy was flabbergasted.

'How much?' he asked again.

'Well, I shall need time to consider your proposal.'

'Fine... I am able to pay by the week, the month... whichever suits. Just send me word.'

He pushed his wallet into his pocket and the action made Ivy concede. 'Very well, Mr Hayward but I shall need some time to work out an arrangement.'

'Very well... but please remember that she's not to be exposed to your other clients. No one touches her.'

Butterfly was hovering in the doorway, pretending not to listen to any of the conversation. She offered William Hayward his hat and smoothed down his cloak whilst he prepared to take his leave.

'I shall return this Wednesday at seven and I think it might be appropriate to discuss the particulars of my membership then. If you need reassurance, I'm sure the Colonel will vouch for me.' Crouching low, he allowed Butterfly to drape his cloak over his shoulders. 'Good night, Mrs Wilson,' he said, following the maid out of the lounge.

Ivy tossed the last beads of brandy down her throat and rushed up the staircase to bedroom number seven. She flung the door open without even knocking to find 'Priya' staring blankly at the wall. 'For what reason are you sitting in the dark, dear?' she barked, turning the oil lamp up full flare. 'And why are the bedcovers not messy and pulled apart?'

'We only talked.'

'Talked?' spluttered Ivy, shrinking in disbelief. 'You must have done something to him… you were a complete success. I declare, he's completely besotted. What did you say to him?' she asked, cocking an ear towards Priya's lips. 'I expect one of the other girls told you to say something seductive and scandalous. You must tell me, my dear… I simply must know!'

'Nothing.'

'Nothing?' scoffed Ivy. 'Very well, I suppose a woman must have her secrets. Nonetheless, I am most impressed and I have some very agreeable news.'

Ivy recounted the discussion downstairs with boundless vigour and then promised her now favourite girl a selection of new outfits and a mound of sparkling trinkets to match. She hastily took her leave after realising the other members were due within the hour and left 'Priya' to make sense of the astonishing events that had unfolded only an hour before.

Jemima rose from the bed and paced the room as a jumble of emotions exploded within her. William Hayward, her former sahib, *William Hayward*, the husband of her former mistress and father of her former charges had asked to be her patron. He had never noticed her back in Calcutta – he had never even looked her way. Now here he was choosing her from a crowd of women and telling her she was beautiful. In Calcutta, she had spied on him and longed for him and loved him in her imagination and now at long last, he had finally taken some notice. But it was not Jemima, the ayah, he noticed. It was the conjured up courtesan with the fabricated name. The conflict in her head was vociferous and strong, and appealed to the ayah that she used to be. It was not right; she was a former servant who had cared for his children and so she must speak to Mrs Wilson and disclose the truth. Perhaps Ivy would allow her to abscond before being discovered; then she could return to India and leave *him* and her shame behind. No, it was not right, the scandal, the children; his wife, Elizabeth Hayward... she had worked for them loyally and they had promised to send her back home. But they had broken the agreement and left her to rot in a shabby strangers' home to suffer at the hands of men like Lawrence and Vikram.

Jemima would have done the right thing but another person had slipped into her shoes and that person would do whatever was necessary to survive. Strangely enough, it was Mehta's face that surfaced in her head and she heard his rousing speech, inspiring her to make a stand against life's injustices. He told her to oust out the browbeaten ayah and fight tooth and nail to make her way in the world. And who caused all of this to happen? Who drove her to such humiliating depths? *Mr and Mrs William Hayward, that's who...* The conflict subsided and Jemima, the ayah, reconsidered her decision to confess. No, she decided, she would not tell Mrs Wilson the truth. She would play the role of 'Priya,' the courtesan and receive William Hayward on Wednesday night and indeed, any other night that he might fancy. She traced his crumpled outline in the bed covers and studied the faint impression of his lips on the edge of his glass. She touched the elbow against which he had brushed his fingers and like Mehta, driven to despair by the inequitable actions of the British, she re-visited the path that had led her to Ivy Wilson's door. And as Elizabeth Hayward's merciless face whirled in her head, only one thought now raged through her mind: *Revenge.*

CHAPTER 46
THE ATRIUM

And so, how did William Hayward come to be at the Atrium? And what were the events that conspired to lead him to Jemima? Well, an abstemious Christmas had passed followed by a rather strained New Year. On both occasions, he had travelled to Leeds to be with his wife and children after trying his utmost to do whatever was asked of him. Any attempts to make amends failed outright; thus the glacial gulf existing between husband and wife deepened further and did not go undetected by their respective family members who queried and speculated on the state of their private lives. Neither William nor Elizabeth divulged their intimate affairs and brushed aside the conjecture with an assurance that all was well. He passed the first days of January alone and sad, and in times of much needed company, turned to Colonel Malvery and his wife, Tara. The Colonel became his trusted confidante and it was at their club, *Whites*, that he surprised William with a little secret of his own.

'How are things, my dear fellow?' the Colonel asked.

'Much the same, I fear,' William moaned. 'I've still not heard from Elizabeth.'

'What can I do to bring a smile to your face?'

'Oh I don't know, Colonel,' he smirked. 'Whisk me back to the East?'

The Colonel looked sheepish as he fumbled inside his breast pocket. He dug out a collection of cards and sifted through them until a particular card caught his attention. He balanced it on one knee, whilst he slotted the others back inside his wallet. Lowering his voice, he said, 'William, I have an acquaintance... an old acquaintance... we're good friends from way before I was married, you understand? She owns an establishment... a sort of private house that caters for gentlemen with tastes... such as yours. It's highly exclusive and one has to be nominated to become a member but I can put your name forward if you like. The woman who runs it is a good sort. Her place is very discreet and I hear that she has women from all over the colonies... *beautiful women...* and I'm sure there will be someone there to make you feel better.'

William hesitated before accepting the card. 'Sir, I'm not quite sure I understand why you are giving this to me.'

'Well, I'm not really sure myself. I suppose it's because you seem so forlorn of late and I thought, perhaps, that it may remind you of the Ivory Palace... you did mention how much you enjoyed it there.'

William glanced down at the card and saw that it bore an image of a birdcage with an address written underneath:

Ivy Wilson
The Atrium
59a Princess Street
London E.1

'East London?'

The Colonel raised his hand. 'Don't let the address put you off, dear boy. No doubt you'll be very surprised when you walk through the door. The decision, of course, is entirely yours. It could possibly take your mind off your present troubles.'

William flipped the card back and forth between his fingers.

'I haven't offended you, have I?' the Colonel asked.

'No, Colonel,' William sighed, 'not at all.' And turning to order another round of drinks, he wondered how *he* could avoid offence if he were to hand the card back.

As William took his breakfast the next morning, Cole entered the dining room, bearing a tray of letters. Elizabeth's handwriting was written trimly upon one of them and he immediately broke the seal to read her news. She had written of Sophie and how she was still getting used to the new governess, Miss Reed. She had even begun to speak a few words of French and was enjoying her language lessons immensely. Elizabeth was now expecting Charlotte to visit her in Leeds. Thus, she ended the letter with news that she would be extending her stay for a further month.

William stormed into his study in search of some writing parchment and found stack in the lower bureau drawer. He pulled out a leaf, dipped a pen into the inkwell and wrote down the following words:

Dear Colonel Malvery,

With reference to the matter we discussed the last I saw you, I would be most grateful if you would recommend my name to your acquaintance in East London. I look forward to your reply.

Your friend, William Hayward

A week later, William Hayward instructed his driver to take him to *Whites*. After arriving at his club, he informed the man that his services were no longer needed but then asked the bemused club doorman to order him a hansom. Whilst waiting for his transport to arrive, he drank a tumbler of whisky and bantered with some other club members. Half an hour later, he climbed into his cab and set off into the night, mulling over the Colonel's tale of Ivy Wilson.

'Ivy is no ordinary bawdyhouse madam. Unlike many of her counterparts in the brothel business, she's avoided languishing in Newgate Prison by honouring her debts and staying one step ahead of the law. Ivy possesses a furtive imagination and a canny business savoir-faire that combined with her unconventional ways has led to the creation of much of her wealth. She's established a business in what she knows best... a high-class brothel house with a difference. You see... Ivy's met all kinds of men with all kinds of tastes and she's decided to cater for individuals lusting after women of differing complexions. Men are prepared to pay generously for ladies other than the usual home grown whores and she's found the perfect place in which these fellows can be fittingly satisfied. You'd think it would be somewhere fashionable like Regent Street or Langham Place, but no! Only Ivy could stumble across an old parchment factory, three storeys high! I hear it has a magnificent circular chamber known as 'The Atrium' that rises from the centre into an elegant dome. Ivy likens it to a giant birdcage... and for those who can afford to pay for its pleasures... she has conjured a haven of shameless splendour. But I tell you, William, the most satisfying aspect of Ivy's new acquisition... the feature that entices her clientele... is that her illicit sanctuary is tucked away in the underbelly of the East End... the last place anyone would expect to find a high-class bawdy house and the last place anyone respectable would want to be seen. She likes to create a sense of excitement...mystery, if you like. It all adds to the experience and it's very exclusive... if you only knew some of the fellows who like to go. Of course, I cannot tell! Let's just say some have seats in

the House of Commons. And you don't have to worry… it's all very discreet. As I said, she's an old friend and she's doing me a favour by arranging a private introduction for you, so you won't brush shoulders with any other members. But even if you do, I hardly think they're going to bandy your name about… not when they're busy partaking themselves! Besides, Ivy has her little tricks and cunning ways to maintain her members' anonymity. Just by having the place in the East End…who would be seen there? It's an ingenious idea, don't you think?'

The cab turned into Princess Street at a quarter to seven. The area was eerily dark but for a few beams of yellow gaslight illuminating the dull concrete pavements. The driver clambered down and looked about the place. 'You sure this is where a gentleman like you wants to go, sir?'

William peeked out and explored the surroundings. 'Yes… I'm meeting an acquaintance here.'

'Watch yourself, sir,' warned the driver. 'This ain't no place for a gentleman… there's thieves and murderers wandering around. Want me to stay about 'til your friend gets here?'

'Thank you but I'm certain everything will be fine.'

'All right, sir… but be careful! You need your wits about you 'round here.'

William handed the driver his fare and watched the cab canter off into the night.

There were several warehouses and disused buildings casting their shadows over the wet, shiny streets. He walked along the pavement trying his best to locate number 59a. The appointment was for seven and he hated being late. Muffled noises spilled out from the adjoining streets but not a soul could be seen or heard. He lurked on the corner and noticed lamplight flickering behind a window of a corner building. He wandered up the paved pathway and found a shiny black door with the brass-plated number

'59' sitting on the front panel. *'Now remember, one enters by the side entrance... around the corner,'* the Colonel had advised.

William returned back down the pathway and turned the corner to discover an iron staircase descending into the foggy darkness below. He stepped down it warily, trying to avoid the loud tap of his shoes against the tinny metal steps. The lane ahead ended at a softly lit door and there he spied the number, '59a,' emblazoned upon the dark wooden panelling. He rang the bell once and heard a bolt slide open and a key release a lock. It only took a second before a caramel-coloured woman appeared and asked for his name. He was distracted by the bright green scarf wrapped around her head.

'Good evening, I am William Hayward.'

'Good evening, sir, Missus Wilson's been expecting you. Please follow me. My name's Butterfly and if there's anything sir wants or needs... you jus' have to call for Butterfly.'

They passed a chair positioned against the wall with a square of embroidery draped over the seat. Butterfly had been there all the time, attending to her needlepoint whilst she waited for him to arrive. The soft glare from her candle illuminated the way down a short corridor. She tottered as she walked and he had to slow his pace several times to avoid running into the heels of her shoes. They climbed a small staircase and walked through a door, which opened out onto an expanse of red carpet flanked by two oak-panelled walls. The scent of sweet oranges invaded William's senses and he felt slightly giddy as Butterfly showed him into the lounge. A cluster of provocative statues greeted his eyes and he noticed the colourful images of scantily clad women draped on the walls. Nervously, he settled into the seat of an ornate ottoman, whilst still the intense scent of citrus floated dreamily in the air.

'I take your things, sir,' Butterfly said. 'And then I go fetch Missus Wilson.' She chewed her bottom lip and rhythmically tapped her foot as she spoke. He stood up and removed his hat and cloak and she took the items and hobbled out of the room.

William sat down on the ottoman again. The cushions propping up his back were over abundant and rather uncomfortable. He displaced a few and leaned back before becoming distracted by a faint pounding noise. He attempted to locate the source of the beat but his scrutiny of the room was hastily abandoned when a rather handsome woman walked through the door. 'Ah, Mr Hayward,' she said.

William jumped up like a spring that had been compressed for a while. 'Mrs Wilson?'

She examined his face and his physique and finally, his smile, and gestured him to relax in his seat. 'I've been so looking forward to meeting you. My, how handsome you are.'

William had been told on many an occasion just how handsome he was considered to be, but this time he blushed ever so deeply. 'Please, Mr Hayward,' she laughed, 'there really is no need to be nervous. Perhaps you would like a drink? Some wine…brandy, champagne?'

'No thank you.'

'Very well, shall we deal with the formalities first?'

'Excuse me?'

'Payment. Since you're a novice, I recommend an introduction followed by an hour with a girl of your choice. And then if you have a pleasant enough evening and wish to return again, we shall think about making you a member. There is even the possibility of spending the night, if you should so wish it.'

One step at a time, thought William. 'An hour sounds fine for now.'

It took some minutes to complete the transaction, during which a fee was extracted and paid in full. Ivy Wilson rose to her feet and ventured over to a table, from which she lifted a rather elaborate looking bell. She rang it three times and Butterfly entered, carrying a mysterious box in her arms.

'Now, Mr Hayward,' Ivy began. 'I'm sure Colonel Malvery has informed you of the extreme pains I take to ensure the anonymity of my clients. That way, the only people who see your face are myself, of course, Butterfly and the girl with whom you choose to spend your time. It restricts the number of people who know your identity and makes it decidedly easy for me to punish anyone who gives you away... I have just as much to lose as you do, but you have my word that my girls are the very souls of discretion.' She waved Butterfly forward with the box. 'Now, would you like to choose a mask? I've just had them brought over from Venice. Aren't they beautiful?'

An assortment of facial camouflages lay in Butterfly's arms. Carefully stacked in order of extravagance, some had feathers and sequins whilst others sported exaggerated noses and were painted in the brightest yellows and reds. William chose the plainest one: a white half-mask that, except for the eyes, hid the upper features of one's face.

'Perhaps I will have a drink after all, Mrs Wilson,' he said, sensing a film of sweat on the palms of his hands. 'A brandy please, if you will.'

'Brandy is a good choice,' she said. 'It calms the nerves. I shall fetch one for you. Butterfly, please help Mr Hayward with his mask.'

Butterfly placed the disguise around his eyes and fastened the cords at the back of his head. Then Ivy returned, holding a decanter and two crystal glasses. She poured a measure of brandy for William and one for herself. 'The masks not only put my clients at ease but they also add to the theatre of the experience. It makes it feel like a little game.' Smiling impishly, she held her glass out into the air. 'Here's to your first visit to the Atrium. Cheers!'

William drank his brandy in one go.

'There's just one last thing, Mr Hayward,' said Ivy, licking her lips. 'I choose not to tell my girls the names of my clients or let them know anything of their background. If you wish to do so, then it is entirely *your* prerogative. You may wish to give your real name or you may use another... like a *nom de plume*, I suppose... either way, the decision is yours. Now, I think that's everything. Would you care to follow me?'

A dark brown door between a bookcase and a second ottoman blended seamlessly with the oak-panelled walls. Ivy unlocked it and guided William onto a path that curled its way around a circular wall. Several narrow points of entry led into the mysterious central chamber but Ivy chose to lead William up a spiral staircase instead. The bizarre pounding grew even louder and the citrus scent seemed more potent than before. Paused on the uppermost step, Ivy wavered before a wooden door bearing the bodies of mischievous angels and cherubs carved into its surface. From the depths of her generous bosom, she extracted a golden key and looking over her shoulder, she smiled the most salacious of smiles. 'Are you ready, Mr Hayward?' she asked, staring into his veiled eyes.

'Ready as I'll ever be,' he replied, faltering on the step behind.

Ivy fed the golden key inside the golden lock and turned it once. The elaborate door opened and overpowered by the rush of orange-scented air, William felt the numinous beat of drums pound his stomach and stifle his thoughts. The far side of the curved balcony was all he managed to see but Ivy insisted that he peer into the space below and at first, it took a minute for his eyes to adjust through his mask. Bright colours and shapes danced below him but as he absorbed more of the curious scene, what a sight seduced William Hayward's shrouded eyes.

Several torches of fire threw halos of mellow light over a spectacular collection of beautiful women placed temptingly about the room. They posed provocatively through outfits barely hanging from their bodies and seduced the beholder with flashes of bare skin. There were Japanese women wearing silk kimonos and Africans floating about in diaphanous tunics of batik. Some girls were wearing a great deal less than others, not in the least bit conscious that their naked bodies were on show for all to see. A cross-legged male musician sat in the centre of the floor, tapping out a rhythm from his painted drum. Another, beside him, produced an array of hypnotic sounds from a long wooden flute perched on his lips. It seemed that Mrs Wilson had arranged her players strategically like chess pieces on a circular shaped board. 'Please, take a walk around,' she smiled, shadowing his moves closely. 'Anyone take your fancy?'

William stared down at the extravagant rainbow of women. 'It's difficult to see their faces. It's so far up.'

Ivy walked over to one of several small cabinets placed around the balcony and delved inside a drawer. She returned, holding two pairs of opera glasses clasped in her hands. 'These should help.'

William waited until Mrs Wilson was seated on one of the wooden settles behind before holding the glasses to his eyes. He adjusted them until the native Indian drummer came into view first and then passed his focus to a black-skinned woman in a yellow scarf and matching *kaftan*. From her, he moved to a Chinese girl in a *qipao* dress, giggling behind a pretty paper fan. The Japanese women hardly looked up, though the Venetian beauties, aware of his presence, exposed their ample breasts through bodices of translucent silk. As sole voyeur of this circular chamber of pleasure, William Hayward realised that he could have the pick of the crop. He beheld a Burmese girl and a Turkish dancer and then his eyes probed the trio of figures lounging on the sedan chairs. How striking they looked in their colourful saris as his glasses lingered on their shoulders and necks. The dark eyes and red lips were particularly enticing but when he traced the outline of the woman sitting in the centre, William Hayward was compelled to stop.

She was looking down with part of her sari covering her head but she glanced up briefly to charm him in an instant. Her hair was curled beautifully and her brown skin shone against the magenta pink sari that bound her body so well. Images of the Ivory Palace spun in William's head as he stared spellbound at the woman who had conjured them for him. Ivy registered his unflinching interest and was up and out of her seat in a second.

'You've seen someone you like?' she asked.

'Yes,' he whispered. 'The Indian girl on the couch... the one dressed in pink.'

Mrs Wilson shifted her glasses to the woman in question. 'Ah yes! Lovely little creature, isn't she? This is your lucky day, Mr Hayward. Her name's Priya and it's her first time too. But mark my word, Mr Hayward, she's eager to please. You can be sure of that.'

Together they descended the spiral staircase and followed the path around the curving wall. Butterfly was already awaiting her orders in the lounge.

'Is there anything we can send up for you, Mr Hayward... drinks, dinner? I have a wonderful cook,' Mrs Wilson said, closing the secret door.

'A bottle of wine will suffice.'

'Certainly. I shall leave you in Butterfly's capable hands and I'll send Priya up to you, shortly. We knock on the door when the hour's up. Butterfly! Show Mr Hayward to Priya's room and fetch him a bottle of our finest wine.'

William trailed Butterfly up the main staircase and along a corridor until she stopped outside a room with the number '7' painted on the door. The space inside was dimly lit and a cluster of fiery dots gave off the creamy scent of vanilla.

'Your lady will be up soon, sir,' she said. 'I go bring your wine.'

He grabbed the lamp by the bed and moved it about to see more of his surroundings. There were incense sticks burning in a dish and a pretty Persian style rug sitting beneath his feet. A painting on the wall told a tale from Indian mythology and the pale pink bedspread smelt of vetiver perfume. Forgetting the present torment in his life, William Hayward sat down and waited patiently for his courtesan to arrive.

CHAPTER 47

KAJAL, INCENSE AND ROSE OIL

Two days after the astounding debut that had brought her face to face with William Hayward, Jemima rose from her bed with thoughts of the sahib playing on her mind. The room was bitterly cold and she wrapped a shawl around her shoulders before dragging the curtains back against the rail. As usual, it was soul-less and dismal in the streets outside but foolishly, she had expected the sun to burst through the clouds and the flowers to have reached full bloom; such was her strange feeling of happiness. Two days ago, she had hated him with a passion and she wanted to strike him for what he and his wife had done. But today she could not bury her excitement, for he was coming to see her again and the mere thought made her head whirl with feverish anticipation.

Lifting her hair away from her face, Jemima noticed a different woman staring back from the windowpane. Perhaps her physiognomy had altered a little, for the person glancing back possessed eyes that were hardened of late. She was slender in the cheeks and leaner around her shoulders but the softness had gone. Yes, it had definitely gone. A knock at the door made her jump. She turned to see Butterfly peering into the room. 'Coals,' she muttered, hovering with a bucket in her hand. 'Missus Wilson says to be down at nine 'cause Mr Sandhu's coming with his wares.' She crossed over to the hearth with the bucket squeaking at her side.

Sandhu was due that very morning; the appointment had slipped from Jemima's mind. She splashed water over her face and pulled off her nightgown, hoping that the merchant would bring her something undeniably special: something that would entice William Hayward into her bed.

Ten magnificent saris and a treasure trove of jewellery took pride of place in Sandhu's collection that morning. The valuables were locked inside a rather intriguing safety box, which was always guarded by his burly manservant, Gopal. Jemima's eyes feasted on the purple garment on top of a pile of saris. It bore silvery-gold threads that plaited themselves around hundreds of tiny pinkish-blue moonstones.

'Isn't it beautiful?' purred Sandhu. 'This is the finest filigree work you will ever see. They say the garment belonged to the Maharajah of Bharatpur's one and only daughter. She took her own life by throwing herself from an almighty cliff. You see, the Maharajah forbade the princess to marry her soldier lover and broken-hearted, she chose to die rather than live her life without him.' Sweeping his fingers across the silk border, he permitted Jemima to do the same.

Ivy was quietly smirking at Sandhu's fanciful tale. His whimsical stories were extremely amusing but she was certain he concocted the fables in order to raise the price of his goods. When he finally left the world of his dubious imagination, he unlocked his chest of treasures and the glare from its contents bounced off his monocle and illuminated his fine-featured face. There were heaps of baubles and piles of semi-precious ornaments. There were pearls, moonstones and pieces of jade. Pretty earrings hung from pins either side of a large silk cushion and necklaces and bracelets sparkled in the secret shelves. There were trinkets it seemed, for every part of the body – waist, nose, fingers, ankles and hands. Jemima ogled the cobra hood brooches and coveted the rings fashioned into tiger heads. Another box held Mr Sandhu's stock of cosmetics and suddenly there were bottles of scented oils, vials of potent attars, boxes of exotic soaps and pots of lip paint, cheek rouge and *kajal* scattered all over the place.

In Sandhu's opinion, the scents of musk and sandalwood proved highly popular with some ladies, but jasmine or rose oil rubbed into the body were favourites among most. He insisted that Jemima sample his new supply of incense and proceeded to open a case overflowing with sticks of vetiver, ginger, aloe bark and myrrh. Mr Sandhu had not disappointed and after reserving the purple sari, a golden headdress and several matching trinkets to complement Jemima's outfit, he urged her to select the opium incense to perfume her room that night. At the end of the appointment, he presented a small tub of *kajal*, which, he guaranteed, would make her look extraordinary. 'I will send her blouse over later... I have her measurements,' he said, placing the purple sari over to one side.

Mrs Wilson nodded and Mr Sandhu proceeded to make a record of his sold and rented goods. Nuwani and Ezrine were waiting outside to make their choices and Jemima wondered whether they resented her sudden favoured treatment. Since becoming part of an exclusive arrangement, she was now offered the pick of Sandhu's finery first. Her special status made her anxious and she made light of her choices in front of the other girls. But Sandhu had so many beautiful items in his collection of treasures that jealousy, so far, had never become an issue. She hoped it would remain that way.

When she returned from her bath that evening, Jemima found the purple sari, its matching blouse and underskirt draped over the back of a chair. She massaged some rose oil into her skin and swept a line of Sandhu's *kajal* across the grooves of her eyelids, ending with an elegant arc that slanted in an upward direction. She had chosen an intense shade of red to rouge her cheeks and lips, and ran her tongue across her mouth to impart a seductive sheen. Butterfly pulled her arms through the sleeves of the blouse and proceeded to fasten the hooks and eyes. Butterfly was adept at dressing the women at the Atrium and just as Elizabeth Hayward had been content to allow her ayah to attend to her attire, Jemima was content to leave Butterfly to her own devices. She combed and plaited a length of gold ribbon around the end of a single braid and then hobbled off to call for her mistress, who subsequently entered the room cradling a trinket box close to her bosom.

Ivy unlocked the box with a tiny key and the jewellery items Jemima had chosen were sitting inside. Ivy passed them over to Butterfly, who then proceeded to fix them onto Jemima. The earrings dangled like crystal teardrops and the bracelets tinkled as Jemima slipped them over her small hands. Butterfly pushed two rings onto her fingers and secured a pretty gold chain around her waist. She then began to light some extra candles but Jemima insisted the room remain dimly lit. 'Don't forget to place it all back into the box when you undress,' Ivy said. 'I have made an inventory of everything,' she clucked, pinning the golden headpiece into Jemima's hair. She crossed the room to admire her creation and gushed as the glimmer of jewellery illuminated Jemima's body like the celestial aura of a heralding angel. 'You look just like a doll, my dear. Just like a doll. He should be here imminently. Work your magic! Work your magic!'

They left her standing before the looking glass, staring at a stunning version of a woman that was not really herself. She *did* look different. She hardly recognised her face. She was breath-taking, that much she could admit, though she could not help but feel a little lost. It was time to banish Jemima from the room, for Priya was waiting to take her place.

The opium incense was pungent and heady. She had lit far too many and they had left her woozy in the warmth of the spitting fire. She must have dozed off briefly before hearing Butterfly's knock, for the noise made her body shudder. A tall, masked figure entered the room. He said nothing and she trembled at the notion that it may not be him. The man freed his disguise and his blue eyes sparkled like sapphires.

'Good evening,' he said, straightening his locks of blonde hair.

'Good evening, sir.'

'I've been so looking forward to seeing you again.'

Out of embarrassment, she giggled and blushed. *'Why am I feeling this way?' she thought. 'I want to hate him. I must hate him.'*

'I've been thinking about you since last we met,' he said, tossing his mask over to the empty chair. 'And I've some good news... at least I hope you regard it as good news.' He reached for her hand and she found herself offering it freely. 'You looked so frightened and nervous the first time we met. I shouldn't blame you... I should feel the same way if I were you... and so I'm sure Mrs Wilson has mentioned the arrangement I made.' She smiled and nodded. 'I hope that's agreeable to you. I only...' He looked down to the floor. 'I only wanted to help you... protect you.'

Jemima's heart was beginning to beat for him again. Faltering a moment, uncertain of what to do, she dared herself to initiate a kiss. It was easy to find the courage to do so as she threw her arms around his neck, for she had yearned to kiss him in her dreams and now she would lead him to her bed for real. She released a corner of her sari tucked deep into her waist and un-wound it until a yard or so was exposed.

'Please,' he said, 'you mustn't feel you have to do that. It's not my intention to make you feel that you owe me anything.'

She pierced him with her kohl-etched eyes. 'I want to,' she whispered. 'Hold tight,' she said, feeding the corner of her sari into his hand. And like a spinning top, she twirled seductively, laughing and feigning dizziness as the sari came loose in his hands. Dizzy for real this time, she snatched the last section away from her waist. It drifted to the floor to reveal her bare navel, which teasingly peeped at him from between her blouse and skirt. The corner slipped out of his fingers, freeing the pathway that invited her towards him. Could she allow William Hayward to touch her? Could she allow any man to touch her after what Sylvester Lawrence had done? This was different. This was no repulsive, drunken maniac who forced his abhorrent body upon hers. This was no disrespectful student activist, who pushed her against an alley wall and insulted her when she fought back. This was William Hayward, the handsome angel, who caressed her elbow ever so gently. He could have had his way with her the first night he came to the Atrium, but no, he only wanted to talk. And so, it only took a second for her to go.

The face of Elizabeth Hayward loomed briefly but there was no guilt or remorse nor strangely, the satisfaction of revenge. She had fantasised about William Hayward on many occasions and now his hands were *really* drifting across her skin. She removed the jewellery pieces from around her face whilst he undid the fastenings on her blouse. He drew its sleeves over her shoulders and she trembled when his warm fingers slid along her arms. She tugged at his shirt and plucked at his waistcoat and he found her awkwardness rather endearing. Lying down against the bed, they rolled and grappled with each other as her hair fell loose and his became tousled. They rid each other's bodies of their clothes and shoes, and writhed together until she felt him slip inside her. Moving gently and then pulsing rhythmically, he looked deeper into her eyes before losing himself in the heady scent of opium perfume. Moaning quietly at first, she then climaxed in a cry of ecstasy whilst, at the same time, he let out a long, soft gasp before dropping his head against the pillow. Try as she might, Jemima had not succeeded in hating William Hayward, for now it seemed her heart wished to run away with his. His lovemaking was tender, warm and sensual, and he held her in his arms as if she were a precious china doll. She rested quietly, enjoying the calm and simple silence but suddenly, she felt overcome with emotion, for William Hayward had showed her that not all men were brutal and William Hayward had showed her that sexual intimacy could be something pleasurable and pure. William Hayward had saved her from believing that she could never be cherished by a man but William Hayward did not witness her tears, for she wiped them away before he could see them.

'Have I made you happy?' she panted softly in his ear.

'Yes, you've made me happy. And you?' he whispered back. 'Have I made you happy?'

'Yes,' she smiled. 'You've made me *very* happy.'

'I'm glad,' he said, kissing her on the forehead.

'Is there anything else I can do for you?'

'Yes,' he mused. 'Tell me about yourself.' He felt her body grow rigid against his.

'What would you like to know?'

'Well, I should like to learn about your family... your parents. Do you have brothers and sisters? I should like to get to know you.'

'He wants to get to know me,' Jemima thought. 'How can this be the same man, who threw me out of his house? I don't understand.'

'I'm waiting!' he teased. 'I should like to know every little detail about you.'

'My parents are dead,' she said after a time. 'I am an only child and I have always been alone.' There was no need for her to lie about that.

'How sad,' he said, kissing her softly on the palm. 'It was never my intention to upset you. Let's speak of other things... where's the wine?'

She pointed to the dressing table and climbed out of bed to bring the bottle over. He replenished both their glasses as she settled beside him again. 'I do not mind talking about my parents... not to you,' she said.

He looked across at her seriously. 'Only if you're quite sure.'

'They were very poor. I did not have many toys or pretty things but they tried their best.'

What would her parents think of her now, she thought? She was a prostitute in bed with her former mistress's husband. 'I have many pretty things now. Look...' She pointed out the glittering bracelets on the bedside table. 'They are not mine really. I have to return them to Mrs Wilson.' William attempted to touch her face but instinctively, she looked away. 'And you? Do you have a wife? Do you have children?'

He lowered his head to his chest. 'Yes, I am married. I have a daughter and a son but my wife and I are presently separated.'

For a fleeting moment Jemima was thrilled. *'Separated?'* she said silently to herself. But his eyes looked exceedingly sad and immediately, she regretted broaching the subject. She was relieved, however, that he had not chosen to lie and sinking further into his arms, she reeled at the incredulity of it all.

It was gone seven o'clock when Butterfly banged on the door. Her shrill voice stung their ears and they stirred, bleary-eyed and worse for drink. 'I wish I didn't have to leave,' he whispered. 'But I must return home.'

'I'll get your clothes,' she said, fighting to break free from his playful grasp.

Daylight danced behind the curtains but she kept them closed as she retrieved his shirt and trousers. Her hair was wild and her eyes smudged with *kajal* and so she dipped a corner of a towel into a pitcher of water and cleaned her cheeks and eyes. Coiling her tresses to one side of her shoulder, she noticed how her features were now fully exposed. Quickly, she swept her hair forward and resumed her task of collecting his belongings that were thrown far and wide in their passion the night before. As she positioned one of his shoes alongside its partner, she noticed a peculiar stare emanating from his eyes. 'What is it?' she asked timorously.

'Come closer,' he said.

'Why?'

'I wish to look at you.'

Clutching his trousers tightly to her breast, she edged towards him. She was not sure if she wanted him to recognise her, for then she could challenge him over what he and his wife had done. But then their glorious passion would end in an instant. *'Why do I feel so confused?' she thought.* Seconds later and quite without warning, he snatched the trousers from her hands and flung them across the room. Her apprehension turned to relief as he dragged her into an embrace. Her relief turned to laughter and then passion all over again.

Again, Butterfly's fist thundered upon the door and William Hayward clambered out of bed, raising a hand to the curtains.

'No!' Please, don't open them!' Jemima cried, startled by the intensity of her own voice

'Very well,' he said, curiously. 'You're not one of those vampires from the Balkans are you? Will you turn to dust or disappear altogether in the sunlight? You do insist on keeping your room so dark.'

'Vampire?' she said curiously. 'What is that?' she asked defensively.

'Never mind,' he smiled. 'Gracious! I'm going to tremendously late!' Reluctantly, he pulled on his clothes and then withdrew a small pouch from inside his jacket pocket. It rattled as he tossed it to her. 'For you,' he said, 'I would like you to buy some pretty things for yourself.' He brought a finger to his lips. 'I shouldn't go telling Mrs Wilson. It's for you and you only. In fact... if there's anything you need... you must come to me anytime.'

Jemima felt uneasy. Days ago, she would have taken money from William Hayward without thinking twice. He and his callous wife owed her more than a passage back to India. But now, as she looked at his face, she saw the kind, sympathetic man she had fallen for staring back at her with genuine concern. He kissed her on the mouth and rose to leave. 'Wait!' she said, pulling him back down. 'Why have you and your wife separated?'

He settled back on the bed and sighed. 'She and I are two very different characters...let's leave it at that, shall we?'

'What do you mean?' she asked eagerly.

'Our wants and needs... our beliefs of life... unfortunately, they're not the same,' he said. 'Heaven knows I've made my fair share of mistakes but she's done one or two reprehensible things herself.'

'Like what?'

William fidgeted uncomfortably. 'Must I talk about her? I come here to get away from thinking about her.'

'Please... tell me,' Jemima insisted.

'Well, it's hardly her fault but she's steadfastly traditional in her ways and then there's India... she couldn't abide the country, whereas... I adored the place. She sent my children's ayah home without allowing them to say goodbye. They were most upset.'

Jemima trembled. *'That's a lie!' she wanted to scream. 'She never sent me home! I'm here!'*

'My children were... and still are...utterly heartbroken. They were extremely fond of their ayah. It was heartless of my wife to deny them their final farewell.'

Then something wonderful emerged from Elizabeth Hayward's lie, for Jemima realised that William Hayward had nothing whatsoever to do with her abandonment. That was another spiteful fabrication.

'I really must depart,' he said, rising from the bed.

'One moment,' she cried, throwing her arms around him. 'Hurry back to me,' she whispered. 'Hurry back.'

'I shall return this weekend,' he said squeezing her hand one last time.

And return William Hayward did to spend evenings of pure pleasure and utter indulgence with his newly found *paramour*. He left her money each time he visited: usually a crown or two, which she concealed under the loose soles of her walking boots. She often caught him staring at her strangely; sometimes after they had made love or whenever her features were free from her face paint. But William was incapable of making the connection and thus unable to identify his courtesan as his former ayah. He left again, unable to say when he would be able to return, for he was working on a last will and testament and she was too much of a pleasurable distraction. He promised not be parted from her for more than two weeks and with a departing kiss, he left her lounging beneath the sheets of their worn out bed.

Ivy was waiting for him at the bottom of the stairs. Her undulating fingers were tapping the banister post. 'It's time to pay, Mr Hayward.'

'Yes of course,' he replied, searching for his pocket book.

'Until the end of the month as usual?' Ivy asked, leading the way into her office.

'The end of the month is fine. I shall be a little busy, so I shan't be able to come as often as I'd like to.'

Ivy opened her diary and studied the pages. 'It makes no difference to me, Mr Hayward. As long as you adhere to the arrangement, you may come and go as you please.'

A frantic knock at the door prevented any further discussion and Butterfly entered, looking rather harassed.

'What is it?' Ivy asked.

'It's Ezrine, Missus Wilson. She's frettin' 'cos her mister ain't turned up.'

Ivy sighed. 'Would you excuse me, Mr Hayward? I have a matter that needs attending to.'

'Of course, how about if I leave a month's money in your diary?'

'That would be splendid. There's nobody about, so you can leave the mask here. Your hansom's waiting for you outside. Butterfly! Please show Mr Hayward to the side door.'

He left twenty pounds sitting in the pages of the bawd's diary and then crossed paths with a dark-featured girl in the hallway outside. Her intense black eyes peered at him lustfully and purposefully, she brushed up against him whilst sweeping her fingers along the folds of his cloak.

'Come along. Ezrine!' Ivy barked, bundling the girl into her office.

William followed Butterfly but stopped halfway through the oak-panelled corridor. 'Blast! I've forgotten my gloves! Carry on, Butterfly... I'll go and fetch them... I'll only be a few seconds.'

Butterfly tottered on, shivering from the breeze blowing through the chinks in the Atrium's side door. It was snowing outside and her bones rattled as she waited for William Hayward to return. She tightened the shawl around her shoulders and as seconds turned to minutes, she huffed furiously. 'Come on, Mister, hurry up! My stump's gonna seize up good and tight if I don't get outta this cold air.'

A quick succession of footsteps grew louder through the corridor. 'You find them gloves, Mr Hayward?' Butterfly asked, noticing his pale face. 'You all right, Mr Hayward? You look kinda strange...'

William Hayward did not answer but strode past Butterfly sporting a look of utter dread. He offered no apology for almost accidentally knocking her to the ground but sprinted up the metal steps only to vanish into his awaiting cab.

'Saints alive!' yelped Butterfly. 'What spooked him? Almos' broke my one good leg too!'

She slammed the door against the icy wind and scuttled back along the corridor, startled by the man's odd behaviour. 'Hmm,' she huffed. 'Didn't have no gloves in his hand neither!'

CHAPTER 48

THE DAGUERREOTYPE

Whilst she waited for William Hayward to return, Jemima drew on her skills as a servant and helped Butterfly dress and arrange the other girls' outfits and hair. Naturally, they were jealous of her exclusive trysts with the handsome blonde gentleman but in a bid to win their favour, she volunteered to mend torn blouses and stitch loose hems, despite their jeers and never-ending taunts. She had been placed in the fortunate position of having to sleep with one man – a man she utterly adored – and it was hugely preferable than having to satisfy several others. Mrs Wilson was ready to come to her defence, saying that when the other girls' clients paid outrageous sums to keep them, then they too could enjoy the benefits of a private agreement. Until then, she advised them to keep their opinions to themselves.

It was while Jemima was in the midst of sewing a trim on Nuwani's blue blouse that Ivy entered her room in a state of excitement. 'Mr Hayward's arrived, dear!' she said out of breath.

'But he's not expected for another week! And I'm not dressed!'

'I'm surprised myself, dear. He always sends word before he comes by but it is his prerogative I suppose... and he does spend an awful lot on you.'

Jemima skewered Nuwani's blouse with her needle and bundled the garment into a chest of drawers. William Hayward would be coming up shortly and she wondered what she could do to make herself pretty in the fleeting minutes that remained. She hardly had the time to neaten her hair when he knocked upon the door and stepped into the room. Saying nothing at first, he noticed that her face was free from paint and examined her features almost obsessively. Bashfully, she held out her arms to him but William Hayward ignored her desire for an affectionate embrace; in fact, it seemed he could barely bring himself to look her in the eye.

'I thought I wouldn't be seeing you so soon,' she said, alarmed by his detachment. 'What is it? What's wrong?'

William removed his mask and plunged his hand into his coat pocket. He withdrew an item wrapped inside a handkerchief and then eyed her most suspiciously. 'Is it you?' he demanded before showing her the *daguerreotype* of an ayah sitting at Robert and Sophie's feet.

But now that William Hayward had asked his question, Jemima could only think of the days gone by, when, as a child, she had ridden piggyback on Subhas's broad shoulders and played 'hide and seek' with the Mukherjee children in their old barn. There was even a recollection of her sitting still in the village temple whilst Madhu offered a *puja* to the gods. Her parents were honest, hardworking people and she had endeavoured to uphold their values throughout her meandering life. Now, looking towards *Ganesh*, the Lord of Beginnings, sitting in judgement upon her chest of drawers, Jemima realised that she must honour her parents' memories and do what was just and right. 'Yes,' she said. 'It is me,' and after that, she could say no more.

When William Hayward returned to Mrs Wilson's office to fetch his gloves the previous week, he had stood outside the door, waiting for an opportune moment to interrupt the conversation arising inside. The knuckle of his index finger was poised only inches away but the two women inside the room were loquacious indeed.

'Stop fretting, Ezrine, I'm sure Mr Asquith will arrive soon. You know he likes to stop at the gin houses ... he'll probably turn up inebriated again and try to beat down your door with his walking stick.'

'This is the second time he's late,' Ezrine moaned, stamping her foot like a spoilt child. 'And I'm losing money. I could have had gone through two fellows by now if not for that fool!'

'There's a party of five arriving at eleven o'clock for the European girls. I'm sure they won't mind if you join them,' said Ivy gathering the money in her diary.

'I wouldn't mind a taste of the blonde gentleman, that's for sure. Isn't it time Jemima shared him?' Ezrine purred.

'She can't share him,' Ivy insisted. 'And she doesn't want to be called Jemima anymore so you must remember to call her Priya. Now hand me my shawl.'

Ezrine plucked Ivy's shawl from the back of a chair and spied something lying on the seat. 'Look, a pair of gentleman's gloves.'

'Oh,' Ivy said. 'They must belong to Priya's patron.'

But Priya's patron was no longer standing outside the office door.

'How could you keep this from me? You were ayah to my children and not only that, you never mentioned a word when I told you what Elizabeth did.'

'But *you* came here... and *you* chose me. I swear I did not know who you were until you removed your mask.'

He stopped pacing the room and remained quite still. 'And how do you explain your actions after that? You were a servant to my wife and children and still... knowingly, you seduced me.'

'Of that I am guilty,' she said, brushing her fingers across her forehead 'But please, understand that...'

'Understand?' William interrupted. 'Understand? I've no idea what to think, let alone understand!' Then, seizing his mask, William departed in haste, leaving the building without speaking to anyone.

Jemima kept the truth of the exchange to herself and spoke of a quarrel that had occurred between her and William Hayward after she had demanded more of his time. She told Mrs Wilson she had been jealous of his wife and he had departed in a fury. But Mrs Wilson did not flinch or fuss. 'I wouldn't worry yet, my dear,' she remarked. 'He's paid up until the end of the month. If he hasn't made an appearance by the beginning of April, then I'm afraid your exclusivity will have to come to an end.'

Previously, whilst she waited for William Hayward, Jemima plaited the other girls' hair, tightened corsets and mended ravaged blouses. She had been bound by a contract that tied her to only one man, but how would she cope at the end of the month when he failed to return? Now she must accustom herself to the notion that she was just like the others and then perhaps, the reality of sleeping with a stranger would not be that bad.

She listened to the tales of Nuwani's men, whose ages spanned from thirty to sixty-six. She heard of the politician who wept whilst climaxing and the property tycoon who bragged about his sexual prowess. There was the young civil servant, who, when drunk, begged Nuwani to marry him, and then there was 'the Major,' who was pre-disposed to bringing his Ceylonese temptress expensive gifts.

The Major – Nuwani's most senior client – had already given her three silk handkerchiefs, a silver hairpin, two figurines and a mound of money. He liked Nuwani to dance for him and often rewarded her at the end of her dance recitals. She had combined some traditional Ceylonese dance movements with the poses learnt from Ezrine, and the Major would find each routine rather delightful and deliver his treat soon after her performance. Most recently, he had surprised Nuwani with a porcelain ballerina and three days later, Jemima found her friend acting in a rather over-excited fashion outside her bedroom door.

'I must speak to you! Come to my room after breakfast,' Nuwani whispered, skipping down the stairs two at a time.

All through breakfast, Nuwani tried to communicate something to Jemima that the others were not supposed to know. Leaving half her toast uneaten and most of her tea untouched, she excused herself from the table and beckoned Jemima to follow her on.

'What is it?' Jemima cried, bursting through her bedroom door.

'Shush!' replied Nuwani. 'I don't want the others to hear.'

'Hear what?'

Nuwani whirled Jemima down onto the bed and beamed a smile as big as the Indian Ocean. Squeezing Jemima's fingers ever so tightly, she kissed her friend jubilantly on both cheeks. 'I did it Jemima. I did it!' she squealed. 'Sometimes I thought I never would but I did. I did it!'

'Did what? What have you done?'

Nuwani's body rippled triumphantly and her face looked pert and smug. 'I'm going home, Jemima!' she proclaimed. 'I'm going home!'

CHAPTER 49
NUWANI'S SECRET

Jemima remembered that momentous day at Mare Street lodging house when she had stood in the Visitors' Room, trying to tell the other women that Mrs Rice-Thomas was taking her back home. Their pain was more palpable now than it was back then and it descended on her in bouts of nauseous waves. Now she could really empathise with the way those women felt, for no matter how thrilled she was at hearing Nuwani's news, the reality of being left behind was hacking away at her heart like a murderous blade. 'I don't understand,' she said. 'How?'

Nuwani hunted around in the bottommost drawer of a chest for something. It jingled as she brought it out into the light of day and jingled again when she placed it onto her bed. Jemima saw a petticoat wrapped and rolled several times and when Nuwani peeled back the last layer, a pile of sovereigns tumbled onto the bedspread. 'Look,' she whispered. 'I have saved enough money to go home.'

Jemima could not quite believe her eyes. 'Where did you get this from?' she asked, drawing her envious fingertips across the shiny coins.

'Remember the Major? And all the gifts he gave me? I sold them.'

Jemima's mouth fell open. 'How could you sell them? We are never allowed to leave this place and when we do leave, we are chaperoned.'

'You will never guess!'

'The Major?'

'Don't be silly!' Nuwani grimaced. 'He bought me the things in the first place! My goodness! He must never find out that I sold them. Guess again!'

'I cannot guess!' Jemima hissed. 'To whom did you sell them?'

Nuwani finally divulged the name. 'It was Mr Sandhu.'

Nuwani's association with the Parsee dandy commenced well before Jemima arrived at the Atrium. She had made his acquaintance on three occasions and it was the fourth meeting that gave her the idea. On account of his very fair skin, Nuwani had not assumed that Mr Sandhu was of Indian descent. She was aware that his name was of Eastern extraction but knew nothing else of his lineage. After summoning the courage to ask something of his background, Sandhu confirmed his Indian ancestry but went onto explain that he had disposed of his Indian ways to fully embrace all things English. He seemed to know everything from the stories behind each item in his assemblage, to the kind of tea Queen Victoria loved to sip. He had travelled extensively and even mentioned visiting the island of Ceylon.

'You have been to my country more than once?' Nuwani asked.

'Oh yes. Twice from India and once from here.'

'From here? You sailed from here?'

The magnified eyeball behind Sandhu's monocle jerked at Nuwani's sudden interest in his travel history. 'Well, I sailed in a ship from Southampton but that was nearly three years ago.'

'How much did you pay?'

'Well, let's see. I paid… if I recall correctly… around fifteen pounds or so… first class, of course.'

'What about a third-class passenger's fare?' she whispered.

'Oh, something in the region of one or two pounds I suppose.'

Mr Sandhu could tell by the way Nuwani's eyes were darting in their sockets that she was trying to calculate the time it would take to save her fare. And knowing it would take a lifetime on the wages Mrs Wilson paid her girls, Sandhu's heart panged with sympathy. 'If you like, I could find out for you… and you don't have to worry… I won't tell *you know who*.'

And so, the next time Mr Sandhu graced the Atrium, he set aside a pot of *kajal*, especially made for Nuwani. 'It's a particular kind of *kajal*,' he said, 'one that will enhance the joy in your eyes!'

Nuwani failed to understand Sandhu's secret code but lifting the lid off the pot later that evening, she found a tiny note lying on top of the black paste, saying…

Third-class deck ticket to Ceylon: £3.00.

Her heart shrunk at the insuperable figure. To save that amount would take even longer than she had first thought. Jemima's unexpected arrival preoccupied her thoughts for a while, but after confessing the truth of her work at the Atrium, she was soon reminded of her quest to go home. She remembered how the Parsee merchant loved to buy beautiful things and searched her room for items he might favour. But most of the valuables belonged to Mrs Wilson and she had purchased them from Sandhu in the first place. Nuwani's own scant belongings were worthless and decrepit but she would not give up; she would persevere.

Nuwani was not in high-spirits when she entertained the Major on his next visit to the Atrium. She danced somewhat sombrely and climbed into bed as rigid as a marionette. He would always be flat on his back, just as he favoured, for there were no other positions his ageing bones preferred. 'What's the matter with my little Ceylonese bird?' he asked, reaching over to tickle her ear. 'You seem awfully sad, today.'

She said it was nothing, yet failed to muster the energy to please him.

'Dear, dear, we cannot have you sporting a face as long as a horse's. Perhaps this will cheer you up,' he said, summoning her to hold out a hand. A steely coldness swept against Nuwani's palm, like a small snake slithering against her fingers. 'Open your eyes!' the Major commanded.

Nuwani's eyes nearly popped out of their sockets as she spied a pearl necklace in her hand. A squeal of delight burst from her lips as she twisted her shoulders so the Major could drape it around her neck. Keen to admire it in the looking glass, she leapt out of bed and scurried over to the dresser. 'You'd best hide it from Ivy, my dear,' the Major said. 'It cost a lot of money and she'll probably steal it!'

The Major's words peeled like bells. '*It cost a lot of money...*'

Naked but for a string of pearls around her neck, Nuwani sprinted into the Major's saggy old arms and thanked him in the way that he was accustomed to being thanked, for unbeknown to him he had shown her the way back home. And as fond as she was of the porcelain ballerina, she hid it inside her shawl and carried it with her when Sandhu made his customary visit. 'Will you buy this?' she asked with big eager eyes.

Sandhu rotated the statue within his manicured fingers and examined it closely with his one shielded eye. A moment later, he offered her sum of one pound. Nuwani then wondered how much Sandhu would pay for the handkerchiefs and pearls. As long as she had acquired enough for her sea and train passages, she did not care if he cheated her out of her dues. Hence, through a series of covert transactions, Nuwani sold the Major's gifts to Mr Sandhu, who effervesced at the thought of having disingenuously procured them.

After sharing her happy secret with Jemima, Nuwani remained in her room, ensconced in a world that saw her reunited with her husband and children. In the forest beyond their hut, her daughters would be playing amongst a spray of avocado trees, whilst her husband, Aruna, would be crouched at a small table, earning a living from making incense. First, he would roll a little ball of perfumed black resin onto a thin wooden stick and then leave it to dry amongst hundreds of others in the sun's thick heat. She would help him mix his attars and then blend the gum that, when dry and ignited, would produce the various scents, and later they would go to the local market, where they would try and sell as many boxes as they could. When she first arrived at the Atrium, Nuwani found it difficult to look at Sandhu's supplies of incense, for not only did it make her wonder if they had come from the shores of Ceylon, but it would have broken her heart to have known they had been made by Aruna's own hands.

The whinnying of horses shattered her reverie and peering through her bedroom window, she saw that Mrs Wilson's carriage had come to a halt on the corner. She hurried down the staircase and found Ivy in the midst of untying her bonnet.

'Nuwi dear, shouldn't you be getting ready? The clients will be here soon.'

'I should like to speak with you in private, Mrs Wilson. It is very important.'

Ivy scowled when a wayward curl would not stay put. 'If it's about the sari Ezrine wanted to wear... let her wear it. You may borrow one of Priya's. Now run along, dear.'

'It's not about the sari.'

Ivy glared at Nuwani. 'Wait one moment,' she hissed, waiting for the driver to deposit her purchases. She then invited Nuwani into her office.

'Now, what's this about?' she asked, removing her gloves.

'I wish to leave.'

'Leave dear? Leave and go where?'

'Home.'

Ivy's eyes glazed over into an unforgiving stare but their vigilance soon returned to issue a harsh warning to the young woman in their focus. She fidgeted madly with her white leather gloves and prickled when Nuwani marched forward and drew her fingers into two tight fists.

'I am going home, Mrs Wilson.'

'My dear, how could you possibly go home? I believe you have to buy a ticket for that and frankly, I don't pay you enough to be able to afford one... not this soon at any rate.'

'I have saved enough, Mrs Wilson. I have saved enough money to buy a ticket home.'

'That's impossible!' Ivy retorted. 'There's absolutely no way you could have saved that much!' Her white gloves fell and accidentally, she trod upon them, leaving a muddy footprint across several of the fingers.

'I sold some of my things...'

'What things and to whom?'

'It doesn't matter to whom I sold them. They were my things to sell. *Mine!* I want to leave. I want to go home!'

Ivy cursed and flapped, agitated that one of her girls had managed to outsmart her. 'You're one of my best girls, Nuwi. Customers pay good money for you!'

'You told me the African woman went home. She saved her money and went home!'

'I lied!' Ivy yelled, her eyes bulging, 'to get you to stay!'

The noises from the office had lured Jemima from her room and Butterfly away from the scullery. Both women exchanged bewildered looks and Jemima leaned further over the banister, trying to improve her chances of hearing the altercation. She heard Nuwani scream, 'Please! Please!'

And then, Mrs Wilson shouted, 'Never! *Never!* You belong to me... and the money for your ticket will pay for your rent and clothes.'

'But I have already bought it!' Nuwani cried. 'You cannot take it!' she hissed, burying her head in her hands and mumbling her words through mangled lips. 'You lied to me. You lied to me! I want to go home. I want to see my husband and my children. My children!' she shrieked, tumbling to her knees, rocking back and forth. She remained that way for several minutes until an icy cold finger lifted her chin.

'I wasn't aware that you had a husband and children,' Ivy said softly, brandishing a hanky to wipe away her tears.

'I was... I am... ashamed,' Nuwani said, looking up through glistening eyes.

The commotion downstairs had drawn the other girls out from their rooms. Some had taken seats on the staircase next to Jemima; others dawdled on the landing, swapping opinions and comments in a series of whispers. Butterfly busied herself with some pretend chores but one ear was poised to learn of the goings on between the Ceylonese girl and the bawd. The pair soon emerged from the office and it was clear that tears had left their traces on Nuwani's smooth brown cheeks. Mrs Wilson's face looked careworn but after spying the little audience gathered on the stairs, she yelled, 'Get back to your rooms!'

The girls dispersed and Butterfly headed back to the scullery. Nuwani brushed past Ivy and began her ascent of the staircase. Before she was able to reach the first step, Ivy grabbed her by the elbow. 'Ezrine will be wearing the pink sari tonight, Nuwi. You may borrow one from Priya,' she said nonchalantly. Turning, she delivered a brutal look in Jemima's direction.

Jemima tilted her head towards Nuwani's and asked in a whisper. 'What happened?'

Nuwani kept her voice low. 'She's allowing me go, Jemima. She's allowing me go.'

An announcement was made over breakfast the next morning: Nuwani would be returning to Ceylon in a week's time but she would be entertaining her clients up until the night before her departure. It was also announced that other than wages, all monies and gifts from customers were to be handed over without delay and, if necessary, Ivy and Butterfly would go through each girl's room with a fine toothcomb and woe-betide anyone if they found anything hidden. Jemima's savings were still stashed under the soles of her walking boots. It never would have occurred to her to sell her possessions like Nuwani had done. But Mrs Wilson had taken pity on Nuwani after learning of her family back in Ceylon, but would she be that sympathetic when Jemima's turn came?

Nuwani never let it be known that it was Mr Sandhu who bought the Major's gifts, but Ivy suspected that it could only have been him. However, she never confronted or accused him of conspiring against her wishes, for theirs was a relationship too advantageous to spoil. She did insist Sandhu make all the travel arrangements to the East and happily, he obliged, offering out his personal carriage and manservant, Gopal, to accompany Nuwani until she set foot on the boat sailing to Europe. He had also taken the liberty to outline every detail of her itinerary; a favour gladly granted for, in his words, 'not letting the cat out of the bag.'

It was a strange farewell – heart-rending for Jemima but undoubtedly heavenly for Nuwani. 'No tears,' she said, wiping Jemima's big brown eyes. 'Be strong. Your chance will come next.' And while the others expressed great sadness to see one of their brightest 'birds' leave, Jemima pictured Nuwani in the arms of her husband and children, and for that reason alone, she knew there was no need for tears.

CHAPTER 50

WITHIN THE HEM OF
THE BLUE CURTAIN

Such was the commotion prior to Nuwani's departure that Jemima had not dwelt much on her acrimonious parting from William Hayward but with Nuwani gone, there was no one with whom she could share her hollow days, for just as she feared, Ezrine had become jealous and aloof. She discovered the Malaysian girl in her room one day, sifting through her clothes and possessions. The drawers were fully open and upturned boxes of jewellery lay scattered on her bed. Luckily, her boots remained untouched by Ezrine's encroaching hands. 'What are you doing?' Jemima demanded.

Ezrine hardly batted an eyelid and rose up from the bed with a tub of Jemima's lip paint in one hand and her ivory comb in the other. 'I have often wondered what it is that's so special about you when it was *I* who taught you how to dance, how to move... how to *really* please a man. If it weren't for *me*, do you think your mister would even look at you twice?'

Jemima shrunk against the door, thinking of the moment when Ezrine and the others would learn that William Hayward had ended their arrangement. What supreme pleasure they would take in her fall from grace, for finally she would be made to take her place amongst them. 'Take them if you want them,' she said, eyeing the items in Ezrine's fists.

Ezrine *did* take them, and she thundered past Jemima with a green fire roaring in her eyes.

From that moment on, the Malaysian girl offered her nothing but stony stares and thorny silences and when twenty-one days turned into a month, Jemima feared the night she would have to share her bed with a stranger.

'I've still not heard any word from him,' Mrs Wilson frowned, lamenting the financial loss of her arrangement with William. 'It looks like he's gone off you. I shall have to put you back into the ring.'

Jemima never really thought of herself as a prostitute. She had had to only satisfy one man – a man she worshipped – and yes, he paid for her sexual services but, in her opinion, she was no different from a customary mistress, so how could she not have enjoyed the exclusivity of their arrangement? Selling her body to more than one man, however, was a thought that re-pulsed her deeply and now that certainty was looming ever closer, she could not rid herself of William Hayward's face. She had tried ousting him from her mind in favour of concentrating on the task of returning home, but enjoying a fling with her former memsahib's husband was a thrilling prospect she could not have turned down, though she had never meant for things to get out of hand, and he was never meant to find out who she really was.

Jemima turned her walking boots upside down and heard the tinkle of coins as they hit the floor. Thus far, her earnings were three crowns and sixpence: less than half of what she needed for a passage home. Like Nuwani, she must save enough until it was possible to leave but after witnessing Mrs Wilson's noxious reaction to Nuwani's departure, she knew the woman would never let her go. Thus, she would have to abscond. She would have to find her way back to the Shadwell Inn and to Ibrahim in spite of the risks involved. He would certainly help her buy a ticket home; in the meantime, she must earn her keep by allowing herself to be mauled by a pack of lusty male wolves. More importantly though, she must keep her savings safe by finding a better hideaway than the flimsy compartments of her old walking boots.

Jemima reasoned that there was no cupboard, drawer, pot or box that Mrs Wilson would not overturn. She climbed onto a chair by the window and peered along the ledge in the hope of finding a nook or cranny into which her money could be effectively stowed. Defeated by the quest, she lowered her foot and felt it catch the hem of the blue velvet curtain. The edge fell open and she cursed herself for doing damage to Mrs Wilson's property. The bawd would surely mend the curtain with money taken from her wages and frankly, Jemima needed every penny she could get.

She contemplated stitching the tear herself before Mrs Wilson came to inspect the room the next day and hunted in her sewing box for a suitable blue colour. She found the cotton used to stitch the sleeves of Nuwani's sapphire coloured sari blouse; it was a shade lighter, still, it would have to do. As she fed the cotton through the eye of the needle, another idea bounded into her head. Here was the perfect hiding place: a place where no one would look – within the hem of the blue curtain. The needle was left dangling as she reached for her secret stash of coins. She pinched one along and left enough space to insert the rest and then sewed with large, loose stitches, which could be easily unpicked if she needed to hide more. The next morning, Mrs Wilson came and went, satisfied nothing incriminating was present and Jemima congratulated herself for outfoxing her keeper.

April loomed and with her next set of wages, Jemima had saved the respectable sum of six pounds, sixteen shillings and sixpence. She could now afford a third-class deck ticket home but she had to consider carriage expenses, train fares and the cost of all the intermediate steamer routes. She could have benefited from the extra money William often slipped into her palm but now their trysts had ended most regrettably, she would have to join the other girls later to be fondled by an assortment of rich but exceedingly strange men. However, she would run away when the first chance arose: during an outing to the market or perhaps when she was taken to see Dr Rose for her regular health check; she was due an appointment the following week.

Sitting alone in her room, mustering some courage to face the approaching night, Jemima considered fleeing the Atrium right there and then. But her daring train of thought dissipated hastily when Mrs Wilson burst into her room, wagging her hands madly. 'You'll never guess, dear! You'll never guess! Mr Hayward is downstairs and he's desperate to see you!'

At first, elated by the news, Jemima then resigned herself to the notion that he had come to punish her for her earlier deceit. Crossing to the farthest corner of the room, she waited for him with baited breath, but when he stepped into her boudoir, Jemima saw a tired and tormented face. 'You're probably wondering what I'm doing here... I'm wondering myself. I came here because I wanted you to know that what Elizabeth did to you was wretched and unforgivable. And not only that, I realise that I was horridly unjust the last time I saw you, and if what happened between us is anyone's fault, then let it be mine.' William's brow creased and his eyes pleaded. 'If you only knew...if you only knew how these past few weeks have been...' he said rubbing his forehead. 'I regret everything that's happened to you and I need you... above everyone else... to forgive me.'

Jemima's relief was so strong that all she could do was close her eyes and hope that William Hayward would say his remorseful words again. Moving in closer, she pulled him into a tight embrace.

'I've missed you terribly, Priya.'

'But I am Jemima,'

'Not anymore.'

He was right. Ayah had gone.

'I forgive you... I forgive you,' she said, holding onto him.

She invited him into her bed and he followed gladly. 'I regret that I cannot stay. I must leave before midnight. In fact, from now on it's going to be difficult for me stay at all.'

'Why?'

'It's Elizabeth,' he said. 'She's come home.'

Appearing suddenly and without prior message, Elizabeth had thrown her husband's world into utter disarray. He had been trying to concentrate on a will and testament that if not for Jemima, should have taken up his entire attention. But unable to blot out his relationship with his wife's former servant, he decided it would be best to go home and refresh his mind before continuing on with his work. It was a little after nine when he returned to Carlton House Terrace. Cole greeted him as usual but there was a subtle change in the butler's demeanour, for it exhibited a rather heightened sense of propriety.

'Is everything all right, Cole?' William asked.

'Yes everything's fine, sir,' he answered, glancing over his shoulder. 'Mrs Hayward has returned, sir... she's in the drawing room.'

William had not seen his wife for almost three months and if he was being entirely honest, the news of her return was not as thrilling to him as it should have been. She was sitting by the fire with a book in her lap and she was wearing her hair differently.

'Good evening, William,' she said.

'Good evening, Elizabeth. You should have sent word that you were coming home.'

'It was all done in haste, William, besides… Sophie wanted to see her father.' She closed her book and reached for a lamp. 'I've been seated here, waiting for you all evening and I'm rather tired now. I do not wish to discuss anything further tonight. Perhaps we could discuss matters tomorrow? I shall tell cook to expect you for dinner. Good night,' she said, rising from the sofa.

William's head began to hurt. He recalled how livid he was to discover that Priya had once been Jemima, his wife's servant, but now his own hypocrisy was impossible to ignore. He had accused his courtesan of lying when he had so often lied himself and he was by far, the worst offender, for he had knowingly deceived his wife and children and he was knowingly deceiving them now. It seemed that Elizabeth's return – no matter how much it irked him – was now forcing him to confront his true feelings.

Meanwhile, upstairs in her chamber, Elizabeth Hayward shook uncontrollably as she sat on her newly made bed. Underneath that fine layer of porcelain skin, a heart was foaming at its mouth and an outwardly confident demeanour was crumbling into un-mitigated fury. William had not rushed over to embrace her, nor had he expressed a desire to kiss her on the cheek. Could he not even pretend to have missed her company? It was highly appar-ent that he could not. Elizabeth buried her nails into her copy of *Jane Eyre* and hurled it across the room.

An awkward atmosphere consumed the pair at dinner the fol-lowing evening. They engaged in the motions of… 'Please pass that…'

'Would you like more of this?'

Elizabeth registered the jittery manner in which her husband stabbed the asparagus and severed his meat into tiny pieces. 'My parents are aware of your little affair, William,' she declared.

'How?' he asked, looking up suddenly.

'I told them.'

William accidentally dropped his knife into his lap.

'Father wanted to know if it was over and I assured him that it was... he insists that I should forget about it. In fact, Mother says that most men take mistresses... even my own father... but I shouldn't like to pursue that now. In Mother's opinion, most women tolerate their husbands' indiscretions as long as the affairs don't interfere with the workings of the family. Of course, I didn't tell them that you'd been cavorting with a filthy little coolie girl... now that would have been far too much for them to bear. Frankly, I don't want anyone knowing that grubby little detail.'

William listened without interrupting.

'I have been a good wife to you, William. Therefore, it would be highly unwise of you to divorce me... unless you accuse *me* of adultery of course!' At that point, she laughed almost hysterically. 'And even if I had proof of your indiscretion, I certainly cannot divorce you. It's most unfair what the women of cheating husbands have to put up with, don't you think? Yes, I believe that we are both in a rather wearisome situation.' She sunk her chin into her hands and peered up at him like a wilful schoolgirl. 'So, William, I'm quite happy to let the gossipmongers think you had some jaunt or another with an army officer's wife... or even that Ettie woman with whom you so loved to gallivant.' She plucked a bread roll from the basket and severed it in two. 'On my father's advice, I shall forget the unfortunate occurrence because I really don't have a choice now, do I?' She looked up at him and smiled. 'For the time being, we shall remain in separate rooms... but we shall be a family in every other sense and who knows, with time, I may even begin to like you again.' A morsel of bread pushed against Elizabeth's throat. 'What are your thoughts?'

'Whatever you think is best, dear,' he said. And then William wondered what his wife could be capable of if she ever found out that he had slept with her recently ousted Indian servant.

Henceforth, he began paying his penance by being present at each and every stuffy social event his wife organized. He played the role of loving husband until her requests almost reduced him to madness. Thus, with much regret and a great deal of consternation later, William Hayward pined for Priya like a lost hound in search of its beloved owner and it really did not matter to him who she had previously been.

Jemima used to enjoy getting ready for William Hayward. She loved the rose-scented baths, the dressing up in saris, the adornment of jewellery and the reddening of her lips. The darkening of her eyes had become part and parcel of a ceremony that would turn her from a dreary caterpillar into a dazzling butterfly but now that pleasure had most definitely faded. Oftentimes, after she had spent hours preparing for his visit, he would fail to appear. Then each earring would be removed with overwhelming sadness and each bracelet squeezed off with a legion of tears tumbling from her eyes. She would wipe the rouge away from her lips in a fury and wash the *kajal* off her eyelids with devastating regret. And then she would revert to the dull caterpillar she had been in another life, wondering whether William Hayward was worth all the trouble. Another time and quite unexpectedly, he would arrive, apologising profusely for his absences. 'Forgive me,' he would say. 'This is the way it has to be.'

Begrudgingly, she accepted the limited time of their assignations but felt a sting from knowing that Elizabeth Hayward was still ruining her plans. 'What do you tell your wife?' she asked him one evening.

Startled by her question, he asked her what she meant.

'When you come here to be with me, what do you tell your wife?'

'That I'm working at the office... that sort of thing. But let's not discuss her... not when we have such little time together.'

She found his treachery satisfying but the thought of Elizabeth Hayward forever controlling her destiny nudged her into a silent rage. She saw herself strolling up to the woman and whispering the truth into her ear. What great pleasure she would take in seeing the expression on the memsahib's face as she writhed in the knowledge that her erstwhile Indian servant was now bedding her husband and, not only that, the man was now completely besotted. Oh, what satisfaction she would feel in taking her revenge, but alas the feeling would always fade as the faces of Robert and Sophie danced about in her head.

Jemima told herself that she was not a bad person but a victim of circumstance brought to despair by forces beyond her control. But the morose feelings always disappeared whenever William Hayward walked through her door. Though their time together was painfully brief, their passion was great and undeniably limitless. But now the time had come for Jemima to leave, the reality of his wife's return had only confirmed the fact that she must go. She would tell him her plans the next time he visited. Yes, despite the overwhelming happiness she felt as she lay in his arms – despite her boundless love for the man – she would tell William Hayward that the time had come for her to return to India's familiar shores.

CHAPTER 51
THE ONE SHE MOST LOVED

William's body was tense and he was especially irritable when he strode through the Atrium doors that evening, but Priya, the courtesan, knew how to remedy that. Inside her room, the balance of power would always swing in her favour and she learned how to wield it when he stepped into her sultry domain. She would undress him slowly and knead his muscular shoulders whilst his head lolled gently across her collarbone. She would kiss him softly along the edge of his ear and then all the way down his neck until ever so nimbly their bodies would twist into one. Sighing, heaving and pinching each other's skin, their fingers would remain locked together until they had perfected the art of lovemaking. Seductively, she would sweep her hair across his stomach as he unwound in the warmth of her soft, fragrant skin. Sometimes, she would fall asleep nestled across his stomach, but not today. There was something else on her mind today.

'William,' she said, resting her chin on his tummy. 'There is something I need to ask you.'

'Yes?'

She rose up and brought her hands across his bare shoulders. 'Before I tell you... do you remember when you said that I could come to you for anything?'

'I remember.'

'Well, I have saved some money... enough to pay for a passage to India.' She paused and looked at him. He said nothing but listened on. 'Mrs Wilson will not allow me leave and so I need your help. Will you help me?'

William turned his gaze towards the ornamental cushions propped against the bedpost.

'Say something please,' she appealed, trying to hijack his drifting gaze. Still, he said nothing. 'What's wrong? Why don't you speak?' She climbed off the bed in a panic. 'Why don't you speak? Why don't you answer me?' He remained silent. 'If you won't help me, I shall run away!' she huffed, pacing the room. 'I'll leave without your help. You'll see. I will get away!'

It was then that William Hayward leapt from the bed and seized Jemima tightly by the arms. 'Stop saying that!' he snapped, 'Heaven knows I would do anything for you but...I don't want you to go. I couldn't bear it!' She felt the pain of his plea in her ribs and urged him to loosen his grip. 'I'm being selfish, I know, but have you any idea what you mean to me? Before...when we parted... my life became so bleak. You mustn't leave. Please reconsider.'

'I told you that one day I would go home. I have been waiting for so long and now I have the chance.'

'I know,' he whispered, wrapping her in his embrace. 'I know... but I have grown especially fond of you. In fact, I love you.'

Only in Jemima's low-class dreams was William Hayward heard to utter such a momentous phrase, but now the reality of hearing him say it was almost too much for her to comprehend.

'Forgive me,' he pleaded. 'But I love you and I will go insane if you leave.'

There, he had said it again. But was it supposed to cause as much pain as it did joy?

'You love me? You love *me*?' she said, finding her voice.

'Yes...'

He had hardly finished his sentence before she flung her arms around him. 'I have always loved you... always... if you only knew.'

'Then you'll remain?'

'Come with me,' she said impetuously. 'Let's leave together.'

William's brow pulsed. 'I wish we could. How I wish we could. But I cannot abandon my children.'

She saw an ache in his eyes as he spoke of his children, yet Jemima had learned to put her needs first. 'I cannot live like this forever.'

'I know,' he said, his brow creasing again. 'Perhaps there's a resolution. I just need time for thought.' He sat on the bed and brought his locked fingers to his lips. 'Yes, that's it,' he said, bouncing up again. 'That's it! I shall take you away.' His blue eyes were glimmering gloriously. 'Do you trust me?'

Jemima's lips twitched but no words emerged. Did she trust him? In the past, she had been foolish enough to trust his wife.

'I'll take you away from here...' he said, 'you have my word. I'll find a place for you... for us... only stay, don't leave.'

'But Mrs Wilson... '

'Blast Mrs Wilson! Leave her to me. If you stay, I'll make everything better. I promise.'

Jemima was flummoxed and flattered by his sudden flight of fancy. 'I don't know...' she muttered.

'Besides,' he said, 'what is there to go back to? You haven't any family.'

He might as well have stamped on her heart but Jemima knew that William Hayward spoke the truth. There was nothing and no one to go back to. She would secure another position as an ayah or a servant, but was it possible for her to slip into a bland lifestyle of subservience after experiencing the glamour of the Atrium? Then again, it was not a matter of having someone or somewhere to return to; deep down, Jemima knew it was a matter of belonging and after the appalling experiences she had endured, she knew she did not belong in England.

'I'll make the arrangements,' he said, pulling on his shirt. 'Please be patient… just a little longer,' he begged. 'Please… say you'll stay.'

He knelt at her feet, offering her the power to crush or delight him. She cradled his face in her hands, wondering how life had become so difficult. Ever since she had been tossed away by Elizabeth Hayward, she had been driven by one goal: to return home. However, fate had thrown a series of horrendous obstacles in her path and now having finally overcome them, she could never have imagined the uncanny turn of events that would make her reconsider her decision. But the fog did clear and the confusion eventually subsided. Throwing caution to the wind, Jemima made her decision… to stay.

William recommended that she say nothing and carry on as normal. He would set about making all the arrangements and swore that she would be leaving with him the next time he visited. He promised her the world and much more besides and Jemima realised that there was another reason why she must stay, for she loved William Hayward and suddenly revenge seemed meaningless.

PART SIX

CHAPTER 52

IBRAHIM'S DREAM

By virtue of his own talent, Ibrahim had transformed the mediocre business of the Shadwell Inn into a thriving overnight success. It had become one of the most popular haunts in East London and life for the Indian chef had sparkled from that moment forth. The elite and the privileged were flocking to sample his food and those averse to travelling to the poorer part of the city sought to hire him as a private cook. They paid him virtually whatever he wanted and the money bolstered the modest income that Mr Meade had only just started to pay. His talent even lured the local press, who sent a fellow to interview him. The meeting was promptly hijacked by Mr Meade, who tended to do most of the talking on his chef's behalf. 'It's the God's honest truth that he came to me first but I could tell just by looking at him that he was a talented fellow. You should've seen the sight of 'im back then... skinny as a rake, hair down to his knees...looking like he'd been dragged through a briar backwards! Heaven knows what would've become of him if I hadn't taken him in! I practically taught 'im everything he knows.'

Despite Mr Meade's stilted version of the truth, Ibrahim was delighted to receive such glowing praise and in theory, he should have been sitting on the top of the world. But without Jemima to share his good fortune, his elation was tempered with unmitigated melancholy.

He had kept her things just as she had left them when she disappeared on New Year's Day. Her old green shawl was strewn across her bed and her valise stood forlornly at the foot of the cellar staircase. The fabric separating their respective sides of the room was still maintained in the event that she may return one night in need of shelter from whatever ordeal she may have suffered. But four months had already passed and there had been no sign of her and as an immense sorrow churned inside him, the encircling darkness told him that Jemima may never return.

Sarah became a great comfort to him. Each night she brought him a cup of tea and he even began to savour her watered down version of the beverage. Their lively conversations fought off any maudlin thoughts and he liked the way she listened intently whenever he spoke of his dreams and ambitions. He wanted to establish an eating house in a better part of the city – a place he could practise his art without Mr Meade constantly shadowing his moves. Sarah told him that if anyone could do it then Ibrahim could and she reminded him how quickly he was becoming a celebrated chef. Ibrahim knew it too and felt proud, but he needed to create a place that most befitted his title.

Endeavouring to describe his vision to Sarah one day, he talked of owning an establishment in the centre of London. 'It will be far from Shadwell and it will have velvet chairs, on which, people can comfortably sit. I will have smart-suited attendants who will present my masterful creations... not like in the common coffee houses. I want it to be like the establishments in Paris, France. They call them 'restaurants' and that is what I will call mine!'

Sarah clapped and swooned, and Ibrahim would beam as she hung onto his every word. In the past, he had thought lustfully of the girl and never more so than when she first brought over his first cup of tea. But as time passed, he grew fond of her in other ways, though she and Jemima were as different as two women could be. Demure and chaste, Jemima worked hard and knew her place. They shared different religions but she and Ibrahim had been brought up in mutual worlds of culture and tradition. As he saw it, Jemima would make the ideal wife, whilst Sarah on the other hand, was like an untamed child. She was pig-headed and coarse at times, but she tantalised Ibrahim with her vibrant laughter and cheeky ways. 'Oh Pa!' she would coo, 'ain't Ibrahim's manners lovely? Not like the skunks that come in 'ere. They wouldn't know a 'please' or 'thank you' from their arses!' Her crudeness made him want to pluck his hair out but it was her ability to uplift him in times of distress that he found endearing. 'You'll be the best chef in the country,' she would often declare. 'You're a genius, Ibrahim!'

It was sweet of the girl to say such things, but if she was right and he was to be the best chef ever, he would have to work harder and be smart about it too. Thus, with a heavy heart, he removed the piece of cloth dividing the cellar and packed it away inside a chest of drawers. He folded Jemima's old green shawl and placed it inside her travelling valise before stumbling across her humble possessions: some crumpled saris, a few bracelets, a comb and a pouch containing some shillings. The tin of *barfi* then caught his eye. It was dented in places and mottled with dirt and dark patches but the sight of it almost moved him to tears. Clasping it tightly, he made a pledge. 'Give me time,' he said, 'I will work hard and I will become a success and if you are alive and safe, Jemima, I will find you and I will make you my wife.' He scratched away the dried dirt and rolled the can within Jemima's shawl. He closed the valise and slid it in a corner and then promptly set about making his dream come true.

CHAPTER 53

COME HELL OR HIGH WATER

O n his last visit to the Atrium, William Hayward had promised Jemima that he would return in three days' time. But
three days turned into a week and a week stretched into fourteen
days and with expectation pummelling her heart, Jemima wondered if he would keep his word. Would William Hayward come
to her rescue and whisk her away? Or would he expose himself
as a cad, who had tampered with her feelings and divulged her
plan to Mrs Wilson?

Jemima entered her room with a month's wages tucked into
her palm. She rummaged inside her dresser drawer in search of
her notebook and pencil, and found both items hidden amongst
various pots of *kajal*, tubs of face paint and vials of rouge. Flipping
through the pages, she found her most recent entry: a figure of
twelve pounds, thirteen shillings and three pence. She drew a
line through the figure and wrote fifteen pounds, thirteen shillings and three pence underneath it. She still had the money
from the work previously done for Mehta but it was hidden in her
valise, which she had left behind at the Shadwell Inn. Adding that
to the amount already saved, and the quantity garnered from her

nights with William, Jemima now realised that she had the funds to make the epic journey home.

However, two weeks had already passed and William had not returned. It seemed he had filled her head with promises that were reckless and empty; it seemed he had unashamedly let her down. Two days later, however, Butterfly entered her room, announcing that Mrs Wilson immediately wished to see her in the office. Thus, when Jemima descended the staircase and saw Mrs Wilson standing in the doorway, frowning, she braced herself for a tornado of abuse.

'Come in,' Ivy said, 'and pray, sit down.' She closed the door and circled Jemima twice. 'It is with regret that I say my following words.'

'This is it,' Jemima thought. 'I've been found out. He must have told her the truth. William must have told her! It's all over now. Mrs Wilson will lock me away and never let me leave.'

She thought of the money stowed away in the hems of the curtains and fretted on how she would leave now that William had given the game away. *'Had he given the game away? Who else could it possibly be?'*

Ivy joined her palms together as if she were about to pray. 'An arrangement has been made for you to leave... tomorrow morning in fact.'

'Leave? Tomorrow?'

'Yes,' Ivy said, tinkering with her curls. 'I'm sorry to see you go. You've been a valuable employee... one of my best.'

Jemima wondered if it were all a cruel joke.

'Whatever's the matter, dear? Does the news not please you?' queried Ivy.

Jemima bounced up from her chair. 'It does... and I appreciate everything you've done for me, Mrs Wilson, but I would very much like to leave.'

'Well,' said Ivy, offended. 'In that case, you might as well start packing your belongings now.' She opened the door. 'And Priya!' she cried, as Jemima passed by and ascended the stairs. 'When he's had his fill of you... you know where to find me.'

She had to have the last word, Jemima thought. *'Say what you like... I don't care! William Hayward has kept his word!'* She burst into her bedroom and threw herself on her bed. 'William Hayward has not let me down! I'm leaving the Atrium!' she laughed.

She was permitted to keep her cosmetics and a few cheap trinkets but most of the saris and valuables had to be returned. She packed away her remaining belongings in only one carpetbag and rested in bed that night, staring at the bare walls of room number seven – a place that had once been alive with love and passion. Now the ghostly emptiness of it all reminded her that once again, she must be brave and step into the unknown. Previously, her feelings of excitement and hope had been mercilessly crushed, but despite the misgivings she harboured for the road ahead, Jemima knew that William Hayward would be waiting for her at the other end.

The morning dawned crisp and new, and Jemima spied a horse and trap trotting up Princess Street. She quickly released the hoard of money concealed in the old curtain hems and tucked the coins underneath the soles of her boots, praying that they would go unnoticed as she trundled down the stairs. The girls were already gathered on pathway, busy admiring the elegant transport that was waiting to take Jemima to a much better place.

'More goodbyes,' she thought. It seemed that she was always saying farewell.

A hand on her shoulder made her shiver. 'There's always a place for you here if you change your mind,' Ivy said.

Jemima hoped – come hell or high water – she would never have to return to the Atrium, but there had been some good times and Mrs Wilson had cared for her, however questionable her motives may have been. 'Thank you Mrs Wilson. Thank you for everything.'

Suddenly, a voice overtook hers. 'Miss! Miss! Wait!'

Butterfly nudged past the girls and pressed Jemima's fingers inside her warm, soft palm. 'Good bye, Miss,' she said, 'now don't you be forgettin' Butterfly!'

'Never!' Jemima declared, hugging the maid tightly.

Now here was someone she would genuinely miss – dear, dear Butterfly, who had nursed her when she had been unwell. She muttered more goodbyes and climbed inside the carriage. She spotted an envelope lying on the buggy seat but ignored it for a moment to say a final farewell. A movement drew her eyes to one of the windows above and she spied Ezrine lurking behind the curtains. The Malaysian girl had refused to come down and say farewell, and her hostility made Jemima feel sad. They had once been friends who had laughed and danced together but now – against Jemima's wishes – they were parting most bitterly.

'Farewell,' Ivy said. Her tone was becoming a little terse and Jemima guessed the lady might be smarting at the loss of her chief money earner. Everyone hollered and waved as the horse made tracks but with no regret whatsoever, Jemima turned her back on the Atrium and allowed the driver to whisk her away from Princess Street.

CHAPTER 54
APPLE COTTAGE

The pseudonym, 'Priya,' was inscribed in fancy black letter-ing on the front of the envelope lying on the buggy seat. Jemima eagerly tore into it and was delighted to see that it was from William. It read as follows:

My Dearest Priya,

Forgive my recent absence and for the delay in my plans for you. The carriage will take you somewhere where we can be together. I shall not say where for now, for I want it to be a surprise. I shall join you later this evening and we shall celebrate your new life together. Words cannot express the utter delight I feel at having been able to fulfil my promise to you.

William.

Jemima cursed herself for ever having doubted William Hayward's word and then wept tears of joy at the thought of finally being free. He had sent a trap that was clean and smart: a far cry from the soiled contraption that had taken her into the misery of the East End streets. Even the driver was good-natured – a man called Samuel – but the fellow preferred not to talk much as he had been instructed not to shed light on where he was taking his passenger. But when the carriage cantered across London's borders, Jemima noticed that the views became glorious to behold. She looked for a sign or clue that would insinuate a destination but soon became enchanted by the sweeping pastoral vistas, whose rivers twinkled under the midday sun. Winding valleys plunged and rose with quaint country churches snuggled between their inclines. Sheep grazed in the green hills, which then disappeared behind expanses of dense woodland. She much preferred this scene to the bother of the city streets, for the air felt clean and fresh, not like the smog-laden air of the East End streets.

Samuel suddenly cried 'Whoa!' and the trap decelerated to almost a crawl.

Jemima peeped out of the window and Samuel noticed her concern. 'It's a deer,' he said. 'We get them strolling into the road all the time. It's best we wait until it goes. God forbid, we don't want to frighten it.'

Jemima lay back in her seat until a sudden motion drew her eye towards the window again. She caught sight of the creature's ears, eyes and slender head, and then followed its journey as it nibbled at the undergrowth and foraged in some bushes ahead. There were many deer back home wandering the grounds of the local temples. As a child, she had stroked one once and cried when Subhas told her that she could not keep it as a pet. The creature stepped further into the woods and briefly looked back at her, but when Samuel whacked the buggy reigns, it bolted into the thicket.

The woods soon parted to reveal a magnificent house nestling amongst a mass of green parkland. Jemima questioned whether the residence belonged to Queen Victoria and she was still staring back at the majestic abode when the trap veered into a leafy lane, bordered by a spray of oak trees. A small timber-framed cottage rose into view and the trap slowed to a halt outside its gate. As Jemima stepped down, a soft blanket of grass caressed her shoes and she noticed the pathway ahead was flanked by a dense scattering of buttercups and daisies. *'How pretty everything looks,'* she thought. *'How pretty and clean.'* Samuel pushed open the little wooden gate, whilst at the same time, the cottage door opened and a girl of Indian appearance – around fifteen years in age – walked out onto the path.

'Good day, Madam,' she said, giggling behind a fist of fingers. 'My name is Champa. Welcome to Apple Cottage.'

Jemima was shocked at the sight of the Indian girl and was certainly not accustomed to being spoken to in such a genteel manner, especially when she had been a servant herself. The Birshingha elders would be more than horrified and what if the girl, Champa, were to find out that she was, in fact, her equal? What kind of insults would tumble from her pretty, young lips? But as Jemima had to keep reminding herself, she was no longer back home and she was no longer a servant. This had to be fate's fault. Yes, the highly inappropriate situation in which she now floundered was nothing else but fate's doing.

After depositing her carpetbag in the modest hallway, Samuel tipped his cap and departed. On Champa's request, Jemima tentatively entered the cottage. The wooden staircase rising to her left was rather old and a little lopsided but the living room to her right was small but welcoming. The scent of eight white roses drew her swiftly to their petals and it was then that she heard a voice say, 'How do you like your new home?'

Jemima turned and feasted her eyes on William Hayward standing in the doorway. She charged towards him, forgetting that Champa was watching from the foot of the staircase. The girl blushed and sniggered.

'Don't mind Champa,' William laughed. 'She giggles at most things. Now, you haven't answered my question. How do you like your new home?'

'I like it very much. But where am I?'

'You are now a resident of a village called Tring, and Tring is in the County of Hertfordshire. This humble abode, Apple Cottage, is where you will live presently. It belongs to a friend of mine, Colonel Malvery... indeed, the whole estate, including the mansion you passed belongs to him.'

'That beautiful house I saw on the way?'

'Yes... and the woods and the parks nearby. In truth, he owns over two hundred acres of land and has very generously allowed me to rent this cottage for you.'

'How kind of him.'

'Yes, it is. He and his wife have been very good to me. Presently, they're away in Europe, but they return next week and you shall make their acquaintance soon.' He sat down on the small sofa and coaxed her to take the seat beside him. 'Finding Apple Cottage was the easy part. Getting Mrs Wilson to release you... that was by far the hardest thing I've ever had to accomplish. That was difficult... *very* difficult!'

William explained how he had to part with one hundred pounds in order to persuade the bawd to relinquish her claims on 'Priya' and that was only after Colonel Malvery had intervened on his behalf. Jemima was staggered that he had gone to such extraordinary lengths but he assured her that she was worth every penny if it meant that she would remain in England to be by his side. She wanted to kiss and hug him and much more besides, but Champa was dawdling in the doorway, looking coy and out of place. Restless in the girl's presence, Jemima raised herself out of the sofa.

'I prepare supper now, sir?' Champa asked.

'Yes, thank you, Champa, I shall show the mistress the rest of the cottage.'

'*The mistress – how inappropriate!' Jemima thought.* It was as if he was referring to someone else. The idea of keeping a servant troubled her deeply but she must shake herself free from years of caste tradition, for her circumstances were shifting and seemed beyond her control. But were they changing for the better? She was not so sure.

Apple Cottage was small and cosy. Two elegant French doors opened out into a fair-sized garden, beyond which, an apple orchard stretched out into the distance; hence the name, 'Apple Cottage.' William and Jemima strolled arm in arm, admiring the rows of trees with their canopies of pink and white blossom. He leaned over and gathered some strewn petals that had blown across the lawn. 'It's absolutely stunning here in the summer and the apples are tremendously delicious. You'll have a lot of picking to do in autumn,' he smiled. 'By the way... how do you like Champa?'

Truth be told, Champa was fine. It was the idea they shared the same caste that bothered Jemima. 'She seems very sweet,' she said, clinging onto his arm.

'Mrs Malvery sent her for you. Oh, and Mrs Jenkins... the housekeeper at the mansion... says that Champa has learnt to make apple pie. What do you think to that?' he chirped. 'She'll come by tomorrow to see how you're settling in.'

He mentioned that Malvery Mansion was only ten minutes away by foot and having already visited the property and its surrounding gardens, remarked on how lovely it all was. 'Colonel Malvery has loaned you his driver, Samuel... and one of his carriages has been placed at your disposal. If you need any help, you must send word to Mrs Jenkins but Champa will stay in the servant's quarters behind the cottage and she'll always be present to lend a helping hand.'

'Please William, I don't need a servant. I shall do everything myself.'

'Nonsense!' he boomed. 'I don't want you to worry about anything.'

But Jemima was worried. In fact she was worried a great deal.

Beleaguered by the day's events, Jemima slowly picked at her supper. William's mind seemed to be racing too with other matters. 'Under the circumstances, it's best your name remains as Priya,' he advised. 'And the story you told me about being a teacher... that shall have to remain the same too. I am due back in London tomorrow but I shall return as soon as I possibly can.'

Jemima was nervous at the prospect of being left alone, but she realised that she was grateful – as awkward as it was – to have Champa for company. She watched William reach for a leather pouch leaning to one side of a bowl of waxen fruits. 'You needn't fret about money,' he said, dropping the pouch by her supper dish, 'and Mrs Jenkins will look in on you from time to time, just in case you are in need of anything.'

'When will you return?'

'I'm afraid I can't quite say,' he shrugged. 'I have an awful lot to deal with at the moment.'

'You mean, the memsahib?'

'I wish you wouldn't call her that!' he spluttered. 'You're not her servant anymore! You're not anyone's servant! And we agreed not to discuss Elizabeth.'

'But there are things I need to know.'

'What things?' he said, frowning.

'I want to know why she did it!'

'Did what?'

'Leave me at that awful place...'

William reached for his handkerchief and wiped his perspiring brow. 'Very well, since you insist, I shall enlighten you. In India, I had an affair with a dancer and the night before Elizabeth made you leave, I told her about my indiscretion.'

'You had an affair with a dancer?' William nodded. 'An Indian?'

'Yes...but I wouldn't want you to think that I make a habit of having affairs,' he said, annoyed with himself.

Jemima felt ordinary and plain. 'Did you love her?'

'I was fond of her... besotted even, I admit that. But it was never love. I have never loved her... or Elizabeth for that matter... the same way I love you.'

She flinched as he brought her hand to his cheek. 'And that is why she abandoned me?'

'I assume so.'

'But she told the children that I returned to India.'

'And me. That's the absolute truth.'

Jemima was furious. 'I still don't understand why she did it,' she said, turning her face away from his. 'What does *your* affair have to do with me? Your wife broke her promise and left me in a dirty lodging house and I don't understand why.'

William rubbed his forehead and sighed. 'I'm afraid, I don't understand why either.'

Left alone the following morning, Jemima attempted to distract herself from thoughts of her former memsahib by getting to know Apple Cottage. She wandered outside to the sound of the trickling river and then encountered a chorus of birdsong rising from the trees. The sky was blue as far as the orchard gate, but beyond it, it had turned grey and the air felt chilly. She returned to the cottage and warmed her hands by the fire, whilst Champa made a pot of hot, spiced tea. Jemima liked the girl but it would take some time adjusting to a world where rules and commands no longer governed her life; except perhaps, the ones she imposed on herself. Freedom had finally come but she was not used to it at all.

William came and went, finding it easier to leave her alone each time. Two or three days at most were all that he could muster and without him, Jemima struggled to fill the monotonous hours. One time, she forgot her new status and endeavoured to dust the cupboards and sweep the floors. Champa's face creased in horror. 'Madam, what are you doing?' she howled. 'I am here to do such work!' And so, with the menial duties no longer her concern, Jemima turned to the books on the drawing room shelves, deciding that if it relieved the mind-numbing boredom, she would read every last one of them. Elated to find *Gulliver's Travels* by Jonathan Swift, she remembered as a child, she had learnt to read from its pages. She had not reached past the first two chapters but she would now endeavour to finish the whole work. Plucking the book from the topmost shelf, she hoped that Gulliver would occupy her thoughts until William came by on his next visit. By the time she had finished reading *The Voyage to Lilliput*, she indeed heard her lover's footsteps bounding up the pathway. And though she was more than thrilled to see him again, she quietly looked forward to perusing the next chapter.

William departed again, conscious that Jemima was simmering with disappointment. This was not the existence she had envisaged for them both and he feared that she would want to return to India. Trapped in a thorny world, where he contemplated leaving his wife, he concluded that it was a decision that could not be made lightly. For all the bitterness he harboured towards Elizabeth, he was painfully aware that it was her *nouveau riche* money that paid for his lifestyle and it was her *nouveau riche* money that now paid for his Indian mistress.

CHAPTER 55

'VOYAGE TO BROBDINGNAG'

Two days after returning from France, Colonel Malvery and Tara invited William to take tea at their house in Berkeley Square. William was keen to thank them for their bounteous help, but found his nerves rattling as he sat making small-talk with the Colonel's wife. 'How did you find Paris, Mrs Malvery?' he asked, wondering just how much she knew about his personal affairs.

Tara poured the tea and smiled. 'I enjoyed it immensely William, but forgive me if I change the subject entirely and ask how the young lady's settling in?'

'She's settling in extremely well,' he said tentatively. 'Mrs Jenkins has made her feel very welcome and Champa is a godsend.'

'It's admirable that you've wanted to help this young woman... and the Colonel and I are very glad that we could help too. It must have been just dreadful being abandoned like that by her employer... and to be in a strange country with no one to turn to for help.'

So *that* is what the Colonel had told his wife. It was hardly a lie. William felt better.

'What does she do to pass the time?' Tara asked.

'Well... I think she might have been reading *Gulliver's Travels* when I left her last.'

'What else?'

'I'm not really sure, Madam,' he confessed, mortified by his own ignorance. 'To be honest, I think she gets a little restless at times.'

'I'm hardly surprised she gets a little restless,' Tara scoffed. 'Tring is a beautiful place but there are limits to what one can do at the best of times.' She thought long and hard for a while. 'I think it's time we met your friend, William. She is a fellow Indian after all! What if I entertain her at Malvery House?'

'That's very kind of you, Madam, and I'm sure Priya will be most happy to accept...'

'But?' Tara interrupted, sensing his lack of enthusiasm. She turned to her husband. 'What do you think to it, James?'

'Well, my dear. Perhaps it isn't wise to entertain the young lady in London,' the Colonel said, acknowledging William's reluctance.

'Why not?'

William's thoughts were running riot. Did Tara know the adulterous situation in which he had – with the help of her husband – become voluntarily embroiled? Or did she simply think he was helping an Indian woman in her hour of need? The Colonel finally spoke up. 'If she were to be seen with William in public, my dear... the scandalmongers would have a field day.'

'I see,' Tara sniffed.

William expected the Colonel's wife to explode in a fit of anger and privately imagined her demanding that he leave after learning of his infidelity to his wife. She said nothing further on the matter, though she was still determined to meet her new tenant.

'What if we were to receive her at Malvery Mansion? What do you think to next Saturday, William? I shall host a dinner.' She did not wait for his reply. 'And we'll invite Mr Kendall and Sir Gregory,' she said, addressing her husband. 'I'm sure they'll get on very well with William. Yes! I shall write to Mrs Jenkins now,' she said, leaving to find some paper and a pen.

William's head grew moist as he rose for Tara's exit. The mere idea that he should socialise quite freely with his Indian mistress was a risky endeavour, even if it was to occur in a village as quiet as Tring. 'My wife, Colonel... what if she learns of this?'

'She couldn't possibly,' the Colonel replied, 'at least not from our friends. Tara and I are extremely pernickety when it comes to our associations. We only trust those who are easy in our company as they do us. We do not waste our time with casual acquaintances and our good friends do not concern themselves with idle gossip. Mark my words, Mrs Malvery is no fool.'

William shifted forwards in his chair. 'Forgive me, sir. I meant no offence...especially after the kindness you have shown me.'

'No offence taken, young man!'

'Colonel, may I ask if Mrs Malvery is comfortable with my predicament?'

Chewing on his cigar, the Colonel nodded. 'I have explained the fractious situation existing between you and your wife... and something of the affection you feel for this other woman. I think Tara understands, although... I haven't told her the truth about how you both met.'

A bitter taste rose in William's mouth. 'What did you tell her, sir?'

'Oh, some tosh about you meeting her in a work agency for colonial women... you know... the explanation Ivy usually offers... but that is the only lie I'm prepared to tell.' Registering William's troubled expression, the Colonel then said. 'Now what's troubling you?'

'What should I tell my wife? Getting away at weekends is especially difficult.'

'Well, what do you normally tell her when you visit the other... young lady?'

'That I have business to deal with... a client... that sort of thing.'

Colonel Malvery looked pensive. 'Go home, William and tell your wife that this coming weekend you will be engaged in the administration of Colonel James Malvery's Hertfordshire Estate. And because the specifics of his affairs are particularly problematical, he has requested that you stay the entire weekend. How does that sound?'

'I think that might work, sir,' William grinned. 'I think that might work!'

Having reached part two of *Gulliver's Travels* – '*The Voyage to Brobdingnag*' – Jemima had become quite riveted by the details of the story after identifying with the protagonist, Gulliver. She had noted how similar their journeys had been and was especially enthralled by the tale of his abandonment. She sympathised greatly when the giant farmer exhibited him as a curiosity for money and chided the Queen of Brobdingnag for buying him like a trinket and keeping him as her favourite at court. The parallels with her own life were rather uncanny, for she could more or less match each character with the individuals in her own journey.

She passed many an hour with her nose stuck between the pages and she only ceased reading when she spied Champa standing in the doorway. 'Is Madam busy?' she chirped.

'Come in Champa. I'm only reading.'

'Madam is reading, reading all the time!'

'It's a very enjoyable story... you can read it too when I'm finished.'

Champa's grin vanished. It was then that Jemima realised that just because *she* knew how to read did not mean that all servants had been taught to. She changed the subject. 'What do you have there?'

'Madam, the postman came and went,' Champa said, handing over a letter.

It was from William and Jemima tore it open to read how the Malverys were arriving on the approaching weekend, eager to make 'Miss Priya's' acquaintance. They would be holding a dinner party in her and William's honour and had also invited some select guests.

Jemima's stomach churned. The Colonel and Mrs Malvery were coming to meet *her* – William's mistress – a once lowly servant parading as a teacher. 'How could this be happening?' she said to herself. 'Is my life meant for this madness?' Sinking deeper in the sofa, Jemima mulled over all the outrageous implications of her and William's deceit and realised that unless she packed her bags and left immediately, she was powerless to change her situation. She loved William without a doubt and desperately wanted to be with him. 'What a mess,' she whispered, 'a terrible mess!' Her eyes rested on the book she had just been reading. 'What would you do Gulliver?' she asked. She already knew the answer. Of course, Gulliver would throw himself into his adventure and so she must do the same.

Her excitement dwindled as she thought of the lacklustre attire in her wardrobe. She rushed upstairs and scrutinized the one sari Mrs Wilson had allowed her to keep: a copper-coloured silk piece bordered with a silver trim. It was not as sumptuous as some of the garments she had worn for William at the Atrium and she considered it hardly fitting for a dinner party. She wondered if she should send him word regarding her dearth of suitable clothes but she preferred not to trouble him with such trivialities. The copper-coloured sari would have to suffice.

Later that week, Champa entered her bedroom, declaring that Samuel had just delivered a parcel. Jemima hurried down the staircase and ripped into the wrapping to find several layers of tissue paper covering an item inside a large white box. Curling back the last layer, she revealed a note saying, '*Love William.*' The message sat on top of a cerise coloured sari and a blouse of richest blush pink. Both were stitched with filigree silver threads that merged delicately into a series of flowers and leaves. A scattering of the palest pink pearls shone softly in the sunlight and Jemima admired its splendour whilst brushing a section of it against her cheek.

'Madam, how beautiful!' Champa sighed. 'The colour looks so pretty on you.' Sighing again, she dashed off towards the kitchen, remembering that she had left a pot of hot coffee simmering on the stove.

Jemima absorbed the sari's beauty. Had William read her mind? The garment proved he knew her well. He *did* love her and it *was* worth being hidden away for him. She counted down the days to his return.

CHAPTER 56

THE GENIUS CHEF

It rained heavily throughout William's journey to Apple Cottage. His hat and coat were heavily soaked but Jemima ran into his arms anyway to thank him for the gift he had sent earlier in the week. He confessed that Mrs Malvery had selected the sari on his behalf, for without her guidance, he would not have had the faintest clue. Tired from his journey, he relaxed on the bed, tinkering with the catches on his smart leather briefcase. A moment later, he delved inside and pulled out a small box, which he promptly delivered into Jemima's lap. Opening it up, she spied two ruby earrings and two gold bracelets glimmering on the cushion inside. 'Mrs Malvery helped choose these too,' he smiled, leaning across to kiss her on the cheek.

'*Will this wonderful madness ever end?*' *Jemima thought.* 'Thank you, William,' she said, overwhelmed by his kindness. She closed the box and hurled her arms around his neck before snuggling down beside him.

The showers subsided by late Saturday afternoon and Colonel Malvery's carriage arrived at seven, ready to whisk the couple away. Deep in thought at the foot of the staircase, William contemplated the implications of the evening ahead, whilst upstairs in the bedroom, Champa made the finishing touches to her mistress's new sari. Jemima emerged, shimmering from head to toe in pink silk and sparkling rubies. She descended the staircase nimbly, taking William's breath away as she reached out for his hand. They both left Champa swooning on the doorstep, waving them off into the rain-soaked night.

The approach to Malvery Mansion was flanked by a parade of fiery torches that pierced the great squares of lawn either side of the snaking driveway. The gloomy air glowed with much light and warmth, making Jemima feel magnificent and worthy as she ascended the smooth, marble steps in all her finery. Kalsi welcomed her and William inside, whilst beyond him in the cavernous hallway, Colonel Malvery paced the floor in anticipation of their arrival.

'Ah!' he cried, 'Good evening, William!'

'Good evening, Colonel… may I introduce, Priya.'

Priya nervously extended a hand.

'Well, well… finally, I have the pleasure, my dear.'

A wealth of Mughal artworks, tapestries and trinkets bore down on Jemima and she wilted under the opulent surroundings. A soft voice called out and turning, she saw a beautiful, dark-haired woman dressed in a midnight blue sari, dotted with pearly moons, silver stars and the tiniest winking diamonds. 'This must be the guest of honour!' the lady said, walking towards the recent arrivals.

'Priya, this is the Colonel's wife, Mrs Malvery,' William said.

'You must call me, Tara,' she smiled, touching Jemima lightly on the arm.

Jemima was astounded. Why had William never mentioned that Mrs Malvery was an Indian too? Had it slipped his mind? Or had he left it as a surprise? It must have been the latter, she concluded, for she was certainly stunned at the sight of the Colonel's wife.

'The sari looks beautiful,' Tara added, stepping back to admire the garment. 'Come. Let me introduce you to the others.' She curled her arm around Priya's waist and escorted her inside the drawing room.

Colonel Malvery winked at his young friend. 'Well, well, William. Now I understand your motives,' he chuckled. 'I understand them completely. She's a beauty!'

Half a dozen of the Malverys' closest friends were invited to dine at the mansion that evening. An assortment of English, Indian and Anglo-Indian guests enjoyed the comfort of the plush interiors whilst revelling in the gaiety brought on from drinking copious amounts of wine. Reclining on a leather sofa, the aforementioned Sir Gregory and his snooty Parsee wife, Rushmee, were engrossed in idle banter with a rather handsome fellow called Mr Kendall. Mr Kendall himself was seated beside a pretty English woman simply known as Nelly. Jemima took a seat beside Nelly and heard her comment on how lovely all the Indian ladies looked in their bright saris and exotic jewellery. Mr Kendall agreed and then turned his attention to William. 'Which part of the country are you from, Mr Hayward?' he asked.

'Surrey.'

'Ah... my wife is from Surrey, Mr Hayward,' said Kendall, seductively placing a hand on Nelly's knee.

'Really?' began William, looking across at Nelly. 'Which part of Surrey are you from, Mrs Kendall?'

Nelly hooted loudly. 'Oh I'm not his wife, Mr Hayward but I was born and bred in Vauxhall!' She then shuffled closer to her illicit partner.

'Forgive me… my mistake,' William muttered, wondering which liaisons in the room were sanctified and which were disloyal. Now he understood what Colonel Malvery had meant when he said that he and Tara chose their company carefully, for looking around at the congregation of guests, he realised that he and Priya fitted in so well.

Kalsi whispered something into his master's ear and the host waved his hands to secure everyone's attention. 'Ladies and gentleman,' he declared. 'In honour of our new friends, William and Priya, my wife and I have decided to bring India to Malvery Mansion… please be so kind to follow me.'

The Colonel guided his guests towards a great banqueting hall situated on the far side of the mansion. Inside, a plethora of candles flickered dramatically whilst slender peacock feathers drooped from a vase positioned in the centre of a vast mahogany table. The angelic voices of two little Indian boys dressed in turbans and suits of Indian silk echoed to the delicate music of a gently plucked sitar. Jemima searched for her name on the elaborate place cards until she found the name 'Priya,' resting between Mr Kendall and Sir Gregory's place settings. She settled down between both men, whilst William took the seat opposite.

Perched at one end of the table, Colonel Malvery resumed his pre-dinner speech. 'To continue the theme of India… a country my wife and I miss terribly… we shall dine on the most sumptuous cuisine prepared by one of the finest chefs India has ever produced. I heard about this chap through Mr Desai here.' He pointed to the bearded Indian businessman seated next to his wife. 'How about telling the story, Mr Desai?'

'Very well, Colonel,' chirped the fellow, bursting to speak. 'Many times, I had heard of this man's genius and so, I went along to see what all the fuss was about. Suffice to say, I came away singing the fellow's praises and I was fortunate enough to secure his services on the Colonel's behalf.'

'And that wasn't an easy feat, you know...' yelped the Colonel, 'for he's now one of the most sought after chefs in London. Kalsi! Go fetch him!'

Jemima's nerves were jangling. *'It couldn't be him,' she thought.*

'Not only that!' the Colonel continued, 'this man has cooked for royalty! The *Nawab* of Awadh of all people! And where was he discovered? You'll never guess! Only in the East End of London of all places... Shadwell would you believe!'

Kalsi was lingering before a partially open door. A second later, he whispered to someone beyond it and whoever it was began preparing for their entrance. The Colonel snatched a spoon from the table and tapped it against his glass several times. 'Dear friends, it is my very great pleasure to welcome the genius chef, Ibrahim!'

The guests applauded but Jemima's appetite had suddenly disappeared.

Ibrahim bowed graciously in appreciation of the generous applause erupting around the table. With his black hair slicked back and his beard cropped neatly, he looked every inch, the sophisticated Indian gentleman. The Colonel proceeded to introduce his visitors and Ibrahim made sure to pass his attention to each and every one of them. Tara explained that the dinner had been held to welcome Miss Priya to Tring and Ibrahim tipped his head towards the guest of honour before observing Mr Kendall seated at her side. Seconds later, his eyes drifted back and were studying the features hidden behind her sari hood. Jemima dared not look up at him, but by the time she felt bold enough to do so, he had completed the pleasantries around the table and left to supervise the staff in the kitchens. She stared at the door through which Ibrahim had entered, praying that he would remain firmly on the other side. Servant followed servant and dish followed dish and she spent the entire meal watching and worrying. Under any other circumstances, she would have been overjoyed to see her dear friend but if he had recognised her face and called her by her ayah name, her and William's integrity would be called into question.

The feasting took over an hour or so, but in Jemima's imagination, it lasted forever. She wholeheartedly agreed with the others that Ibrahim's cuisine had been a roaring success and was hugely relieved when the Colonel asked everyone to return to the lounge for liqueurs and brandy. But Jemima simply had to know if she had been recognised and that meant getting to Ibrahim first. She made the excuse of mislaying a bracelet and made her way back to the banqueting hall, passing the servants who were clearing the table of left-over food and crockery. She opened the door through which Ibrahim had entered and immediately came face to face with Kalsi. 'May I be of some assistance?' he asked, surprised to find her wandering about. 'Is Madam lost?'

'Ibrahim, the chef,' she said. 'I wish to congratulate him on his cuisine.'

'He is in the kitchen, Madam. To your left,' said Kalsi, finding her manner rather odd.

She followed the sound of banging pots and splashing water and saw a collection of brown and white faces that ceased babbling as she entered the room. She approached a small boy standing on an upturned bucket. He was scrubbing dirt from a huge copper pot. 'Where is the chef, Ibrahim?'

The boy raised a soapy hand towards a figure in the corner, immersed in the task of wiping utensils on a cloth. Ibrahim was whistling a tune and did not hear her footsteps creeping over to him. She raised a finger and tapped him on the shoulder. He stopped whistling and turned around. 'Yes, Madam?' he said after a tentative pause.

Jemima's rigid spine relaxed. 'Don't you recognise me, Ibrahim?' she whispered.

Ibrahim dithered in front of the pretty lady who had to raise her toes to reach his lofty height. Relieved, she lifted a hand to her lips to mask the words she had been bursting all evening to say. 'Ibrahim... it's me, Jemima.'

CHAPTER 57
MEHTA REMEMBERED

Ibrahim's face danced with a variety of expressions. First he frowned and his eyes shrivelled to half their size; then his eyebrows leapt in utmost astonishment. Finally, his mouth hung open like a freshly caught trout as the remarkable image of the woman before him started to make sense. A thousand coherent questions raced through his mind. Where had she been? What was she doing here? Why was she dressed like that? But instead of voicing them, he could only stand – lips agape, tongue in limbo – and mutter a series of nonsensical sentences. 'You look so different... so beautiful! But what have you... when I saw you I thought... where have you been?'

Jemima hushed him. 'Ibrahim, you must listen carefully. I don't have time to explain... but you mustn't tell anyone who I really am. You must pretend that you do not know me... that you have never seen me before tonight. They all know me as 'Priya.' I will explain everything to you later, I promise. Do you understand?'

Ibrahim added another facial expression to his collection by twisting his top lip to meet his nostrils. 'Of course but...'

'When do you leave for London?'

'Tomorrow.'

'I am staying in a place not far from here... a place called Apple Cottage. Can you come tomorrow at ten o'clock?'

'Yes, I think so...'

'Good. I will explain everything then, I promise. And if anyone asks why I came to see you... you must say that I have asked you to come and cook for me. I must return now.'

Shocked and speechless, Ibrahim watched as she took her leave.

Back in the drawing room, she apologized for her prolonged absence and confessed that she simply had to congratulate the chef on his wonderful cuisine. William patted the empty seat beside him and she crossed over and sank down in it a good deal calmer than she had been during supper.

'Are you enjoying yourself, Priya?' Tara asked, handing her a liqueur. 'You looked a little preoccupied during dinner.'

'Oh Madam,' she said. 'I am overwhelmed by your kindness and I am having a wonderful time. Thank you so much for everything... the cottage, this sari and Champa.'

'Yes Champa is sweet isn't she? She is the daughter of my father's former servants. Unfortunately, they both died when a cyclone swept away their hutment. Champa was only a small child at the time but she was saved by a villager and brought to live at my father's house in Calcutta. I grew very fond of her and decided to bring her here with me. It's difficult for her when the Colonel and I are away... and she grows a little restless in the house back in London. That's why I thought she'd be most suitable company for you at the cottage.'

Jemima tasted liqueur on her lips and coughed a little before answering. 'Champa has been most helpful and I am very grateful to you and the Colonel.'

'It's a pleasure, dear. My husband and I have grown very fond of William and welcome any of his friends. He tells me he must return to London in the morning. Is that correct, William?'

'It is Madam,' William replied, a little tipsy from the Colonel's brandy.

'Well then, Priya must join us for tea tomorrow... then I can get to know her much better.'

She agreed to Tara's request but found her nerves beset again after seeing Ibrahim walking into the room. He had changed out of his chef's uniform and was wearing the clothes of an Englishman. It was strange for Jemima to see him that way, as it was for him to see her bedecked in such finery. The host instigated another round of applause and Ibrahim shared a few words with everyone he passed. Conscious of Jemima's request, he played along with the charade of not knowing who she was, but his face sagged greatly as he noticed the fingers of a blond gentleman inches away from the back of her neck. He thought it best to retire early and mentioned that he needed to rest after a long day's work. And since he had an appointment with Miss Priya the very next morning, he said his *adieus* quickly and followed Kalsi to a private apartment where he was to spend the rest of the night.

By and large, Jemima would not have been content seeing William climbing into the carriage that would take him back to London. But the morning after the dinner party, she welcomed his hasty departure, for it allowed her to concentrate on Ibrahim. After sending Champa out on several errands, she set a pot of coffee steaming on the hob and just after ten o'clock, wandered out of the cottage to wait for him by the little wooden gate.

Ibrahim was walking by the nearby thicket, eager to unravel the mystery that once again involved Jemima. '*Who was that man sitting next to her? And why was she allowing him to touch her?'* He had sat up all night thinking about her predicament. He had worried that she had become embroiled in something beyond her control. The stream gurgled gently as he ambled along its banks and he soon spied chimney smoke tainting the sky's bright blue air. She was offering a squirrel a piece of bread when he finally caught sight of her. Her hair was loosely tied into a braid and she appeared more like the old Jemima he had grown to cherish. She looked healthy and happy, he thought, as he watched her from afar.

'Ibrahim!' she cried, spying him through the trees. 'This is where I live now. This is Apple Cottage!'

They sat in the kitchen with two cups and a pot of hot coffee set down on the table. Ibrahim confessed that after being introduced to 'Miss Priya' the previous evening, there seemed to be a familiarity in her painted features that he could not quite place. And since he had several mouths to feed and a reputation to maintain, he had set aside the riddle in favour of presenting his extravagant menu. He took her back to New Year's Day and spoke of how news had reached the inn of a political meeting that had been disrupted in a warehouse nearby. He told her that he had searched for her frantically and had never given up hope that she might be alive.

'I read in the paper that Mehta's trial date had been set,' she said.

Frustration filled Ibrahim's sighs. 'It was last week, Jemima. I was there... I wanted to know what happened to you, so I went along.'

Tuesday, the twenty-third of April 1867. Handcuffed and dressed in grey prison uniforms, Mehta and his co-conspirators stood in the dock whilst the judge read out the charges. 'Navin Mehta, you have been brought to trial on charges of treason against

Queen, country and Empire. On the first of January 1867, you did wilfully deliver a speech with content that can only be described as highly seditious with intent to incite members of Her Majesty's armed forces, amongst others, to rebellious and violent behaviour against England and her subjects. How do you plead?'

Mehta seemed unperturbed. In fact, he had been chatting merrily without a thought for the consequences coming his way, but he did have this to say: 'Your honour, I refuse to accept your description of my conduct as "treason against Queen, country and Empire." She is not my queen, this is not my country and I detest your Empire and everything it represents!'

The gallery of spectators gasped and seated on the settles behind them, Mehta's parents – who had made the journey over to save their son – shook their heads in utter despair.

'If I am guilty of anything,' he continued, 'then let it be of loyalty to India, the Motherland, and justice for India, the Motherland!'

Mehta's father shook his head as he mourned the loss of his once respectful son whilst his anguished wife soaked three handkerchiefs with her tears. Viswanath, Bonnerjee and Seth, however, cowered when the judge's attention turned to them.

'Amithav Seth, Raju Viswanath and Vikram Bonnerjee... on the first of January 1867, you did wilfully aid and abet Navin Mehta to incite members of Her Majesty's...'

And so it went on, with all three of them pleading, 'not guilty.'

Had he not been handcuffed and separated from the others by two policemen, Navin Mehta would have attempted to rip off all three men's heads with his bare hands. 'Not guilty? Not guilty?' he yelled. 'Traitors! Cowards! Bloody traitors to the Motherland!'

The jury took minutes to deliver their guilty verdicts and Vikram's eyes were blinded with tears as the judge read out their sentences. 'Amithav Seth, Raju Viswanath and Vikram Bonnerjee, you have been found guilty of aiding and abetting Navin Mehta in his mission to incite hatred and violence against England and her Empire. Henceforth, you will be expelled from this country and transported to the Andaman Islands to serve time doing hard labour in a penal colony for the rest of your natural lives.'

There was whooping and cheering from the more jingoistic members of the audience but the judge put a stop to their jeers when he brought the gavel down several times. Mehta's mother buried her head into her husband's shoulder when the judge turned his fierce eyes to her son. 'Navin Mehta, you have been found guilty of preaching and inciting treason against England and her subjects. In the interests of this country's national security, this court recommends that you be taken to Pentonville prison, where, at a later date, you will be hanged until dead.'

The spectators in the gallery jumped to their feet. Some shouted, 'Hang them all!' whilst jabbing their fingers in the sentenced men's faces. Mehta's father tried to steady his wife but she lost her footing and collapsed in his arms. And whilst the judge's gavel came down over and over again, Mehta looked on, unrepentant.

'Do you wish to say anything?' the judge asked, once all had quietened down.

'Yes,' said Mehta, 'write this in your English newspapers... Navin Mehta defended the honour of the Motherland and was proud to sacrifice *his* life for *her* chance of freedom.'

English patriots began heckling loudly and Mehta, still defiant as he was taken away, did not notice Ibrahim's concerned face amongst the crowd.

'I never liked the fellow, Jemima, but even I thought his sentence was harsh. They could have transported him with the others but they chose to make an example of him. It was his family I felt sorry for...his poor mother and father knew nothing of his conduct.

They are decent people... even loyal to the Raj... they were deeply ashamed of his actions but they never thought he would be sentenced to hang. I heard that he refused an offer of a solicitor and acted as if he had no fear. Meade told me that many of his associates have gone into hiding... we have never seen them at the inn since. Even Jacob has disappeared!'

Jemima considered how fortunate she was to have run away that night, for her previous fears of possible arrest were now confirmed. Still, she could not help but feel a little sympathy for the man who helped her in the alley that day. 'Can he not appeal? He did not kill anyone.'

'No, but it would have only been a matter of time,' Ibrahim declared. 'Meade says that his parents have asked for clemency but Mehta has refused this too.'

'He wants to die?'

'He wants to die a martyr.'

People's passions were varied indeed, Jemima thought. There was Ibrahim who had a passion for food, she, with her passion for William; and then there was Mehta and his passion for India's independence but was his passion more compelling because he was paying for it with his life? Or was he just a young, impetuous student who had taken on more than he could handle? Either way it was a shame, she thought, a shame for a promising life to be cut so short.

'I thought you had come to some harm because of Mehta,' Ibrahim said. 'I prayed that you were alive and well... but what happened to you that day? Where did you go?'

She resumed the story from when the police stormed the meeting and watched Ibrahim's face crease in anger when she told him how she had escaped from Vikram's clutches and ran until fate somehow had led her back to Nuwani. She mentioned Mrs Wilson and how she had kindly taken her in, but just as she failed to speak of Sylvester Lawrence, she neglected to tell

Ibrahim about the child she had lost. The circumstances surrounding the creation of 'Priya' were particularly difficult to recount and then revealing herself as an Englishman's mistress seemed to push Ibrahim to the point of despair. 'He rescued me, Ibrahim... and he has taken many risks. The Malverys are good people... they would not have helped him if they doubted his character.'

'Is this the man who was seated beside you last night?'

Jemima nodded and then stressed that William Hayward had freed her from Mrs Wilson and brought her to live at Apple Cottage. She hoped that Ibrahim would understand the workings of their relationship, but he sat brooding in a stony silence, alarming Jemima with his peculiar mood.

'Are you ashamed of me?' she asked. 'I would not blame you if you are.'

She expected his condemnation at any given moment but his contempt softened somewhat when he spied the tears welling. Squeezing her hands, he stared deeply into her dark, wet eyes and said. 'You have suffered greatly, Jemima. You did what you needed to survive... just as I had to steal from the ship and the stallholders in Suez. I cannot pass judgement; only God can do that and I like to think that God would understand. But you do not need to stay with this man any longer. Come with me.'

'Wait Ibrahim,' she said, wondering whether he would be so sympathetic after confiding in him further. 'There is something else... and it is something that has come to be such a burden to me.'

Ibrahim assured her that she could tell him anything.

'Remember my mistress?' she said, 'the one I came to England with? The woman whose children I looked after in Calcutta?'

'The woman who abandoned you,' he said, reminding her of the bitter truth.

'William is her husband.'

He almost fell from his chair. 'You were ayah to his children and he does not know?'

'At first he did not know... but now he does.'

Ibrahim struggled to look Jemima in the eye.

'I met him at Mrs Wilson's place. I never imagined that he would fall in love with me,' she pleaded, hoping Ibrahim would not leave in disgust.

'He loves you?' he answered, growing more bewildered with each revelation.

'Yes. He is a good man, Ibrahim. He treats me very well and he has done many kind things for me.'

Ibrahim was baffled. How could Jemima trust a man who visited brothels and had a wife and children waiting for him at home? 'Do you love him?' he demanded, hauling her out of her chair.

Jemima recalled the first day she came to William Hayward's house in Calcutta and her head rocked with the inconceivable notion that she was now his mistress. 'I have always loved him and I cannot leave him.'

Ibrahim burned to tell Jemima about his feelings for her, but her devotion to this 'rogue' of an Englishman was evident and angered him greatly. 'So, you are staying here in England? I thought you wanted to go home.'

'Not anymore,' she replied, breaking away from him.

He paced the kitchen floor trying to calm his temper. If William Hayward were to walk in right now, he imagined himself knocking the scoundrel to the floor. He watched Jemima dry her tears with a corner of her napkin and she watched him hammer the ground with his angry feet.

'Do not think badly of me, Ibrahim. I could not bear it if you did,' she whimpered, contemplating life without her good friend by her side.

His rage softened again and locking away his hurt, he considered that short of perpetrating the most heinous crime, there was nothing Jemima could do to make him despise her, not after she saved him that night on the *Bengal Star*. It took a while for him to simmer down and for the sake of their friendship, he reluctantly accepted Jemima's aberrant situation, hoping for her sake alone that William Hayward was worth all the trouble. After promising to keep her secrets, he forced a change in the subject by informing Jemima that it was not only her life that had transformed since they had last seen each other.

'I wish to open my own eating establishment,' he announced.

'That's wonderful, Ibrahim,' Jemima gushed. 'You deserve to do well in life!'

'As do you, Jemima,' he replied, smarting at the thought of the Englishman. 'The places in London are very expensive, but I will work hard and find the money somehow. You wait and see.'

Jemima took a lingering look at Ibrahim. 'My brother, you are destined for great success... there is no other path for you. Our friendship will last an eternity, I am sure of that.' She raised herself up out of her chair and continued. 'Wait here, I have something for you.'

She rushed up the lopsided staircase and minutes later, rushed down it, carrying an old cigar box. 'I want you to have this,' she said placing it upon the table.

Ibrahim lifted the lid and saw an assortment of sovereigns, guineas, crowns, half crowns and shillings inside the container. It was all the money she had scrupulously collected and she would have used it to pay for her journey back home.

'There is almost twenty pounds here and I want you to use it to make your dream come true.'

It was a respectable sum but not enough to make his dreams come true. Touched by her gesture, he nudged the box back towards her. 'I cannot accept, Jemima. This is your money and you may need it one day.'

She pushed it back towards him. 'I have everything I need and William takes care of me. Mr and Mrs Malvery have been very kind to me too... so, I have no need for this money and it would make me very happy if you were to take it for your business. I want you to be a wonderful success!'

Ibrahim sighed. 'Very well, I shall take it... but I will invest it and you shall be... as they say in England, my silent partner. And I will work hard, Jemima, and I *will* be a success. As *Allah* is my witness, I *will* be a success!'

Ibrahim gathered his emotions and thanked her a thousand times before announcing that he had to leave. The trains to London left on the hour and if he were to hurry, he would be able to catch the next one. Walking along the pathway and onto the grassy road beyond, he turned around to look at her once more. 'Now I know you are safe. I can rest more easily. I shall call on you soon.'

He strode towards the stream and vanished through the thicket, leaving Jemima to wander back into the cottage, relieved that a huge burden had been lifted and happy in the knowledge that a loose end had been tied. But above all, she was delighted to know that her good friend, Ibrahim, was once again back in her life.

Ibrahim returned to London nursing his wounded pride. Jemima had no idea of his feelings for her and furthermore, it was clear that she did not feel the same about him. She had used the words 'brother' and 'friendship' and was blinded with love for another man. Why had it not occurred to her that *he* might want her too? He fingered the coins in the old cigar box and the sight of them saddened him even more. But when all had been said and done, he could only be pleased that she would be staying on in England, though he was relieved to have kept his feelings to himself. He already knew her answer if he had asked her to be his wife and so, after returning to the Shadwell Inn, he brooded behind a mountain of work.

Sarah noticed his sudden irritability. Soon after his arrival, she rose early knowing he would be busy preparing food in the kitchen below. She left her younger sister snoring in the small bedroom they shared and descended the stairs to find him immersed in the task of chopping carrots and slicing potatoes. He failed to hear her pass through the doorway.

'Morning, Ibrahim!' she cried, shattering his thoughts.

Startled, he stopped slicing and looked up. 'Morning, Sarah. You are up very early today.'

'Couldn't sleep... fancy some help?'

Ibrahim cleared the space beside him and fetched another knife. She sauntered over and paid close attention to how efficiently he severed the carrots. He watched her intently as she endeavoured to do the same but noticed that she looked different, for she had pinned her curls over the side of her ears instead of to one side of her face. The scent of cologne drifted over from her soft heaving cleavage and he caught an invisible wisp of it as it wafted under his nose. 'That scent. What is it?'

'Neroli,' she replied. 'I got it from the market in Whitechapel.' She bit into her plump lower lip as she continued to chop and pierce the vegetables with the tip of her knife.

'Where is your father today?'

'Oh, he's gone to the brewery...won't be back for ages,' she replied, brushing past his shoulders.

He imbibed her scent again and found that he had suddenly grabbed her by the waist. He pushed her up against the table and hitched up her skirts. Whilst pressing his lips against hers, he thrust his hand inside her undergarments until he touched her soft ivory skin. Carrots rolled across the counter top and an avalanche of potatoes tumbled to the floor. The racket made

Ibrahim pull away. 'Forgive me, Sarah,' he panted. 'I'm sorry. Forgive my vulgar behaviour.'

'Don't stop!' she gasped. 'There's nothing to forgive!' and she hastily loosened her corset. Next, she reached for his hand and guided it under her flimsy camisole. She urged him to caress her warm pert breasts; her nipples were firm and his penis grew hard. 'I love you, Ibrahim,' she said, unfastening his trousers. 'Don't you know that I love you with all of my heart?'

CHAPTER 58

TARA

'In Midnapore, I worked as a teacher. I taught young children how to read and write in Bengali, Hindi, and sometimes, English. We had discussions... I was given many books by a doctor friend of mine.'

Jemima was lying again and this time the charade was being played out before the Colonel and his wife, who, keen to know more of her background had invited her to spend the day at Malvery Mansion. But her story was gathering superfluous layers of deceit and now it was pilfering truths from the lives of those she had known in the past. She relied mostly on childhood memories: memories in which Jagatterini had pointed to the letters on a blackboard and she had sat – back straight, legs crossed – repeating out loud the letters of the English alphabet. Outside the house, Subhas would be crafting an article from a piece of wood in the yard, whilst Madhu swept the kitchen floor, listening to her daughter's strains of '*ayeee, beee, ceee...*'

And Jemima had also invented another story; one that explained her journey to England. As tutor to the daughter of an Indian banker, she described how she had accompanied the family to Europe but had subsequently quarrelled over her wages and had since been abandoned.

'Gracious, times are changing,' Tara stated, 'Indian families hiring female tutors? It's nigh on unheard of. Still, it was horrid of your employer to desert you like that. What is his name? The Colonel and I might know the fellow.'

Jemima's cup tinkled in its saucer. '*Think of a name! Think of a name quickly!'* 'Mukherjee,' she said.

'Mukherjee?' Tara replied, cogitating on the name. 'My father had many banker friends, the Desais and the Dhaliwaals, but I never heard the name Mukherjee spoken in those circles.'

'I wouldn't suppose he would have been familiar with every banker in India, dear!' the Colonel chuckled.

'Well of course,' said Tara, grimacing. 'According to William, you both met at a work agency for women of the colonies?' she said, turning back to Jemima.

The Colonel coughed purposefully and Jemima took the hint. 'Yes, that is correct.'

'I believe that he was with a friend, who was searching for a maid to accompany his wife to Africa and that's when he met you?'

'*So many questions,' Jemima thought.* Guilt was pummelling her conscience. Even the Colonel was lying on her behalf and he knew as much as William had told him, that is, she was a teacher, a victim of circumstance, who, out of desperation, had turned to Ivy Wilson for help. Fortunately, Kalsi entered the room bearing a tray of tea and lemon cake. He severed the cake and presented the slices on some dainty dishes.

Tara waved away his offer. 'Teaching is an honourable profession. I once entertained the thought of becoming a teacher myself but my father insisted that I be... as the English say... an educated lady of leisure.'

'*If only I were a teacher,*' Jemima mused. Would the Malverys be so sympathetic if they knew her true heritage? '*What would they think of me if they knew the truth?*'

Her tea had gone cold but she drank it anyway wondering how life had become so tortuous since fate had bound her to William Hayward. Every conversation, every little detail and everyone's opinion – no matter how insignificant that person may be – seemed to matter a great deal. Tara insisted that she help herself to more cake but the Colonel's wife sported a most curious expression as Jemima attempted to nibble her way through a second slice.

After tea, they toured the mansion's bright and magnificent rooms and Tara recounted the history behind the art on the walls. The lady's passion for culture and beauty came to the fore when she reminisced back to her early days in Calcutta. 'I was six years old and my father took me to swim in the sea at Puri. The Maharajah of Jaipur and his wife, the Maharani, were also visiting Puri on a weekend retreat... indeed, their villa was very close to my parents' apartment and I was told that the Maharani often listened to my laughter from her window. One morning, she saw me splashing in the waves and summoned her attendant to bring me and my parents to her villa. Well, my father told me that while I was being pampered and petted, I pointed to a small painting of a *nautch* girl hanging on the wall behind the Maharani's head and naively asked whether the lady portrayed in the image was the queen herself. Well, the handmaidens gasped and almost fainted over my accidental insult and my father feared what would happen next... but the Maharani chuckled at my innocence and rewarded me with toys and sweetmeats for making her laugh out loud. She also gave me that very painting, which has instigated the immense love of art that I have carried in my heart ever since.'

Tara's eyes sparkled as she spoke of the kind-hearted Maharani and Jemima felt privileged to have been told the tale. When the Colonel rushed off to attend to some business, both women walked the grounds of the magnificent estate, exploring the beautiful secret gardens and far-reaching parks. As Tara drifted in and out of the snaking trees, Jemima thought her to be cultured and bohemian in thought. She moved gracefully and spoke in a voice that was bewitchingly serene and interestingly enough, she reminded Jemima of Jagatterini. The two had much in common and now Jemima would strive to emulate them both. By remembering Jagatterini's passionate beliefs and observing Tara's elegant ways, she would learn to walk and talk in a manner befitting a lady, though she would have to be a scandalous one at that.

They strolled for some time, enjoying the afternoon sunshine but then Tara's carefree mood changed. 'My dear, where did you teach? What was the name of the school?'

Jemima's mind emptied and her lips floundered. Not only that, Tara was studying her face as if trying to catch her out. *'No more questions please,' she silently begged*. Her mouth went dry and her eyes shifted. A moment later, she blurted out, 'Birshingha... Birshingha School.'

Tara's intense stare festered. She dropped her shoulders and straightened her back. 'My dear,' she said, 'you're not a teacher are you?'

Jemima's brain turned to mush and ashamed, she lowered her gaze to the ground. 'Forgive me, Madam, forgive me!' she spluttered, falling at Tara's feet. 'I'm not a teacher! I'm a servant... a common servant! I lied to you, forgive me.' Genuflecting absurdly, she then seized Tara's ankles. 'Please forgive me, Madam!'

'My dear, get up! Please get up!' Tara exclaimed. Her face turned red as Jemima burst into tears. 'Forgive *me*, I never meant to upset you so.' Raising her distraught companion from the ground, she guided her to nearby bench.

'I'm sorry for lying to you and your husband. I don't deserve to be in your company... a fine Brahmin lady like you,' Jemima gasped. She did not hear Tara's ironic laugh. 'I should be serving a lady like you. I shouldn't be here at all.' She tried to leave but Tara threw an arm across her waist and nudged her back into her seat.

'My dear, I may be a fine lady in the eyes of some but I'm not a Brahmin, I can assure you of that.'

Perplexed, Jemima listened on.

'You should know that my great grandfather was a humble farmer, who learned a few words of English and became a *de-wan*... an interpreter and mediator to the British merchants in Calcutta. He helped set up bazaars and hutments for artisans and labourers in Black Town and was then able to invest in land and business himself. He soon became one of the few men to manage all the mercantile business in Calcutta and he left his descendants a profitable landed estate, as well as the rents from bazaars and slums, which to this day, keep my family in an extremely privileged position. But he hailed from a *lower* caste, Priya, yet rose to become a man of position and wealth, just as my husband's predecessors did. You see, some think it is nobility of birth and caste that sets people apart from others... and some think it is money and wealth. But what *really* sets people apart is kindness, honesty and charity to their fellow man and one caste cannot claim that over another. My great grandmother learned to become a fine lady and she had to learn quickly. And who knows what may have become of me if my great grandfather had not made his fortune. So you see, you and my great grandmother are not really so different, Priya... and you don't have to worry... your secret is safe with me.'

An explosion of flapping bird wings rocked the branches of a huge oak tree behind them, and Jemima – exhausted but hugely relieved – smiled a fragile but grateful smile.

Dusk fell and the Colonel called for his carriage to take Jemima back to Apple Cottage. Just before she took her leave, the Colonel took Tara aside and informed her of his sudden idea. She then insisted that he share his thoughts with their guest.

'My dear, what are your plans for the coming week?' he asked, taking Jemima by the arm.

'I have nothing important planned, sir.'

'There is to be an exhibition in London... it's to do with the colonies.'

'Yes,' interrupted Tara. 'We're lending a few of our Mughal pieces but unfortunately the Colonel will not be able to attend.'

'I'm away viewing beachfront properties in Sussex and I was wondering whether you would be so kind to accompany Tara?'

'I would love to,' she cried.

'Wonderful!' Tara exclaimed. 'We shall attend the exhibition together and we will have such fun. Such fun!'

As she returned to Apple Cottage that night, Jemima felt secure in the knowledge that she had made the right decision in confessing the truth of her caste to Tara. She mulled over the story of Tara's great grandmother and revelled in the thought that she had more in common with the lady than she ever dared imagine. Having a woman like Tara as a confidante made her feel secure and worthy, and as she blew out the candle on her bedside table, she sensed that the seeds of a life-long friendship were quietly being sewn between herself and the Colonel's lovely and most understanding wife.

CHAPTER 59
THE PAINTING AND
THE LETTER

As a continuing retrospective of 'The Great Exhibition' of 1851, the World Fair of Culture and Arts was set to show-case an assortment of colonial literature and art to the general public in Regent's Park. There were over one hundred thousand objects on show and the area was heaving with all classes of day-trippers and tourists, eager to see the exotic spectacle. Tara's particular interest lay in the pieces of Mughul art and sculpture, to which she and the Colonel had loaned many of their prized possessions. After obtaining their tickets, she and Jemima studied artworks from the Americas and then moved onto the tribal costumes from the continent of Africa. Intrigued to see how their homeland was portrayed, they heeded the sign pointing to the 'Indian Room' and excitedly passed through its doors.

Tara was thrilled to hear so many visitors complimenting her Mughul portraits and subsequently expressed a desire to scrutinize the Sanskrit scriptures. She wandered off to the appropriate section, leaving Jemima to admire the Indian costumes pinned on the mannequins behind a large glass wall. She continued to roam the galleries until a room entitled, *'Impressions of the Colonies and its subjects'* attracted her eye. There, she saw images of maids, servants, maharajahs; *nawabs,* soldiers and seamen. Around another corner, she was met by a sea of paintings: some depicted elephants, tigers and snakes, others depicted people such as musicians caught in the middle of a recital. Then further along, she noticed a crowd assembled before an immense artwork. Having overheard their favourable comments on the artist's use of light and shade, she peered beyond their shoulders and glimpsed a portrait of an Indian woman reclining on an opulent couch. She was dressed in a fine red sari and loose locks of hair tumbled around her face. The inscription in the corner said, *'Maharani'* and Jemima almost fainted when she read the signature etched underneath: *'Sylvester Lawrence.'*

Several distinct differences existed in the face but the eyes were large and undeniably hers. There was no doubt Lawrence was a talented painter and the comments Jemima heard were entirely flattering. Trembling, she wrapped her hands around her waist and retreated among the onlookers, praying that the insidious man was not somewhere nearby. A perverse compulsion to examine the portrait again drew her to it like a pin to a magnet. She spied the *'For sale'* sign hanging to its side and heard people around her commenting on the price. But suddenly in Jemima's head, they were taunting her with the idea that they all knew her secret. Yes, they all knew what happened to her at the artist's studio that day, and they pointed and laughed, and knew it was her.

A hand on her shoulder made her jump out of her wits. 'My dear, are you all right? You've turned rather pale.' It was Tara.

'Madam, I'm fine...'

Tara stepped forward. 'What a magnificent portrait. I wonder who she is.'

'I think it's a princess. It's called *'Maharani.'*

'Sylvester Lawrence... I've never heard of him. He's quite a talent, don't you think?'

Jemima felt sick. 'Yes...'

Now that her shame and debasement were hanging on a wall for everyone to see, Jemima wanted the painting to be taken away and destroyed. She pictured herself hacking it to shreds and setting fire to the lacerated remains. She read the *'For Sale'* sign over and over again and considered the contentious idea spinning in her head. 'Mrs Malvery, may I ask a favour?'

Tara cocked her head with interest.

'I should like to purchase this painting but I haven't enough money on me. May I borrow some from you? I will return it as soon as I am able to.'

'Of course. And pay me back whenever you are able to, my dear.'

And so, Tara went off to purchase the painting.

Jemima wondered what on earth possessed her to buy the portrait. *'I want it removed. I want it taken away... that's why,' she told herself.* As she departed to find Tara, she almost collided with a woman, who suddenly came careering through the gallery.

'Forgive me!' the woman said, looking exasperated. 'There you are!' she cried, glaring at someone hiding behind a pillar. She wagged a finger angrily. 'You mustn't run away like that! The carriage will be here soon and I shouldn't like to say that you've misbehaved.' A young girl giggled and then squirmed before looking over to Jemima as the woman grabbed her arm. 'It's rude to stare, Sophie, Come along now!' the woman spat.

Jemima rocked on her heels. Immediately, she turned her face away as the pair departed but felt compelled to follow them as they headed towards the ticket hall.

'Miss Reed!' a boy called, galloping up the main stairs. 'Mother's arrived with the carriage!'

Miss Reed looked flustered. 'One mustn't raise one's voice, Robert!'

'Cole told Mother where we'd be and she's not very happy that you brought us here. She hates India and everything to do with the East, you know.'

Jemima panted with shock as they scurried out into an awaiting carriage and there she was too, sitting by the window, given away by the slant of her nose, the haughtiness of her cheekbones and the exceedingly serious brow. Elizabeth Hayward raised a reproachful finger to the woman – the new nanny Jemima assumed – and looked as though she were delivering a harsh lecture of some sort. The horses cantered on and Jemima began to pray that Sophie had not recognised her face.

The warm winds of June cleansed the quaint rooms of Apple cottage with the kinds of mellow breezes that accompanied the quintessential English summer, however, Jemima spent her days gloomily after seeing the children's faces again. Ten months had passed since she had been in their company but she had noticed the extra inches they had grown and the sudden sleekness of their once cherubic features. Elizabeth Hayward had not changed. No, she had not changed at all. But like a rat at a rope, guilt gnawed away at Jemima and she wandered the orchard grounds, misplaced and remorseful. Punishing her former memsahib meant she was punishing the children too, and they had done nothing wrong. Yet, she had knowingly beguiled their father and now the shame of her wrongdoing was crushing her reasons to be by his side.

Confined within the cottage walls, she considered the colossal lie her life had become and fell deeper into turmoil when the postmaster arrived with a letter that had meandered some distance before reaching her hands. The address of the Atrium had been struck out and replaced with that of Apple Cottage.

My dear Jemima,

I hope this letter will reach you. I had to travel to another village far from mine to have it written and sent to you. I must tell you that I am finally home in Ceylon. The journey was long and hard, Jemima. I had to live and sleep amongst other passengers in the filthy lower deck of the ship. We could hardly breathe and there was no room to walk about. There were many storms around the western coast of India but somehow I arrived safely to catch a second boat from Bombay, which sailed all the way to the port of Colombo. I cried when I saw my husband and children, for my daughters had grown so much and they are so beautiful. Thankfully they had not forgotten me, as I feared they would. I wish, one day Jemima, that you will be able to meet them and know them, for I know that you would love them just as I do.

How is Ezrine? And Mrs Wilson and Butterfly? I hope they are well. Please send everyone my very best wishes. And what of you Jemima, are you still there? If you are, then I cannot be truly happy knowing how sad you must be. Words cannot express the joy I feel now that I am home with my family, and I pray that you will be able to leave and reach your village as safely as I have done. I pray every night that you are well and that you will one day return home. I also pray that we will meet again, dear sister. Do not give up hope.

Your friend, Nuwani

The sentiment in Nuwani's words was too much for Jemima to bear. She staggered upstairs to her room and wept with abandon, blaming herself for every little thing that had gone astray. Convinced that life would consist of nothing but strife, she concluded that she must pay for her sins, for her misfortune was well deserved and of her own making. Then, when she could feel no worse, a knock at the cottage door heralded the arrival of the painting.

Jemima ignored it at first and resisted Champa's exuberant requests to see what was hidden beneath the brown paper. It claimed most of the space in the cottage's modest lounge and remained propped up against one of the walls, tied up with string. That evening, unable to relax, Jemima tip-toed barefoot downstairs and grabbed a knife from the kitchen drawer. She hacked through the twine under the light of a candle and ripped away the paper. The image before her looked strange under a hazy glow; its eerie qualities seemed to mirror everything she had been through so far. She chided herself for wasting good money on it, for she had not bought it out of vanity, of that she could be sure. It was a reminder of Lawrence and how he had violated her and so there had to be another reason why she had summoned it into her possession.

He had captured her eyes perfectly but there were subtle variations in the slant of the jaw and the curve of the chin. Had he tried to commit her features to memory or had he chosen another model to sit in her place? In Jemima's view, the face bore no resemblance to hers, but if she really looked hard enough, there was something in the eyes that told her bitter tale.

Morning dawned and Champa's comments began to irk Jemima; the girl said the woman in the painting looked like her Mistress Priya, and because of Champa's astute observation, Jemima banished the painting to the depths of the cellar, well out of sight.

The July sun soon melted the dark disposition that ruled Jemima's existence for a while and the delights of the countryside lured Ibrahim to her side. He had stayed away for months and had only been communicating by the rare letter, but this time he came carrying her old valise and the belongings she had left behind at the Shadwell Inn.

'What is your news?' Jemima asked. 'Is life treating you well?'

He wondered if he should mention Sarah and how they had both enjoyed a series of passionate trysts since their lustful encounter on the kitchen floor. He wanted to tell Jemima about the explosive spark that now flickered between them whenever they passed each other: the lingering looks and secretive smiles. His blossoming ardour for Sarah amounted to more than just sexual satisfaction, for the girl confessed to loving him as far back as the day she brought him his first cup of tea. But could Ibrahim say he felt the same way? Nothing would have given him more pleasure than to break Jemima's heart, as she had done his, but would his revelations make her jealous enough to leave William Hayward and marry him instead? Only time would tell. But if he was completely honest, Sarah *was* vivacious and very, very lovely. He had enjoyed thinking of her during the train journey to Tring. In fact Ibrahim found that he was thinking of Sarah almost all the time.

He spoke of several properties in London that had recently caught his eye. He told Jemima, he wanted to prosper and fill his home with pretty trinkets and artworks such as those seen in Malvery Mansion and it was these disclosures that gave Jemima the idea to bring the exiled painting out into the light of day.

Ibrahim swooned when he saw it and asked why she had hidden the artwork away. She told him she had bought it from an exhibition but it had been simply too big to hang on the walls.

'Do you have room for it?' she asked. 'I would like you to have it.'

'You have already given me enough. I cannot accept,' Ibrahim gasped.

'Then I shall be most upset. It is a gift to a beloved friend.'

Only moments before, he was damning Jemima for unknowingly forsaking his love. Now he felt ashamed, for he would never want her to suffer. He wanted the very best for her, even if she was meant to be with someone else. 'Are you absolutely certain?' he asked.

'Absolutely,' she replied.

A few days later, Jemima watched the *Maharani* embark on her journey back to London, where she would one day reside on a wall in Ibrahim's new house.

CHAPTER 60
THE HERTFORDSHIRE CLIENT

The month of August arrived and back at Carlton House Terrace, William spent an hour of his free time soaking up the remainder of the late morning sun. He was not alone for long, for Elizabeth entered the room and settled into a chair on the other side of his desk. She prodded her curls for a time, forcing him to ask the purpose of her visit. 'Does a wife need a reason to sit with her husband?' she said, stooping forward to play with the quills on his desk.

William gripped both arms of his chair and prepared for whatever it was his wife had come to say.

'Truth is,' she continued, 'there is a reason why I'm here.'

'Well..?' he said, growing more agitated by the second.

'I should like to know about your client.'

'Client?'

'Yes, the one in Hertfordshire... the one who summons all your time.'

William had not imagined his body would tremble so as he explained that his 'client' was in fact a very good friend with many affairs that needed thorough legal attention.

'What is his name?'

'Colonel James Malvery… you wouldn't know him.'

Elizabeth fingered the inkbottle. 'Perhaps it's time I got to know him. I could accompany you on the next occasion you make a trip to his estate? He wouldn't mind, would he? Especially if he has a wife. Does he have a wife?'

'Yes, but I expect you'll find it extremely tiresome, Elizabeth, for I shall be dealing with the affairs of his estate.'

'Still, I should like to meet him… and *her*.'

William could feel the heat rising in his face. 'He's just a client.'

'But you just mentioned that he was a very good friend and I'm sure Mrs Malvery won't mind having a female companion. I've never visited Hertfordshire. I hear it's lovely.'

William glared at her.

'Whatever's the matter? Anyone might think you didn't wish me to accompany you. They might even think you had something to hide.'

William's day had begun exceptionally well. The parks outside were lush and green; the flowers were out in full bloom. Children scurried and laughed, playing hopscotch and spin the hoop. Agitated, he rose from his chair and pulled back the curtain in a fury.

'You really are a man with secrets.'

'Say what you really mean, Elizabeth,' he replied, still facing the window.

'You have become quite skilled in the art of lying, haven't you?' she said, wrapping her fingers around the inkbottle.

The chilling tone in her voice told William that he must face Elizabeth again, but he only turned when he heard the inkbottle smashing against the floor. Black fluid splattered against the walls and splodges of velvety black liquid ran down the skirting boards. She swept the journals from the top of his desk and rocked forward on her hands to spit out her subsequent words.

'I took it upon myself to visit the office while you were away, William. Well, that pleasant clerk of yours, Mr McKay, told me some rather interesting facts. I mentioned this client of yours in Hertfordshire... and do you know what he said?'

At that juncture, she paused, as if anticipating a great rush of agony in his eyes but he stared back without as much as a blink.

'Mr McKay had no knowledge whatsoever of any such client. Well, I told him that he must be mistaken but if anyone should know, he certainly should since he arranges all your appointments. He checked the callers' books... even those belonging to the other partners... and oddly enough, there was not one iota of information on your Hertfordshire friend.'

William sunk back into his chair. 'Congratulations Elizabeth!' he said, applauding her with a serious of slow, weighty claps. 'You've found me out again! And now, I shall tell the truth and I shall leave no stone unturned.'

He mentioned the woman he had met whilst Elizabeth was visiting her parents in Adel. He told her that he called on her regularly and she had since become his mistress. They were very much in love; in fact, it pained them to be apart. He prepared himself for a vicious reaction: screaming perhaps, a slap across the face, or a hard object hurtling in his general direction, but Elizabeth's manner surprised him, for she rose from her chair and walked out of the room without even slamming the door.

She was in the midst of lifting a foot to the staircase when she heard his voice. 'Elizabeth,' he said calmly. 'What are you going to do?'

Ignoring him, she carried on.

'Elizabeth, I demand an answer.'

'Nothing,' she said, continuing on.

'*Nothing?*'

'Everything remains the same,' she said. 'By the way, I've invited Charlotte and Frederick to tea this weekend. They're looking forward to seeing you, so I'd appreciate it if you were home.'

William made up his mind to deliver the final blows. 'My mistress is Indian, Elizabeth,' he said, overtaking her on the staircase. 'I met her here... in London.'

Elizabeth's heart shrivelled as she pushed past him on the steps. 'Everything remains the same,' she said through gritted teeth.

William seized his wife's wrist and hauled her up the staircase.

'Unhand me!' she gasped.

'There's something I'd like you to see!' he bellowed, hauling her towards his chamber. She was still resisting when he kicked open his bedroom door and hurled her inside with an almighty heave. He warned her not to leave and she dared not disobey him. She watched him pluck out a key from his dresser drawer and stride over to the corner of his room to unlock one of his travelling chests. He delved inside and retrieved an item wrapped inside a handkerchief, which he then thrust under his wife's eyes. 'Look closely,' he said. 'This is the woman I love.'

Elizabeth smiled and then began to laugh. 'Oh William! How amusing! Must you come up with some fanciful tale about Jemima just for revenge? Did I not already say that I sent her back to India and still... you invent this silly notion in retaliation?' She laughed out loud. 'Is this the best you can do?'

'But you never sent her back, did you?' he spat. 'You abandoned her in a squalid lodging house!'

Elizabeth's laughter subsided.

'I met her you see,' he said, 'and she told me what you did. Still I'm rather grateful to you, Elizabeth... because if you hadn't left Jemima stranded in that place, she and I would never have fallen in love.'

Elizabeth's head whirled in madness. 'How absurd! She's a servant! You're lying... '

'It is true,' he said, placing the picture back into the chest. 'I regret to say that our particular union was doomed from the start, Elizabeth, and we cannot go on living in contention... it's hardly fair on you or the children. It aggrieves me to say this, but I do not love you and I'm certain that you do not love me.'

Elizabeth failed to reign in her tears and her sudden distress concerned William. Stepping towards her with a sensitive hand, he said, 'Come, come, Elizabeth. We could both be happy if we admit that our marriage has been a calamity. We could even be friends... in time.'

'Friends?!' she screamed, striking his hand away. 'Are you insane? You must be! You should be committed! I loathe you and I loathe your black whore of a mistress. You'll suffer for what you've done! By God, I swear I'll make you and *her* suffer... your black bitch of an Indian whore!'

Reeling at his wife's rancour, William departed, leaving her to contemplate her life from that devastating moment forth. Spasms of disgust pulsed through her body and she tightened every muscle in an attempt to restore some self-control. But it was no use, for Elizabeth's tears were lamenting the loss of William as she considered his love affair with Jemima as possibly being true. But what damaged Elizabeth Hayward the most was not the scandalous repercussions of his relationship with the children's former ayah. What damaged Elizabeth Hayward the most was that, in spite of it all, she *did* love her husband... with a passion in fact. But unfortunately, for Elizabeth Hayward, he did not love her back.

William passed his time at the offices of Simeon & Howarth, feigning interest in law reports and practices. In reality, he dreaded what course of action Elizabeth would take now that his scandalous secret was out in the open. He did not have to wonder for long because Mr McKay knocked on the door, announcing the arrival of William's older brother, Raymond.

'What brings you here, Raymond?' William asked, springing up from his chair to shake his brother's hand. 'Is everything all right...Mother and Father?'

'They're fine,' Raymond replied rather sternly.

'Then to what do I owe the pleasure?'

'I highly doubt you'll regard it a pleasure when you hear what I have come to say.' Raymond frowned and tossed his coat over a chair. 'Do you really have no knowledge of the reason I am here?'

William shook his head.

'Father and I received a visit from Elizabeth's parents this weekend gone. They spoke of how you've taken leave of your senses and started some absurd affair with a native woman from India.'

Raymond went on to say that the Hayward family had defended him of course and that William's mother had insisted that Elizabeth must have made an unspeakable mistake. Thus, Raymond had been sent to hear his younger brother's side of the story.

'Please say it's not true, William.'

'It is true.'

Raymond cringed and collapsed into a chair.

He knew his brother would not understand. Raymond had always been under the control of their father, Victor, who had consequently wiped away any trace of independent thinking from his eldest son's mind. Raymond pleaded with him to give the other woman up and make amends with Elizabeth but after confessing that their marriage had been dead for a long while now, William explained that even if he wished to return – and he did not – Elizabeth would never take him back. Hence Raymond opened his briefcase and withdrew some papers. 'Father and I have discussed the matter with Elizabeth's parents and... in the absence of any reconciliation on account of the rumours being true... then here are the terms of the separation as specified by Elizabeth on the advice of her father's solicitor.'

She was demanding a divorce on the grounds of mental cruelty but as this would be incredibly difficult to prove in a court of law, which almost always favoured the husband, George Marshall's solicitor suggested that it would be in both parties' interests if William agreed to sign a written affidavit placing the breakdown of their marriage squarely on his shoulders.

'Do you understand, William?' his brother asked grimly.

'Of course, I understand,' William laughed. 'I'm a lawyer my-self, remember?'

Riled by his brother's impudence, Raymond continued to convey the sentiments of the contract in a sober tone of voice.

'Since it was Elizabeth's money that has kept you in the style in which you have become accustomed, they demand that you rescind all claims to her fortune and pay back all monies spent on the upkeep of... shall we say... of this other woman.'

'That's an awful lot of demanding.'

'I think it's highly reasonable under the circumstances. Naturally you are not obliged to grant Elizabeth any privileges at all, but she and her family agree not to reveal the particulars of the affair and drag the Hayward name through the mud if you agree. I urge you to consider the effect of this senseless, despi-cable dalliance on our family, William. Mother and Father are mortified enough as it is... and as for the children...'

'What about the children?' William interrupted.

'Elizabeth asks that you do the noble thing by the children and permit them to live with her in Adel. She also requests that Robert and Sophie never be exposed to the company of the oth-er woman.'

'Raymond,' William frowned. 'What did Elizabeth tell the family about this other woman?'

'Only that she's some unknown native woman from India... that's all she knows because that's all you've told her. Why? Is there anything else we should be prepared for?'

William had already guessed why Elizabeth had omitted the detail of his mistress being their former ayah. She could not bear any further embarrassment if that outrageous aspect were to be divulged.

'What if I decide I want the children here with me?'

'Well,' replied Raymond. 'You have the final decision but think of how your selfish actions will influence Robert and Sophie. They will have to grow up in the knowledge that their father left their mother for a ...'

Raymond struggled to find an appropriate word.

William concluded that the children would be better off living with their mother and when they were older, he would explain his decision to break the family apart. However, for now, he would give Elizabeth what she wanted. He signed the affidavit.

'This isn't finished, William,' scoffed Raymond. 'I must return and tell Mother and Father that Elizabeth speaks the truth.'

'Then that is what you must do, brother.'

'You fool,' sneered Raymond, slamming his briefcase shut. 'You could have saved yourself this ruin... even your marriage... if you kept a white mistress like the rest of us.'

Raymond fastened his briefcase and departed without saying goodbye.

Following Raymond's visit, two letters arrived for William. In the first, George Marshall's solicitor, having written on Elizabeth's behalf, stressed that since he had signed the affidavit, Elizabeth was now at liberty to sell the house in Carlton House Terrace and consequently, William had one week to vacate the premises. In the second, William's father had asked if the Indian woman in question had cast a spell over his youngest son in the 'evil way Indian natives are known to do.' He begged his son to give the 'vile creature' up and enticed him with the promise of a position in the family business with a generous allowance to boot. However, if William were to disagree, then he would no longer be welcome in the family home and would thus be held accountable for his mother's present illness. In short, the Hayward family would sever all ties. The final blow occurred at work, where it was politely explained to William Hayward that he must collect his belongings and vacate the premises forthwith.

CHAPTER 61

A MATTER OF URGENCY

Jemima reluctantly settled into the treacherous existence she had carved out in Tring and as the days grew shorter, she allowed herself to enjoy the oftentimes elusive English sun. She had not seen William for almost a month but she had grown accustomed to his sporadic visits and spent the last days of summer witnessing the ever-changing vistas of the rich Hertfordshire countryside. Then autumn crept in, making its mark by colouring the landscape several shades of brown and red. The pathways were layered in shimmering golden leaves that crunched beneath Jemima's feet during her early morning walks. And when William did return, the circumstances of his arrival were rather strange, for he did not forewarn Jemima of his visit and he appeared when she and Champa were out at the local market.

She heard him calling out to her as she walked through the cottage door. He was sprawled in an armchair, shoving an open decanter of whisky back and forth across the small mahogany table. His normally sparkling blue eyes were lazy and bloodshot, and Jemima smelt a strong whiff of alcohol on his breath. Champa grimaced too at the sight of her scruffy master and cowered as she offered him a slice of cake. His temper was uncommonly short that morning and he growled at her unnecessarily to go away. His brusqueness upset the girl's sensibilities and she scurried to her quarters, where she spent some time sulking in her room.

The trauma in William's face was discernible and deep. Wearily, he explained the reasons for his sudden and sorry appearance. Jemima feared he had agreed to his father's demands and had come to end their affair. She could not blame him if he did, for he had lost so much because of her, and so, whatever he had come to do or say next, she would courageously accept the consequences. Lord Hayward's letter lay crumpled at William's feet. She rescued it and smoothed down the edges. Within seconds, William had grabbed it from her fingers and ripped it up before scattering its fragments onto the sooty hearth.

'I'm afraid I'm no longer in a position to spoil you, Priya,' he said, looking disappointed. 'Agreeing to Elizabeth's contract means I now owe a substantial amount of money to her family. I have also been cut off from my own parents and I am currently without a position of employment. We shall have to move out of this place as I cannot afford to pay the rent.' He rested his hand on her knee. 'I am a poor man now, Priya. Do you still love me? I would not blame you if you wished to leave, although I'm not sure what would become of me if you did.'

'You have given everything up for me?'

'I'd rather that than live without you,' he whispered, nestling his head against her chin. 'We have two weeks left before the rent is due. I shall visit the Colonel and let him know that we'll be leaving soon. Perhaps, he will be kind enough to permit us to stay until we find a room. Unfortunately, it shall not be as pleasant as Apple Cottage... I suppose I could go to him now or later this afternoon,' he said sleepily. 'Yes, I shall visit later this afternoon, for I would like to sit here for a while longer with you. Will you stay with me a while?'

'Yes William,' Jemima said, through her tears. 'I will stay with you for as long as you wish.'

A tangle of voices pouring in from the partly open French windows woke William from a heady sleep. Yawning and stretching, he ambled towards the garden to find the Colonel and Mrs Malvery sitting at a table with his lover by their side. The early evening air danced with a sprinkling of bluebottles and midges, and the Colonel waved a cluster of them away from his nose. 'My dear fellow, you're awake!' he boomed, spying William in the doorway.

William cringed in the sunlight. 'Forgive my appearance, sir... Mrs Malvery... Priya should have woken me up.'

'Stuff and nonsense! I insisted that she let you rest,' the Colonel barked. 'From the sight of you, you looked like you needed it!'

He stood up and his chair legs screeched against the stone ground, rattling William's brain in the process.

'Now get this down you and come for a walk. I have a proposition for you,' he said, pushing a cup of tea in William's direction.

William gulped down his tea and crossed the lawn in pursuit of the Colonel. He resolved to turn his fortunes around by finding a place to live and then trying for another position as an attorney at common law. If the Colonel were to be kind enough to permit him and Priya to remain at the cottage for a few days longer, he would garner the confidence to battle whatever life threw at them. The wind puffed the remaining sleep from his eyes and facing his good friend, he proceeded to speak of the matter foremost on his mind. 'It's fortunate that you're here, sir. I meant to visit you earlier but foolishly, I fell asleep. I needed to talk with you urgently.'

Colonel Malvery kicked a fallen apple out from his path. 'Well there's the funny thing... I needed to speak with you too.'

'Perhaps you would be so kind to permit me to go first?' insisted William, his head sore with alcohol. 'The matter is quite urgent.'

'So is mine,' the Colonel professed, disregarding William's plea. 'Do you remember Cecil Richards, my accountant?'

William scratched his head. 'The fellow I met at the club?'

'Yes, that's him. Well, I've had to dispense with his services.'

'I regret to hear that, Colonel.'

'I'm not! His charges were getting rather high and frankly, I'm at a loss to know what the scoundrel was doing for me anyway. Well, it happens that I'm now in search of an overseer of some sort, somebody to keep an account of my expenditure, write my letters, keep my papers in order for immediate reference. You're aware, I've just purchased a townhouse in Brighton and there's a tremendous amount to deal with... decorator's estimates, furniture estimates, business transactions with coach-makers, horse-dealers and harness-makers et cetera, et cetera... an awful lot of bother, truth be told. So, I was wondering whether you would take the post of general manager of my estates and since you're a solicitor by profession, perhaps, you could combine both positions and heed my legal affairs too. Of course that would mean that I would have to dispense of Mr Campbell's services,' the Colonel laughed, 'which would make my wife extremely happy. Tara was never too fond of Richards and Campbell in the first place. Come to think of it... neither was I. She's been badgering me to find someone trustworthy to keep my affairs in order... you know... ensure everything runs smoothly here and back in London and now Brighton of course, but mostly here in Tring. But I'm afraid that would mean you having to stay on at the cottage, you understand?' The Colonel grinned. 'Rent-free, of course... since that would be part of the arrangement. But there shall also be a wage of three hundred a year. So what do you say? Do you accept?'

A jumble of confusion, happiness and alcohol swirled in William's brain and his stock of dismal thoughts began to scatter like leaves in a breeze. 'I accept, sir,' he said incredulously, 'and I promise to be as zealous over your affairs as if they were my own.'

'Wonderful!' yelled the Colonel, whacking him on the back. 'Now, there's a load off my mind. Now, what was it you wanted to speak to me about, dear boy?'

William looked up to the waning sun. 'Nothing, sir... it really doesn't matter now.'

Colonel Malvery's compassionate eyes made William understand what had passed between them in the orchard that day. And short of embracing the man and whooping cries of joy, all William could do to show his gratitude was to shake his loyal friend's hand in the most vigorous of fashions. To celebrate his new appointment, Colonel Malvery requested another pot of tea and suggested everyone raise their cups in a toast to the future. Jemima's relief was telling and William recognised what she had done on his behalf, though at first, his pride was wounded after learning that she had spoken to the Colonel when it should have been him. But remembering the sacrifices she had made to remain at his side, he squeezed her hand lovingly in a silent thank you.

In spite of the Colonel's generous offer, the subsequent weeks proved a struggle for William, for every pound he earned went straight back into the Marshall family's pockets. But as a man once accustomed to living a modest lifestyle, he eventually settled into his new existence and quickly learned how to cope. Jemima – no stranger to scrimping and saving – did her best to keep costs low. She pawned her saris and a few items of jewellery but never regretted giving her savings to Ibrahim. Of course, he would have returned the money if he had known of her troubled circumstances, but she vowed to keep her suffering financial affairs to herself and decided she would never ask for the money back, no matter how hard life became.

When October passed, Jemima realised that she had been in England for over a year now. When November dawned, she discovered she was carrying William's child. She wondered how they could possibly improve their chances in life with an extra mouth to feed but when she told him, he roared with delight and immediately sent word to the Malverys. 'Perhaps this is my chance to be a proper father,' he declared, embracing Jemima tightly in his arms.

The Colonel and Tara continued to proffer their support in any way they could, despite their concerns for the child having been conceived out of wedlock, but Jemima's happiness was tempered by thoughts of Elizabeth, for the child would be a brother or sister to *her* children and she feared the lady's reaction if or when she heard the news. Those worries lurked like a beast as the days raced by and as the year finally came to a close, Jemima realised that she was struggling to keep up with the speed at which her life was now hurtling.

CHAPTER 62

TEA AND BARFI

'Dear Jemima,
1868 will be a momentous year!'

The statement came from a letter written by Ibrahim, in which he described how the successful Indian businessman, Mr Desai, (Colonel Malvery's friend) and two of his rich Anglo-Asian associates were expressing their desires to invest in his restaurant venture. The wealthy patrons had witnessed how Ibrahim had single-handedly turned the fortunes of the Shadwell Inn around and were now clambering all over themselves to encourage him in his new enterprise. With their influential testimonies and promises of financial support, Ibrahim had garnered a loan from the bank and now only needed to locate some suitable premises.

'I was invited to cook for a writer fellow living in Bedford Square and I had taken refuge beneath the canopy of an old coffee shop when it had begun to rain very heavily. The windows were steamy and it was difficult to see inside but there was a notice hanging above the door that said:

To Let
Contact L. Smithers & Son.
No. 48 Tottenham Court Road, London W1

I made an appointment to view the property the next day. There was a little damp but nothing a little care and attention could not fix. In fact, the building is in a fairly good condition and there is even a spacious cooking area perfect for preparing large quantities of food. The front quarters are perfect for seating my customers and the place is ideally located with businesses and smart houses spread out along the way. Just imagine it full of people enjoying my food! I told my investors that this had to be the place and they were more than happy to secure the deal. The premises need to be decorated and furnished and I have written to seek your advice.

Ibrahim'

Jemima was thrilled to know that Ibrahim valued her opinions. She suggested red velvet pelmets and curtains for the windows and insisted the walls be furnished with eastern-style art. In her opinion, dark mahogany floorboards were stylish and much more preferable to the dreary concrete ground. She recommended the wood be varnished and covered with oriental rugs and after studying the great portraits hanging in the rooms of Malvery Mansion, she drew sketches of furniture made in the times of the great Indian kings.

Ibrahim was delighted with her ideas and set about making his plans. Soon word spread that his 'restaurant' would open in the summer of 1868. When the work was completed and the invitations duly sent, Ibrahim subsequently effervesced over the fare he would serve to his customers. 'I cannot wait,' he declared on one of his visits to Apple Cottage. 'I am preparing the menu now. I was thinking of serving dishes of lamb, chicken and fish... amongst others and I am working on a new lentil dish that will be named after my father, of course... and you shall be one of the guests of honour!'

As Ibrahim mused on his *carte du jour*, it dawned on Jemima that the scheduled opening of his restaurant would prove most inconvenient and she would most definitely not be able to attend.

'Why can't you come?' he cried. 'Are you concerned about Sarah and Mr Meade? I told them that Jemima has returned to India. 'Priya' will be able to fool them as she did me.'

Jemima then explained that Mr Meade and his daughter were not the problem.

'I don't understand... why can't you come?' Ibrahim asked again.

She patted her stomach and Ibrahim sighed. It pained him to remember that she was carrying William Hayward's child. 'Forgive me,' he said. 'In my excitement I had forgotten.'

Jemima was just as disappointed, for the occasion meant as much to her as it did to him. But William would never approve of her travelling to London so far on in her confinement and so, she could only assure Ibrahim that she would be there in spirit.

Over the next weeks, Ibrahim visited less and less and Jemima correctly surmised that he was busy preparing for the restaurant's grand opening. William and Colonel Malvery had recently departed for Brighton and so she spent her time relaxing under Tara's watchful eye or reading books with Champa fussing at her side. *Great Expectations* had already come to an end and it was time to choose another epic. She plucked *Oliver Twist* from the shelf and was about to read the tale of the unfortunate orphan boy when she glimpsed Champa sitting alone in the kitchen, staring into space.

'Is everything all right, Champa?' she asked.

Startled, Champa turned around. 'Yes, Madam... everything is all right.'

'What are you doing?'

'Nothing, Madam... all my work is done.'

'I see. Why don't you go out somewhere?'

Champa shrugged. 'Nowhere to go, Madam.'

Jemima sympathised. Many a time in Carlton House Terrace, she had sat alone in her room, feeling lonely and bored. 'Come sit with me,' she said, beckoning the girl into the drawing room.

'But Madam is reading.'

'Yes... but I shall read out loud and you shall listen.'

Champa ambled into the drawing room as Jemima settled into a sofa. 'May I ask Madam a question?'

'Yes.'

'Is it hard... to read?'

Remembering Jagatterini, Jemima said, 'Not if you have the right teacher.'

Champa settled on the floor and drew her knees to her chin.

'I could teach you if you like? You're a clever girl,' smiled Jemima.

Champa smiled back bashfully. 'Oh no! Madam is clever... not Champa!'

Jemima opened the book of *Oliver Twist* and glanced down at the first page. *"Among other public buildings in a certain town, which for many reasons it will be prudent to refrain from mentioning, and to which I will assign no fictitious name, there is one anciently common to most towns, great or small..."*

As she read on, Jemima glanced down at Champa, whose big brown eyes glowed as she listened to her mistress's voice. And it was the very same glow that she, as Anupriya, bore all those years ago when she was first told that she could be anything she desired. And as she registered the content expression on Champa's face, Jemima felt for the first time that she had a real purpose in life, and that alone made her exceedingly happy.

A few weeks later, Jemima received another letter from Ibrahim but on this occasion, he had written in a rather cryptic fashion, stating that he would be sending a carriage to fetch Jemima from Apple Cottage the next day. She was to catch a train to London, where another carriage would bring her to meet him in Bedford Square. He was adamant that she make the trip and would never forgive her if she declined his invitation. And since it was still safe for her to travel in her current stage of confinement, she packed her old brown valise and took Champa along for company.

Ibrahim was waiting on a corner, looking dapper in his English suit. 'The restaurant is ready,' he proclaimed, helping Jemima out of the carriage. 'No one else has seen it yet... I want you to be the first.'

He guided her into a yard at the rear of the building and unlocked the door that led into his new domain. He swept a hand across the new work surfaces and gushed over his gleaming copper pots and sparkling new pans. He proudly pointed out the new stoves and ovens before letting it be known that he had employed two kitchen hands to help cook and three attendants to serve his dishes out front. Ibrahim then escorted her into a world of red velvet and gold, where mahogany chairs fitted beneath handcrafted tables and crystal oil lamps flickered on their smooth shiny surfaces. A large chandelier illuminated the walls, decorated – just as she had recommended – with murals of India and depictions of Awadh.

'Gracious, Ibrahim!' she cried, 'how did you manage to afford all this?'

'Those investors were richer than I first thought!' he boasted. 'Now turn around,' he said, nudging her arm.

She turned around and her eyes spread quickly at the shock of seeing Sylvester Lawrence's painting hanging on the wall ahead.

'What are your thoughts?' he asked, his face beaming. He did not wait for her to answer. 'Wait,' there is one more thing I have to show you,' he said, throwing open the bolt on the main door.

He beckoned her out onto the street, where passers-by stopped to peer through the window, interested in the new establishment opening up in their vicinity. Ibrahim asked that they spread the news and then pointed to the word written across the golden canopy: '*Maharani.*' Jemima leant against the window for fear that she would faint.

Seated at one of the tables, drinking tea, Jemima hesitantly asked why Ibrahim had chosen to hang Lawrence's painting in his restaurant. He confessed that it was *she* who had spurred him on to realise his ambition after he had deposited the money she had gifted him into an account at the bank. He bolstered the amount every month with a quota of his earnings and soon found the discipline paying off. With time, he had garnered a handsome sum that, in turn, initiated the plans for his elaborate restaurant and so it seemed only fitting that the portrait hang inside, for it reminded him of their friendship and how far they had ventured in the world.

His reasoning made sense to Jemima but she reeled at his subsequent declarations. 'I tried to contact this fellow, Sylvester Lawrence. I wished to invite him to the grand opening and reveal his creation to everyone.'

'*No! No! Never! Not that man!*' she wanted to shriek.

'I spoke to a painter who knew of him, Jemima...the fellow drinks regularly at the inn. He told me a terrible story.'

'What? What did he tell you?'

Ibrahim reached for Jemima's hand. 'Are you feeling all right? You look ill. Is it the baby?'

'No, I'm fine. What did the man tell you?'

'He said that this Lawrence fellow died two months ago.'

'Died?'

'Yes.'

'Are you sure?'

'Yes. He drank heavily and recently had become very ill... a problem with his skin, the other fellow said. One of his servants found him dead in his bed with two empty bottles of whisky beside his pillow.'

Jemima was stunned. But the news of Sylvester Lawrence's untimely death soon filled her with pure relief. Never would she fear an encounter with this man again, for fate had dealt with him, it seemed, in its own karmic way. She was unable to spare an ounce of sympathy for him. Indeed, she hoped he had suffered and that his last hours were spent in agonizing pain. She pictured him drowning in his own filth and vomit. Still, it would never match the torment she had had to endure.

'Such a shame, Jemima... he was a talented fellow,' Ibrahim sighed.

Jemima could say nothing but soon the knots in her stomach began to untangle. Ibrahim left her alone momentarily and she digested the news with vengeful vindication. He returned with a pen and inkpot clasped in his hands, and then slid an official-looking document under her nose.

'Sign your name there, please,' he said, pointing to a space halfway down. Four signatures were written on the paper, three of which bore the names of Ibrahim's investors whilst one bore his own.

'Why must I sign this?' she asked, bemused.

'Well,' he began, 'I did say that I would make you a silent partner, did I not? So you will now have a share of the profits my restaurant makes.'

Jemima wondered whether she could take any more surprises. Overwhelmed, she thanked Ibrahim as enthusiastically as her pregnant belly would allow. She remembered how Colonel Malvery had toasted William's appointment that memorable day at Apple Cottage and requested that she and Ibrahim do the same. She wanted to toast something else too: the death of Sylvester Lawrence. But since there was no more tea in her cup, she flicked open the catches on her old valise and reached for Ibrahim's tin of *barfi*. 'It's about time I tasted some of this.'

Ibrahim threw his head back and laughed before leaving the table to fetch the tin cutter.

What a jumble of emotions Jemima felt as she glanced around the beautiful restaurant. First, her heart leapt with pride; not just for Ibrahim but for herself too. Then, revisiting the memory of Sylvester Lawrence, she recalled the violence, anguish and shame she had suffered but figured that somehow, in spite of it all, she had survived the ordeal to win the love of William.

The painting caught her eye again but she found that she could stare into the face of the *Maharani* without being forced to look away. No longer did it signify sexual brutality; no longer did it represent her never-ending pain; no longer did it symbolize her bitter tears of abandonment, for now she saw something else in the *Maharani's* eyes. It reminded her of her friendship with Ibrahim and how they had overcome their turbulent journeys to embrace life once again. But Ibrahim had most definitely found his place in the world, whilst she was still searching for that elusive peace of mind. She tentatively etched the name, 'Priya Datta,' on the contract and wondered who on earth that person could be. For months, she had waged a battle on her own integrity and now it insisted that she speak the truth.

'What should I do Ibrahim?' she asked on his return. 'I have lied so much and now I am carrying a child, the guilt feels so much stronger.'

Ibrahim dragged the tin cutter around the edge of the can. 'To me, honesty is an important virtue, but sometimes things are not that simple. You are not the same person you were when I met you on the *Bengal Star...* neither am I. You are no longer an ayah... a person whose life only made sense when she heard a command from a master or a mistress... and I no longer work for a *nawab* or slave on a ship that made my life miserable. I have a different spirit now and what has gone before is not important. It is what you mould from life this day forward that really matters.'

'So you think that I should remain as Priya?'

'Only you know the answer to that.'

'But I don't, Ibrahim. I don't...'

Ibrahim sniffed the exposed *barfi*. 'You will know when the time is right. Fate will guide you. It has always done, has it not?'

'What would I do without you?' she smiled. 'You have always been my dear, dear friend.'

'And I always will...' he whispered, fixing her in his deep, dark stare.

'I am proud of you Ibrahim. You have accomplished so much. Now all you need is a good wife.'

'Really?'

'Of course! Our children must grow and play together.'

Ibrahim remained quiet.

'I must ask Tara if she knows of anyone.'

'That will not be necessary.'

Jemima sat up in her chair. 'Is there someone you like?'

Sarah's face flashed before him.

'Perhaps...' he replied. Then changing the subject, he spun his head towards the kitchen and cried, 'Champa! Come out here and try some of this.' And emptying the sweetmeat out onto a plate, Ibrahim urged Jemima to taste the *barfi* that had travelled just as far and wide as they both had.

CHAPTER 63

HOME

In the days leading up to the birth of her child, Jemima could not help but reflect on the baby she had lost almost two years before. She had not sensed its presence within her body neither had she confronted her feelings when she learned of its demise that day. But she regarded the unborn child that presently thrived as an essence of the one she briefly carried and finally, she was able to understand why Madhu had loved her as passionately as she did.

In July 1868, she gave birth to a blue-eyed, olive skinned daughter, whose name, Isabella Madhumita Hayward, blossomed from the union of William's favourite grandmother's middle name and that of her own dear mother's first. Bonding with her offspring was exceedingly special, for unlike the children Jemima had cared for in the past, this one was truly her own. She was, however, keen to learn how Ibrahim had coped on his grand opening night and just as she had thought, the occasion was written about in every London newspaper.

People had flocked from all over London to taste the cuisine served at the *Maharani* and Ibrahim had had to turn customers away on a promise that they would be allowed to enter the next day. The night was a triumphant success and as the toast of London, the *Maharani* was never without its glut of customers. By spring the following year, the restaurant's profits were higher than predicted. Jemima was duly informed that the partners would be purchasing the adjacent property to enable the business to expand and when she finally told William of her secret partnership with the Indian chef, he applauded the ingenuity shown by the pair and encouraged them wholeheartedly in their business endeavours. Thus, Ibrahim tentatively put aside his secret disliking for William Hayward and for Jemima's sake alone, considered becoming his friend.

For the first time in her life, Jemima had money of her own and she offered it to William to help him pay his debts. Of course, male pride prevented him from accepting her contribution, for it was a responsibility, he later declared, that he must shoulder alone. But with or without Jemima's help, William knew he would be paying his debt to Elizabeth for the rest of his life.

'In time, we should be able to afford a larger house,' he said, sheltering his daughter's eyes from a ray of sunlight shooting across the bedroom.

'I like it here,' Jemima replied. 'It's our little home.'

His mood darkened somewhat. 'Elizabeth still hasn't told Robert and Sophie everything.'

'What do you mean?'

'They are only aware that their father left their mother to be with another woman. In fact, that's all Elizabeth's told anybody. Our respective families know that I'm living in sin with an Indian woman...but they do not know that I'm living in sin with the children's ayah. Robert and Sophie do not know that it's you and I'm bound by my word to never let them know. I *have* decided to tell them they have a sister and I'm going to tell them when I see them next.'

'Do you think that's wise?'

'I'm not ashamed of us...or Isabella and I'm sure the children will be thrilled to meet her.'

Jemima was not so certain.

The day after William departed, Jemima dwelt on how Robert and Sophie would take his revelations. And were it not for the needs of a thirteen-month-old child, she would have surely gone insane waiting for him to return. It was shortly after three in the afternoon when she heard him striding up the stairs. He commented on how many apples there were in the orchard and she dismissed his trivial banter with an impatient huff. 'Did you tell them?'

'Yes,' he replied. 'Fortunately there were no tears or tantrums. Robert didn't ask very many questions. He was just a little worried that I wouldn't be his father anymore... poor little chap. I reassured him though.'

'And Sophie?'

'Well, she was delighted at the thought of having a little sister but I'm not sure Elizabeth will approve of the children knowing. I hear she spends most of her time in Leeds and there's even talk of her having an admirer.' Leaning over his baby's cot, he smiled and pulled a face. 'I hope she does,' he said. 'I'd like her to be happy. Oh... Sophie wants to meet Isabella. She even said that if we plan to keep a nanny... we should find an ayah. Then she gave me this.'

He withdrew an item from his case and handed it to Jemima. It was the *daguerreotype* of Jemima Ayah sitting next to his children. She remembered finding the portrait under Sophie's pillow that night on the *Bengal Star*. She had been more than happy to see it then but the sight of it now upset her terribly.

'She has asked to meet you,' William sighed, 'but I did try to explain that it wasn't possible for now.'

'Not possible for now? Not possible ever, you mean. Don't forget the promise to your wife.'

'Elizabeth need never know. Remember, you're Priya now; not Jemima, and I'm willing to wager that Sophie won't even recognise you.'

Jemima blinked in disbelief. 'Won't even recognise me?' she reeled. 'I bathed and clothed your daughter every day for almost three years. I carried her in my arms and sung lullabies whilst she slept. She knows the shape of my face, the scent of my skin and most of all... she knows my eyes.' Sinking back against the bedpost, Jemima despaired at the thought of her former charges hating their once beloved ayah.

'I know how much *Jemima* meant to them both and I am most grateful for everything *she* did. But they believe that she has returned to India and it's not as if they've seen you since.'

'Sophie *has* seen me,' Jemima stammered. And then she recounted the events that had transpired at the World Fair to William.

'Why didn't you say?' he asked.

'I was frightened,' she said, 'I still am.'

Jemima began to panic.

'Let's go back to India... you, me and Isabella.'

'One day perhaps,' he said, wrapping his arms around her, 'but what makes you think life in India will be any easier? Besides, I cannot leave Robert and Sophie... I've disrupted their lives enough. But I pledge to stand by you and by us... so you must cease worrying... and we shall face things together... when and if there's anything to face. Until then, I shan't worry too much about it. I'd rather stroll in the orchard and enjoy the splendid weather.' He kissed Jemima on the forehead and crossed over to his daughter's cot. 'We shall look at the apples, won't we my angel?' he cooed, clutching Isabella gingerly to his breast. 'And you should come too,' he said, before departing from the room.

Jemima studied the *daguerreotype* in her hands and realised that the creature in the image was nothing but a ghost. Rising from the bed, she pulled her dresser drawer open and grabbed the diary she had never begun to write. She slipped the portrait between the blank, white pages and then slammed the drawer shut. The sun's rays had cast the room in hazy yellow light and she stood quietly, soaking up its warmth. Crossing over to the open window, she spied Champa in the garden below, struggling with one too many apple baskets in her arms. One tumbled and bounced across the lawn.

'Wait there, Champa!' Jemima called, 'I'll help you.'

She descended the lopsided staircase and passed through the French windows, where Champa was waiting to be relieved of her load. Together they wandered across the garden with their arms full of baskets and Champa nudged the orchard gate open with her foot. 'Madam!' she declared. 'So many apples to pick today!'

'Yes there are, Champa,' Jemima said, placing her share of baskets on the ground. 'Perhaps, you can make a pie.'

'Yes Madam,' the girl said, hesitating somewhat. 'Madam,' she said again, her eyes dipped low. 'Can I also learn to read?'

Jemima's heart bulged with pride. 'Well of course, Champa. We can start tomorrow.'

The girl nodded and skipped off to collect as many unspoiled fruit as she could.

Balancing on her toes, Jemima picked an apple from the first tree in line and wondered what life had in store for her next. She envisaged the child, Sophie, telling all and sundry who her father's mistress really was and shuddered at all the possible repercussions of her scandalous union with her former sahib. Beyond the trellis of tree branches, she saw his handsome figure drifting about without a care in the world. How easy it was for men to forget their troubles, she thought. It was not so easy for her. She watched him move amongst a carpet of green and red apples rolling hither and thither as his shoes shifted them out from his path. His sleeves were rolled up and his cravat was draped loosely about his neck and he appeared so like the image of when she first saw him in Calcutta. And in that one blissful moment in time, Jemima chose to abandon her burden of worries in favour of admiring William Hayward cradling the child she bore him tenderly in his arms. She took a deep bite into the apple and found that it was crisp and tasted incredibly sweet. '*What a beautiful day,' she thought. 'It really could not be any more wondrous.*'

And slicing through the mayhem and seemingly insurmountable strife, Jemima thought of home and all its possible meanings to realise that home would always be by William and her daughter's side.

END

GLOSSARY

ayah	Indian nanny/nursemaid
bhadralok	Bengali middle classes
barfi	Indian sweetmeat
budgerow	sailing barge
caranchie	native carriage
chi chi	native
dhoti	a loincloth of varying length
ghat	wharf
ghat serang	lascar recruiting agent
kajal	kohl
kameez	loose shirt

khudafiz	goodbye in *Urdu*
lascar	Asian sailor
memsahib	mistress
nabob	disparaging term for the British who made their fortunes in India
nautch girl	dancer
nawab	prince
paan	betel leaf palate cleanser
panchway	four-oared passenger boat
peelers	police
punka	cloth fan
sahib	master
serang	Indian boatswain
tindal	lascar petty officer

ACKNOWLEDGMENTS

I would like to thank those who helped shape Ayah into the story it is today. I am blessed to have collaborated with some extremely talented people, some of whom, I am proud to count as my friends.

Danny Scheinmann – *Actor, Director and Best-selling novelist*
Thank you for your generous advice, support and endorsement of *Ayah*. You are a great mentor, friend and an all-round good human being. I don't think I would have taken myself seriously as a writer of fiction if not for you.

Lionel Schneider – *Graphic Designer*
What can I say, Lio? You are a genius and a treasured friend. I love you dearly for all that you have done. Thank you, thank you... thank you!

Jim Zuckerman – *Photographer*
What a privilege to use your stunning image on my cover again. You are a gentleman – a real pleasure to do to business with. Thank you.

Stella Kamugino – *Film-maker*
You gave up your time and expertise to help me make my '*Ayah*' promo film. You are kind and generous beyond measure. Thank you.

Thanks to the following, who gave their time, support and encouragement in the development of this book: Jasprit Singh, Paige Birnie (author photograph), Edina Imrik, Rochele Mitchell and Camilla Aitken. And last but not least, my family and friends.

Though *Ayah* is essentially a piece of fiction, much of its inspiration comes from the scant history of the Indian servants and lascars (sailors) brought to England during the glory days of the British Empire. I discovered their stories whilst researching a similar character from history for the Museum of London. Much of the information came from two excellent and fascinating books: *Ayah's, Lascars and Princes*, and *Asians in Britain: 400 years of History*, both written by Rozina Visram.

My research for this novel also came from the following books:

The Parlour and the Streets. (Elite and Popular Culture in 19th Century Calcutta) by Sumanta Banerjee

Social Life in England from the 19th Century to the Present Day by John Finnemore

London, The Wicked City (A Thousand Years of Vice in the Capital) by Fergus Linnane

The London Underworld in the Victorian Period (Authentic First-person Accounts by Beggars, Thieves & Prostitutes) by Henry Mayhew & Others